DYING GAMES

A Jefferson Tayte Genealogical Mystery

DYING GAMES

A Jefferson Tayte Genealogical Mystery

by

STEVE ROBINSON

 THOMAS & MERCER

Text copyright © 2017 by Steve Robinson
All rights reserved.

No part of this book may be reproduced, or stored in a retrieval system, or transmitted in any form or by any means, electronic, mechanical, photocopying, recording, or otherwise, without express written permission of the publisher.

Published by Thomas & Mercer, Seattle

www.apub.com

Amazon, the Amazon logo, and Thomas & Mercer are trademarks of Amazon.com, Inc., or its affiliates.

ISBN-13: 9781477848265
ISBN-10: 1477848266

Cover design by @blacksheep-uk.com

Printed in the United States of America

For my wife, Karen

Prologue

When the woman awoke, she was instantly aware of two things. The first was that she felt cold, the kind of cold you feel deep inside your bones. It made her teeth chatter uncontrollably, and she wanted it to stop. She had to be quiet, or the man would find her.

The second thing she felt was fear.

She couldn't recall why she felt so afraid, but she instinctively knew she was. She was terrified. It was dark, absolutely dark. She was sitting in a crouched position with her knees pulled up close to her chest, hands by her feet. She tried to move, her cold limbs stiff and aching, but there wasn't enough room. Wherever she was, she thought she must have gone there to hide. Yes, that was it. She was hiding from the man, and she must have been there for some time to feel as cold as she did.

But where had she hidden, and why was she wearing only one shoe?

She tried to think. She wished she could remember. Her hands wandered up from her numb feet, and she began to run them over the smooth walls around her, which were so close she couldn't even straighten her arms. She imagined she must be in a box of some kind, and the idea caused her to catch her breath as claustrophobia gripped her. She wanted to smash her way out of there. She wanted to scream, but she knew that would be bad.

An image flashed through her mind, and it startled her. It was the man. He was angry, and she was running from him, trying to find somewhere to hide. She supposed he was the reason she was hiding in the box now, but was she hiding? She shook her head as the answer came to her. In her mind she could see her other shoe. It was on the floor at the back of the garage at her home. She was lying on her back a few feet away from it, reaching out for the hammer she'd seen just moments before the man caught up with her. She was kicking out at him as he pulled her back, away from the hammer. Her shoe had come off in the struggle. She had not found a place to hide. She had not managed to escape.

So why was she crouched inside a box?

A fearful shiver ran through her as she realised the man must have put her there. At last she screamed.

'John!'

Her husband had not been home when the man came to the door, but then she thought the man must have known that. She began to cry as she thumped on the walls, which resounded with a low, hollow note. Wherever the man had put her, she was starkly aware that it was with no good intent. She had to get out. She pushed at the wall in front of her and felt her spine brace against the wall at her back. A moment later she thought she heard a crack. Then she heard another sound and froze. Somewhere beyond her confinement, a door had clicked open. She heard echoing footsteps, becoming louder. Her breath quickened.

It was the man.

Silent again in the darkness, she listened until the footsteps fell silent with her. Then she heard the man sigh, and her eyes were suddenly blinded by light. She blinked and tried to focus. A small square, no bigger than a matchbook, had opened in the wall to her right. Light was cast into the box, and she saw her surroundings for the first time. There were pictures on the walls—miniature pictures. She could see a bookcase and several fireplaces. There were tiny portraits of indistinguishable people, and above her she saw the interior of an apex roof with a tiny chandelier hanging down. She touched it in disbelief. She was inside a doll's house, with all the floors removed to accommodate her.

The light at the small window the man had opened was suddenly interrupted, and she turned towards it. What she saw startled her. It was an eye—his eye—as grey as steel and easily recognisable by the scar that cut a deep line across his left eyebrow, cleaving it in two. The woman caught her breath again, still uncertain of the man's intentions, fearing she would soon find out.

The eye blinked as the man focused on her.

'I wanted to be sure you were awake,' he said, showing no emotion, no nervousness or excitement in light of what he had done, or was about to do. 'The others were awake when it happened. You can be sure of that.'

The others? What others?

'When what happened?' she asked, but the man gave no answer.

The eye at the tiny window withdrew, and the interior of the doll's house became bright again. A moment later, she caught the distinctive chemical smell of gasoline. She heard it splashing on to the roof above her. She saw it dripping in through the window.

'What do you want?' the woman asked, panic in her voice. 'Why are you doing this?'

The only sound she heard in reply was the unmistakable striking of a match. It scratched and fizzed, and then the man's eye returned to the tiny window.

'Jefferson Tayte knows why,' he said as he offered up the flame.

Then he dropped the match inside.

PART ONE

Chapter One

Ten days later.

Sitting in the back of the car that had just picked him up from Dulles International Airport, courtesy of the federal government, Jefferson Tayte felt a sense of satisfaction to be home in Washington, DC—although the seriousness of the situation that had called him back meant the feeling didn't last.

Twenty-four hours ago he'd been in London with his fiancée, Professor Jean Summer, enjoying their last evening together before she had to set off to Scotland for a seminar on the early years of the Scottish monarchy. Now he was keeping company with the Federal Bureau of Investigation. He didn't yet know exactly why, and the lack of information was beginning to frustrate the hell out of him. All he knew was that someone was dead, and the reason had something to do with him. That had been more than enough to get him on the plane, but so far, he wasn't entirely sure whether he was there to help out, or because he was a suspect.

The seat next to the driver was vacant. Sitting beside Tayte, on the other side of Tayte's briefcase and suit carrier, was the man who had personally greeted him off the plane, Special Agent in Charge Jordan Reese—the man tasked with leading the investigation. He was a big man, like Tayte, but lean and muscular. He was African American with close-cut hair and a shadow of a beard, whose dark-grey three-piece suit put Tayte's perennially creased tan-coloured two-piece to shame.

'Thank you for your patience, Mr Tayte,' Reese said, straightening his tie, which was ink blue like his shirt. 'I'm sorry I've not been more forthcoming with information just yet, but I'd like to show you what we're up against before we get down to the details.'

They were two miles north of the Capitol, driving alongside McMillan Park, which had been fenced off and closed to the public on all but a few special occasions since World War Two. It was almost dusk. Through the fading October light, beyond the barbed-wire fence, Tayte could see the concrete silos of the former sand-filtration site upon which the twenty-five-acre parkland had been created. It was adjacent to the McMillan Reservoir, the vast catacombs beneath it now dormant and abandoned. He imagined it was the perfect place to stage a murder, and if the FBI was involved, it had to be more complicated than a straightforward homicide.

The car pulled up by a black mesh gate, which was promptly opened by a man wearing the familiar dark-blue uniform of the DC Metropolitan Police Department. Just inside the gate were two MPD cruisers, and the lack of any flashing lights on the vehicles told Tayte that the situation was thankfully now under control.

'Is this where the man was murdered?' Tayte asked, still taking the area in as they drove towards the first of the silos. 'Is this the scene of the crime?'

Reese nodded. 'Two men were murdered here in the early hours. They were twins.'

'A double homicide,' Tayte said under his breath.

Reese gave a sour laugh. 'It's a whole lot more than that.'

When the car stopped, they were outside one of the silos, which, like all the others they had passed, was partially covered with ivy. The driver remained in the car as Reese got out.

'Please follow me, Mr Tayte,' he said as he went.

Leaving his briefcase on the seat, Tayte followed Reese to a tall archway opposite the silo. It had a heavy grey wooden door that was open and hanging aslant from a single rusty hinge. The entrance was guarded by another officer of the MPD. Reese flashed his badge and they passed through on to a wide concrete slope that took them underground into the catacombs where the sand-filtration process once took place, settling and purifying most of the city's drinking water. Beneath his loafers, Tayte could feel the compacted sand, still there after all these years, and the air smelled of damp concrete. The immediate area was dimly lit, but further in, Tayte could see where they were heading by the lights that had been set up around the scene of the crime.

'Are the bodies still here?' Tayte asked, a little apprehensively, meaning to prepare himself for the shock if they were. He was surprised at first that his voice carried no echo whatsoever in such a hollow space, but he quickly realised it was because of the many pillars and the curvature of the cell-like ceiling sections they supported just a few feet above him.

'No, we're about done here,' Reese said. 'I thought it might be useful for you to see how the victims died before the apparatus the killer used gets taken away for further examination.'

Tayte could see the apparatus Reese was referring to. It was a clear tank of about four feet square by six feet high, which appeared to have been constructed from heavy-duty Perspex panels, strengthened at each corner and along the sides by a steel framework. There was a water hose attached to the left side of the tank, which had a lid that was raised open about two feet. As Tayte approached, he noticed that the ground was wet, and he imagined the tank had been filled with water, which would have been drained by the police after the bodies were discovered. Inside the tank was another thick layer of Perspex, to which a chair was bolted. It had leather straps at the ankles and wrists, and another larger strap across the middle. There was an identical chair just outside the tank, only this chair had no straps, and it wasn't bolted down.

'See the box on the side of the tank there,' Reese said, pointing. 'It houses a sprung hinge, and there's a winding mechanism to release the catch and crank the lid open. Once closed, it can't be opened from the inside.'

'What happened here?' Tayte asked, scrunching his brow as he tried to imagine.

'Both brothers drowned,' Reese said. 'When their bodies were discovered, one was gagged and strapped to the chair. The other was floating loose, suspended in the water. Their killer tapped into an old water supply to fill the tank.'

Reese picked up the chair in front of the tank and shook it. 'Our best theory is that one brother woke up sitting in this chair. It has a pressure pad, set to trigger the flow of water when he gets up off the chair. As he does so, he hears the water and turns to see his brother in the tank, struggling to free himself as the water begins to rise. He quickly weighs his options. He pulls at the hose, thinking to stop the flow of water, but it's secured too well and he can't stop it. He thinks to go for something sharp to cut the hose with, maybe to get help while he's at it, but at the rate the water's rising, he knows that will take too long. If he leaves, his brother will drown. He sees the straps that are binding his brother to the chair and thinks he can stand on his own chair to help get himself up into the tank. Then all he has to do is undo the straps and they can both climb out. Only that's exactly what the killer expects him to do. He wants him to jump in and try to save his brother.'

'And lose his own life in the process,' Tayte said, almost to himself, knowing he would probably have done the same thing.

Reese nodded. 'There's another sensor inside the tank. When the brother on the outside got into the tank to effect his rescue, that sensor triggered the lid to snap shut, sealing the twins inside. The tank filled and they both drowned.'

Tayte felt a shudder run through him as he imagined the fate of the two victims. The whole setup was horrific. 'Seems a convoluted way to kill people,' he said as he studied the apparatus again. He frowned. 'How did the killer get all this gear down here?'

'That's an excellent question, Mr Tayte. Our killer has clearly been planning this for some time. He probably brought it all in here piece by piece, hiding it away until he needed it. He must have assembled it in situ. There's no way he could have gotten that tank down here in one piece.'

'What about security? Are there any cameras?'

'Not down here. He gained entry through the wire fence, where it's become overgrown with ivy. If he fixed the mesh back temporarily each time he left, the breach could have gone unnoticed for some time. He probably chose this particular filtration unit out of the twenty that are here because of its location, knowing he wouldn't be seen.'

Another question popped into Tayte's head. 'Why here?' he asked. 'I know it's a quiet location—someplace he could go about his business undetected once he was set up, but there must be a hundred more suitable places in DC with easier access for all this equipment. A disused warehouse, for instance.'

Reese turned away from the tank. 'That's where I'm hoping you can help us, Mr Tayte.' He began walking back towards the exit. 'Let's get out of here. There's something else I need to show you.'

Tayte followed, glad to get out into the fresh air again. As they climbed back into the car, he asked, 'Are you going to tell me what all this has to do with me?'

'Yes, I am,' Reese said, 'but you're not going to like it.'

Reese worked out of the FBI field office in DC, located on 601 4th Street Northwest. He took Tayte to a small, sparsely decorated room inside the building, where a woman sat waiting for them with an attaché case on her lap. She set the case on the floor and stood up as they entered.

Reese acknowledged her with a nod. 'This is Ms Mavro, one of our analysts,' he said to Tayte, and Tayte offered her a smile.

'Jefferson Tayte,' he said, almost dropping his suit carrier as he awkwardly switched hands with his briefcase, wondering whether or not a formal handshake was in order.

He still hadn't quite decided when Reese said, 'Mavro has read your file. She knows who you are.'

'Of course,' Tayte said.

He didn't like to think that the government had a file on him, but he supposed that was the case to some extent for most of the people living in DC. He couldn't help but wonder what was in it. Nothing very exciting, that was for sure.

Reese took off his jacket and hung it over the back of his chair. Tayte watched him take out a long silver cigar case from inside his jacket and place it on the desk in front of him. He did so with great care, as if it were something precious to him. Tayte looked on with fascination as Reese meticulously lined up the engraved silver tube with the edge of the desk until the two were perfectly parallel.

'Mavro here is one of our finest intelligence analysts,' Reese added, seemingly oblivious to the attention his little ritual with the cigar case had drawn.

'I bet you say that about all the analysts you draft in from HQ,' Mavro said, playing the compliment down.

'Well, maybe I do,' Reese said with a half-smile. To Tayte he added, 'Anyway, Ms Mavro is going to be working closely with you until we crack this.'

Tayte took Ms Mavro in more fully once they had all sat down. She appeared to be in her early thirties and wasn't very tall, only about five four, and quite stocky with it. She was big boned, he thought, much as he was. She had short dark hair that had a slight curl to it, which was almost black like his. It was clipped back off her brow to one side, framing a round face that had a smooth and pale complexion, probably on account of her being cooped up in an office most of the time, crunching numbers. She was dressed in black trousers and a white short-sleeved shirt. He liked her dress sense. Nice and simple.

Reese had a folder with him. He opened it on the desk and pulled a few papers out. 'Okay, let's get you briefed and up to date with our problem. Our twins back there at the sand-filtration site weren't the killer's first victims.'

'Serial killer?' Tayte said. He'd guessed it had to be something like that for the FBI to be involved.

'I'm afraid so. The twins were murders three and four.'

Reese slid a photograph across to Tayte of a blonde-haired woman sitting on a sunlit bench with a river twinkling behind her.

'Is that the Potomac in the background?'

'Yes, it is. The picture was taken right here in DC about two months ago. It's the most recent image her husband had. She was our killer's first victim—Annabel Rogers, aged thirty-one. Her remains were discovered when the fire department attended a house in Northwest. The odd thing about it was that the fire was barely underway when they arrived. It's doubtful anyone outside the house would even have noticed it so soon. We can assume, then, that the 911 call was made before the fire was started.'

'By the killer,' Tayte said, pre-empting Reese. 'Was the call recorded?'

'Yes, it was. I listened to it myself. All I heard was the sound of a woman screaming. Her killer never spoke. The phone number was quickly traced to the address where Rogers was found. When the fire department arrived, the fire had been going just long enough to kill her, but not long enough to make it too difficult to identify her. We believe it was important to the killer that we knew who she was. The other odd thing about it was that before she was set on fire, she'd been placed inside a doll's house. Pieces of it were found still intact at the scene, and there was a pile of miniature furniture on a nearby coffee table.'

Tayte shook his head. It was a gruesome reminder of a story he'd been told while working on his family history in Germany a few months ago. 'Who would do something like that? Why a doll's house?'

'Once again, Mr Tayte, I'm hoping you and Ms Mavro are soon going to be able to tell me.'

Reese slid another photograph towards Tayte. 'This is the killer's second victim, Randall Edwards. He was fifty-nine, shot dead five days ago after being gagged and tied to a tree in Lincoln Park.'

'I live near Lincoln Park,' Tayte said, sounding shocked at the idea that someone had done this so close to his home.

'We know,' Reese said. 'The odd thing about this murder is that Edwards effectively shot himself.'

'Suicide?'

'No, most definitely not suicide, assisted or otherwise. Edwards was no willing participant. A log was found at his feet. His arms had been left free so he could hold the log up. Attached to the log was a length of fishing line. The other end was fixed to the trigger of a sawed-off shotgun, mounted on a branch four feet away. When Edwards' arms became too weak to hold the log up, which I doubt was long given his age and size, and the weight of the log, the gun went off.'

'Long enough for his killer to clear the park, though,' Tayte said.

'Yeah, long enough. Someone reported hearing the gunshot and Edwards' body was soon found.'

Reese slid a third photograph to Tayte. 'That brings us to murders three and four, our twins, Bobby and Lee Masterson, aged twenty-four. You've seen where and how they were murdered. Both were football scholars and were, no doubt, their father's pride and joy. Their parents' home was full of trophies of one kind or another.'

The photograph showed both brothers padded up in their football shirts, bent over towards the camera, arms locked around each other as if they were facing off against their opponents. Tayte only saw the loss the photograph now represented, and with all his heart he did not want this killer to chalk up a fifth victim.

'How do you know these murders were all committed by the same person?' he asked. 'I mean, apart from their unusual and clearly pre-meditated nature, they're all so different.' The bizarre nature of the murders, their locations, and close timing was perhaps enough to give the FBI the idea that they were dealing with a serial killer, but there was something about the way Reese spoke that told Tayte he was absolutely certain. There had to be more to it. 'What else do you have?'

Reese sat back in his chair. He placed a palm over his cigar case and began rolling it slowly back and forth. 'This is the part where you come in,' he said. To Mavro he added, 'Would you care to show Mr Tayte what you've been working on?'

Mavro reached down beside her chair and pulled her attaché case up on to the table. 'We know the murders were committed by the same person because he left a calling card at each of the crime scenes.' From her case Mavro withdrew three printouts. She slid them across to Tayte, placing one beside each of the photographs, indicating the order in which they were found. 'Family trees,' she said. 'At least, they're sections of family trees. The names are all different, but they were written by the same hand in the same manner, and on the exact same paper.'

Tayte leaned closer, suddenly aroused by this connection to his profession as a genealogist. His eyes narrowed as he began to scrutinise them. There were several names written on to incomplete genealogical wheel charts, each chart fanning out from a central name that instantly drew Tayte's attention, as it was no doubt supposed to. None of the names rang any bells for him. They also appeared to bear no obvious relationship to the victims whose bodies they had been left with.

'We began working on these soon after the second murder,' Mavro said, 'once the MPD had matched the murders of Annabel Rogers and Randall Edwards to the same killer.'

'Does the FBI always get involved in cases of serial murder?' Tayte asked her.

'Not always, but often. In this particular case, apart from the extra manpower and the advanced forensic science the FBI can provide, it was clear that specialist skills would also be needed to bring this killer to justice.'

'Because of the connection to genealogy?' Tayte said, glancing down at the wheel charts again. 'What have you learned?'

Mavro shook her head. 'So far we don't have much. We've looked into the names in the middle of each chart, and we've been focusing on trying to make a connection between them.'

'But the only connection we've made is you,' Reese said.

Since Reese had first called him, Tayte had been wondering when he would get around to telling him specifically what this had to do with him. It appeared that now was the time. Reese had his full attention.

'When we spoke to the families of the victims and showed them what had been left for us at the scene of each murder, indicating a possible connection to family history, your name came up every time. Annabel Rogers' husband told us she'd once hired you to compile her family tree. Randall Edwards' daughter, Mrs Andrea Hutchinson, said she'd asked you to work on her husband's ancestry. With the Masterson twins, their mother said that her sister, Mrs Wanda Delacruz, was into family history. Mrs Delacruz was able to confirm that she'd also used your services in the past. It appears, Mr Tayte, that someone is killing your past clients, or close members of their family.'

The revelation knocked Tayte back into his seat. 'Why?' he said under his breath, utterly confused. 'How does this killer even know who my past clients are?'

'Those are two very good questions,' Reese said. He leaned forward, crossing his arms in front him, his muscles stretching the sleeves of his shirt. 'I'd love to have you answer them for me, but I don't suppose you'd know anything about it, would you?'

There it was: the body language and the tone of voice that confirmed to Tayte that Reese still had his doubts about him, even now, after he'd voluntarily flown all the way from England to see him.

He narrowed his eyes. 'You think I'm somehow involved in this, don't you?'

'Right now, Mr Tayte, I don't know what to think. Excuse my frankness, but if it was down to me, I'd keep you at arm's length until I was sure.'

'I told you before—I was in England with my fiancée when these murders took place.'

Reese picked up his cigar case and pointed it at Tayte. 'We've satisfied ourselves that you were out of the country,' he said, waving the case like a baton as he spoke. 'And believe me, if you didn't have such a strong alibi we'd be having a very different conversation right now. So tell me—just how does our killer does know so much about your past clients?'

'I don't know,' Tayte said honestly. 'But I'll find out if you'll give me the chance.' He didn't like to think that Reese suspected he had anything to do with these murders, whether he was out of the country at the time or not. He wanted to set that right if he could, and above all, he wanted to help stop whoever was doing this.

Mavro spoke then, cutting through the tension. 'Do any of the names on these charts mean anything to you, Mr Tayte?'

Tayte drew a deep breath and turned to the charts again. 'Two of the surnames you just mentioned are here,' he said. 'Hutchinson is on the chart that was left at the scene of the Rogers murder. Delacruz is on the chart found with Randall Edwards.'

'We worked that much out,' Reese said.

'The names match your clients,' Mavro added, 'but they're not your actual clients.'

'No,' Tayte said. 'The first names are different and the dates against them are too far back.'

'Does anything else stand out?'

Tayte shook his head. 'I don't know. Maybe.'

'Maybe?'

Tayte tapped the centre of the chart that had been left at the scene of the Rogers murder. 'Simmonds seems familiar, but I can't place it. I guess if I've worked on the ancestry of these families, that could be why, but I look at so many names in my line of work. It's all about names and dates, and I've been a professional genealogist for more than twenty years—over half my life. During that time, I've had hundreds of clients, most of whom have lived in or around DC.'

'You asked why anyone would want to murder your past clients,' Reese said. 'Do you have any idea, however remote it may seem?'

The thought made Tayte feel sick. He wanted some fresh air.

'Do you piss many people off in your line of work?' Reese continued.

Tayte almost dismissed the notion out of hand. He did good things for people. He connected them with their wider families, with their ancestral past. How could that possibly upset anyone enough to make them want to kill his former clients? But he had upset people. In uncovering the past, as he so often did, he'd come across those who would rather the past remained buried. Some of those people had forcibly tried to stop him, while others had taken a more passive approach and simply refused to help with his research. One way or another, he'd certainly upset a few people over the years.

'This is clearly personal, Mr Tayte,' Mavro said. 'The killer must have known that sooner or later we'd link the victims to you.'

That worried Tayte. 'I don't know why my clients are being murdered,' he said, thoughtfully, still a little shell-shocked. 'Yes, I've upset people from time to time as a result of my work. But no, I don't know who would do this.'

'Can you think on it?' Reese said. 'Let me have a list of names? It'll give us somewhere to start.'

'Of course,' Tayte said. He eyed Reese seriously. 'I want to do everything I can to help.'

'I'm glad to hear it, because you can be damn sure our killer is at the very least already looking for his next victim. We may not have much time. The current pattern is every five days, but let's not take anything for granted. We need to work fast, starting with your list. Ms Mavro will call by your apartment to work on the charts with you first thing in the morning.'

Tayte nodded. 'I'll go through my files as soon as I get home. I'll put something together for you.'

'Good. Just bear in mind that while around seventeen percent of serial offenders in the US are female, our killer on this occasion is most definitely male. The nature of the Masterson murders in particular also suggests that we're looking for a man with greater than average physical strength. And don't make the mistake of thinking that serial killers belong to any particular ethnic group, as the entertainment industry might have you believe. Serial killers are not all Caucasian. They do, however, like familiar territory—a comfort zone. They tend not to kill interstate unless their work happens to take them farther afield, but that's rare with pattern killers. So far, these killings have all taken place in DC, so I suspect that's where our killer lives. They often operate close to home, or near their place of work. You're probably not looking for some weirdo or misfit—not on the outside at least. Our killer is more likely to be the friendly family guy next door who always helps his old neighbour take her trash out. Or the working mom sitting next to you at the office. Fitting in so well with the rest of society is often why serial killers go undetected for so long, so keep an open mind. Right now, our killer could be just about anyone.'

Reese stood up, indicating that the brief was drawing to a close. 'If you find anything,' he added, 'anything at all, I want to be the first person to know about it. And I don't want either of you acting on your own initiative, putting yourselves in harm's way. I've got plenty of highly trained field agents ready to do that.' He paused. Then directly to Mavro, he said, 'I'm well aware that you used to work in the field, Ms Mavro, but that was a while back. I want you to stay in the background. Help us find out who's doing this.' He turned to Tayte. 'Given what we have here, I'd say our killer is someone you know, or at least someone who knows you.' Reese handed him a card. 'Anything you need, just let me know.'

Someone I know . . . It was an unnerving thought, and one that made Tayte all the more keen to go outside for some fresh autumn air. *Stay in the background,* Reese had said, and Tayte fully intended to do just that.

Chapter Two

So many questions preoccupied Tayte's mind as he opened the door to his one-bedroom ground-floor apartment on tree-lined North Carolina Avenue Northeast and stepped inside. He hadn't been home in months, not since the summer, and he had to concede that he hadn't much missed the place. He'd made it a loner's paradise, sparsely decorated with off-white walls and hardwood floors, and no room for guests to sleep over, not that that had been a problem. The doormat was tellingly covered with junk mail. He kicked his way through all three months' worth, knowing he'd have to sort through it all at some point just in case there was anything important. There rarely was. He set his briefcase and suit carrier down, thinking that it made the decision of where to live with Jean once they were married all the more straightforward. He'd happily live wherever she wanted to, and in any kind of home she wanted them to make for themselves.

But that was all for some other day.

As was the research he'd been conducting into his own family history since discovering the names of his biological parents. All his plans had come to a shuddering halt when Special Agent Reese had called. He remembered exactly what he'd been doing at the time. He was with Jean at her apartment in London, part way through helping to clear the table after the romantic meal they had shared. He even remembered the smoochy love song that had been playing on the stereo, courtesy of Luther Vandross.

'Mr Jefferson Tayte?' Reese had said when Jean came in from the kitchen and handed him his phone.

'Yes, I'm Tayte. Who's this?'

'My name's Jordan Reese. I'm with the FBI.'

'The FBI? How can I help you?'

The music stopped playing at that point, and suddenly Jean was holding his arm, listening in. Her concerned expression matched his own.

'I'm sorry to disturb you, but I need to ask you a few questions.'

'What's this about?'

'I'll get to that. First, can you tell me if you've been in England long?'

'How do you know where I am?'

'Your cell phone. Have you been there long?'

'A few months.'

'Can anyone confirm that?'

Tayte didn't like where this conversation was heading. 'Yes, my fiancée. She's right here beside me. Do you want to ask her?'

'No, that's okay for now.'

'For now? Look, are you going to tell me what this is about or not?'

'Mr Tayte, I'm in charge of a murder investigation that concerns you. That's as much as I can say for now. We'd appreciate it if you could come in and talk to us.'

'In DC?' Tayte couldn't quite believe it.

'Yes, in DC. I can get you on a flight tomorrow.'

Tayte paused, looking into Jean's eyes before he spoke again. He was supposed to be going to Scotland with her for the week-long Scottish monarchy seminar she was attending. They had a double room booked. He'd planned to spend the evenings with her. How could he do that now? If he didn't go back to DC to help the FBI with their enquiries, it would only serve to implicate him in whatever was going on. He also wanted to know why the FBI thought this concerned him.

'Let me have the details,' he said, sighing as he spoke. He could already see the disappointment in Jean's eyes. He felt the same way.

When the call ended, Tayte kissed her and went over to the CD player. 'At least we have tonight,' he said as he pressed the play button. Then as Luther Vandross's silky tones filled the air, he embraced her and they danced in slow circles, two bodies entwined as one.

'You will be careful, won't you?' Jean whispered in his ear.

'You know me,' Tayte said with a smile.

'That's what I'm afraid of.'

Tayte kissed her again. 'Don't be afraid. I'll be just fine. I'll call you as soon as I land.'

That was only yesterday, but he missed her already.

It was just after six in the evening, and night had begun to fall on the streets of DC. Tayte hung up his jacket, switched on the light and the heating thermostat, and made straight for the coffee machine, still ruminating over everything he'd seen and heard that day. Much as he loved to think of Jean and the times they spent together, right now he had other people to focus on, and there were lives at stake—his former clients' lives, for whom he felt an overwhelming sense of responsibility. There was a small flat-panel television on the kitchen counter, the only set he owned, used just for the news channels. He stared at the blank screen, lost in his thoughts.

Who's doing this?

It was someone he knew, or at least someone who knew him. But who?

How does he know who my past clients are?

That had Tayte stumped.

What do these pieces of genealogical wheel chart mean? What message is the killer trying to send?

The charts he'd seen were not his own. They had been crudely drawn, and they were far from complete, containing only a handful of names. He needed to have a better look at them as soon as Mavro arrived in the morning. He poured his coffee, strong and black, wondering how he was going to begin figuring out all the answers.

Why my clients?

He knew that was where he had to start—with the list of names he'd promised Reese. At some point in his career, as a result of one of his assignments, he'd seriously upset someone. That had to be it. He opened one of the kitchen cupboards and took out a fresh bag of Hershey's Miniatures to help keep him going through what he imagined was going to be a long night ahead. He tucked the bag under his arm, picked up his coffee, and went into his filing room, where he paused to take in all the tall wall-to-wall grey cabinets he'd collected over the years.

Tayte had begun his career in the days before digitisation and online access to archives really took off, and although now fully acquainted with the digital world, he'd been slow to adapt. He had some digital files, dating back several years, but in his filing room he also kept paper copies of everything. When it came to his files, he'd always been a hoarder, unable to part with anything in case he ever needed to look something up or cross-reference a name, never knowing when one client's family history might overlap with another, saving him time. He had so many paper files that he needed an entire room to store them in.

He drew a deep breath through his nose. He liked the smell of all that old paper inside those cabinets and in the many lever arch files he had on shelves higher up. It reminded him of countless archive reading rooms and old libraries. His files were meticulously arranged in alphabetical order. He figured he just had to work his way through them all, from A to Z, familiarising himself with his past assignments.

'All twenty years' worth,' he told himself.

He whistled, knowing it was going to take time. He wished he could draft in a handful of FBI agents to help out, but no one else knew what to look for. He had made no records of any of the people he might have upset over the years as a result of one assignment or another.

Those names were all in his head. He just had to hope that something, or someone, stood out enough to jog his memory.

He put his coffee and the bag of Hershey's down on the small desk that stood beneath the window, where a heavy net curtain hid the view of a tree that had grown so tall and so close that it obscured much of the street. He popped one of the chocolates into his mouth and turned to the first cabinet, which had a big letter A on the front. He pulled open the bottom drawer, figuring he'd take a high-level glance through everything first, hoping it would save time. Maybe it would be enough to recall whether he'd upset anyone on that particular occasion.

He began flicking through the files, starting with *Abbot*, then *Ackerman* and *Adams*, through *Arrington* and *Ashworth* to the last file in the drawer, *Avery*. Nothing stood out. He couldn't even place half the names and he supposed that was okay. He imagined if he had upset someone during an assignment, he would remember at least something about it. Those others he couldn't recall had to be run-of-the-mill assignments where nothing particularly memorable had happened.

As he turned to drawer B and began to flick through more files, he thought back over some of his more recent engagements. Sure, he'd upset a few people, and some of them were now serving prison sentences as a result. But the only noteworthy cases he'd had of late had been in Europe, mostly in England where he'd met Jean. He opened drawer C, reminding himself of what Reese had said about the typical profile of a serial killer.

They tend to operate close to home or their place of work.

According to Reese, serial killers rarely travelled interstate to perform their nefarious activities, let alone intercontinental. But perhaps this serial killer didn't conform to the typical profile. He was killing his former clients, after all. Just his. That made it about him. It made it personal.

Keep an open mind . . .

Reese had also said that, and Tayte planned to follow his advice. He couldn't rule anyone out, and neither was it his job to do so. He went to the desk and took a notepad from the drawer. Then he wrote down all the names he could think of from his recent travels abroad in case Reese wanted to check them out. Against the names he wrote all the reasons why they were on the list. If the people his actions had put in prison were still inside, Reese could rule them out. That only left Tayte's US assignments. Until recent years, ever since his adoptive parents were killed in a plane crash when he was in his teens, his morbid fear of flying had kept him stateside. It was from those assignments that he expected to find clues to the kind of people Reese was looking for.

Tayte went back to his filing cabinets, and by the time he'd reached the back of drawer D, he had one more name for his list, but he thought it only a weak possibility. It concerned a middle-aged man who lived in Northwest called Ronald Dorsey. While researching the Dorsey family tree for Mrs Dorsey, Tayte had unwittingly shown her husband to be a three-times bigamist, which, Tayte had learned soon after the end of that job six years ago, had led to their divorce. Mr Dorsey had good reason to dislike Tayte, but it was hardly something to trigger a killing spree.

Fresh coffee to help keep him awake came and went with the hours that passed as Tayte went through cabinet after cabinet on his trip down Memory Lane, writing names down whenever he recalled an assignment where he felt he might have made an enemy. Tired as he was, and jet-lagged from the flight, he wanted to put that list together for Reese tonight so he'd have something for him when Mavro came by in the morning. He checked the time on his new wristwatch which, although similar to his old timepiece, he was still getting used to because he'd worn his old watch for so long. It was an original 1980s digital watch with glowing red LEDs that Jean had found for him on eBay, an engagement present to replace the watch he'd been forced to part company with in Germany that summer. It was midnight, and the jet lag he'd been trying to ward off with more coffee and Hershey's Miniatures than he knew was healthy for him was finally winning.

It was almost one in the morning by the time Tayte had finished compiling his list. There were close to forty names on it, none of which he'd have pegged for a serial killer, but what did he know? He thought he could have added a few more if he'd dug deeper into his files, but these were the names that stood out. And as he'd previously supposed, if nothing did stand out, it was a pretty good bet that the assignment in question hadn't made a big enough negative impact on anyone's life to turn them into the monster that had so far killed four members of his former clients' families. Tayte closed the last of his filing cabinet drawers and sat down at his desk, slumping forward on his elbows, too tired to keep his eyes open. He was ready to call it a night right there, but something was bothering him. It was Annabel Rogers, the killer's first victim. Going through his files he'd come across the assignment and it had stirred a memory. He couldn't quite place it, but he recalled that something very bad had happened in that family bloodline and he wanted to take a closer look before he turned in for the night. However tired he felt, he knew he wouldn't be able to sleep unless he did.

He rubbed his eyes and forced himself out of his chair, draining back the lukewarm dregs of his last cup of coffee as he rose. He located the file and took it through into the lounge, where he slumped on to an old, beaten-up walnut leather couch, thinking he'd be more comfortable falling asleep there if the sandman came for him while he was reading through it.

He was halfway through the file when the thing that had been niggling him revealed itself at last. It was triggered by a child's death certificate from 1920. He gave a deep yawn as he continued to study it and, as his tiredness finally overcame him, a slow smile spread across his face, knowing that he had just worked out a key part of the sadistic game this killer was playing.

Chapter Three

Tayte awoke the following morning with a stiff neck and a mild pain in his lower back. He was still on his couch, having fallen into a deep and dreamless sleep, or so it seemed because he couldn't recall anything beyond reading the assignment file for Annabel Rogers. He rolled on to his side and saw it on the floor beside an almost-empty bag of Hershey's Miniatures. He picked up the file, noting from the light at the window that the day had already begun. At that moment his door buzzer sounded and he drew a sharp breath, realising that had to be what had awoken him. He checked his watch: it was just before eight.

Ms Mavro.

'Just a minute!' Tayte called.

He sat up, still in the tan suit trousers and shirt he'd been wearing when he'd flown in the previous day. He swung his legs off the couch and stood up, stretching as he rose. He straightened his unkempt hair as he went to the door, thinking there was nothing he could do for the rest of his appearance, which was as creased as an old bank note. When he opened the door, Mavro greeted him with a perky smile. She had a folder tucked under her arm—her case file, Tayte supposed—and a paper bag in her hand. She held the paper bag up.

'You like bagels?'

'Sure, who doesn't?'

Mavro didn't look much like a member of the FBI today, Tayte considered, and he imagined that was because she didn't want to draw attention to herself in the field. She was wearing blue jeans and a navy polo shirt beneath an olive-green army-style parka. Her coat was open and he could also see that she was carrying a sidearm, reminding him of the seriousness of the situation—as if any reminder were needed.

'Agent Mavro,' Tayte said, rubbing the sleep from his eyes. 'Come in.'

'I'm not an agent,' Mavro said as she stepped inside. She sounded far more chirpy than Tayte felt. 'I'm an analyst, remember?'

'Right,' Tayte said, fighting a yawn. 'I thought all you people were called agents.'

'It's a common misconception.'

'Do you all carry guns?'

'No, and I don't usually get to carry a badge any more, either, but Reese insisted. Special circumstances. You just woke up?'

Tayte nodded. 'I couldn't wait to get stuck into that list I promised Agent Reese. It turned into a longer night than I'd expected.'

'How did you get on?'

'Great, I think. I've got around forty names.'

'Forty!' Mavro whistled at hearing the number.

'As I said, I stayed up awhile. It was a good thing I did, too—apart from finishing the list, I mean.'

'You found something?'

'I think so. Let me fix you a coffee to go with those bagels. Then I'll explain.'

Tayte led Mavro into the kitchen. He still had the Rogers file in his hand, which he set down in front of her as she made herself comfortable on one of the two stools at the breakfast bar. He tapped the folder. 'I found an interesting coincidence in here. See if you can spot it while I freshen up. I'll be as quick as I can.'

He was only gone ten minutes, during which time he'd hurriedly showered and changed into a fresh shirt and a lighter shade of tan linen suit from the selection of similar garments he kept in his wardrobe. Mavro was chomping on a bagel, eyes buried in the Rogers file, when he went back into the kitchen.

'Here's that list, before I forget,' Tayte said, handing it to her with one hand as he continued to comb his damp hair back with the other. Mavro took it and placed it inside her folder.

'Did you spot it?' Tayte asked. 'The coincidence?'

Mavro shook her head. 'I'm not even sure what I'm supposed to be looking at.'

Tayte poured himself a coffee and sat beside her. 'This,' he said, singling out the certificate of death from 1920 that he'd found the night before. 'It's not easy to see it amongst all these records. I doubt I'd have made the connection myself if this had been someone else's assignment file. Note the cause of death.'

'Smoke inhalation.'

Tayte nodded. 'It could have been due to a number of reasons, but I know from memory that it was because of a house fire. Up until 1999 the majority of fire deaths were put down to smoke inhalation, whether the deceased also died of burns or not. I remembered as soon as I saw the record. It was widely reported by the press at the time, and I'd read an article in the newspaper archives. A nine-year-old girl was killed. The fire was thought to have started in her bedroom. I can't recall the precise details, but I remember reading that it quickly raged out of control. By the time the little girl's parents knew anything about it, it was too late to save her. It was a tragic accident.'

'You think that's why our killer used a doll's house in the killing of his first victim? Because one of her ancestors—a child—died in a house fire?'

'It's a pretty big coincidence, don't you think? The girl had a brother. He was several years older and he was away from home at the time of the fire. He was Annabel Rogers' great-grandfather. Can you tell me where in Northwest Annabel Rogers was murdered?'

'Columbia Heights,' Mavro said, not needing to check her files. 'The house was on Otis Place.'

Tayte fetched his laptop, helping himself to a bagel as they waited for it to boot up. 'I don't recall the address, and I don't appear to have kept a copy of the newspaper report, but I'm sure it must have been noted at the time.'

He logged on to the Library of Congress digital newspaper archive, which contained over ten million newspaper pages from 1789 to 1922. Using the information from his assignment file he was soon looking at the report.

'There it is,' he said, hovering his index finger close to the screen so that Mavro could see the match. 'The house fire was also at Otis Place. That's where the little girl lived. It can't be a coincidence.'

'No, it can't,' Mavro agreed. 'The killer rented a room at the house where he killed Annabel Rogers. He used an alias and gave false details so we wouldn't be able to trace him.'

'Did anyone get a good look at him?'

'Sure. The landlady told us she saw him briefly when he first came to the house. She said he paid upfront in cash. After that, he kept to himself.'

'So what did he look like?'

Mavro smiled to herself. 'Big man, dark hair, tan suit. He looked just like you in sunglasses. It's easy to see it now for the disguise it was.'

Tayte frowned. 'He looked like me? No wonder Reese was suspicious of my involvement.'

'I've heard he can be a bit of a bear,' Mavro said. 'I shouldn't take it too personally. I've worked with a few ex-military agents in the past. They're not always the easiest to get along with.' She opened her folder and took out the piece of genealogical wheel chart that had been left at the scene of the Rogers murder. 'If this is the pattern,' she said, moving on, 'then the killer is as good as telling us who he's going to kill next.

He's left these charts at the scene of each murder to let us know where and how he plans to kill again.'

'If we can't stop him in time,' Tayte said. 'We should be able to prove the pattern easily enough.' He took a big gulp of coffee, collected his laptop and stood up. 'Would you care to follow me with those wheel charts?'

Tayte led Mavro into his file room, where he set his laptop down on the desk.

'My, my. You *have* been busy,' Mavro said as she took in all the cabinets and stacked shelves.

'You're looking at my life's work,' Tayte said. 'I guess I've had little else to do.'

'Right. Unmarried and no kids. I read that in your file.' Mavro laughed to herself. 'Same here, more's the pity.'

'Maybe it's not all it's cracked up to be,' Tayte offered, thinking about Jean, hoping he was wrong and knowing he was soon going to find out.

'Yeah, maybe,' Mavro said, somewhat unconvincingly.

Mavro handed Tayte the wheel chart from the first murder. 'Here. See what you can do with this.'

Tayte studied the name in the middle of the wheel. 'Wilbur Simmonds,' he read aloud. 'Born March 1895. Died August 1938.'

'That makes him forty-three years old at the time of his death,' Mavro said, taking no time at all to work it out.

'Right. I guess I must have come across him during my research at some point. He's the subject of the chart, so let's suppose for now that this is who the killer wants to draw our attention to.'

'And if we're on the right track,' Mavro said, 'if this theory about the first victim and the little girl who died in the house fire is correct, we should find that Wilbur Simmonds was shot dead in Lincoln Park back in 1938.'

Tayte nodded, thinking that by choosing a victim whose name couldn't be directly associated with one of his assignment files, as it was with Annabel Rogers, it made the puzzle a little more complicated, which was just how he imagined the killer had planned it. He studied the wheel chart further. Something struck him as odd.

'This isn't the way wheel charts generally work,' he said, offering the chart up so Mavro could see it more clearly. 'In the semi-circle beneath the subject, Wilbur Simmonds, you'd usually write his wife's name, and in each quadrant of the circle you'd write in the parents and grandparents, and so on for each person, going back in time.'

'I see what you mean,' Mavro said. 'The dates on this chart go forward, not back.'

'Yes, and that has to be significant, as must the names themselves, or why fill in only a few?'

There were five other names on the chart, and Tayte was immediately drawn to one of them. 'Hutchinson,' he said, recalling the conversation with Mavro and Reese the day before. 'You said that someone called Hutchinson was my client for the Edwards murder.'

'That's right,' Mavro said. 'Andrea Hutchinson. She was Randall Edwards' daughter. She hired you to compile her husband's family tree.'

'So Randall Edwards and Wilbur Simmonds are connected through Andrea Hutchinson's marriage.'

Tayte hurriedly stepped over to the drawer marked H and found the Hutchinson file. He took it to the desk and leaned over it with Mavro at his elbow. There were the usual vital record copies of births, marriages and deaths that he'd collected during the assignment, but for now he was only interested in the family tree he'd put together for his client's husband. He unfolded it and smoothed it out, scanning it for Wilbur Simmonds. A moment later he saw the name and stabbed his index finger at it to show Mavro.

'This is it,' he said. 'The other names on the killer's wheel chart are here, too.'

'Can we see how Wilbur Simmonds died?'

'Sure, a copy of his death certificate should be right here in this file.'

Tayte began to go through the file's contents. He kept his files neat and tidy, arranged chronologically for each ancestor, going backwards from death to birth, which is how he liked to work as it was often easier to find records that were more recent. It took less than a minute to single it out, and as soon as he looked at the cause of death he knew, without a doubt, that his theory was right.

'*Gunshot wound to head,*' he read aloud.

'Now we just need to confirm where he was shot,' Mavro said, the excitement of the chase for this serial killer evident in her voice.

Tayte went back to his laptop, and knowing the date of Wilbur Simmonds's death, he was quickly able to find the news article from 1938 he was interested in. It was in the form of an obituary that had been printed in the *Evening Star*, a former daily afternoon paper of the capital that ran from 1852 to 1981. Tayte expected that if he'd kept looking, he'd have found other reports of the shooting of Wilbur Simmonds, but his obituary was enough to tell him what he wanted to know.

'Gunned down in Lincoln Park,' he said. He thought perhaps Simmonds had been attacked for his wallet, or maybe he'd offended someone and got into a fight. The reason wasn't important. 'There's no question here that the manner of Randall Edwards' death was intended to replicate that of Wilbur Simmonds.'

Mavro was smiling broadly when Tayte looked at her. 'Good job!' she said. 'But we need to be absolutely sure of the killer's pattern. See if you can do it again for the Masterson twins with the wheel chart the killer left at the scene of the Edwards murder.'

Mavro handed Tayte the chart, and this time he went straight to his files beginning with D for Delacruz. Wanda Delacruz had been his client, aunt to the murdered Masterson twins. As before, he was soon able to match the Delacruz family tree with the rest of the names on the wheel chart. Ten minutes later, they were looking at another newspaper article, this one from 1951.

'It's clear now why the killer chose to murder his third and fourth victims where he did,' Tayte said. 'The Masterson twins were related to a man who worked at the McMillan Filtration Plant. He died in an industrial accident of sorts. It says here that he drowned in the reservoir while trying to save his brother.'

'I don't know about you,' Mavro said, 'but the fact that our killer just forced the Masterson twins into the same deadly scenario sends a chill right through my bones.'

'Let's have a look at that last clue,' Tayte said. 'I think we can confidently say it's going to lead us to the next victim, and with any luck you can get to him or her before the killer. It's not been long since the twins were murdered. This has to give us an advantage.'

'Reese is really going to like this,' Mavro said. 'These clues—these genealogical wheel charts—have had us confused from the get-go, but you've literally cracked it overnight.'

'You couldn't have known what they meant,' Tayte said. 'And even if you did, it would have taken too long without my files, and this.' He tapped his temple. 'The important connections are all up here. These are my past assignments—my clients. You'd need to know something about them.'

'That's worrying.'

'How do you mean?'

'I mean the killer must have known we'd need your help to work this out. That tells me he's wanted you on board from the start for some reason. Now we've played right into his hands. He'd have known we'd talk to the victims' families, and he could be sure your name would come up.'

'And that it would keep coming up until you got the message.'

'Right. And now we've brought you back to the District. Exactly where, I suspect, our killer wants you.'

Tayte shivered at the thought. It had been clear to him that this was personal for some reason ever since Reese had first called him, but Mavro had just none too subtly punctuated the reality of the situation— that a cold-blooded killer was prowling the streets of Washington, DC, bent on some kind of revenge against him. But for what? What had he done, and to whom?

———

Somewhere in DC, a man was standing in front of a wardrobe, staring at a photograph of Jefferson Tayte, scratching irritably at the scar that cut an angry chasm across his left eyebrow. He was irritable because he was having trouble concentrating again. It had become quite a problem for him.

He'd worked several jobs in recent months. He just couldn't seem to hold any of them down. They weren't particularly rewarding jobs, requiring no skills that couldn't be taught during the first day, but they had helped to get him back on his feet, and they paid the rent. He knew the problem was in part due to his temper, but that was just the thing that ultimately got him fired. It all stemmed from the fact that he couldn't stay focused on anything long enough, and the reason he couldn't focus was because his mind was so often elsewhere, in a very dark place. He was there now and he didn't like it. He wanted it to stop, and he knew there was only one way that was going to happen.

He had to kill Jefferson Tayte.

The man was forty-three years old and in the best shape of his life. He was a little over six feet tall, and while he'd always had an athletic physique, spending the last twenty years in one state prison or another, at the behest of the Maryland Department of Public Safety and Correctional Services, had turned him into a muscle-bound behemoth. In prison he'd had a goatee and used to shave his head, but now, because of the jobs, he was clean shaven with mid-brown hair cut short, but not too close. It was all part of trying to fit in with normal life after prison, his counsellor had told him. He didn't care much for her advice, but fitting in suited him well enough for now.

'Twenty miserable years . . .'

He was going to end Jefferson Tayte all right, but Tayte had to suffer first, as *he* had suffered. He continued to snarl at the overweight cause of his despair—at the photograph he'd taped to the wardrobe mirror to remind himself why he was doing this, as if he needed any reminder. He'd taken the picture through the wire fence as Tayte was leaving the McMillan sand-filtration site with the FBI the day before. Now he spat at it and turned away into a dimly lit flea-pit of a room that was barely more accommodating than the prison cells he'd become so accustomed to.

He'd rented the room three weeks ago, just as soon as he'd walked out on his last job, no fuss or fight this time. He just hadn't turned up one morning. The rent had been paid up front in cash, and he'd given false details because he didn't want anyone to know where he was, or who he was. There was a single bed against the wall, and a small stained sink by a barred window, which his eyes now wandered over to. He'd come to loathe bars, even if these bars were not there to keep him in, but were to keep out the dregs of DC's Southeast quadrant; not that he imagined there was anything in the entire building worth stealing.

Just let them try, he thought to himself, with a degree of relish as he continued to dress.

He pulled on a pair of faded grey jeans, his muscular thighs stretching the fabric. Reaching down to pick up his blue denim shirt from the bed, he caught the reflection of his broad back in the cracked mirror over the sink behind him. It bore a tattoo, and the sight of it reminded him of the gang he would always now be a part of: Dead Man Incorporated—a predominantly white prison gang. The tattoo showed the gang's name in bold lettering, arching around the initials, DMI. The letter M was in part made up from the tip of a pyramid into which was set a depiction of the Eye of Providence. The gang was anarchistic in nature, and its members often referred to themselves as *Dawgs*, an acronym for DMI Against World Government.

He hadn't joined the gang to bring down the government, although he imagined his actions of late were tying up more than a few federal resources. No, he had joined DMI for the protection that being part of a gang offered—safety in numbers. He buttoned up his shirt and refocused on the wardrobe mirror in front of him. He scratched at his scar again, something he'd picked up in a particularly bloody fight during his first few months inside. He'd been beaten and raped time and again during those days, but only in the beginning. After joining DMI he'd been left alone, and he'd muscled up. Then it was he who gave the beatings.

He put on a pair of black leather chukka boots and took another long and hateful stare at Tayte's image before he made for the door. He had work of another kind to do now—dark work to match the darkness in his mind, and this was a job he would absolutely stay focused on. Making Jefferson Tayte pay for what he'd done was all he could think about.

Chapter Four

Excited by Tayte's solution to the genealogical wheel charts the killer had left at the scene of each of the murders, Mavro strode into SAC Reese's office on 4th Street Northwest with Tayte at her heels, clearly anxious to give him their news. Reese was hunched over his desk looking at the front page of the *Washington Post* as they entered.

'Just look at this,' he said, offering up the front cover for Tayte and Mavro to see. He slapped the front page, angered by the headline. 'How did it get out so fast?' He shook his head. 'They're calling this killer the "Genie", for Christ's sake, because of the genealogy charts he leaves with his victims. Have either of you spoken to anyone about this?'

'No, sir,' Mavro said. 'Not a word.'

Tayte quickly shook his head.

'Probably some rookie cop leaked it,' Reese said. 'So what have you got for me?'

Mavro smiled. 'Good news. Might even cheer you up.'

'The Lord knows I could use some,' Reese said, his tone softening. 'Take a seat.'

Mavro sat at the desk facing Reese, and Tayte pulled another chair over and sat beside her, setting his briefcase down between them. From her folder, Mavro handed Reese the list of names Tayte had previously given to her, and Reese studied it with wide eyes.

'You appear to have upset a lot of people over the years, Mr Tayte.'

Tayte gave him a sheepish smile. 'It's been something of an occupational hazard.'

'That's not all we've got,' Mavro said. 'The really good news is that Mr Tayte has worked out what these charts mean.'

Reese looked surprised. 'Already?'

'Yes, and it's not because I drew up those charts in the first place,' Tayte said. 'If that's what you're thinking.'

'I didn't mean to insinuate anything,' Reese said. 'Tell me what you've got.'

'Actually, it was pretty straightforward—for me at least. I literally had all the records I needed right there at my fingertips. It would have taken anyone else far longer.'

There was a hint of a smile on Reese's face, as if to suggest that he was coming around to the idea that it was a good thing to have Tayte on board. 'So, what do these charts mean? What's our killer telling us?'

'In broad terms, he's telling us who the next victim will be, and how and where he's going to kill them.'

'Broad terms?'

Tayte nodded. He reached into his briefcase and brought out the details he'd put together for the first murder. With Mavro's permission, he'd made copies of the wheel charts the killer had left for them. He pointed to the name in the centre of the chart that was left when Annabel Rogers was murdered. 'The name in the middle of the chart indicates from whose family tree the next victim will come. So far, as you know, they've all been clients of mine, or a close member of their family.' He tapped the name. 'The location and manner of death of the person in the centre of this chart is basically being replicated by the Genie here in the present day.'

Reese sighed at hearing Tayte use the moniker the press had given this killer, clearly still aggravated by it. 'So you know who the next victim is going to be?'

Tayte and Mavro looked at one another, as though for assurance. Then they both nodded.

'More or less,' Mavro said. 'We know it will either be Tayte's former client, a Mrs Jennifer Walters, who lives in Northwest, or a member of her family.'

'And the manner and location of death?'

Tayte brought out the chart that had been left at the scene of the Masterson murders and slid it across the desk to Reese. 'As you can see, the wheel chart left at the scene of the Masterson murders contains a woman's name, the names of her three children, and a question mark alongside those three children, suggesting a fourth child. It was clear from this that I had to work out how and where the mystery fourth child died. I found the corresponding file I had for this family, and at first I wondered how on earth I was going to work it out because I had the exact same information in the file—three names and a question mark.'

Reese looked intrigued. 'How did you work it out?'

Tayte produced another piece of paper and handed it to Reese. 'Turns out I already had. At the back of the file was this newspaper cutting.'

Reese looked at it. He read out the headline. '*Infant remains found in Georgetown attic.*'

'The baby had been wrapped in newspaper and sealed inside a cardboard box,' Tayte said, saving Reese the trouble of reading the full article. 'The newspaper in the box was printed in 1935, during the Great Depression. It was thought that the child had been the result of an unwanted pregnancy and had become one too many mouths to feed. The discovery was made during the redevelopment of the Georgetown slum area where the family lived.'

Reese looked incredulous. 'My God. I've come across some things in my time.' He shook his head. 'So you believe the killer is planning to murder his next victim at the same address?'

'That appears to be the pattern,' Tayte said.

'Only the house is no longer there,' Mavro added.

'Right. Area redevelopment. Do we know what's there now?'

'Generally speaking, yes,' Tayte said. 'Before we came to see you we checked with the Library of Congress Geography and Map Division. They have a freely available online map collection.' Tayte paused and reached into his briefcase again. He took out a current map of the city and indicated a section to Reese. 'I marked an X here in Georgetown, roughly where the house was in 1935.'

'The satellite image on Google Maps shows a large structure there now,' Mavro said. 'Using Google Street View we were quickly able to determine that it's a parking garage.'

Reese sighed. 'So how on earth are we going to pinpoint the location of the house?'

'We haven't figured that out yet,' Mavro said.

'Maybe we should visit the location,' Tayte added, keen to get involved beyond looking at records. If he could work out exactly where the house was in 1935, he figured they would have a much better chance of catching the killer.

Reese gave a nod. 'Okay, you two get on it. It's probably too soon to expect another body. In the meantime, I'll send a team over to talk with your former client, Jennifer Walters.' A satisfied expression washed over Reese as he sat back in his chair. 'Mr Tayte, I believe myself to be a fair man, and it seems I owe you an apology. It's a habit of the job to be suspicious of people, but my early instincts about you were clearly wrong. I'm sorry, and I want to thank you. As of right now, I believe we're ahead of the game for the first time.'

Reese reached inside his jacket pocket and took out his cigar case. He opened it, put his nose to the open end, and drew a long breath through his nose. He offered the open end to Tayte. 'Take a sniff.'

'Thanks, but I don't smoke.'

Reese pushed it closer. 'I don't want you to smoke it. Just take a sniff. Go on. It won't bite you.'

Tayte leaned closer and drew in the aroma. It smelled like tilled soil after rain, of barnyards and old leather.

'You know what you're smelling right there?'

Tayte screwed his face up, as if it were obvious. 'A cigar?'

Reese shook his head. 'No, that's not a cigar in there.'

'It isn't?' Tayte offered, feeling somewhat bemused.

'Not to me it isn't. It's a symbol of success, and its aroma is the smell of success. I don't smoke as a rule, either, but at the start of every big case like this, I buy myself a fine cigar and put it in this case. I'll smoke it, and I'll savour every breath of it, but only when I've earned it—once this killer sees the justice that's coming to him and the case is closed.'

'I see,' Tayte said, not knowing what else to say.

Mavro began to stand up. Tayte followed her lead, but Reese hadn't quite finished.

'I don't want any heroics, remember. Just see what you can find and report back to me as soon as you have something.'

Mavro drove a silver Jeep Cherokee SUV. She parked up as close as she could get to the garage facility she and Tayte were interested in and they walked the remaining distance. Staring up at the red-brick and smoked-glass building, Tayte couldn't see how it was going to be possible to know exactly where the house from 1935 had stood, and he could see from the look on Mavro's face that she was thinking along similar lines.

Mavro shook her head. 'It would take a team from city planning all week to tell us exactly where that house was located. Looks like the street's been widened at some point, too. We could be standing on top of it right now.'

'I don't suppose the Genie works for city planning,' Tayte offered as they strode up to the garage entrance. 'Come to think of it, he probably couldn't know exactly where the house stood either. I guess the simple answer is that the house stood where this parking facility now stands.'

Mavro agreed. 'But where would he choose to kill his victim? What's he thinking?'

Trying to get into the mind of a serial killer wasn't something Tayte wanted to do, but he had to try. 'One thing's for sure,' he said. 'Once he's killed again, he wants us to find the body. I doubt he'd want to make it too difficult once we'd worked out where to come.'

There was an office beside the entrance barriers. Through the glass, Tayte could see a young man in a shirt and tie reading a book with his feet up on the desk.

'I know I told you I'm not an agent,' Mavro said, 'and technically that remains true, but I've got a badge and right now I aim to use it.'

Tayte smiled. 'Good,' he said. 'Authority suits you.'

He knocked, the sound seeming to startle the young man, as if he wasn't used to people calling in person. He clearly wasn't too busy. He sat bolt upright as Tayte opened the door and followed Mavro inside. She'd taken out the badge Reese had given her before she'd crossed the threshold.

'I'm Agent Mavro. I'm with the FBI,' she said, holding her badge up for the young man to see. 'We need to take a look around this facility. Do you need to call someone for authorisation?'

'No, I can authorise it,' the young man said. 'What are you looking for?'

'That's federal business,' Mavro said, her tone uncharacteristically surly. 'It shouldn't take long. Do you have any co-workers on site?'

The young man shook his head. 'Only when there's a problem. Everything's automated.'

'Any locked rooms we might need access to?'

'There's a small equipment room in back.' He went to get up. 'I can show you.'

'No, that's okay for now. Anything else?'

'There's the plant room beneath the lower ground floor. It's mostly for the ventilation system.'

Mavro raised her eyebrows at Tayte. She turned back to the young man. 'Can you show us?'

The young man sprang to his feet, as if eager to help. He opened a drawer and grabbed a bunch of keys. 'Sure, I can lock up the office awhile.' He snorted a laugh. 'I doubt the phone'll ring any time soon.'

They were led across the ground-level parking area, where most of the parking bays were full. The overhead lights were typically bright. No cars had come or gone since Tayte and Mavro had arrived.

'There's not much activity here,' Tayte said as they walked, heading around the perimeter of the facility towards a set of double doors that he imagined gave access to the stairwell.

'It's mostly long-term parking,' the young man said.

They took the concrete stairs to the lower-ground level. Beyond the double doors that led out to the parking bays was another door, which the young man unlocked. The stairwell on the other side only led down and there was a further doorway at the bottom of the steps.

'It's right in here,' the young man said, raising his voice so he could be heard over the hum emanating from the ventilation slats.

They went through and the noise grew louder. Inside was a matrix of steel pipework and cables, switch boxes, and other electrical and mechanical plant equipment.

'Not much to see,' the young man said, taking them further in.

'Who else has access to this room?' Mavro asked.

'There's only two sets of keys I know of. The set I have, which is kept in the office for whoever's on shift, and the manager has a set.'

'And do you know if anyone's been down here lately?'

'No, not lately. If they had I'd have seen it in the log book. Last time was just a regular inspection about a month ago.'

The tour of the plant room was brief. There really wasn't much to see, and it was clear to Tayte, as it must have been to Mavro, that there were no signs that their killer had tried to set up any of his diabolical apparatus. If this was the room where the Genie intended to murder his next victim then, as Reese had supposed, they were well ahead of the game.

Mavro threw the young man a smile. 'Thanks,' she said, and they all made for the exit.

Back on ground level, Mavro said, 'We're going to take a look around before we leave. I'll drop by the office and let you know once we're done.'

'Oh, sure. Okay,' the young man said, sounding a little disappointed that his services were no longer required.

Tayte followed Mavro back into the stairwell, where they took the stairs up a level. Apart from the entrance and the office, it looked just the same, but with a few more vacant parking spaces.

'Anything stand out here for you, Mr Tayte?'

Tayte shook his head. 'Just more cars and concrete pillars. That plant room would appear to be the only place the killer could go about his business unnoticed. That's good, right? That has to be the place.'

'I don't know,' Mavro said as they followed the ramp up to the next level. 'Reese will probably have the place staked out. Maybe someone will show.'

'Does protocol allow you to call me JT?' Tayte asked. 'Most people I know do. Mr Tayte sounds kinda stuffy.'

'Sure, I could manage that. And maybe you could stop calling me Ms Mavro, which, in case you didn't know, is short for Mavrothalassitis.'

'Greek.'

Mavro nodded. 'From my father's side. It's quite a mouthful. My first name's Franchesca, but I go by Frankie—Frankie Mavro.'

Tayte smiled and offered out a hand. 'It's nice to meet you, Frankie.'

'Likewise, JT,' Mavro said, shaking his hand firmly. 'So how did you end up being a genealogist?'

'I found out I was adopted when I was in my teens, after my adoptive parents died. They left me a letter, telling me what little they knew. In short, my birth mother abandoned me and I wanted to know why. I wanted to find her so I could ask her. I got into genealogy as a means to find my family.'

'How did that work out for you?'

'Until recently it wasn't working out at all. I only found out about my biological parents a few months back.'

'That's great,' Mavro said. 'Better late than never, right?'

'Perhaps. I was told they both died in the 1970s.'

'Oh, I'm sorry.'

'That's okay. The cloud has a silver lining. I also found out I have a brother, recently confirmed with a sibling DNA test. We've been corresponding since we met and I've visited with him a couple of times. I was also able to find out more about my wider family. It's all I've been doing for the past few months. And even if she has passed on, it's good to know about my mother after all this time. I'm glad to be able to put a name to the woman in the photo I've been carrying around in my wallet for so many years.'

Tayte could feel the weight of the conversation bringing his mood down. He had no doubt that his father was dead and he'd come to terms with that, but it upset him to think of his mother in the past tense. He'd heard a compelling story about how she died, but so far his research had turned up little to corroborate the story. Maybe that's all it was—in part at least: a story. It was Tayte's fantasy, perhaps, but he liked to believe she was still out there somewhere, despite everything he'd heard, and despite the fact that she had never come back for him. He wanted to change the subject, but his mind had become too caught up in his own recent past to move on.

Thankfully, Mavro moved the subject on for him. 'As we're getting better acquainted,' she said, 'can I ask how come you made it to forty-one years of age without getting hitched?' She smirked. 'Are you gay? I mean if you are, I have no problem with that, just so you know.'

'No, I'm not gay,' Tayte said, smiling. He laughed to himself and was glad to do so. 'Even if I was, I still wouldn't have found the time or the commitment for a relationship. That's been my problem. I'm always working and I have a tendency to shut people out. It took me a long time to realise that, but now I have a fiancée. She lives in England.'

'Well, good for you.'

Tayte smiled again. 'I can honestly say she's the best thing that's ever happened to me.'

'How did you meet her?'

'Under somewhat tragic circumstances. We met in London just over a year ago. It was on the day a good friend of mine was killed.'

'I'm so sorry to hear that.'

'Yeah,' Tayte said again, and then he turned the question around before his mood darkened again. 'What about you? I picked up earlier that you're not married either. What was it you said? *More's the pity?*'

'I don't think I'll be hearing any wedding bells anytime soon,' Mavro said. 'I'm afraid I recognise too much of myself in what you just said.'

'There's no one?'

'No, not really.'

'Not really? Is that a maybe?'

'Well, there's this guy I used to work with off and on when I was in the field—Special Agent Jerome Martinez. Our paths still cross from time to time, and . . .'

Mavro's phone began to buzz and she trailed off. She checked the display. 'It's Reese.'

She took the call and Tayte waited to hear what he had to say. By the time the call had ended, he thought she looked a little pale and there was urgency in her eyes as she looked up at him and said, 'We need to get out of here. Right now.'

They walked back to the stairwell at a brisk pace.

'What's happened?' Tayte asked.

'Reese just heard back from the team he sent to see your former client Jennifer Walters.'

'Has something happened to her? Is she okay?'

'She's okay. It's her daughter. She's been missing for the past three weeks.'

Chapter Five

Special Agent in Charge Jordan Reese arrived outside the garage facility ten minutes after his call to Mavro. With him were two other men, both wearing blue jackets with large yellow FBI lettering on the back. They were introduced as Special Agents Woods and Farrier. Tayte imagined they were there for support if any were needed, although he figured that if Reese thought they were in any immediate danger, he would have told him and Mavro to keep out of the way. They were all now heading back inside and Reese was clearly upset. He'd been sighing and shaking his head since he'd arrived.

'I really thought we were ahead of this killer,' he said, sighing again as they passed the barriers that led into the garage complex. 'As soon as I heard that Kelly Uttridge, your former client's daughter, was missing, I wanted you both out of here as quickly as possible in case our killer was around. I didn't want him to get spooked and choose another location. As she's been missing three weeks, however, I now believe that whatever our killer had planned for her has already happened. Why else take her so early? It would be an unnecessary risk on his part.'

'You think she's here?' Mavro said. 'There aren't many places to hide a body without someone noticing it, and we've checked the only room offering any kind of privacy.'

Reese stopped walking outside the office and gave her a bemused look, as if to suggest she'd overlooked the obvious. 'There are literally hundreds of places to hide a body here, Ms Mavro.' He waved a hand towards the parked cars. 'Take a look around you. How many vehicles do you see?'

Mavro gave no answer. She just nodded her head to let Reese know she understood what he meant.

'And that's just on this level,' Reese continued. 'Did you manage to locate the exact position of the house from 1935? Maybe he put Kelly Uttridge's body in a car parked on the same spot.'

'No, sir,' Mavro said.

Tayte joined the conversation. 'I don't believe the killer could have known the exact location of the house,' he said. 'I think he just wanted us to come here to this garage.'

Reese laughed. 'So we've got to check every car and pop every trunk in the place to find out if we've got another body on our hands?'

'No, I don't think he'd have made it that difficult. The genealogical wheel chart brought us here. That was the puzzle. If there is a body here, finding it should be relatively easy.'

'You have something in mind? If you do, I'd love to hear it.'

'Not really,' Tayte said. 'Just follow your procedures, I guess.'

'Follow my procedures. Okay.'

Reese turned away and without knocking he walked into the office where the young parking attendant was already standing expectantly, no doubt having seen the FBI lettering on the jackets of Special Agents Woods and Farrier outside his window. Tayte and Mavro followed Reese into the office. The other agents waited outside.

Reese showed his badge. 'I need to see your records for every vehicle still in this facility that's been parked here within the last three weeks. Can you do that?'

'Yeah, sure,' the young man said with enthusiasm. He sat down and began tapping keys on the computer keyboard in front of him. 'It shouldn't take long.'

Reese turned back to Tayte and Mavro. 'This Genie would have to be pretty dumb to leave a car here in his own name, but it's not something we can afford to overlook.'

Tayte didn't think they were dealing with someone of low intelligence. Quite the opposite.

'On the other hand,' Reese added, 'people make mistakes, and that's ultimately what gets them caught. Maybe we'll find a match with one of the names on that list of yours.'

The printer behind the desk the young man was sitting at began to whir and he sprang to his feet. 'Here it is,' he said, snatching up the sheets of paper it had just churned out. 'These are all monthly leases. That just means the parking space has been paid for in advance for the month, not that the car in question is currently here. The owners can come and go as they please.' He handed the printouts to Reese, who glanced over them.

'There must be close to three hundred names here,' he said, scanning through them all. 'I'll get some copies made of your list, Mr Tayte. We can all then take a sheet apiece. It shouldn't take too long to—' He stopped suddenly and began to look more closely at something he'd noticed on the printout. 'Would you believe it?' he said. 'Take a look at this.' He handed one of the printouts to Tayte. 'See anything familiar?'

Tayte did. He was staring at his own name, right there against a vehicle registration and parking bay allocation. He looked up from the printout. 'The Genie couldn't have left us a bigger sign than this.'

The young garage attendant's ears pricked up. 'The Genie?' he said, bright eyed. 'Is that the case you're working on? I read about it in the paper this morning.'

Reese didn't answer the question. Tayte had made it so obvious that he didn't have to. He took the printout back and tapped the entry against Tayte's name. 'It would save us time if you could take us to this parking bay,' he told the attendant.

Tayte knew which vehicle they were going to long before they got there. He'd recognised the licence plate number on the printout, and he saw the car as soon as they all left the stairwell and turned towards it. It was his car. The torch-red 1955 Ford Thunderbird stood out amidst the comparatively dull modern vehicles around it like a bright splash of paint on an empty canvas.

Tayte's jaw dropped at the sight of it. That car was his pride and joy. He'd have known it anywhere, even without the licence plate, which he could now just about make out. It was the first car he'd bought and the only car he'd ever wanted to own.

'That's my car,' he said, as if unable to fathom how it came to be there. He realised then that the Genie must have stolen it. Tayte had a rented lock-up a few blocks from his apartment. He kept it there whenever he was away on business, and he'd been away a lot lately, giving the Genie plenty of opportunity.

Tayte began to run to it, but strong arms held him back. It was Woods and Farrier.

'Take it easy, sir,' one of them said.

'It could be dangerous,' the other man added.

Reese stepped in front of them. 'You'd better stay back,' he said to Tayte. 'Do you have a key?'

Tayte kept one on a key ring with the keys to his apartment. He fished in his pocket and handed it to Reese, wondering how his car could have been stolen. The lock-up where he kept it was secure and manned twenty-four seven, which is why he'd chosen the place. When he was in England earlier that year, he'd left his keys at Jean's apartment during their visit to Germany, but Jean's apartment was thousands of miles away.

'He must have broken into it at the lock-up and hot-wired it,' Tayte said. Then a chilling thought occurred to him. 'Or he's somehow gotten the spare key from my apartment.' He could see no other possible explanation. He kept his only spare in a kitchen drawer at home.

'We'll be sure to look into it,' Reese said, 'but right now I need you to stay exactly where you are while we go and take a look at your car. You too, Mavro.'

Tayte nodded. Then, as the three Special Agents headed towards Tayte's car, he said, 'Shouldn't you call the bomb squad in? What if it's booby-trapped?'

Reese turned back. 'That crossed my mind, but I'm pretty sure this killer wants us to find a body, not blow us all to kingdom come.'

'Right,' Tayte said, automatically taking a step back, just in case Reese was wrong.

'It's a nice car,' Mavro said. 'Lots of chrome, whitewall tyres. I love the white hardtop.'

Tayte knew Mavro was trying to take his mind off what was going on, to calm him down, but it wasn't working. He took two steps closer as the agents reached the vehicle, his eyes wide with anticipation as Reese snapped on a pair of latex gloves. Tayte watched him move around to the driver's side of the vehicle and look in the window. He seemed to study the lock area briefly before he came around to the back again.

'He's opening the trunk,' Tayte said a moment later.

'Yeah, I can see,' Mavro said.

As it popped open, all three agents reeled back. Tayte's nerves were so on edge that he reeled back with them, but nothing exploded. Instead, all three agents instinctively covered their mouths and noses, and at once Tayte knew they had found another body. He watched them step closer again. One of the agents shone his torch inside, his free hand still firmly over his face. Tayte saw Reese produce what appeared to be a penknife just before he leaned further in. A few seconds later, Reese recoiled again and slammed the lid shut. The sound echoed around the otherwise quiet space, jarring Tayte's nerves further. Reese came back after that, leaving the other two agents by the car. One of them was on his radio, calling it in.

The sour expression on Reese's face said it all. 'I don't want to disturb the scene, so right now I can't tell you for sure if that's Kelly Uttridge in there, but I have little doubt that it is. There's a cardboard box inside, sealed with duct tape. From the glimpse I had when I cut the corner of the box open, I know it's a woman. The blonde hair I saw fits with Kelly's description, and I don't need a coroner's report to tell me she's been dead for some time. We never had a chance to save her.'

'She was sealed inside a box and suffocated,' Tayte said under his breath. 'Just like the infant in her family tree from 1935.'

'So it would appear,' Reese said. 'As far as your car's concerned, none of the locks appear to have been forced, so maybe the killer did steal the key from your apartment. And he chose his parking bay well. The car's parked right next to one of the ventilation ducts to mask any smell that might have escaped as the body began to decompose—not that I could smell anything untoward before I opened the trunk.' He paused and looked directly at Tayte. 'Mr Tayte, there's a large envelope taped to the box. It has your name on it.'

Chapter Six

As soon as Tayte returned home with Mavro he went straight to the drawer in his kitchen where he kept his spare car key, anxious to know whether it was still there. The second thing he did was call Reese.

'My spare car key's right here where I left it,' Tayte said, dangling the key in front of him as he spoke. 'If whoever put that poor woman in the trunk of my car used this key to steal it, then they put it right back where they found it.'

'That doesn't sound too likely,' Reese said. 'Unless our killer is deliberately trying to mess with your head. Any sign of a break-in?'

'Nothing obvious. I was tired when I got home last night, though, and I was focused on putting that list together for you. I'll take a better look around with Ms Mavro now.'

'Okay, well you let me know if you find anything. I'll have the lock-up where you keep your car checked. Someone might have seen something.'

'They have CCTV.'

'Great. Maybe they picked something up. Stay put until I call. I'll let you know as soon as the lab's done with that envelope.'

'I will,' Tayte said, eager to know what it contained, and why it had specifically been addressed to him this time.

He ended the call and started thinking over what Reese had just said about the killer messing with his head. If that was true, then it was working. His clients and their relatives were dying left, right and centre, and somewhere deep inside him that really hurt. The Genie could have stolen just about any car to stage the murder of Kelly Uttridge, but he'd chosen to take his Thunderbird, possibly with the spare key from his apartment.

What if the killer really has been here?

It was still the only way Tayte thought anyone could know so much about his former clients. Whoever was doing this clearly had good knowledge of his victims' family histories.

Mavro was working the coffee machine as Tayte turned to her. 'Can we put a hold on that coffee while we check if anyone's been in my apartment?' He went to the window, keen to know the answer.

'Sure,' Mavro said. 'It looks pretty clean though. If anyone was here while you were away, they did a very good job of tidying up behind themselves before they left.'

'Yeah, but I'd like to be absolutely certain.'

They checked each room together on the principle that two pairs of eyes were better than one; if either of them missed something, the other might not. The apartment was in a small three-storey corner block with windows on three sides. The kitchen and file room backed on to one another and both looked out on to a side street, the view to which was mostly blocked by trees. The living area had a window above a lawned space and the steps that led down to North Carolina Avenue. Finally, there was a small obscured window in the bathroom at the back of the apartment that faced a tidy, but featureless, communal garden Tayte had never used.

It was an older property with quarter-panel sash windows. They checked the thumb bolts on each window and all were locked down tight and secure. The glass panes were all intact. Nothing was broken. They checked the main door to the apartment last as they came back into the living area that was home to Tayte's couch, his crowded bookcase, and a few paintings here and there of Native Americans that he kept as a reminder of his country's history and its people, respectful of the land in which he lived, and of those who had lived there before him.

'Nothing amiss here, either,' he said, closing the door that led into the hallway outside. The door was solid and showed no signs of damage or forced entry.

'We should talk to your neighbours,' Mavro said.

'I don't really know anyone too well.'

'It doesn't matter. We just want to know if anyone saw or heard anything unusual or suspicious while you were away.'

Tayte nodded, doubting anyone even knew he'd been gone. 'Do you want to grab that coffee first?'

'Sure, why not.'

Tayte marched back into the kitchen and returned a moment later with two cups. Mavro was sitting on the couch. He handed her one of the cups and slouched down beside her. Neither of them spoke as they sipped their hot coffee. Tayte just stared at the bookcase in front of him, deep in thought, trying to think if there was any other way the Genie could have known who his clients were. Nothing came to him. He didn't even keep a list. There were just his files. Lots of them. A moment later, Tayte's eyes focused on one of the books in the bookcase. What he saw made him sit bolt upright. He stood up and went to it. It was one of his favourites: an old copy of *The Adventures of Tom Sawyer*, bound in a plain blue jacket.

'I don't know how he got in, but he's been here,' Tayte said. His eyes fell on another book, further along. It was a well-thumbed copy of *Gentle Ben* by Walt Morey: another cherished title from his childhood. 'These two books aren't level with the rest. I always put them back so they're flush.'

He was about to push one of the books in to line it up with those to either side when Mavro stopped him. She was suddenly beside him with her hand on his arm.

'Don't touch it,' she said. 'There could be prints. Are you absolutely sure these books aren't how you left them?'

Tayte nodded. 'I'm very particular about it, bordering obsessive, like Reese with that cigar case in his office yesterday. I like things in their place; neat and tidy. These books aren't. I never would have left them like that. Someone's taken them out and not put them back straight.'

'Could someone else have moved them—someone who's been here with you at some point? A friend? Or maybe your fiancée?'

Tayte didn't need to think about it. He shook his head emphatically. 'I don't really have any friends. My fiancée hasn't been here in a while, and I know I dusted everywhere and generally tidied up before I left for Europe three months ago. These books were all in a neat line.'

'Okay, so someone's been here, and whoever failed to put your books back right before they left must have gotten in somehow.' Mavro peered at the two books again. 'Maybe he wanted to draw our attention to them for some reason.'

'You think he left us a note inside one of them?'

'It's possible. Or perhaps he was just passing the time while he copied your files. Anyone else have a door key?' Mavro smiled to herself. 'Scratch that. Of course they don't. You're a loner. I get it. Let's take another look around. Whoever it was is either good at picking locks or we must have missed something.'

The windows were the obvious answer, so they inspected them all again. Those at the side were vulnerable on account of the trees outside, which not only obscured the view looking out, but also the view looking towards the house from the street, making it difficult to see anyone who might be trying to gain entry. As before, they saw nothing unusual. It wasn't until they went into the bathroom that something now stood out as odd.

It was Mavro who spotted it. 'Your windows aren't too clean, are they?'

'I haven't had a chance to clean them since I got back.'

'Right.'

Mavro stepped closer to the window. She opened it and leaned out to take a better look at the outside of the glass. 'I didn't notice it before.

Maybe the light's changed, but wouldn't you say that this particular pane looks cleaner than the rest?' She tapped the pane in question with her fingernail as Tayte stood beside her.

'What are you saying?'

'I'm saying I think maybe this pane has been replaced.' Mavro was still scrutinising the glass. 'Yeah, that's exactly what I think,' she added. 'Although there's no difference in the paint coloration. The area around this pane is just as white as the rest, but that doesn't mean much. The whole frame could have been repainted.'

'Three months is plenty of time to replace a broken window and repaint the frame,' Tayte offered.

'I'm going to call it in,' Mavro said, taking out her phone.

They went back to the couch and Tayte listened as Mavro spoke with Reese. When the call ended, she said, 'He says we're to sit tight and not disturb anything more than we already have. He's sending over an Evidence Response Team. They'll check the place for prints and collect forensic material.'

'And check out those two books?'

Mavro nodded. 'It'll take a while, so Reese suggested we head back to see him as soon as they get here. He's expecting that envelope back from the lab any minute.'

'Great,' Tayte said. 'If there's another clue in there, I'd really like to get started on it.'

There was little doubt in Tayte's mind that the envelope contained a clue to the Genie's next murder, and he found himself wondering which of his former clients' families the killer was going to target next. How and where would that person die if he couldn't work out what was going on in time? He had no idea where this sick game was heading, or what was coming next. All he knew was that he had to stop it.

Within the hour, Tayte and Mavro were back at Reese's office. It was just after midday, and the envelope was on the desk waiting for them as they entered the room—as was Reese's cigar case. He was staring down at it, his brow set in a deep furrow as if he were somehow trying to channel positive energy through it. He looked far more troubled than Tayte had so far seen him.

'It's going to be a while before the lab techs are fully finished with everything,' Reese said, 'but it's been confirmed that it was Kelly Uttridge's body inside the trunk of your car, Mr Tayte.'

Tayte had already convinced himself that it had to be her, but this cold confirmation left him feeling numb all over again. As with the rest of the victims, Kelly had died simply because she was related to someone who had previously employed Tayte's services, and he was having trouble coming to terms with that. He took a deep breath as he sat down with his briefcase.

'This has to end,' he said, his dark eyes fixed on Reese's, his hands making fists beneath the desk as numbness turned to raw anger.

Reese gave a solemn nod. 'Maybe we can do that this time. We didn't have a chance with Kelly Uttridge. She wasn't the Genie's fifth victim. She was his first.'

Tayte's eyes sank to the envelope on the desk between them and settled on his own name, scrawled on the front in black ink. 'The killer knew I'd be involved at this point,' he said. 'He's very calculating.'

'Yes, he is. Either that, or he'd written your name on this envelope so we'd get you involved if you weren't already by now. Either way, it confirms he wants you to partake in his game. I'm going to have you relocated to a safe house, especially since you believe someone's been inside your apartment while you were away. You can work on stopping this from there.'

'What about my files? I'm going to need them.'

'I'll have everything moved once forensics are finished. You'll have all you need.'

Tayte sighed and nodded, thinking it was probably a good idea under the circumstances.

'The clock starts again, Mr Tayte,' Reese said. 'And we can be damn sure our killer already knows who his next victim is going to be. Maybe he or she has already been abducted. The MPD is trying to find out whether any of the families of those reported missing recently have had any dealings with you in the past. That's going to take time, though, and it could prove fruitless.' Reese slid the envelope closer to Tayte. 'Our best hope is inside this envelope. Take a look. See what you can make of it.'

Tayte picked up the envelope. It was a plain white letter envelope with no distinguishing features. He found himself holding his breath as he opened it, expecting to find another piece of genealogical wheel chart—but not this time. Inside the envelope was a small piece of paper, not much bigger than a business card, and Tayte was momentarily bewildered by what he saw written on it. He hadn't really known what to expect, but seeing his name on the envelope had made him think there would be some kind of personal message. Maybe something from the past that only he would understand, but that wasn't the case. He read it out.

'*Ream EBH 4/30/2.*'

'I was hoping it would mean something to you,' Reese said with disappointment, clearly having noticed the lost expression on Tayte's face.

'The last part could be a date of birth or death,' Tayte offered. 'Or it could be something else. It might make better sense once we know what the first part means.' He took his notebook out from his inside jacket pocket and wrote everything down. 'Whatever this refers to, it appears the Genie just changed the nature of the game. I suspect he's made it relatively easy up until now just to get me involved, and he wanted us to know the rules. Find the ancestor, find the victim.' He looked at the obscure clue again, and now that he was on board he had the feeling that this deadly game had begun in earnest.

'Whatever it refers to,' Mavro said. 'It's gotta be something to do with family history, right?'

Tayte put his notebook away, nodding. 'If I've understood the rules well enough, this clue should point to someone in one of my clients' files, just as before. Up until now, the killer's made it obvious who that was—the name in the centre of the genealogical wheel charts he was leaving at the scene, whose death he intends to replicate. Now we've got to work that part out, too. I'd like to get started on it right away.'

'Of course,' Reese said. 'You and Ms Mavro can work here while we relocate your files.'

'I could use some air, if that's okay,' Tayte said. 'And some lunch. I don't think so well on an empty stomach.'

'Whatever works best for you, but stay in contact. I've got other people trying to crack this. If they get a breakthrough I'll let you know, and I want you to do the same. Once everything's set, I'll have someone drop you at the safe house. You can collect whatever personal items you need from your apartment along the way.' He paused and drew a sharp breath. 'I'm sure I don't need to tell you that time is critical here. We don't know how long we have.'

Tayte and Mavro both gave a sombre nod. As they left Reese's office, heading for the stairs, Tayte wondered just how long it would be before another body was found. Twenty-four hours? Forty-eight? The Genie surely knew Tayte was involved by now, and Tayte didn't imagine the killer would give him very long.

Who's doing this? he thought again, wondering what the Genie was doing right now. Had he already gone to work on his latest victim? What terrible fate did he have planned for him or her this time?

⌣

The man with the scarred eyebrow was troubled.

'Decisions, decisions,' he said to himself. He just couldn't choose.

He was sitting in a blue Ford Econoline camper van, which he'd stolen that morning. It was parked between several other vehicles beneath the shade of a tree whose red and gold leaves threw him into shadow. He offered his binoculars up to his eyes again and continued to look at option number one through one of the windows of the house he was watching.

Pretty little black girl, he thought. She was four years old, hair bunched up in a ponytail. *Don't you have the cutest smile . . .*

He drifted the binoculars across the house to his right, to another window, where he saw her father, option number two, preparing their lunch. How different, and how difficult he imagined it must have been for the man since his wife had died. The house was in Kensington, one of DC's commuter suburbs in Montgomery County, Maryland. The town was purported by many to be the safest in the DC area.

But not today.

He shook his head. He couldn't afford to sit there all day while Jefferson Tayte was busy solving the next puzzle he'd set for him. He'd heard about the discovery of Kelly Uttridge's body earlier that morning on his handheld radio scanner, and he knew Tayte was good at what he did. He'd seen just how good he was first hand, and he didn't think the latest clue he'd left for him would take the genealogist too long to solve. He had to be quick this time. He had to choose right now.

But which one?

If he chose the father, he would leave the little girl without any parents at all, perhaps in the care of her grandmother, the woman who had once employed Tayte's genealogical services. He smiled wryly to himself.

How could she have known what that would someday lead to?

If he chose the little girl, on the other hand, the father would be left to grieve the loss of both of the people he loved most in the world. The little girl was young. She would have been no more than a year old when her mother died, and he doubted she even remembered her.

But she looked so adorable, sitting there colouring in her picture book, nodding her head to whichever nursery rhyme he imagined she was humming to herself.

He lowered his binoculars again, careful not to use them too long at any one time in case someone saw them and began to wonder what he was looking at. So he sat, idly gazing at the double-fronted house, and he began to think about the nice house he once had—a better house even than this. But then, he'd had so much going for him before Jefferson Tayte came along with his unwavering sense of right and wrong, digging into his client's family history without giving a thought to those who might suffer as a result of what he found.

'I've suffered,' he muttered to himself, picturing the genealogist in his bright tan suit the day he'd first clapped eyes on him. At the same time, he slammed his fist into the passenger seat. 'Now it's your turn.'

He didn't need his binoculars to see the little girl's father join her at the table she was sitting at. They began to eat their meal, the last meal for one of them, and he thought about tossing a coin to decide which. He didn't really care. Maybe he'd base his decision on opportunity. It wasn't as if either of their lives had any meaning or purpose beyond their own imaginations and the propagation of a species that was already beginning to outstay its welcome in this world. So what if the little girl might someday go on to cure cancer? It wouldn't save him. Not where he was heading.

He refocused his thoughts and considered how he would abduct her. Movies and crime novels had had him believing that a chloroform-soaked cloth would do the trick just fine in a matter of seconds, but that mistake had almost got him caught the first time around. He recalled how he'd had to hold that cloth over the mouth of Annabel Rogers a full five minutes before she passed out. And she'd bucked and thrashed the whole time while her children were watching television. It had taken way too long, and its effect was short. It was only down to luck that the family had been so engrossed in their viewing, the volume turned up so high, that no one came out to the kitchen to see what was keeping her from returning with the bowl of potato chips she'd gone for, and that no one had seen him chase her down to the garage when she'd come round. It was pure luck no one had seen him drag her to his vehicle, still kicking and thrashing and trying to scream for her life. Now he mostly used a needle on his victims, injecting them with a concoction of drugs he'd learned about while he was serving time. He'd made many connections on the inside, largely through his association with Dead Man Incorporated. Through them, he knew people who knew people who could get him just about anything.

He thought ahead to how he was going to kill his victim this time. The way he would do it was already decided. That was part of the game. He thought about where he would do it—the predetermined location, also chosen by the game—and he stiffened in his seat, drawing a deep, excited breath at the thought of Jefferson Tayte trying to get there first. It made him want to get out of his van and go up to the house right now. Maybe he would, but he had to be patient. He had to wait for the right opportunity.

Chapter Seven

Tayte and Mavro were sitting opposite one another at a restaurant in Chinatown, just around the corner from the FBI field office. Not wanting to take long over their lunch, they both ordered from the express menu, although as Tayte imagined that any kind of express meal was going to be small, he ordered a side of pork dumplings to go with his. They had talked about the contents of the envelope on their way there, coming up with nothing remotely promising. Now Tayte's notepad was open on the table between them, and they were still staring with thoughtful expressions at the killer's latest clue when their meals arrived.

'*Ream,*' Tayte said, reading the first part of the clue for the umpteenth time. 'Something to do with paper? A paper mill?'

'A ream of paper is five hundred sheets,' Mavro said, almost to herself as if thinking aloud. 'Used to be four hundred and eighty. Could those numbers mean anything?'

Tayte put a large forkful of rice noodles into his mouth and sighed as he chewed and swallowed them. He'd passed on the chopsticks, preferring to use a fork when he was hungry. 'They could,' he said, turning his fork on his plate as he continued to think. 'They don't mean anything to me, though, genealogically speaking. What about the letters, EBH?'

'An abbreviation or an acronym for something?'

'Or they could be someone's initials,' Tayte offered. 'Ream could be a surname.'

Mavro agreed. 'And if those numbers at the end, 4/30/2, mean April 30th, 1902 or 1802, maybe that's relative to whoever "EBH Ream" is.'

'Let's suppose for now that it's a date of death,' Tayte said, holding one of his pork dumplings in mid-air as he considered the possibility. 'That's the kind of thing we're looking for here—the death of one of my clients' ancestors, which the Genie plans to replicate here in the present. I don't recall any clients by the name of Ream, but maybe it was a small assignment, easy to forget.'

'Too bad your files are in transit. We won't be able to take a look at them for a couple of hours yet.'

'So let's keep at it. We can't afford to wait, and I don't imagine for a moment that this is going to be as easy as checking my files for someone with the name of Ream. Otherwise, the Genie might just as well have used another genealogical wheel chart, like before.'

They continued eating in silence for several minutes, each caught up in their thoughts. Then Mavro said, 'If it is a person, and it's not one of your former clients, who else could it be?'

Tayte reached down into his briefcase and pulled his laptop out. 'Let's ask Wikipedia.' He began tapping keys and was soon looking at a page for the word *Ream*. It showed several possibilities, but the one that interested him for now was 'Ream (surname)'. He clicked the link and was presented with just five notable people. He turned his laptop around to show Mavro.

'There aren't many links, so we could take a look at all of them,' he said, clicking the first, which was for Dwight Ream, American football and basketball coach. There was very little information, and nothing to suggest a connection to the puzzle they were trying to solve. He clicked the next and the next, reading along with Mavro until the meal was finished and they had reached the last name on the list.

'*Vinnie Ream,*' Mavro said, reading from the screen. '*Lavinia Ellen Ream Hoxie, American sculptor.*'

Tayte clicked the link, thinking there was something familiar about the name. When the web page presented itself, he saw why. 'Of course,' he said, edging closer to the screen. 'Vinnie Ream created the statue of Abraham Lincoln that's in the Capitol rotunda. I came across her Hoxie name during an assignment a while back. I have a client with connections to the same Hoxie family.'

They read on and several seconds later Tayte slapped his palm down on the table, rattling their bowls. 'There,' he said pointing to a name part way down a list that appeared under the heading, 'Works'.

'*Edwin B. Hay,*' Mavro read out. 'That's gotta be our EBH.'

There was another link. Tayte clicked it and was surprised to see that it wasn't a link to the life of the man himself, but to a bronze bust Vinnie Ream had sculpted in his image in 1906, which marked the gravesite of the Hay family. He smiled to himself when he read that the bust was located at the Rock Creek Cemetery, right there in DC's Northwest district. He picked up his notepad, knowing now what the numbers he'd written down were.

'These numbers at the end of the killer's clue aren't a date of birth or death,' he said, still smiling. 'It's not any kind of date. It's a burial plot reference for a grave at Rock Creek Cemetery. Section four, lot thirty, grave two. We need to go and see who's buried there.'

They took Route 29 north, and within thirty minutes Tayte and Mavro had reached Rock Creek Cemetery. It was a fine afternoon, Tayte thought, as they traversed the car park. October was one of his favourite months in DC, when the skies were mostly sunny and the heat and crowds of the summer months had passed. His assignments had often brought him to Rock Creek, and at any other time he could happily have spent a few hours amongst the cemetery's famous sculptures, but not today.

On the way there, he'd been wondering what they would find at the grave marker they were now looking for. The obvious answer was a burial plot and a headstone, and from that they would have another name to work on—someone from the past whose death was going to be replicated here in the present; in a matter of hours, for all Tayte knew. The thought made him quicken his pace as they left the car park, heading for the red-brick church that was located roughly in the centre of the cemetery's eighty-six acres.

'You think there could be something important at the location of Ream's sculpture of Edwin Hay?' Mavro asked.

'No, I'm sure that was just a cryptic way to get us here. The burial-plot reference is the important thing now. I have a map of this cemetery in my files, but that's not much good to us just now. Fortunately, there are copies available online.'

Tayte was about to reach into his briefcase for his laptop, but he saw that Mavro was ahead of him. She had her phone out.

'You know the website?'

'Find A Grave has one.'

Mavro entered the search and they were soon looking at a copy of the cemetery layout.

'We're looking for section four,' Tayte said. 'If memory serves, it's on the west side. That's where most of the numbered sections are.'

Mavro found it. 'Take a left here,' she said as they reached the church, where there was a fork in the path.

They took the path to their left, and as they walked Tayte asked Mavro something he'd been curious about since first meeting her. 'Reese said something about you having worked in the field before. How was that? I imagine it can get pretty intense.'

'I started out in the field,' Mavro said. 'When I was in college my father became a victim of violent crime. My parents owned a small convenience store in Southeast where we used to live. He was shot point blank in the chest for the money in the cash register.'

'I'm so sorry to hear that.'

'Yeah. He was a kind, hard-working man, and he deserved better. He was always working, but he more than made up for it on the rare occasions when he did manage to find time for Mom and me. The day after the shooting I applied for a placement in the FBI Honors Internship Program, and that was that.'

'You wanted to fight crime because of what happened?'

Mavro drew a long breath. 'I guess I did at the time, although if I'm being totally honest, I was running away.'

'From what?'

'My mom. We didn't get along so well, and things became a whole lot worse after my dad was gone. I knew it would and I didn't want to stick around to deal with it. She didn't handle his death at all well. Pretty soon she stopped taking care of herself. Then during my first year as a field agent she got sick. She died before we could reconcile our differences.'

'That's too bad,' Tayte said. 'So that's why you left the field?'

Mavro nodded. 'I could no longer perform my duties. That's how I saw it. I started to screw up. I knew it, and I think my supervisor knew it. Although no one directly asked me to step down, I decided it was best to get out before I got someone killed.'

Tayte knew what it was like to lose your parents at an early age. He hadn't known his biological parents—he'd been too young to know what was going on when he was abandoned—but he still missed his adoptive parents: the love and the fun times they used to share. He felt for Frankie Mavro. He sensed she was a lonely person, much as he had been before he met Jean. Half the time he'd paint a smile on his face and get on with his life as if it didn't matter to him, but it did. That's why he was always so wrapped up in his work, to keep himself busy and so tired that he'd fall into a deep sleep as soon as his head hit the pillow at night. He imagined it was much the same for her.

'Here we are,' she said, putting her phone away and interrupting his thoughts. 'This is section four.'

Section four backed on to New Hampshire Avenue. It was a wide rectangular section, and although it was a relatively large area, Tayte was familiar with how the system worked. It didn't take long for him to find the lot and the grave they were looking for.

'John Bedford,' Tayte read out. '1852 to 1885.'

'It doesn't say much.'

'No, but perhaps it says enough.'

Tayte saw that there was another grave on plot thirty for this section, which also carried the Bedford name. It was for a woman called Mary Bedford, and because of the older dates engraved into her headstone, he figured this was the resting place of John Bedford's mother. There was no grave for his father, and nothing for a wife or children.

Tayte set his briefcase down, took out his notebook, and wrote in the details. 'Unless the rules of the game have changed along with the type of clue this killer's leaving for us,' he said, 'I believe this is the equivalent of the name in the centre of those genealogical wheel charts. In which case I really need to see my files. The name doesn't ring any bells, but if John Bedford's name is among them, maybe it contains information about how and where he died.'

'What if you don't have a file for Bedford?' Mavro said. 'I mean, we had other names to look up from those wheel charts before. All we have here is one name—Bedford. If you don't have a file for this family, we can't exactly go through every record you have looking for mention of a John Bedford. It would take too long.'

'Yes, it would, but we still need to know if I have a file in this man's name. It could save a lot of time if I have.'

Mavro took out her phone again. 'I'll call Reese. Unless your files are in transit, I'm sure he can have someone check.'

Mavro made the call and Reese picked up straight away.

'Ms Mavro. What have you got for me?'

'Nothing yet, sir, but we have a lead. We need to know if there's a folder under the name of Bedford in Mr Tayte's files.'

The man with the scarred eyebrow was getting a real kick out of the game now that Jefferson Tayte was back in DC. It gave him even greater pleasure than the snatch he'd just made in Kensington. That had given him a wonderful adrenaline boost, but with Tayte the rush was more sustained, as if he were plugged into a drip feed that was steadily keeping him high.

He was driving south on Route 185, heading back to Washington, wondering how close Tayte was to solving his latest clue, thinking that Tayte had better hurry because he was almost ready, and he wasn't about to cut the genealogist any slack. It was all he could think about, despite the banging that was now coming from the back of his van, letting him know that the injection he'd given his victim had worn off—and much faster than he'd expected.

He turned up the volume on the stereo and let Van Halen drown out the noise—not that it really mattered. The traffic was flowing well and he was close to where he was heading. He had another needle primed and ready to silence his catch again as soon as he stopped. All he had to do was feign a breakdown, pull over and take care of it.

He wound down his window and turned the volume up a little louder as he arrived at the next crossroads, which had forced him to slow down. He knew he was drawing attention to himself, but all anyone outside the van could hear was the music. As he took a right turn his mind began to wander ahead to how his next victim was going to die, concluding that it was both simple and ingenious. The game was going exactly to plan.

Another Van Halen track began to play and he smiled to himself as he sang along with the music as if he didn't have a care in the world. He thought the song lyrics were never more poignant. He really was living his life like there was no tomorrow.

He was 'Runnin' with the Devil'.

Chapter Eight

Before Tayte and Mavro left Rock Creek Cemetery, Reese had been able to advise them that there was no folder in Tayte's files under the name of Bedford. Tayte was disappointed, but Mavro's call had saved them a trip to the safe house where the files were waiting for him. For now, Tayte saw little point in checking in. He had to find out specifically where and how John Bedford had died in 1885, and to do that he needed to see Bedford's vital records. It was already late afternoon, and they were in Northeast at a building on North Capitol Street, the home of DC's Department of Health Vital Records Division.

'They keep death certificates dating back to 1874 for deaths in the DC area,' Tayte said as they headed up to the first floor. 'That's when civil registration of vital statistics in DC began.' He was glad John Bedford hadn't died sooner as that could have made the task ahead more complicated than it already was, particularly if he'd died between 1861 and 1865, during the Civil War years, for which no death records existed.

'It should help that we called ahead,' Mavro said.

Tayte smiled. 'And that we have the weight of the federal government behind us. I usually have to wait days, sometimes weeks. That's where the Internet can come in handy, although even when I get lucky online, I still like to see the original records if I can. In this case we can't afford to make any assumptions or mistakes.'

They were met by a middle-aged woman in a light-blue skirt suit. 'I'm the head of department, Pamela Bryant,' she said, ushering them into an office. 'Please take a seat.'

Tayte imagined Bryant had already been informed that the FBI needed to see a record, and that it was literally a matter of life and death for someone, so she'd wanted to oversee the matter personally.

'We're locating the record for you now,' Bryant said, a little nervously, Tayte thought, as though being in the presence of the FBI made her uncomfortable.

'Will it take much longer?' Mavro asked. 'I can't stress enough how urgent this is.'

Bryant paused before answering. Then, as if unable to think of anything positive to say in reply, she smiled and said, 'I'll go and see how it's going.'

Tayte took his laptop out as soon as Bryant left. 'I want to run a quick newspaper archive check while we wait,' he said. 'We don't have much to go on yet, but you never know.'

All he had was the subject's name, date of birth, and date of death. As he was interested primarily in the man's death, Tayte entered the information, '*John Bedford, 1885*', into the search field. He whistled at the results when they came back.

'Eight thousand ninety-eight results nationwide.'

He narrowed it down, choosing only newspapers covering the District of Columbia.

'One hundred fourteen results for DC. That's more like it, but it could take hours to go through them all, and with no guarantee of finding what we're looking for. Not that we know what we're looking for with any certainty yet. We need more information.'

'Maybe the death certificate will help.'

'I sure hope so.'

Bryant was only gone fifteen minutes, although to Tayte, who was growing more and more impatient to find out how and where John Bedford had died, it felt more like an hour.

'Here it is,' Bryant said as she came back into the room, waving the copy of John Bedford's death certificate above her head like a parade flag. She was all smiles now, clearly happy to be of service. 'I'm sorry it took a while to retrieve it, but—'

'That's okay. Thank you,' Tayte said, cutting her short. He was on his feet before she had fully entered the room, his eager eyes following the record as she handed it to him. He took it to the only table in the room, set it down and leaned over it with Mavro at his side.

'*Cause of death, hanging*,' he read out. It was annotated with the word '*extrajudicial*', reminding him of times when unlawful hangings were still carried out by the citizens of America.

He was about to discuss the record further with Mavro, but he could sense Bryant was now at his other elbow and he thought it best that their discussion should be private, given the nature of their purpose there.

He turned to her. 'Could we use this room for a short while?' he asked her. 'Privately, I mean. Do you mind?'

'Oh, sure,' Bryant said, sounding a little disappointed that she couldn't stay to find out why the FBI wanted to see the record she'd brought in. 'Just leave whenever you're ready.'

Tayte gave her a smile. 'Thanks again for your help.'

As soon as Bryant had closed the door behind her, Tayte turned to Mavro, and in a low voice said, 'Now we know how the Genie plans to kill his next victim. The hundred-dollar question is, where?'

'There's no place of death shown on his death certificate?'

'No, but it's given us something else to search the newspaper archives for.'

Tayte opened his laptop again and returned to the website he'd visited when they arrived. He added 'hanged' to his search and this time there were thirty-seven entries in newspapers from the DC area.

'That's not so many,' he said, forcing an optimistic tone. 'Most, if not all, of these results are likely to be from newspaper pages containing the keywords we're looking for, but it doesn't mean they'll be related to one another. It shouldn't take too long to read through them all to find out.'

They sat down again, huddled around Tayte's laptop as he clicked the link to the first of the newspaper pages. It was from the *National Tribune* and he was quickly able to dismiss it. The reference was to a John Banks of Bedford City. There was an entry in another column that matched the keyword 'hanged', but that was for someone else altogether. He moved on and was presented with a page from the *Washington Critic*. This was under the sub-heading 'Marriage Licenses' and not what he was interested in. He went through each newspaper page in this manner and the minutes zipped by. He found nothing but disparate matches to the keywords he'd entered. Many were related to hangings that took place outside the District of Columbia.

An hour was lost all too quickly, but Tayte knew he had to be thorough so as to avoid missing anything important. It wasn't until he came to the twenty-ninth newspaper page that he sat up from the slumped position he'd settled into. It was from the *National Republican*, dated August 1885.

'This is it,' he said, indicating an article in the fourth column. He read it out. '*Ravisher lynched on the Potomac. Washington, August 11. John Bedford, the negro who assaulted Miss Katie Spencer on the ninth instant, was captured last night while hiding out along the river. News of the assault created such intense excitement that he was duly lynched from Chain Bridge. His hiding place was told by a negro who had promised to protect him.*'

Mavro's phone was already out when Tayte turned to her.

'Good job,' she said. 'I'll let Reese know.'

Half an hour later, Tayte and Mavro were sitting on a bench in the late-afternoon sunshine outside a coffee shop on nearby Georgia Avenue, waiting to hear back from Reese.

'I hope we were in time,' Tayte said as he sipped his double espresso, absently watching the rush-hour traffic. He didn't like waiting around to find out. A big part of him would sooner have gone to Chain Bridge with Reese and his team, but they had been told to stay out of harm's way, so that was how it had to be.

'You did great,' Mavro said. 'I don't see how anyone could have worked that clue out any faster.'

'What if we're wrong? What if there was more to it and Chain Bridge isn't the right place?'

'Stop worrying. I was there with you. Everything pointed to Chain Bridge.'

Tayte sighed and took another sip of his coffee. 'I hope you're right,' he said, noticing that Mavro still had her phone out. She was tapping it on her jeans, suggesting she was just as nervous about this as he was.

There was a low wooden table in front of them with several news-papers and magazines arranged on top of it. Tayte hadn't had time to catch up on DC's general news since he'd arrived home, so he picked up a copy of the *Washington Post*, thinking it might provide a little distraction while they waited. He had to sit up in disbelief when he saw the front cover of the publication that was lying beneath it. It was the latest edition of the *Washingtonian*, a local monthly magazine that described itself as 'The magazine Washington lives by'.

'You've gotta be kidding,' he said as he reached for it, at the same time reading out the main feature heading: '*Family history meets CSI.*'

'What is it?'

Tayte was shaking his head at the image associated with the heading. 'Michel Levant,' he said under his breath. He sounded as if he couldn't quite believe it, but he could never forget that face. Nonetheless, it had come as something of a shock to see the skinny Frenchman on the front cover of a Washington magazine. He laughed sourly to himself as he took the image in. Levant was in his sixties, but there he was, more than a year after Tayte had first met him, still trying to look half his age, with his over-styled fair hair and his flamboyant dress sense. He had a crowd-pleasing smile on his face, and looking back, Tayte wished now that he had punched him on his pointy little nose when he'd had the chance.

'Who's Michel Levant?' Mavro asked, sitting forward with him to get a better look at the magazine cover.

'That's a very good question, and I'm not entirely sure I know the answer. From what I know about him, he's a probate genealogist—an heir hunter. I met him in London, just over a year ago. It was the day I met Jean, the same day a good friend of mine was murdered—Marcus Brown. Apparently Marcus and Levant had been friends once, but I don't know how deep their acquaintance ran. I'm sure Levant had something to do with Marcus's murder, not that I could prove anything. Levant's one slippery character as far as I'm concerned, and right now I'm wondering what the hell he's doing in DC.'

'What's the article about?' Mavro asked. 'I expect that will explain it.'

Tayte opened the magazine, glad to be rid of Levant's image. He quickly found the cover feature and began to read it. 'He's running a series of events here in DC at the National Archives Museum about genetic ancestry—how DNA can be used to help trace our roots.' He noted the event dates. 'The first event is the day after tomorrow.'

Mavro smiled to herself. 'I somehow doubt you'll have time to attend.'

'Don't get me wrong,' Tayte said. 'I have no interest in hearing what the man has to say.'

Mavro's phone interrupted the conversation. 'Excuse me,' she said as she took the call.

Tayte knew it had to be Reese. He knew from the way Mavro's eyes were suddenly locked on his as she spoke, although she didn't say much.

She mostly listened. Tayte felt his palms becoming clammy in anticipation of what Reese was telling her. He wondered again whether they had been right about Chain Bridge, and if they had solved the puzzle in time. A moment later Mavro began to shake her head. He saw a single tear roll down her cheek, and knew the news was bad.

'Are you okay?' he asked her as soon as the call ended.

Mavro nodded and sniffed back her emotions. 'Now you know why I can't cut it as a field agent.' She wiped her cheek. 'Reese wants to see us. He's at Chain Bridge. I'm sorry, JT. There's another body.'

Chapter Nine

DC's Chain Bridge was located at Little Falls, where there had been a bridge across the Potomac River since 1797. Currently in its eighth version, it was named after the chain suspension bridge that had been built in 1808 after the two wooden bridges before it were destroyed, first by rot and then by fire. The present version was of a continuous steel girder construction, sitting on piers built in the 1870s. It supported a pedestrian walkway and three lanes of traffic, carrying over twenty thousand cars a day.

Dusk had begun to fall by the time Tayte and Mavro arrived at the small parking area on the Virginia side of the bridge, which had now been reduced to two lanes to facilitate the numerous emergency services vehicles Tayte could see coming and going. It seemed the whole area was alight with their red and blue flashing lights, although as he stepped out of the car he sensed that any urgency that had existed had now passed. He saw Reese standing by a low wall facing the river, with the bridge to his right. He was talking to two heavily armed men wearing FBI tactical vests. When he saw Tayte and Mavro he waved them over, dismissing the two agents.

One of the agents, a dark-haired, dark-eyed man, smiled and nodded at Mavro as they passed. 'Hey, Frankie.'

'Hi there,' Mavro said in a chirpy voice that seemed a little forced to Tayte. Or embarrassed. He couldn't decide which.

'Is that Jerome Martinez, by any chance? The guy you told me about?'

'Yes,' Mavro said, and Tayte thought she was blushing.

'He seems to like you.'

'You think?'

'I'm no expert, but he didn't have to smile at you, did he?'

'I guess not.'

They arrived at the low wall.

'We were this close,' Reese said, pinching his thumb and forefinger together. He shook his head. 'If we'd been any closer we'd have caught the Genie in the act. Roadblocks have been set up, but they take time. I expect he's long gone by now.'

Tayte felt wholly responsible. 'I'm sorry,' he offered, but Reese quickly stopped him.

'Mr Tayte, the team I assigned to this didn't even come close. You did remarkably well, so I don't want to hear any apologies. If it hadn't been for you and Ms Mavro, we wouldn't have known a damn thing about this until someone reported it. You gave us a chance and that's all we need. Sooner or later this guy's going to run out of luck.'

'What happened?' Mavro asked, peering down over the wall towards the river, where most of the activity was focused. 'The victim was hanged, right?'

Reese nodded. 'He was still twitching when the response team arrived. We can't have missed his killer by much. We found the victim's wallet on him. His name was Samuel Shaw.' He paused and threw his head back. 'Christ! The press are going to love this. It's been a long time since a black man was lynched so close to our nation's capital.'

Reese led them around to the walkway. 'His killer slipped the rope through these railings and threw the ends down by the support pier so he could reach them from the bank below. He'd have had plenty of opportunity to set everything up unnoticed before the rush-hour traffic built up.'

He leaned over the railing and Tayte and Mavro followed suit. Tayte could see the Evidence Response Team, still busy below. The rope had been left hanging for now, but Shaw's body was no longer there. Looking across the river, Tayte could see that once the killer had taken his victim below the bridge, no one could have seen them from the far bank, which was distant and shrouded by trees and shrubs.

Reese pointed back to the low wall they had just left. 'We believe our killer took Samuel Shaw down over that wall, through the bushes and over the rocks to the bank where he put the noose around Shaw's neck and pulled him up. The loose end of the rope was tied to that tree you can see down there. Once he'd done that, it was just a matter of scrambling back up to his vehicle and off he goes. We don't believe Shaw was thrown off the bridge. There was no drop, as often happens with a hanging. That would have been too risky. Shaw was literally strung up and left to suffocate, and he was no lightweight. We're dealing with a very strong killer here.'

'Do we have another clue?' Tayte asked as they headed back to the low wall. 'Can I see it?'

'I was just coming to that,' Reese said. He shook his head. 'There isn't one. Not this time.'

Tayte hadn't expected that, but it was Mavro who asked the obvious question.

'What does that mean?'

'Right now, I don't know,' Reese said. 'But you can be damn sure this isn't over. Maybe the Genie didn't like the close call we just gave him and he didn't have time to leave his next clue. Whatever the reason, we need to stay sharp. Your temporary accommodation's all set, Mr Tayte. Mavro can take you there. I suggest you both get some rest.'

'Was anything found at my apartment?' Tayte asked, wondering whether the Genie really had been there while he was away.

'I can confirm that one of the glass panes in your bathroom window has recently been replaced. The glazing putty wasn't fully set. I'm still waiting to hear whether the paint was the same type as the rest of the window, but given the fresh putty, I suspect not. It's clear that someone broke into your apartment while you were away, and they didn't want to make it obvious. For now, we have to assume that person was the Genie, so if you need to go back there for any reason, I want you to call me first. I'll have someone go with you. Personally, I'd stay away for now if I were you.'

Tayte planned to. 'So there was no message inside those books? Were there any fingerprints on them? Apart from mine, of course.'

'No, there was no message, and there were no prints. Not even yours. The books were *too* clean, if you know what I mean. He probably just got bored, took a look at them and got careless putting them back. Or maybe he was messing with you again, knowing you'd be the only person who would know someone had been inside your apartment.'

The way things were stacking up, Tayte figured the latter most likely. 'What about my neighbours? Did you check with them?'

'Yes, we did. No one heard anything unusual, and no one saw anyone coming to or going from your apartment other than the mailman. Most of them didn't even know who you are.'

'I keep to myself most of the time. How about the lock-up where I keep my car?'

'That was interesting. If I didn't know you were out of the country when your car was last driven out of there, I'd have sworn it was taken by you. The surveillance recordings show a man who looked just like you getting into the car. Not facially—he managed to keep his face hidden from the cameras—but he was a big man, like you, and he was wearing a suit exactly like the one you're wearing now.'

'Just as he was when he rented the apartment he used to kill Annabel Rogers,' Tayte said under his breath.

It was disquieting to think that the killer had dressed up in his clothes in order to rent that apartment and to steal his car, but where his car was concerned it made perfect sense. Whoever had taken it had waltzed into the lock-up pretending to be him, and he'd taken the keys right out of his kitchen drawer. He pulled a sour face, and he held on to the expression as he continued to walk on heavy legs that felt suddenly numb beneath him. His personal space had been violated, and it angered him to know that there was nothing he could do about it. Whoever broke into his apartment must have been there for some time, going through his files, copying what he needed from them, and in between, sitting on his couch, perhaps watching TV with the volume low, eating with his knives and forks, and worst of all, maybe even sleeping in his bed. Wherever he and Jean were going to live once they were married, he was now absolutely sure that it wasn't going to be in his apartment.

They were back at the low wall overlooking the river. Tayte was about to ask Reese whether the booking at the parking garage where Kelly Uttridge's body was found had turned anything up, thinking that her killer had most likely made it online from an Internet cafe, when his phone rang, playing one of his favourite show tunes, 'Defying Gravity' from the musical *Wicked*. It sounded far too upbeat given the circumstances. He quickly took his phone out and checked the display, wondering if it was Jean. With the time difference, and because he'd been so tied up, he hadn't managed to call her since landing at the airport the day before. There was no caller ID, ruling Jean out, along with everyone else in his phonebook.

'Excuse me,' he said to Reese and Mavro, turning away as he took the call. 'Hi, this is Jefferson Tayte.'

'Tayte.'

'That's right. Who's calling?'

'Oh, you know me.'

'I do?'

'Sure you do, but not as well as I know you.'

Tayte tried to place the man's voice, but he couldn't. It sounded deep and hollow, and he spoke slowly with no particular accent, his tone laid back and calm. As Tayte began to realise who this man was, he began to feel anything but calm.

'Look, who is this and what do you want? I'm kinda busy.'

'Oh, I know you are. I've been keeping you very busy, haven't I?'

Tayte felt the blood rush to his feet. He felt so light-headed he had to sit down on the wall. He waved wildly at Reese and Mavro, and when he had their attention he repeatedly stabbed his forefinger at his phone. Then he covered it with his free hand as he mouthed, 'It's him! It's the Genie!'

Reese took the phone from Tayte. 'This is Special Agent in Charge Jordan Reese. I—'

The call ended.

'Damn!' Reese said. 'He's gone.'

Tayte's phone rang again, and this time Reese answered it. The call ended before he could get two words out. When it rang for a third time, Reese handed Tayte's phone back to him. 'Here. He's not going to talk to me.'

Tayte's throat felt suddenly dry as he answered the call. 'This is Jefferson Tayte.'

'That's better,' the caller said. 'I don't want to talk to the FBI. I want to talk to you.'

'What about? Why are you doing this?'

'Keep playing the game and you'll find out.'

'How can I? You didn't leave a clue for me this time.'

'Now you've joined the game, I thought I'd call you instead—make it more personal.'

Given that this man had invaded Tayte's home, and that he'd no doubt used it while Tayte was away in Europe, Tayte didn't think things could get any more personal. 'Okay, so tell me,' he said. 'What's the clue?'

'So keen to play. I like that.'

'I'm keen to stop you killing people.'

'Maybe you will, but you'll have to be smarter and faster than you were today. You could have saved poor Samuel Shaw, but you let me kill him, didn't you?'

Tayte clenched his jaw and took a deep breath to calm himself. He knew this man was goading him. He'd done all he could, hadn't he? 'Just give me the damn clue.'

The line was silent for several long seconds. Then the caller said, 'Not yet, but I will, and soon.'

With that the call ended, leaving Tayte thinking that this wasn't over at all.

Chapter Ten

After collecting a few personal items from Tayte's apartment, Mavro drove them to the FBI safe house that was to be Tayte's accommodation for the foreseeable future. As they came to a busy intersection, she slowed for the red light ahead and asked, 'Do you like Italian food?'

'Sure,' Tayte said. 'I love Italian. Got any recommendations near this safe house we're heading for?'

'It's not a good idea to go out once you're there. There'll be a well-stocked refrigerator and everything else you need to get by. Only go out when you have to. That way there's less chance for anyone to spot you coming and going.'

'That makes sense.'

'And when you do have to go out, keep an eye open for anyone paying you too much attention. It's also a good idea to come and go via different routes. Only a handful of people at the Bureau will know you're there and you'll always get a call before anyone comes to see you—myself included. If you don't get a call first, don't answer the door. Call Reese.'

'Got it,' Tayte said as they waited at the light. 'So why did you want to know if I like Italian food?'

'I'm into Italian. I thought I could cook us a meal. I get it from my mother, God rest her. It wouldn't be any bother and I can promise you it'll be a whole lot better than you'll find in the refrigerator at the safe house, unless you're a good cook.'

'No, not really,' Tayte said, and put like that he could hardly refuse. The thought of being alone in an unfamiliar apartment after everything that had happened that day was also less than inviting. It wasn't as if he had anything to do with his time either, until he had another clue to work on. He was desperate to talk to Jean, just to hear her voice again, reminding him that there was a normal life waiting for him when this was over, but given that it was now past eight in the evening, and that the UK was five hours ahead of DC, that window had closed for the day.

'Sounds great,' he added, and as they passed through the intersection, Mavro smiled and made a turn, heading for Route 29 and home.

A moment later she said, 'We're not far away. Do you want to know what I'm making, or do you like surprises?'

A year ago, Tayte would have wanted to know. Surprises led to the unexpected, and he liked to know exactly what to expect from his day, down to every detail if possible. But that was before he'd met Jean, from whom he'd learned to let go of his old predictable self.

'Surprise me,' he said, and then turning the conversation back to the case, he asked her about the phone call he'd had with the Genie. He hadn't really been able to stop thinking about it, any more than he could stop wondering when he would call again.

'I guess Reese is going to find out where that phone call came from.'

'He will, but I don't think our killer's likely to have used his own cell phone. And if he's using someone else's, or an unregistered unit, he'd be a fool to use the same phone twice, or to hold on to it, but you never know. If he used a payphone, we should be able to find out which one easily enough, but I expect he was careful not to leave any forensic evidence for us to find.'

'What about street cameras?'

'If he did make the call from a payphone, any cameras in that vicinity will be checked, but he didn't give us much to go on when he was caught on camera taking your car, did he? I don't expect we'd see enough of him to get a positive ID with anyone on the list you gave Reese this time, either.'

'No, he's smart,' Tayte said. 'At least, if he isn't, he must be working with someone who is.' The notion made him think about Michel Levant again. 'You know—it doesn't sit too well with me that the Frenchman I told you about is here in DC.'

'How do you mean?'

'I mean, I don't like the coincidence that Levant just happens to be here at the same time these murders are taking place, even if he does have a reason.'

'You think he's involved in this? Is his name on that list you made for Reese?'

'No, but perhaps it should be. I denied Levant what was arguably the greatest prize an heir hunter could ever hope to find. And he's a genealogist. It would take one to come up with these puzzles.'

Mavro pulled a face. 'I don't see how the little fella on the cover of that magazine you showed me could be the Genie. I know appearances can be deceptive, but don't you think he's a little too old and frail? The Masterson twins must have weighed over four hundred pounds between them, and as Reese just pointed out, the killer would have to be a strong man to do what he did to Samuel Shaw.'

'I don't imagine for a moment that Levant is killing these people,' Tayte said. 'From what I know about him, he's not the kind of man who likes to get his own hands dirty if he can help it.'

Mavro drew a thoughtful breath. 'Okay, let's not rule anyone out. If he's someone you've upset in the past, for whatever reason, we'd better add him to your list and have him checked out.'

As they joined Route 29, heading north, Tayte wondered how things were going with his list, and he made a mental note to add Michel Levant to it as soon as he next saw Reese, which he thought would be soon. What if Levant was the genealogist behind the crime? Tayte had suspected his involvement in the murders of several people during their first encounter in London the year before. Was that the case again now? The more Tayte thought about it, the more the possibility made sense to him.

＊＊＊

Frankie Mavro lived in a small, three-bedroom, two-bathroom house in Silver Spring, Maryland, which formed part of DC's metropolitan area to the north. It was a charming yet unassuming Cape Cod-style property that she'd bought with the inheritance left to her after her mother died. Tayte was trying to make himself useful in the kitchen, although he thought he was mostly getting in the way.

'I could really use a drink right now,' Mavro said as she continued to chop the tomatoes. 'I've got to drive again later, but hey, don't let me stop you if you want something. I've got beer, wine, bourbon. You name it.'

'No, that's okay, thanks. A soda will do just fine if you have any. I want to stay sharp.'

'Yeah, me too. We don't know when this creep's going to call again. There should be something in the fridge, and there's ice in the freezer if you want any.'

The meal was ready in under half an hour, and not long after nine they were sitting at the table in the dining room.

'I don't often eat in here,' Mavro said. 'Makes a nice change.' She raised her glass to Tayte and smiled as they touched glasses. 'Thanks for letting me cook for you.'

'The thanks are all mine,' Tayte said. 'The meal looks wonderful.' He tapped her glass with his again and added, 'And here's to catching the Genie. We can do this.'

'Amen to that.'

Tayte took in the wide bowl of food set before him, and the aromas made his stomach groan. 'What's this pasta shape called? I don't think I've seen it before.'

'It's castellane. I hope you like it al dente.'

'Is there any other way?' Tayte said with a grin. He took a mouthful. It was still a little too hot, but he didn't care. 'Wow, that's a great-tasting sauce. Did you put anchovies in there?'

Mavro nodded. 'Capers, too. I wish I could take the credit, but it's my mother's recipe. Do you want some Parmesan to go with it?' she added, pointing to the cheese and the grater she'd set out.

'Absolutely. You can't beat fresh,' Tayte said, still smiling as he shaved the cheese back and forth several times over his pasta.

Once they had settled into the meal, Mavro said, 'So tell me some more about your fiancée. What's she like?'

Tayte thought that was a huge question, and he didn't quite know how to answer it. His first thought was to say, 'She's wonderful. Just wonderful,' but he didn't think that was what Mavro had in mind.

'Well,' he began, hesitating as he continued to think about it. 'Did I tell you she's a history professor?'

'No, you didn't. That's quite an achievement.'

'Yeah, her folks are very proud of her, too. I met them a couple of months back.'

'How did that go?' Mavro winked. 'Did you get their approval?'

'I don't know. I guess so. We got along fine. They live just outside London, to the northwest.'

Tayte thought back to the pleasant week he and Jean had spent with her parents towards summer's end, with nothing on their minds but each other.

'Are you planning to have any kids? You're not too old yet, you know.'

Tayte felt himself blush. 'Who knows,' he said. 'We've only been engaged a few months, so it hasn't exactly come up yet. She has a son already. He's called Elliot, from her previous marriage.'

'Divorced?'

Tayte nodded. 'Her ex was cheating on her, so she did the right thing and left him.'

'Good for her. And that's serendipity for you.'

'How do you mean?'

'Well if her fella hadn't been cheating on her, she would never have left him, and if she hadn't left him, she wouldn't have been available when you came along.'

'I suppose so,' Tayte said, thinking back to the first time he'd seen Jean. A moment later he laughed. 'Would you believe she was a blind date? I'm not even sure we liked each other to begin with. Now it's like all the things I thought really mattered no longer do. As long as Jean's there with me, everything else seems secondary and somehow unimportant.' He laughed again. 'I'm not sure I'm articulating myself very well here, am I?'

'Oh, you're doing great,' Mavro said. 'They say you can't miss what you never had, but I don't think that's true. It sounds real nice.'

'Yeah. Although I never knew what I'd been missing until we met.'

'Maybe it's different for men.'

'I'm sure it's just the same. I think I'd just become too comfortable with my own company over the years. It's the nature of all living things to want a partner.'

'Ain't that the truth.'

Tayte nodded. 'Which brings us to you and Special Agent Jerome Martinez.'

Mavro looked down at her food. 'What about him?'

'He likes you. I could tell.'

Mavro laughed to herself.

'You're too embarrassed to ask him on a date, aren't you?'

'Isn't it the men who usually do the asking if they're interested?'

'Maybe he's shy. I'm talking from experience here. Would you believe that it was Jean who proposed to me? She knew I'd never find the courage. She probably thought I'd be too scared that proposing would ruin the friendship we already had, and she'd have been right—I was. Someone has to take the first step.'

'I guess.'

'So, are you going to ask him out, or do you want me to ask him for you?'

Mavro sat bolt upright. 'Don't you dare!'

'Well, like the Nike advert says, just do it. You're no worse off if he turns you down. It's not like you're still working together and have to see him every day.'

'Okay, okay, I give in. I'll ask him when I get the chance. How about that?'

'How about you go ahead and make the chance? Don't wait for it.'

Mavro sat on her hands, as if she were already nervous about it. She let out a long breath. 'Okay, I will.'

Tayte threw her a playful smile. 'Just make sure you do, because if you haven't by the time I head back to Jean, I'm asking him for you.'

Chapter Eleven

The sound of the telephone that woke Tayte the following morning was as unfamiliar to him as it was unwelcome. Still half asleep, he rolled over and tried to ignore it, wishing in his dream-like state that the phone's owner would hurry up and answer it so he could get back to sleep. But the phone kept ringing, forcing Tayte more awake until he realised where he was. He sat up with a jolt, shielding his eyes from the bright daylight at the window that caused the blinds to glow an intense shade of yellow. With his eyes half open he scanned the unfamiliar surroundings of the safe house he'd just spent his first night in and located the source of the trilling he could hear. The phone was on a low table by the bedroom door beside a large flat-screen television that seemed to dominate the wall opposite the bed. He peeled back the bedcovers, and in his stars-and-stripes boxer shorts, he dragged himself to the phone and answered it.

'Hello, this is Jefferson Tayte.'

'JT, it's Frankie. It's best not to say your name when you pick up. If the caller's legit, he or she will know who you are. You don't want to go announcing you're there to anyone.'

'Right,' Tayte said as he tried to take in what Mavro had just told him. He still felt half asleep.

'Did I wake you? It's gone nine.'

'I didn't sleep too well,' Tayte said in his defence. 'Then I slept a little too heavy. You know how it goes. So what's up?'

'I'm coming over,' Mavro said. 'Reese too. He wants to talk to you about the list you gave him.'

'How long do I have?'

'About thirty minutes. Maybe less.'

'Right,' Tayte said. 'Thirty minutes. I'm on it.'

As soon as the call ended, Tayte wandered out of the bedroom, looking for the kitchen. He couldn't function properly before his first caffeine kick of the day. There was a small hallway off the bedroom and several more doors. When Mavro had dropped him off the night before, he hadn't taken the time to explore the place much. He opened one of the doors and saw all his assignment filing cabinets lined up in neat rows. Then he opened another door and found the vaguely familiar bathroom he'd used before he went to bed. Further along the hall he looked in on what was evidently the living room, where there was another big television set, hinting at the boredom he imagined was synonymous with safe houses. He saw a set of glass French doors leading off this room and he went over to them, finding the kitchen beyond. He spent several more minutes gathering all the necessary items he needed to fix himself a strong pot of coffee.

He was thinking about Jean again as he poured the hot liquid into an oversize cup, which seemed to fit his large hand perfectly. Because he'd had a fitful night, he'd called her around three in the morning, DC time, hoping to catch her before she got caught up in her day. It had been just after eight in the UK, and Jean had been getting herself ready for another day of Scottish royal history.

'You'll never guess who's in town,' he'd said.

'Who?'

'You remember that slippery Frenchman, Michel Levant?'

'Are you kidding? I still think he was behind my son's kidnapping. He's in Washington?'

'Yes, he is. He's running a series of lectures about genealogical DNA over at the National Archives Museum.'

'It's a small world.'

'Yeah, in this case a little too small for comfort. I hope I don't bump into him anytime soon. Anyway, how's your seminar going?'

'Oh, you know. The usual exciting stuff. Yesterday we discussed Kenneth MacAlpin, "King of the Picts", who reigned during the mid-ninth century. He was the son of—'

'Okay, I give in,' Tayte said jokingly. 'No more, please.'

'I've bored you already? That was too easy.'

'It must be the late hour. I hope Scotland's not too cold for you.'

'It's chilly, but I don't mind. It's wet, too. I don't think it's stopped raining since I got here.'

'That's too bad. I don't suppose you get much time for sightseeing though.'

'No, not much, but I was hoping to do some before I head back to London at the end of the week. I'm really going to miss you.'

'You mean you don't miss me now?'

'You know what I mean. I'll miss you all the more when I'm back in my flat and you're not there.'

'I was just teasing,' Tayte said. 'I miss you, too. Maybe when I get back we should start planning our wedding. We could set a date if you like.'

'I'd like that very much. How about sometime in the spring?'

'Sure. I don't really mind when, although being away from you like this has made me realise just how much I love you.' He paused, laughing. 'I'll marry you as soon as I get back. How about that? We could take off somewhere and come back as man and wife.'

Jean laughed then. 'JT, are you turning into a romantic?'

'It doesn't come easy, but I'm trying.'

'It's a lovely idea, but I know for a fact that my mum would never talk to me again if we did that.'

'Okay. So we'll get married where and when it suits your mom.'

'Stop being facetious.'

'I'm serious. I wouldn't want to come between a mother and her daughter. You can decide the date and venue between you. Just make it soon.'

'Perfect.'

Yes, you are, Tayte thought, and once the call ended he'd drifted off to sleep with a smile on his face and a warm feeling inside him.

Now, as he drained back the last of his coffee and headed for the shower, he hoped all the more that this killer the press had dubbed the Genie would soon be brought to justice. He wished he would hurry up and call so he could get to work on trying to identify the next victim and the location of the next potential crime scene before he had the chance to kill again.

Tayte was just buttoning up his shirt when the front-door buzzer sounded. He went to it, looked through the fish-eye peephole and saw the distorted faces of Reese and Mavro.

'Come in,' he said, opening the door. He immediately noticed the weighty folder Reese was carrying as he entered behind Mavro.

'How was your first night?' Reese asked him.

'I've had better,' Tayte said. 'Then again, I've had worse.'

Reese gave a small laugh. 'I expect you'll soon settle in. Did you manage to find everything okay?' he added as they went into the living room.

'I'm getting there. I managed to make a pot of coffee. It's still hot if you'd like some.'

'Thanks. Black, one sugar.'

Tayte nodded. 'Frankie?'

'Sounds good to me. No sugar, though.'

'Yeah, I remember.'

'It's good to see you two are getting to know one another,' Reese said as he and Mavro sat down.

Tayte was only gone a few minutes. When he returned with the coffee, he sat on the armchair opposite Reese, who already had his folder open on the low table between them.

'As I suspected,' Reese said, 'last night's roadblocks yielded nothing. The Genie no doubt had his route worked out well ahead of time, and he was gone long before the MPD were able to set things up. You might be interested to know that we managed to trace the origin of last night's call.'

'You did?' Tayte said with enthusiasm.

'Don't get your hopes up,' Reese said. 'It was made from Samuel Shaw's own cell phone.'

'He used the victim's phone?' Tayte hadn't thought of that, but it made obvious sense to him now. 'Why did he bother to withhold the number?'

'Most likely just to screw with us. He would have known we'd try to find out where the call came from. Why make it easy for us when he can tie up our resources? We're unable to locate the phone. He probably destroyed it soon after making the call, or threw it in the river. I somehow doubt we're going to find him through a phone trace, but as a matter of procedure, I've gone ahead and had the phone company put a tap on your cell phone.'

'You have?'

'I trust you have no objection? DC law requires one party to be aware that calls are being recorded. Under the circumstances, I—'

'No,' Tayte cut in. 'I have no objection at all.'

'Good, and who knows? Maybe we'll get lucky.'

Reese put his coffee down and opened his folder. 'Right now, I'm more interested in your list.'

'About that,' Tayte said before Reese had a chance to continue. 'There's someone else I'd like to add to it.'

'That might not be necessary. I think we may already know who the Genie is.'

'You do?'

Reese nodded. He reached into his folder. 'It's not yet confirmed, but one man on your list just became our prime suspect.'

He pulled out a report and held it up for Tayte to see. Along with the words, which were too far away for Tayte to clearly make out, was a head-and-shoulders portrait of a bald man with a dark goatee. Judging from the size of the trapezius muscles to either side of his neck, Tayte thought the man had to be huge, which was in keeping with the profile the FBI had put together for the person they were hunting. It was all well and good, but Tayte wasn't ready to move on without mentioning his concerns about Michel Levant, so he put aside his curiosity about this new suspect for now.

'Before you go on, do you think it's possible that the Genie could have an accomplice?'

The notion seemed to surprise Reese. 'Anything's possible, but I think it's unlikely in this case. Almost every serial-killer duo ever caught were partners, heterosexual, gay or lesbian, and in most cases their crimes were sexually driven—typically the abduction, rape, and murder of young people. Our prime suspect is way outside the typical duo profile.'

'But it's not impossible that the Genie could be working with some-one else?'

'No,' Reese conceded. 'But only one duo comes to mind outside of the parameters I just mentioned. They were two male friends, dubbed the Speed Freak Killers because of their methamphetamine abuse. Who's on your mind?'

'He's a Frenchman called Michel Levant. I'm sure he was involved in a series of murders in England a little over a year ago.'

'Was anything proven?'

'No, but he seems the type who doesn't like to get his own hands dirty, and I don't like that he just happens to be in DC right now.'

Reese took out a pen and wrote Levant's name down. 'I'll have him checked out.'

'He's also a genealogist,' Tayte added. 'Does your prime suspect have any genealogical expertise? Whoever's doing this knows his stuff, or he knows someone who does.'

'Not as far as I know, but he's had twenty years to learn. His name's Adam Westlake—Adam Peyton Westlake III, to be precise. He was released from prison three months ago.'

'Westlake?'

Tayte recalled the assignment well enough. He hadn't long turned professional when their paths had crossed. During the course of his research into his client's ancestry, he'd unwittingly uncovered a trail of political corruption that ran all the way back to the forefather who had settled the Westlake family in America—Peyton Westlake, after whom the town of Peyton, Maryland, was named. Tayte hadn't followed up on what had become of Adam Westlake and his family after their corruption had been exposed. He did know that Adam Westlake had tried to kill someone, and had come close to succeeding, in his attempt to keep his family secrets safe.

'You're saying Adam Westlake served a twenty-year sentence for what he did, because of my assignment at the time?'

'That's right. He has enough reason to want payback, but there's more to it. His father committed suicide soon after the trial. His young wife divorced him when his sentence began, and his mother died while he was in prison. She slowly killed herself through drinking and drugs, squandering what remained of the family's wealth after the courts had finished with them. There's no other name on your list that comes close to how much Adam Westlake must blame you and hate you for what he must surely believe you were ultimately responsible for. And get this—he violated the conditions of his parole a month ago when he failed to report to his parole officer. That was just days before Kelly Uttridge was reported missing. He's no longer at the halfway house that was set up for him. No one knows where he is.'

Tayte swallowed the lump that had risen in his throat at hearing what Reese had just told him. To think that such a man was on the loose and unaccounted for made his mouth all the more dry. He took a big gulp of coffee to quench it, glad that he was there at the safe house and not his apartment, where Adam Westlake could come for him whenever he became bored with the sick, vengeful game he was playing. Adam Westlake was a smart and highly educated man as Tayte recalled. His wealthy family had seen to it that he received a first-class education. He had been primed for a political career, just like his father before him, and when Tayte had shown the world that the family had earned, and continued to earn, its wealth and position in the community, not through hard work, but through just about every illegal and immoral activity they could make money at, he'd brought their entire dynasty tumbling down around them.

Yes, Westlake was an intelligent man, but a genealogist? As Reese had pointed out, Westlake had had plenty of time to learn the tools of the trade, but he doubted he would have been able to obtain sufficient material whilst in prison, and he certainly would not have been able to practise any of the theory in order to build the required experience. Tayte started to think that he'd been here before, and his mind was once again taken back to London a year previously, when he'd told the detective in charge of the murders then that he believed there had to be a genealogical mastermind behind the killings. More and more he believed the same was true now, but how could he prove it? It was certainly possible that Westlake, if he was the Genie, had had the time to learn all he needed to know from Tayte's assignment files after he'd broken into his apartment.

Tayte sat back with a sigh. 'So what do I do now?'

'You sit tight,' Reese said. 'Wait for the Genie to contact you. When he does, call me. And I don't want to scare you, but keep in mind that because this is about you and your work, you're probably the only person qualified to solve the clues he's setting for us in time. That means you're in the best position to lead us to him, and he knows it. I don't believe he wants to be caught. Remember that. He's probably getting a kick out of letting us believe we have a chance, but as far as he's concerned, we don't. If the odds start to shift in our favour, who knows what he'll do?'

Tayte had a pretty good idea, and he didn't like it at all. If it came down to it, he thought the Genie would most likely decide to stop the only man capable of stopping him. It sent an uncomfortable shiver running down his spine.

It was almost ten o'clock, and it was raining heavily as Adam Westlake climbed the steps to the front door of the townhouse he'd been watching in Washington's Downtown neighbourhood. He thought the rain was good. It was a quiet time of day, midweek, when most people were already at work, but the rain helped to keep the streets even quieter; the few people he'd seen as he'd headed towards the property were all hiding beneath their umbrellas, paying him no attention. The man Westlake was going to see wasn't at work yet. He worked shifts, and today his shift began at midday, which gave Westlake two hours to go in and set things up. When he reached the door, he took another casual look around, and then knocked.

The door was opened a few seconds later by a small, dark-haired boy who looked no more than five years old. He was barely tall enough to reach the catch. He stared up at Westlake with his mouth agape, and Westlake could tell that his eyes were transfixed by the scar across his left eyebrow. The staring was nothing new to him. He smiled down at the boy, trying not to scare him. Not yet.

'Is Daddy home?' Westlake asked him, knowing full well that he was.

Another voice answered from further along the hallway. It was the boy's mother. 'Who is it, sweetie?'

She was at the door in seconds, still buttoning her blouse as though she was getting ready to go out, which was too bad.

She looked up at Westlake as he stood on the porch, dripping wet from the rain. 'Can I help you?'

Westlake continued to smile. 'Yes, you can,' he said, and then with sudden force he reached out and put a hand around the woman's neck. At the same time, he grabbed the boy and stepped inside, clapping his other hand around the boy's mouth to stifle his cry as he kicked the door shut behind him. 'Make a sound and I'll snap your neck,' he added to the woman. He could see the fear in her eyes; fear for herself and for her boy. He liked that.

Fear breeds obedience.

Westlake forced them both back along the hallway, heading towards the first door he could see, which was on his right. As he reached it, he paused, hearing the woman's husband call out to her from the room beyond.

'Honey, don't slam the door like that. Who was it?'

As the man came through into the hallway, Westlake saw the fear in his eyes, too, but this time he could see that his fear was about to make him do something stupid. He let go of the woman and her child, and without a moment's hesitation he hit the man hard in the face, knocking him to the ground before he could say or do a thing.

'You broke my nose!' the man wailed, his hands clutching his face as blood began to drip on to his shirt.

'No talking,' Westlake said, 'or I promise this will get worse for you and your family. I don't want to hurt you. You're not why I'm here.'

'Why are you here?'

Westlake leaned down and hit the man again. 'I said no talking. Now get up! Do exactly as you're told and you'll all live through this.'

The boy began to cry.

Westlake turned to his mother. 'That goes for the boy, too. Shut him up, or I will. Is this the living room?' Westlake added, indicating the room her husband had just appeared from.

The woman nodded, holding her son close to muffle his crying.

'Get in there! All of you!'

Westlake followed after them, and once they were in the brightly furnished room, he took a roll of duct tape out from his coat pocket and tossed it to the woman. 'Hands and ankles. The boy, too. Use your teeth if you can't tear it. Where are your cell phones?'

'My pocket,' the man said.

'Mine's on the coffee table there,' the woman added.

Westlake took them both and proceeded to smash them beneath the heel of his boot. He knew he couldn't use these phones to call Jefferson Tayte with the next clue, or he would risk the FBI tracing it back to the home he'd just invaded. It didn't matter. He had plenty of other phones he could use. He continued to watch the woman bind her husband with the duct tape. Once she'd finished, she turned to her boy.

'We're going to play a little game, sweetie,' she said softly, her voice trembling. 'Everything's okay.'

Once she'd finished, Westlake snatched the tape from her and bound her hands and ankles. Then he sat them all down on the couch and tore off a strip of tape for each of their mouths so they couldn't call out. He used the rest of the tape to bind everyone together, like flies in a spider's web, so no one could get up again or go far if they did. Then he calmly sat down opposite them and lit a cigarette. 'You don't mind if I smoke, do you?' he said mockingly. He inhaled deeply and sat back. 'That's better. Now I just need to borrow your home for a short while.'

At the safe house, Tayte was in the temporary filing room the FBI had set up for him, in what he imagined was ordinarily an extra bedroom. It was a quarter past five in the afternoon, and he'd been in there most of the day, going through his old files in part to reacquaint himself with some of his previous assignments in case anything proved useful later on, but mostly to relieve his boredom. With so many files, he knew the odds of reading anything valuable to the case were slim. He'd been drawn to them initially by the need to find out which of his former clients Samuel Shaw, the Genie's latest victim at Chain Bridge, had been related to, and it pained him to think that his innocent research during that assignment had now led to this man's murder, bringing the total number of deaths he felt responsible for to six.

After that he'd wanted to look up the assignment that had led to the incarceration of Adam Westlake, the FBI's prime suspect in the case. It had involved his discovery of a land rights battle, and he'd helped to set things right for his client after the corrupt and formerly powerful Westlake family had effectively stolen that land from his client's ancestors, and many other Maryland families besides. If Reese was right about Westlake, from those ashes a monster had now risen.

Tayte put away the last of the files he'd been looking through and went to the kitchen to fix himself a coffee and a sandwich. He wasn't particularly hungry—he'd already eaten more than usual that day. He just didn't have anything else to do. He was part way through making his sandwich when he heard familiar show-tune music coming from the living room where he'd left his phone. He put down the kitchen knife he was holding and ran to it, wondering whether the call was from Jean or the Genie. It wasn't Jean. There was a number on the display, but he didn't recognise it. If it was the Genie, he hadn't withheld his number this time, in which case it clearly didn't matter to him. It would be an untraceable phone that he'd destroy as soon as he was finished with it.

'Hello?' Tayte said as he took the call, aware that his heart rate was already climbing. What he heard in reply made his pulse kick harder.

'Are you ready to play another round, Tayte?'

Tayte didn't answer right away. He sat down on one of the armchairs and tried to compose himself. He'd thought over what he wanted to say to this man many times since he'd last called, but right now he couldn't think straight.

'Do I have any choice?'

'Of course. We all have choices, but we also have to live with the consequences of our choices, don't we? Now, are you ready to play the game again, or not?'

'Yes, I'm ready.'

'That's more like it. Would you like to know where I am?'

'Yes, I would.'

'Good, because I want to tell you. I'm sitting in a vehicle I just stole, across the street from a DC realtor. They have a store front, and through the window I can see a smartly dressed woman in a green business suit. She's thirty-four years old. She has a husband and two children, and she arrives here at work around a quarter after eight, Monday to Friday. She leaves promptly at five. That's in about ten minutes. The only difference today is that she won't be able to make it home tonight. And guess what?'

'What?'

'It's all your fault.'

It was a bitter pill to take and Tayte swallowed it hard. A moment later, he said, 'I know who you are. Your name's Adam Westlake.'

'Bravo. But then I didn't expect it would take long to figure that out—not once you were in the game. You might think that gives you some kind of advantage, but it doesn't matter who I am.'

'Why doesn't it matter? There's nowhere you can hide where the FBI won't eventually find you.'

Westlake gave a sour laugh. 'Where I'm going, no one can follow. My life was over the day you destroyed it. Do you think I care anything for the pathetic existence you've left me with?'

To hear that Westlake had no desire or expectation of living through this sent an icy chill through Tayte. It made the man all the more dangerous.

'I'm going to stop you.'

'Do you think you're good enough?'

'Just give me the damn clue and we'll find out.'

Westlake laughed again. 'Your blood's boiling, isn't it, Tayte? I like that.' There was a brief pause. Then Westlake said, 'When this call ends you'll receive a text message containing the clue. I wouldn't want you to write it down wrong or lose it. You have until noon tomorrow. If you and your FBI friends can't work it out in time, the woman in the green suit will die.'

'You're not going to kill her!' Tayte said, his voice raised to a defiant shout. 'Not this time. I'm going to stop you—you hear me?'

With that, Tayte ended the call. He didn't want to waste another second talking to this creep. He fell back into the armchair with a heavy sigh, hoping he was right and that he could stop Westlake in time to save this woman. He had little time to think about it before his phone beeped, startling him, despite the fact that he was expecting the text message. His hands were shaking as he opened it. It contained two letters, followed by a series of numbers: GJ 28027590. Tayte's eyes narrowed in puzzlement as he began to wonder what it meant. Then he called Reese.

Chapter Twelve

Tayte's next call after phoning Reese was to Mavro, and within thirty minutes she was knocking on the safe house door. During that time Tayte had been chain-eating Hershey's Miniatures from a new bag he'd opened as soon as he'd received Westlake's text message, all the while staring at it, trying to understand what it referred to.

He and Mavro sat down in the living room, where Tayte had drawn the blinds against the fading early-evening light.

'So, it's not another burial plot reference?' Mavro said.

Tayte shook his head. 'No. At least if it is, it's like none I've ever seen. GJ 28027590. Two letters and eight digits,' he added, thinking aloud as he popped another chocolate into his mouth. 'Could be an index reference to something.'

'Those letters could be someone's initials, like before.'

'Yes, they could,' Tayte agreed. 'Although, I don't think we can know for sure until we know what the numbers are. I guess it has to be a reference I'd be familiar with in my line of work.'

'Something genealogical?'

'Or maybe something I'd know about because of my research. There has to be some logic to it. I can't see why Westlake would make it too difficult to get off first base.'

'So what kind of eight-digit numbers do you deal with?'

Tayte had to think about that. A moment later, he said, 'National Archives Identifiers can be eight digits. Maybe it's a reference to a document they hold.'

'Can we look it up?'

'Yes, we can,' Tayte said, getting to his feet. 'Help yourself to those chocolates.'

He went into the kitchen where he'd left his laptop and a moment later he returned with it, waking it up as he walked. He sat beside Mavro now so that she could see what he was doing as he brought up the page for the National Archives Catalog. He entered the eight-digit number into the search field and pressed the enter key with his fingers crossed. A second later he saw the results and read them aloud.

'*There are no search results found using the search term: 28027590.*'

'That's too bad,' Mavro said.

'Yeah, I thought maybe we were onto something there.'

'Anything else?'

Tayte sat back with his thoughts. Several quiet seconds later, he sat forward again. 'I'm going to put a fresh pot of coffee on. You want some?'

'Definitely,' Mavro said. 'That's a question you never need to ask me.'

Tayte was smiling to himself as he headed back into the kitchen, thinking that her coffee addiction was right up there with his own.

When he came back, he was still smiling. 'The Library of Congress,' he said as he handed Mavro her coffee. 'They use an eight-digit or ten-digit identifier, which they call a control number or LCCN.' He sat down and referred back to the digits Westlake had sent him. 'Depending on when the control number was allocated, the first two or four numbers refer to the year. It's two digits up until 2000 and the full four digits of the year after that. The six digits that follow represent the sequential serial number for that record.'

'So, if this is a Library of Congress Control Number,' Mavro said, 'it was allocated in 1928?'

'That's correct. I come across these LCCNs whenever my research takes me to the Library of Congress to see a publication. Being the fastidious researcher I am, I typically make a note of them in my assignment files for easy referral should I need to go back to them.'

'It sounds like an LCCN would be something Westlake could be sure you'd know about, doesn't it?' Mavro said, with a look in her eye that told Tayte she thought they could be on the right track.

Tayte nodded back, knowing there was every chance they were. He opened his laptop again and brought up the Library of Congress Online Catalog, into which he entered the eight-digit number, and this time he didn't feel the need to cross his fingers so hard as he clicked the search button. When the associated catalogue entry displayed, a wide smile spread across his face.

'There it is,' he said. 'Gertrude Jones.'

'GJ,' Mavro added. 'The initials Westlake sent in his message.'

'He wanted us to know when we were looking in the right place, just like before at River Creek Cemetery.'

'So the reference points to a book,' Mavro said, scrutinising the contents of the screen. '*Tales of Romance: A Volume of Short Stories* by Gertrude Jones.'

'1908 to 1930,' Tayte said as he read Jones's year of birth and death. He quickly wrote the details down in his notebook. 'She died age twenty-two, two years after the book's publication,' he added, wondering whether the close proximity between her death and the book's release, or the fact that she had died young, might come to yield any significance.

'She might have lived locally,' Mavro said. She pointed to the screen. 'It says here that her publisher was in Richmond, Virginia.'

Tayte sat back with his coffee. 'So we know whose death Westlake plans to replicate. Now all we need to find out is how, and more importantly where, Gertrude Jones died in 1930. To do that, we need to take a look at her vital records.'

'That's not going to be easy,' Mavro said, checking her watch. 'The Department of Health offices closed over an hour ago. Under the circumstances, I'm sure we could persuade them to open up for us, but it could take half the night to get access to the records we need to see.'

'There could be another way.'

Tayte led Mavro to his temporary filing room at the back of the apartment. 'There's a good chance that copies of Gertrude Jones's records will be in here somewhere. If she was related to a former client whose surname was also Jones, it shouldn't take too long to find out.'

'I bet you have plenty of files for people called Jones,' Mavro said. 'It's a common surname.'

Tayte went to the cabinet containing surnames beginning with J. 'Last time I checked, Jones was ranked the fifth most common surname in the US.' He pulled open the drawer and turned back to Mavro with a raised eyebrow. 'At least her name wasn't Smith.'

Mavro stood beside him as he began to flick through the files. 'How many are there?'

Tayte was still counting. A moment later, he said. 'Fourteen, and they're all bulging. All we have to do, though, is check the index at the beginning of each file—the client's family tree. If Gertrude Jones is in the file, she'll be listed.'

'Let's get to it then. Half each. We can spread out on the table in the kitchen.'

They each carried a pile of files to the kitchen and set them down on the floor at either end of the table. As Tayte sat down, Mavro took her phone out.

'I'm going to call Reese,' she said. 'I think it's best that he at least informs someone high up at the DoH that we may need access to the Vital Records Division this evening.'

'Good thinking,' Tayte said. 'If Gertrude Jones's records aren't among these files, it would take more time than we have to go looking through all the rest.'

Mavro wandered out of the kitchen to make the call as Tayte opened the first of the Jones files. He expected to find the client's family tree index right there on top of the pile, telling him the names of all the people the file contained, but it wasn't there. He quickly flicked through all the records in the file in case he'd put it in the wrong place, or slipped other records on top of it at some time, but he knew he hadn't. He was far too meticulous when it came to his records. When he reached the end of the file, he sat back in his chair, dumbfounded.

Mavro came back into the kitchen, putting her phone away as she walked. 'It's done,' she said. Then when she looked at him she added, 'What? What is it?'

Tayte had already opened the next Jones file from his pile. There was no family tree index there either. 'The indexes are missing.' He opened another of the files and it was the same story. 'Westlake must have taken them when he broke into my apartment. Not all of them, though,' he added, recalling that he'd checked a couple when he first became involved in the case. He slapped the file down on to the table and sighed. 'He's only taken the ones he knows I need to see, to make things harder for us.'

Mavro shook her head. 'At least that tells us something.'

'It does?'

'Sure it does. Gertrude Jones's records must be in one of these files or he wouldn't have felt the need to remove the indexes in the first place.'

'Good point, but it's going to take longer than I thought.'

'We've got all night,' Mavro said as they set to it.

Tayte carefully began to thumb through the first of his files as Mavro did the same with hers. Tayte had to try hard not to let his mind wander as he recalled detail after detail from each past assignment. Without the copies of the family tree indexes it was slow going, but they had to be thorough so as to avoid missing that one vital record. Each had to be inspected for mention of Gertrude Jones, or a date later than 1930 when she had died, thus ruling it out. Depending on the type of record, it wasn't always clear at a glance, necessitating close scrutiny of each document they came to. They sustained themselves on coffee and another bag of Hershey's, which Mavro had also now taken to. Neither voiced any desire to take a break to fix something more substantial or nutritious to eat. Almost two hours passed without success, and it was after nine o'clock before Mavro sat up in her seat. She had a record in her hand and a broad smile on her face.

'Here she is!'

Tayte was already on his feet. He pulled a chair up beside Mavro and sat down as she slid the record in front of him. It was a copy of Gertrude Jones's birth certificate.

'Born 1908,' Tayte said. 'That's her all right. Is there a certificate of death?'

Mavro singled it out and handed it to Tayte. 'That's all there seems to be for her,' she said. 'No certificate of marriage.'

Tayte studied the death certificate. The place of death showed the District of Columbia, and it stated that she had died in 1930, which again confirmed that he was looking at the same Gertrude Jones who had written the book Westlake's clue had led them to. The document was otherwise unremarkable in all but one respect: the cause of death.

'*Suicide*,' Tayte read out. '*Arterial hemorrhage*.'

'She cut her wrists?'

'Looks that way.'

'The poor thing. Why? She was so young.'

'*Why* is a good question,' Tayte said. 'But *where* is the question we have to answer.' He was thinking about the woman in the green suit Westlake had spoken of when he'd called earlier. 'At least we now know how Westlake plans to kill his next victim, but that's no use to us unless we know where he plans to do it.'

'Maybe why leads to where,' Mavro said. 'There has to be a story behind this girl's suicide.'

'True, but maybe we can play a hunch here. If Gertrude Jones cut her wrists, there's a very strong possibility she did so at home. She wasn't married, so it's likely that she lived with her parents, whose address at the time is right here in these records. It's in the Downtown neighbourhood.'

Mavro had her phone out before Tayte had finished speaking, calling Reese.

'And you can tell Reese whose family Westlake's next victim will come from,' Tayte added, sorting through the file to find his former client's details. 'When I called him before you got here, I told him it was a woman who works for a DC realtor. He should be able to identify her now.'

He thought perhaps a missing persons report had already been filed for the woman, who had in all probability not made it home from work that day. As Reese picked up the call and Mavro began to give him the details, he hoped the location was right. He could already feel his anxiety levels begin to rise at knowing he would once again have to wait to find out.

⌣

Adam Westlake was back at the Downtown home he had recently forced his way into. It had a traditional bathroom with a large claw-foot bath beneath the window. He was sitting on the rolled top at the tap end, looking contemplatively down at the woman in the green suit he'd abducted on her way home from work. She was lying on the black-and-white-chequered tile floor just inside the door, still unconscious. He was wondering when the injection he'd given her would wear off. He knew now that he'd given her far too much of the concoction of potentially lethal barbiturates and benzodiazepines. He'd almost killed her before the next part of the game had begun, and that would never do.

He was waiting to run a nice hot bath for his guest, which would help prevent her blood from clotting once he'd cut her, but he wanted her awake before he began. Not too awake, though. Docile, yet aware of what was going on, her blood pumping at a decent rate, which he imagined would not be a problem once she came around and realised what was going on. He was already anticipating her fear. He had suffered. Now they had to suffer, and it was all because of Jefferson Tayte.

His eyes wandered to the glass shelf over the washbasin where he'd put the knife he planned to use. It wasn't his knife. He'd found it in Tayte's apartment. It was an old bone-handled carving knife he knew the genealogist couldn't fail to recognise. He thought that was a nice touch. Knowing that Tayte's own knife had been used in the gradual exsanguination of the woman in the green suit would surely inflict a few psychological scars on the man himself—an added bonus as far as Westlake was concerned.

He stood up and went to the woman. Then he stooped down beside her and cupped her chin in his hand, lifting her face to his. She looked pretty, just his type, and so calm and peaceful. How all that was about to change. He slapped her face in an attempt to wake her. He was keen to get started, and this really wouldn't do at all. He was about to slap her again, harder this time, but he heard something that forced him to stop and listen.

It was getting late. Outside, the street had been quiet for the past hour or so. He could hear the raised engine notes of several vehicles approaching, clearly in a hurry to be somewhere. A moment later his breath caught in his chest as he heard the vehicles screech to a halt. They sounded right outside. He shot to his feet as car doors opened and were slammed shut, wondering whether Tayte had worked his latest puzzle out already. The idea angered him. Then a sense of panic sent his pulse racing and he left the bathroom, heading for one of the bedrooms at the front of the house to find out.

Tayte and Mavro had not been idle while they waited for Reese to call back with news about the Downtown address they had given him. They had been sitting in the living room, checking the newspaper archives, supposing that the suicide of a young author would be a newsworthy story. The only match they had found was in the obituaries section of the *Washington Herald*, which they were looking at now.

'It doesn't really add anything to the story of Gertrude Jones's death, does it?' Mavro said, pinching the tiredness from her eyes.

'No, not much,' Tayte agreed. 'Apart from telling us where she was buried, and giving us a few names of the friends and family who were in attendance at her funeral. I'll take a screenshot for my files.'

Tayte stood up. 'Let me refill your coffee. You look as if you could use some.'

Mavro passed Tayte her mug. 'Thanks. And you're not looking so fresh yourself,' she added with a grin.

'I'll sleep when this is over,' Tayte said as he made for the kitchen, but the sound of Mavro's phone ringing stopped him cold.

He turned back to see Mavro answer it, her eyes locked on his as she spoke. He knew right away that it was Reese. He sat down again, waiting to hear the news. The call was brief, and when Mavro ended it with a firm shake of her head, Tayte's heart sank.

'I'm sorry, JT. Looks like Gertrude Jones didn't die at home.'

Tayte gave a heavy sigh. 'Then I've just wasted everybody's time—time we don't have.'

'Don't beat yourself up. It was a solid hunch.'

Tayte thumped the chair he was sitting on. 'No, it would have been too easy. I should have realised that. Westlake wouldn't have given us until noon tomorrow if it was that simple.'

'So go and get those coffee mugs refilled and let's find out where Gertrude Jones *did* die,' Mavro said. 'There has to be a way we can find out. We just have to keep looking.'

Tayte's shoulders were slumped low as he entered the kitchen. As he poured their coffees, he began to contemplate something Mavro has said earlier. *Maybe why leads to where.* If they understood why Gertrude Jones had wanted to end her life, then perhaps they would be in a better position to work out where she had died. There had to be a reason why she had felt so despondent. By the time Tayte went back into the living room, he thought he knew where the answer could be.

'The book,' he said, setting their drinks down on the coffee table. 'Westlake's clue led us to it. Maybe the answer to why Jones killed herself is wrapped up in the pages of her book.'

'A book of romantic short stories,' Mavro said. 'Maybe that's the reason right there. It sure wouldn't be the first time someone killed themselves in the name of love.'

Tayte agreed. 'I think we need to see a copy of the book. If only to rule it out.'

'I expect it's long out of print by now.'

'The Library of Congress has a copy,' he said as he brought up the web page he still had open. His session had timed out, so he entered the search again and was soon looking at the title information. He pointed to the lower half of the screen. 'It says here to request it in the Jefferson or Adams Building reading rooms.'

'There won't be anyone there now, of course,' Mavro said. 'I could call Reese. Maybe he can get someone there tonight, but as I said earlier, it could take some time and it's already late. When do they open for business?'

'Half past eight,' Tayte said, having no need to look the information up. 'Once you've had your coffee, why don't you go home and get some rest. I want to look into the newspaper archives some more, but I can do that by myself.'

'You should get some sleep, too. We'll only have the morning to solve this. You'll need to be sharp when the sun comes up.'

'I know,' Tayte said. 'Just another hour or so.'

'Okay. I'll pick you up at half past seven.'

Chapter Thirteen

The Library of Congress was home to more than 160 million catalogued items, and with almost thirty-eight million books, it was the largest library in the world. As soon as Mavro had picked Tayte up from the safe house early the following morning, they headed for the Thomas Jefferson Building, which was located on 1st Street Southeast between Independence Avenue and East Capitol Street. It was built in the 1890s and was the oldest of the three Library of Congress buildings. In the car on the way there, Mavro had told Tayte that to save time she'd asked Reese to call ahead to set things up for them. On their arrival they had been taken through to the Main Reading Room while they waited for one of the librarians to locate the book they needed to see.

It was a circular, domed reading room at the heart of the building, lavishly galleried and softly lit from above by high arched windows, and at ground level by the many reading lamps that lined the desks. As they sat down, they found themselves surrounded by bronze statuary on the upper level, which seemed to gaze down at them, as if to inspire and encourage their learning. Tayte thought some inspiration was just what they needed. He yawned, still waking up after another fitful sleep, despite having had three large mugs of coffee already that morning.

'I'm surprised I didn't find anything in the newspaper archives after you left last night,' he said, 'given that Gertrude Jones committed suicide, I mean.'

'Maybe her family wanted to keep her name out of the papers.'

'Maybe,' Tayte agreed. 'That would certainly explain it.'

The librarian wasn't long finding the book they had requested: *Tales of Romance: A Volume of Short Stories.* Tayte opened it, not at all sure what they were looking for, or whether they were even on the right track. He figured if they were, then whatever it was that they were expected to find, it had to be something that would seem obvious to them when they saw it. He turned the title page and glanced over the copyright information. When he turned the page again he saw the dedication and read it out.

'*For MAK. The love of my life.*'

'That's nice,' Mavro said. 'She writes a book of romance stories and dedicates it to the man she loves.'

'I wonder who MAK is? It's not spelled like a first name, and being capitalised like that, I'd say those were someone's initials.'

Mavro shrugged. 'There was no marriage certificate for Jones in your files, so we know he wasn't her husband.'

'Maybe that's it,' Tayte said. 'MAK was the love of her life, but maybe her love wasn't reciprocated.'

'Maybe MAK was married, and Jones killed herself because she couldn't have him. That could be the *why* we're looking for.'

Tayte thought the scenario they had just painted between them fitted the situation well, although it also occurred to him that MAK could have been another woman. In which case, back in 1928 when the book was published, Gertrude Jones would have had every reason to be cryptic about MAK's identity. He turned another page and the first of the stories began. He turned another and another, and then he flicked to the back of the book, where he saw a typical acknowledgements page and an author biography. They read them both together, but neither passage sparked any conversation between them—nothing stood out enough to be of any interest. Tayte had been looking for someone with the initials MAK, or just MK, but no one with those initials was mentioned, and he soon realised it would have been pointless to be so cryptic in the dedication if the person's name was printed in the back of the book. He wished it was. It would have saved time trying to find out who MAK was, but Tayte knew that was just what they had to do. As always, he had to keep following the clues in the hope that they would eventually yield the answers he was looking for. He turned to the dedication again.

'Let's say for now that you're right about MAK being a married man,' he said. 'If that's the case, it's understandable that Jones felt the need to be cautious and to only use her lover's initials. We need to find out more about him.'

'How are we supposed to do that just from his initials?'

Tayte reminded himself again that there had to be a way to find out who MAK was, or the sick game Adam Westlake had forced him to play would be utterly futile. He didn't believe that was the case. All the answers had been right there in the records so far. He just had to find them.

'Unless Gertrude Jones was living some kind of fantasy,' he said, 'I think it's safe to say that MAK was at least a friend of hers—someone who knew her.'

Mavro smiled at the understatement as she clearly saw it. 'In all likelihood, MAK was a *very* good friend.'

Tayte nodded, still thinking. A moment later, he looked at Mavro wide-eyed and said, 'Of course! And what do good friends do when someone they know, and probably love in this case, die?' He reached down into his briefcase and took his laptop out. 'That person would, if possible, attend the deceased's funeral. Maybe he's mentioned in the list of attendees noted in Gertrude Jones's obituary. Those names I saw didn't mean anything at the time, but I took a screenshot. We'll soon see.'

It took less than a minute to confirm.

'Mark Knight,' Tayte said, smiling broadly. 'There's no middle name, but that has to be him.'

'*Monsieur* Tayte!'

Those two words sent a shudder down Tayte's spine. It wasn't so much the words themselves, but the unmistakable soft French accent of the man who had just spoken them. Tayte turned around to see the slight form of the exuberant Michel Levant pacing excitedly towards him. For reasons Tayte could not fathom, his face was full of smiles, as though he had just seen an old friend, only Tayte knew he was anything but. Levant was wearing a close-fitting ruby velvet suit that shimmered as he walked, in that effeminate way Tayte had come to loathe almost as much as the sound of the man's thin, melodious voice. He was every bit the twenty-first-century dandy Tayte remembered him to be. He was speechless as Levant approached them.

'But what are you doing in Washington?' Levant asked with obvious surprise. He stepped closer still, as if to embrace Tayte, which got Tayte to his feet just in time to step away, bumping into Mavro as he did so.

'What am *I* doing here?' Tayte said, frowning. 'I live here.'

'You do? I had no idea.'

'Really?' Tayte said, utterly unconvinced.

'And who is this? You have a girlfriend, I see.'

Tayte didn't want to get into his personal life with this man, so he just sighed and shook his head. Being rude didn't come easily to him, regardless of whom he happened to be talking to, so he turned to Mavro and introduced her. 'This is my associate, Ms Mavro.' He waved his hand between the two of them. 'Ms Mavro, this is Michel Levant.'

They went to shake hands, but as they did so Levant leaned in suddenly and kissed the back of Mavro's before she had the chance to object. 'You have me at a disadvantage, *mademoiselle*.'

'I do?' Mavro said, almost laughing at Levant's flamboyant gesture.

'You know my first name, but Michel Levant does not know yours.'

Mavro glanced at Tayte, who was holding on to his frown. 'I don't think I know you well enough.'

'Perhaps not yet,' Levant said, smiling through that sing-song voice of his, just as Tayte stepped between them.

'Perhaps not ever,' he said, able to feign politeness only up to a point where Levant was concerned. 'We're kind of busy here, if you don't mind.'

Levant's smile dropped. 'You don't like me very much, do you?'

Tayte wanted to say that he didn't like him one bit, but he kept it to himself.

'I don't know why this is,' Levant continued. 'I saved your life, after all. Surely you could not have forgotten.'

Tayte remembered the occasion only too well, but he was sure Levant had only done so to further his own cause.

'Come, come,' Levant continued. 'Let's have some coffee together, shall we? Forget about the past and put everything that happened in London behind us. What do you say?'

Tayte couldn't do that. His friend had been murdered and he didn't want to forget about it. He didn't want to stand around talking to this man any longer than he had to, either, but as he was there, Tayte thought he'd throw a pertinent question at him.

'Do you know a man called Adam Westlake?'

Levant pulled a face as he seemed to think about it.

'Adam Peyton Westlake III,' Tayte added, knowing a name like that would be hard to forget.

Levant slowly began to shake his head. 'No, the name is not familiar. But who is he? A friend of yours?'

Tayte couldn't hold back a derisive laugh. 'No, he's not. He's been murdering people here in DC—members of my past clients' families. But you wouldn't know anything about that, either, would you?'

Levant gasped, and it seemed a little theatrical to Tayte. '*Mon Dieu*, Mr Tayte! You must dislike me more than I thought. I'm here on business, that's all. I'm hosting an event tomorrow at your National Archives Museum and—'

'Yeah, I know,' Tayte cut in. 'I read about it in the *Washingtonian*.'

'Well, perhaps you and your friend would like to come along,' Levant said with a thin-lipped smile. He reached into his inside jacket pocket. 'I have several spare tickets, and you're most wel—'

Tayte cut in again, blocking Levant's hand as he began to pull the tickets out. 'No thanks,' he said, more than a little assertively. 'Now, as I said, we're very busy here, if you don't mind.'

Levant tut-tutted and pursed his lips. 'Very well,' he said. 'Michel Levant knows when he's not welcome.'

He turned away and Tayte watched him go, thinking that he'd got that right. As far as Tayte was concerned, Michel Levant wasn't welcome at all.

He was shaking his head as he turned back to his laptop and the obituary that had given him the name of Gertrude Jones's lover.

'Remind me not to piss you off,' Mavro said through a smile.

'I'm sorry,' Tayte said. 'The man just gets under my skin, that's all.'

'I can see that, and I know what you were trying to do when you mentioned Adam Westlake just then, but I'm sure Reese would go nuts if he knew you'd leaked the Genie's real name.'

'Levant knows his name.'

'You can't be sure of that. So what exactly did Levant do to you in London last year—apart from saving your life, I mean?'

Tayte could tell Mavro was teasing him with the remark. He stared up at the circular window in the cupola above them and tried to come up with an answer, but apart from a gut feeling about the Frenchman, which he knew was based on little more than a series of hunches and suppositions, he had to confess that Michel Levant hadn't actually done anything to him. He also had to remind himself that he'd landed himself in trouble before for accusing Levant of things for which he had no proof.

'I don't know,' Tayte said, shaking his head again. 'He just makes me uneasy. Where I'm concerned of late, he always seems to be where the trouble is, yet he's got an alibi or an explanation for everything. It's all rather too convenient for my liking. Apart from the fact that he happens to be in DC at the same time Adam Westlake is murdering members of my former clients' families, don't you think it's an odd coincidence that he just happened to be here at the Library of Congress this morning, right when we are?'

'He couldn't have known we'd be here.'

'Yes, he could. If he's the genealogical mastermind behind these murders—if he's the one setting us these puzzles—he'd know we'd have to come here to look at Gertrude Jones's book.'

'Okay, I can see that,' Mavro conceded. 'But alternatively, as he's in town running a genealogical event at the National Archives Museum, maybe he's just here to do some research. I'll ask a member of staff to see whether he made any requests while he was here. Not that it will prove anything if he hasn't.'

'I shouldn't waste your time. Knowing Levant as I do, I'm sure he'll have asked to see something just to cover himself.'

Tayte turned back to his laptop for a second time, reminding himself that they had to stay focused. If Levant was behind these murders, Tayte wouldn't have put it past the man to have forced the interruption on purpose, just to slow them down. He tapped a few keys and brought up his preferred newspaper archive website.

'Let's see what we can find out about Mark Knight,' he said. 'Gertrude Jones might not have made the headlines back in 1930, but maybe the love of her life did.'

He typed Mark Knight's name into the appropriate search fields, entered 1930 for the year he was interested in, and ticked the checkbox for newspapers distributed in the District of Columbia, where he knew

Gertrude Jones had lived, and Virginia, where her publisher at the time was based. Only two results came back, and his eyes were immediately drawn to the first article, which was from the DC publication, the *Evening Star*, dated January 1930.

'Touchdown!' he said as he began to read it. He was a big Washington Redskins fan, although he hadn't had the opportunity to see a football game in a while.

Mavro leaned in and read out the headline. '*Woman's body found in lover's bathtub.*'

'That's our guy,' Tayte said. 'His middle name's Alexander, which fits with the book's dedication to MAK.'

The article was brief. It told them that Mark Alexander Knight was forty-six years old—a much older man than Gertrude Jones—and that he was indeed married, as previously suspected. It also stated that Mark Knight had two children by his marriage and that he'd been having an affair with the deceased, a local author whose name was not mentioned.

'But we know who she was,' Tayte said. 'And after she was rejected by the love of her life, Gertrude Jones killed herself in his bathtub so his wife would discover their affair.'

'It amazes me how you can draw a picture of people's lives like this,' Mavro said.

'It's all in the records. You just have to find the pieces and put them together to see how our ancestors lived, and in this case, how they died.'

'And now we not only know how Jones died, but where.'

Tayte picked up on the excitement in Mavro's voice at knowing they were so close to solving the Genie's latest clue. He nodded. 'All that remains is to find out where Mark Knight lived in 1930.'

'Will that take long?' Mavro asked. 'I hate to rush you, but it's a quarter after ten. We don't have much time left.'

'The 1930 census will tell us,' Tayte said with confidence, knowing that the census enumeration that year began in April, three months after Jones had taken her life. He tapped at his laptop's keyboard again and brought up an online census search for that year, glad the required seventy-two-year privacy period for this census had passed. 'We should have this wrapped up in a matter of minutes,' he added as he began to enter the search details for Mark Alexander Knight.

When the results came back, Tayte froze. Knight's address was in DC's Downtown neighbourhood. He had lived right next door to the address Mavro had passed to Reese the night before. Gertrude Jones had been having an affair with her neighbour.

Chapter Fourteen

Tayte and Mavro were driving to meet SAC Reese, and it seemed to Tayte that Mavro couldn't get to the meeting point fast enough. Her impatience to punch through the lunchtime traffic had Tayte clutching at the grab rail above his window with one hand, and the edge of his seat with the other. Following Mavro's phone call to Reese, they had spent an uneasy hour in the coffee shop on the Jefferson Building's cellar level, waiting to hear whether the address they had given Reese this time was right, and if it was, whether they had been in time to save the woman Adam Westlake had chosen as his next victim.

The wait to find out had been torturous. Tayte had felt so useless and frustrated the whole time, and the strong coffee he'd consumed as he and Mavro waited for the call seemed to put him all the more on edge. When Reese's call eventually came through it was brief. He'd confirmed it was the right address, but so far that was all he'd confirmed, having chosen to save the details for when they met. They were heading west on Independence Avenue. Reese had said he'd meet them at the George Washington University Hospital.

'She has to be alive,' Tayte said, with more than a hint of hope in his voice. 'Why else would Reese want us to meet him at the hospital?'

'It's a good sign,' Mavro said as she turned the car north on to 17th Street, 'but try not to get your hopes up too high until we know more. We're almost there.'

Tayte thought back over the research they had conducted over the last twelve hours and he shook his head. 'I can't believe how close Reese's team must have been to Westlake last night. He was probably right next door when they showed up.'

'We'll get him, JT. The team would have arrived at the second address we gave them well before the noon deadline. Maybe they already have him.'

'Wouldn't that be something.'

It wasn't long before Tayte had the answers they were so anxious to hear. On their arrival at the George Washington University campus area, Mavro parked up and they met Reese in the hospital foyer. He was sitting with his head in his hands when they arrived, and as he rose to greet them, Tayte immediately noticed that his shirt, which today was light blue, was stained with blood. He wasn't wearing his jacket.

'Are you okay?' Mavro asked him, clearly concerned and as yet uncertain as to whose blood it was.

Reese looked drawn. He sat down again. 'I'm fine,' he said. 'It's not my blood. It came from Westlake's latest victim, Tiffany Nelson. I really thought we had him this time, but now . . .'

Tayte sat in the chair beside Reese as Mavro sat to the other side. 'Were you in time to save her? Is she okay?'

'It's too early to say. She was alive when I carried her in here, but she's lost a lot of blood.'

'What happened?' Mavro asked.

From the manner of Gertrude Jones's suicide, Tayte had a pretty good idea, but he let Reese explain.

'When we arrived we found the family the home belonged to bound together in the living room—a little boy and his parents. Apart from the shock of the ordeal Westlake had put them through, they were more or less unharmed. The child's father is being treated for a broken nose, but they got off lightly, all things considered. I wish I could say the same for Tiffany Nelson. We found her upstairs in the bathroom.

She was lying naked in a half-full bathtub. Her body was cut in so many places, her life was slowly bleeding away from her. She was unconscious and close to death. I expect by noon she would have been.' He turned to Tayte. 'You might have saved her life.'

Tayte was in no mood to celebrate just yet. 'Was there any sign of Westlake?'

Reese shook his head. 'Bleeding his victim slowly to death like that meant he only had to remain with her until she lost consciousness. The cuts he'd inflicted on her, some pretty deep, would have taken care of the rest. We know he has to be in DC somewhere. There's been a full-scale manhunt in progress for the last twenty-four hours. If he stays active in the area, we'll find him.'

'Anything useful found at the scene?' Mavro asked.

'He left us the knife he used. It's an old bone-handled carving knife.' Reese turned to Tayte. 'There was a short note attached to it that said it was your knife, Mr Tayte, and that we should return it to you.'

Tayte screwed his face up. 'My knife?' he said, subconsciously clenching his hands into fists. 'Why the hell did he do it with one of my knives?'

'It clearly wasn't an attempt to frame you, so I can only assume he did it to upset you.'

'Well, it worked,' Tayte said, his tone unexpectedly snappy. He drew a deep breath to calm himself. A moment later he said, 'Someone should let my past clients know what's going on here. They all need to be extra vigilant. I have all their contact details. It won't all be up to date, but maybe you could—'

'It's already taken care of,' Reese cut in. 'An announcement was made to the media this morning.'

'To the media? That's kind of impersonal, don't you think?'

'We don't have time to be personal, Mr Tayte. You've had too many clients to let them all know individually.'

Tayte sighed. He knew Reese was right. After a pause, he asked, 'Did Westlake leave another clue?'

'No, so you can expect him to call.'

Tayte sat back and wondered what it was going to take to catch this man. How many more innocent people had to die before they did? Westlake always seemed to have a way out, long before the intended time of his victim's death. Tayte knew he was going to have to work much faster if he was to have any chance of stopping this killer.

'Can we go and see Tiffany Nelson?' he asked. He wanted to apologise to her for the pain and suffering he felt more than a little responsible for. 'Or can we at least find out how she's doing?'

Reese drew a deep breath, summoning his energy. 'We can go and ask,' he said as he seemed to haul himself to his feet again. 'She'll need rest, though. I'll be here until she's able to talk, but I'd suggest the two of you go and unwind somewhere. I want you to be ready when the Genie calls again.'

Having satisfied himself that Tiffany Nelson was in a stable condition, and that the prognosis for her recovery was good, Tayte left the hospital with Mavro, heading for a sports bar Mavro knew on G Street Northwest called the Exchange Saloon, which she'd told him was about half a block from the White House. It wasn't far from the hospital, so it didn't take them long to get there. The promise of a cold beer, a large plate of buffalo wings and highlights from last Sunday's Redskins game seemed to Tayte to be just the way to follow Reese's advice to unwind and get himself ready for the next clue. Tayte obviously had no idea when that call would come, but he doubted it would be so soon. Westlake had to prepare, and the idea that he was somewhere in DC right now, planning to abduct his next victim, to goodness knows what heinous end, turned Tayte's stomach.

They sat on stools at the bar and ordered two beers from the vast selection on offer. The place was lively with late lunchtime trade, and as Tayte picked up his beer and allowed his shoulders to relax for what felt like the first time all morning, he thought it was good to be surrounded by normality again. It made for a welcome change.

'Here's to you,' Mavro said, raising her glass to him. 'You saved a woman's life today.'

Tayte touched his glass to Mavro's. 'Right back at you,' he said, but despite the fact that between them they had, indeed, saved Tiffany Nelson's life, he couldn't stop himself from feeling, yet again, that it was he who had ultimately put her life at risk in the first place. It gave his first sip of beer a bittersweet taste.

There were many television screens at the Exchange Saloon. You couldn't look in many directions without seeing at least one, and that was especially true of the area behind the bar Tayte was facing. He had a clear view of no less than five screens, and while the Exchange Saloon didn't appear to be showing any highlights from last Sunday's Washington Redskins game, the screen closest to him was showing a game featuring their biggest rivals, the Dallas Cowboys, whom Tayte also took an interest in, if only to cheer on the other side in true, good-natured sports rivalry fashion.

'Do you follow the game?' he asked Mavro.

'Hell, yeah,' she said. 'I hope we have a good season. We've had too many duds over the past few years.'

'Last season wasn't so bad.'

'Not too bad,' Mavro agreed. 'At least we finished strong.'

'Did you see the game between—' Tayte began, but the conversation was interrupted when he felt a hand on his shoulder.

Tayte spun around to see who it belonged to and saw a man in a business suit, whose tie was hanging loosely around his neck. He had froth in his beard and a half-full beer glass in his other hand.

'It is you!' the man said, his face beaming as though he'd just bumped into an old pal. From his somewhat slurred speech and overfamiliarity, Tayte got the impression that he'd been in the bar for some time.

'Who?' Tayte asked him. 'I don't think I know you, do I?'

'No, you don't know me, but I've seen you. You're the guy I saw on TV before I went to work this morning.'

Tayte's eyes wandered over to Mavro as he thought about the media announcement Reese had told him about.

'Man, I wouldn't want to be in your shoes,' the stranger continued. He came closer, invading the space between Tayte and Mavro. 'Someone's bumping off your customers, eh? That's a real bummer.'

Tayte didn't know what to say. He wanted his former clients to know what was going on—it was their right to know—but he hadn't expected his face to go out on local TV.

'Let me get you a drink,' the man said. 'You gotta need it.'

Tayte began to turn away. 'No thanks. We'd like to be left alone, if you don't mind.'

The man laughed. 'Go back to drowning your sorrows, you mean.'

Tayte turned back to him, meaning to ask him a little less politely to leave him alone, but he saw that the man was already leaving.

'Remind me not to hire you anytime soon,' the man quipped as he went.

Tayte drained his beer, and as he came up for air it was Mavro's hand he felt on his shoulder this time.

'I know it's not easy, JT, but try not to let it get to you.'

Tayte sighed. 'I am trying,' he said. 'Believe me, I am. It's just so personal that it's hard to distance myself from what's going on.'

'Will you let *me* get you another beer?'

'Sure,' Tayte said. 'As it's you.'

Their buffalo wings arrived and they each had another drink to wash them down. Halfway through eating them, Tayte's phone started playing its show tune and he looked at Mavro with a degree of alarm as he hurriedly began to wipe his fingers, eager to find out whether the call was from the Genie, yet hoping it wasn't. As Tayte took his phone out, he relaxed again.

'It's Reese,' he said, and he saw Mavro's shoulders relax, too. He pressed his phone to his ear and took the call, raising his voice to match the lunchtime hubbub as he spoke. 'Agent Reese,' he said. 'What can I do for you?'

'Mr Tayte, I'm afraid I have some bad news for you.'

'What is it? What's wrong? Did Tiffany Nelson die?'

'No, she's doing okay. It's your apartment. I'm here with the fire department. It doesn't look good.'

Tayte swallowed hard as he continued to listen. 'I'll be right over,' he said as soon as Reese had finished.

When the call ended, Tayte's heart sank to what he felt must have been its lowest ebb. He looked solemnly at Mavro, who appeared ready to receive the bad news he'd just been given.

'My apartment's on fire.'

'Someone set fire to it?'

'Reese told me he believes so. Maybe saving Tiffany Nelson's life pissed Westlake off. One way or another he's systematically destroying my life. Maybe that was his plan all along.' Tayte looked up at all the spirits behind the bar and thought he could use a double Jack Daniel's about now, but he resisted. 'I now have no home, and I'll have no career left after this, either. I don't even mind that so much, but if it's me Westlake wants why doesn't he just come after me and be done with it? Why does he have to kill all these innocent people?'

'It's like you said, he wants to destroy your life. He wants you to feel responsible for the lives he's taking, but it's not your fault.'

'I just want him to stop.'

'Of course you do, but the only way to make him stop is to be strong and keep going until we catch him.' She eyed Tayte seriously. 'And we will catch him.'

By early evening, Tayte was back at the safe house, having turned down Frankie Mavro's offer of another good meal and some company. In light of everything that had happened that day, she'd told him she thought it might be good for him, but Tayte just wanted to be alone. He was sitting on the bed, waiting for Jean to answer his call, having already tried her number three times in the past hour. Given the time difference, he imagined she was having dinner with the other seminar attendees at the hotel she was staying at. He was about to hang up again when at last she answered. Just hearing her voice instantly lifted him.

'Jean! I'm so glad you picked up. I've been trying you awhile now. How is everything?'

'Sorry, JT,' she said. 'There was a late dinner.' She yawned. 'I was just getting ready for bed. I'm shattered.'

'I won't keep you up long. I just wanted to hear your voice.'

'That's sweet. Has something happened?'

Tayte drew a deep breath, not sure where to begin explaining his day, or even if it was right to burden Jean with it at all, but he figured she should know. 'Things aren't going so well over here,' he said. 'We've still not caught the man who's doing this, although we were able to save his latest victim this time. She's in bad shape, but she's going to live.'

'That's great. So why am I sensing something wrong?'

'I'm worried that I won't be able to save his next victim, or the one after that. I have to try, and I know it's probably the only way we're going to stop him, but it's eating away at me. On top of that, my apartment was burned out today.'

'What? How?'

'The fire department confirmed it was arson,' Tayte said. 'Everyone thinks it's the same guy, although there's no proof. A window was smashed and some kind of incendiary was thrown in. It's all gone. Everything apart from the few things I brought here with me. I still have my briefcase, thank goodness, and a couple of suits, my files, too, not that they're going to be worth keeping once this is over.'

'That's terrible. Look, my seminar finishes the day after tomorrow. Do you want me to get on a plane and come over?'

'No, definitely not. I don't want you anywhere near this man. I'd rather not be here either, but I have to be. You don't, and that's how I want it to stay.'

'Okay, in that case I'm going to drop in on my parents for the weekend on the way back. And don't worry. When all this is over and we're married, we'll make a completely fresh start somewhere. How about that?'

'That sounds good to me. I'll let you get to bed now. I love you.'

'Be careful, JT. I love you, too.'

Tayte held on to the phone after the call ended, as if by doing so he was holding on to Jean just a while longer. Then he decided to follow suit and go to bed himself, thinking that if he lay there long enough, he might even get what amounted to a proper night's sleep. He knew he was going to need it. He imagined that tomorrow was going to be another stressful day.

Chapter Fifteen

When Tayte awoke the following morning, his heart was pounding. He'd been woken early by his phone's ringtone, and still in a state of half-sleep he could only imagine it was the Genie calling with the next clue to another murder he would soon commit—if Tayte couldn't stop him in time. The sudden rush of adrenaline caused his hand to shake as he reached for his phone. He hoped it was Jean, but the number he saw on the display told him it wasn't.

'Hi,' he began, coughing to clear his throat. 'This is Jefferson Tayte.'

A woman answered. She sounded agitated. 'Mr Tayte, I'm sorry it's so early, but I've been awake half the night. I'm worried sick.'

'Who is this?'

'It's Marjorie Oakes. I hired you to research my family tree a few years back.'

'Mrs Oakes,' Tayte said, sitting himself up. 'Yes, I remember you. What is it I can do for you?'

'What can you do for me? You've heard what's going on, haven't you—about this serial killer they're calling the Genie?'

'Yes, of course. I'm helping the—'

'The news report said to be extra vigilant,' Mrs Oakes cut in. 'It said this man is targeting your former clients and their families. Why? Why would he do that?'

Tayte wanted to tell her that it was all because of him, because he'd ruined the man's life during one of his early assignments twenty years ago, not that Adam Westlake hadn't deserved what was coming to him for what he and his family had done, but for now he thought better of it.

'He's a sick man, Mrs Oakes,' he said. 'The authorities are doing all they can to stop him.'

'Is my family going to be next? Is he coming after me?'

Tayte honestly couldn't say. If there was any kind of pattern or purpose to how Adam Westlake was selecting his victims from the vast pool of Tayte's former clients and their families, he couldn't see it. 'Look, try not to worry yourself too much,' he said, and he instantly regretted it. Of course she was worried, and she had every reason to be. 'I'm sorry, Mrs Oakes. What I mean to say is that I've had a great many clients in the DC area over the years. The odds of any harm coming to you or your family are very slim. Just do as the news report said and be extra cautious. I'm sure you'll be just fine.'

'But you can't guarantee that, can you?'

Tayte sighed. He couldn't guarantee it at all. 'I'm truly very sorry,' he said, not knowing what else to say. Then he ended the call.

His legs felt extra heavy today as he threw them off the bed and went into the bathroom to take a shower. It was only just light outside, but he figured he'd been in bed long enough, and he was glad to get an early start on the day—not that he knew what he was going to do to fill the time until Westlake's call came in. It could be days for all he knew, but he somehow doubted it. He'd just denied the killer his kill. He didn't think the man would let him sit back and revel in his victory for long. Tayte ran the shower until the water started coming through hot, but just as he was about to remove his boxer shorts and step into it, his phone started ringing again.

It has to be him this time, he thought. He felt his pulse quicken again as he hurriedly shut the water off and sprinted back into the bedroom to answer the call. He didn't check the display this time. He didn't want to waste any time and this was a call he couldn't afford to miss.

'Jefferson Tayte,' he announced.

'Tayte!'

Tayte didn't answer right away. It wasn't the Genie this time, either. It was a man's voice, though, and he sounded angry.

'Tayte, are you there, goddammit?'

Tayte screwed up his face as he said, 'Yes, who's calling?'

'It doesn't matter who I am, Tayte. My daughter came to see you way back when, and now she's afraid to step outside the house. The papers are saying this mess is all your fault.'

'They are?'

'Sure they are. And I want to know what you're going to do about it?'

'Well, I'm trying to—' Tayte began, but it seemed that the caller wasn't really interested in hearing what Tayte was trying to do about it. He sounded as if he just wanted to vent some steam.

'Don't give me any of your bull-crap, Tayte. I don't want to hear it. You've put good folks' lives at risk, and I want you to know that if anything happens to my daughter as a result of this, I'm holding you personally responsible. You hear me?'

Tayte heard the man loud and clear.

'I'll sue your ass, Tayte, and I'll make damn sure you never work in this town again.'

Tayte opened his mouth to cut in, but no words came out. He lowered his phone and continued to listen to the caller's faint but angry diatribe for a few seconds longer, then he ended the call, thinking that if this kept up it was going to be a very long and challenging day whether the Genie called him or not. He trundled back to the bathroom, taking his phone with him this time.

During Tayte's first waking hour that day, he took close to a dozen phone calls from past clients or their close family members, many of whom appeared to be angry and upset with him to one degree or another. They were all understandably worried for their safety in the light of the news that was now all over the press and local TV stations following SAC Reese's announcement the day before. Tayte's heart went out to every one of them, but he could find no effective words to assuage their fears.

He was dressed and in the kitchen fixing an omelette for his breakfast when his phone rang for the umpteenth time, although by now the sound did little to set his heart racing. Instead, it caused his heart to sink as he prepared himself for yet another unpleasant conversation with one of his former clients. He casually slid the pan off the stove and accepted the call.

'This is Jefferson Tayte,' he said, already impatient for the call to be over. He just wanted to eat his omelette before it got cold. This time, however, it was not one of his clients calling. It was the Genie.

'Tayte.'

Hearing Adam Westlake's hollow voice again made Tayte's skin crawl. He swallowed hard before he spoke again, by which time he was sitting down at the kitchen table.

'You're not wasting any time, are you Westlake?'

'I don't want you to get bored with my little game. Actually, I tried you five minutes ago, but the line was busy. That's five minutes off your time, Tayte, not mine. They could mean the difference between life and death for someone.'

'I'll just have to work faster.'

'Oh, you're pretty fast already, aren't you? Fast enough to save Tiffany Nelson, our mutual friend in the green suit. Are you sure you can work any faster than that?' Westlake laughed drily to himself. 'You're going to have to this time. I'm giving you until noon today, which gives you just under four hours.'

'Four hours?'

Tayte couldn't stop himself from repeating what Westlake had just said. Had he heard the man right? He was afraid he had, and he was suddenly in a hurry to get started. He already wished he could have back the five minutes he'd lost. He rushed his next words out.

'What's the clue?'

'Wouldn't you like to chat awhile first? Maybe you'd like to know something about the next life I plan to take if you can't stop me in time.'

'Just send me the damn clue,' Tayte said. 'We'll have plenty of time to chat once you're back behind bars where you belong.'

The line went quiet. Then the call ended.

Christ! What have I done?

Getting sassy with a serial killer was perhaps not such a good idea, Tayte now realised. He'd just lost himself more precious minutes. What if Westlake decided not to bother with a clue at all this time, just to teach him a lesson? He got up and went to his omelette. He chopped into it and shoved a large forkful into his mouth, then another and another until it was gone. He'd barely tasted it. He sat down again and stared at his phone, willing it to beep, letting him know a new text message had arrived. Another five minutes passed before it did, and Tayte couldn't bring the message up fast enough. It was short like the rest.

'*R71/S261,*' he read aloud.

He called Reese straight away, to let him know he had the next clue and that he only had until midday to solve it. Then he called Mavro, who told him she was on her way over. Despite now having less than four hours to solve the Genie's latest clue, Tayte was feeling more upbeat about the prospects of working it out in time than he had been when Westlake first told him how long he had. He was upbeat because he recognised the reference he'd been sent as soon as he saw it. He figured Westlake knew as much, which was perhaps why he'd allowed Tayte so little time.

The reference was a marker to another burial plot, and this time it needed no further clue to help identify the cemetery it belonged to. Tayte had seen a thousand references just like it in his time as a DC-based genealogist, which was not surprising given that the cemetery was so close to where he lived, or used to live, before his home had been burned out. The reference belonged to the Congressional Cemetery, where over 65,000 people were interred or otherwise memorialised, and where all the burial plot references began with the letter R, standing for range, and were often followed by an S, standing for site. Rather than identifying each area of the cemetery, as was the case at River Creek, the entire area was laid out as one large matrix, each plot being identified by the range and site numbers allocated to them.

As a first step, all Tayte had to do was find out who was interred at this particular burial plot. Then he could go on to discover how and where he or she had died. His first thought was to use the cemetery's online search facility, but he quickly remembered that the interment records database at the Congressional Cemetery was no longer searchable by range and site reference. Now, you had to know the name of the person whose plot you were looking for, which was exactly what Tayte had to find out. Nevertheless, he remained upbeat because he knew it didn't matter. He had the right cemetery. All he had to do was wait for Mavro to arrive, and then they could go and take a look for themselves.

Chapter Sixteen

Washington, DC's Congressional Cemetery was located eighteen blocks from the Capitol in the Southeast district on the west bank of the Anacostia River. Originally called the Washington Parish Burial Ground when it was established in 1807, the cemetery had rapidly expanded from under five acres to its current size of almost forty acres by the last quarter of the nineteenth century. There was no other cemetery on earth that Tayte was more familiar with, but because of its size, he was none-theless glad he'd thought to put his map of the grounds in his briefcase before Mavro arrived to pick him up. She was wearing a mint-green polo shirt today, with the same blue jeans and green parka she'd been wearing when she'd first called at his house.

They parked alongside the kerb on 17th Street by a black iron gate, which Tayte had already identified as the cemetery entrance closest to the burial plot they had gone there to see. It was a fine, cool morning. Stepping out of the car, they were instantly greeted by birdsong coming from the trees along the street and from those further into the cemetery. It helped Tayte to relax a little, following his particularly stressful morn-ing full of phone calls from upset former clients. He'd put his phone on silent before leaving the safe house. They could leave a message because right now he had other things to focus on.

Tayte took his map out as they entered through the gate on to Prout Street. 'It's going to be on our immediate right,' he told Mavro.

'According to this grid layout, it's eleven rows back from that junction up ahead.'

They walked to the junction at a fast pace and counted back to be sure they found the right burial plot when they came to it. As they went, Tayte noted how quiet it was, which was why he often came here, sometimes just to think and take in the history of the place and the people buried there, many of whom had helped define the city. He saw a woman walking her dog, and there were one or two indistinguishable figures in the distance, but for the most part they had only each other and the birdsong for company.

Tayte counted eleven rows and stopped walking. 'This is range seventy-one. Site two hundred sixty runs right along this street.' He turned to face the opposite side of the street and walked across to where range seventy-one continued. He set his briefcase down, knelt, and began to brush at the grass, revealing a small ground stone.

'This is it. R71/S261.'

Mavro pulled up the knees of her jeans and knelt beside him. 'It's not too clear, is it?'

Tayte agreed. The horizontal nature of the stone meant that the engraving had eroded over time, but he'd seen far worse and he didn't think it was so bad that he wouldn't be able to read it. He scratched at the ground until he had a handful of soil, which he brushed over the lettering to darken the words. The transformation was instant, if still a little patchy in places.

'John P. Alexander,' he said, wondering what the P stood for. 'June 1877 to July 1922.'

'Forty-five years old,' Mavro said.

It was a simple memorial, and it told Tayte that John Alexander had likely been a man of modest income. He checked the graves around it to see if any other family members were buried nearby, which would help him to identify this particular John Alexander when it came to looking for him in the records, but there were none. He took out his notebook and wrote the details down, still feeling upbeat about his chances this time around because, although he and Mavro only had until noon to solve this puzzle, it was still only half past nine and all he needed to find out was where this man had died.

'I know I have files for an Alexander,' he said. 'Maybe they're not for this family, but it's worth checking.'

He got to his feet again and put his notebook away. 'Before we head back, though, I'd like to run a quick check to see if John P. Alexander here made the newspapers. He died prematurely. That's often a good indicator that the cause might have been newsworthy.' He had his laptop with him in his briefcase. 'Let's head back to the car and take a look.'

Within minutes Tayte was sitting in the passenger seat with his laptop open on his knees, looking at the familiar Library of Congress newspaper archive website, Chronicling America. He selected to view results for the District of Columbia, and the date range he was interested in, covering 1922 when Alexander had died. Into the search field he entered the man's name, and then he clicked 'Go'. The search returned fifteen results for pages containing the keywords he'd entered, and he was quickly able to dismiss most of them because they contained unrelated instances of the words John and Alexander. Two, however, contained perfect matches. Both publications were from the *Evening Star*, dated 1922. The first was in the obituaries section. Tayte read it to Mavro.

'*Funeral arrangements for John P. Alexander, forty-five years old, 816 Tenth Street Northwest, who died Tuesday as the result of his electrocution while working for the Potomac Electric Power Company, have now been completed.*'

Tayte paused. 'There's something familiar about this.'

'A past assignment?'

'It's gotta be.'

He read on. '*The deceased had been in the employ of the company for the past twenty years and is survived by his wife, Mrs Hattie Alexander. A verdict of accidental death was returned by the coroner's jury late yesterday in the inquest over the body.*'

'So he was married?' Mavro said. 'I guess his wife must have moved away before she died.'

'It's possible, given she wasn't buried alongside her husband, although if this is related to the assignment I'm thinking of, I believe she remarried and was buried with her second husband.'

The second article bore the bold heading 'CITY NEWS IN BRIEF' and it began telling a similar story to the obituary, but halfway down there was more information, and it was just the kind of thing Tayte hoped to find. There was excitement in his voice as he read the section out.

'*John P. Alexander, Electrical expert who was shocked to death in a manhole of the Potomac Electric Power Company at Euclid and Champlain Streets Tuesday night.*' He turned to Mavro with a broad smile on his face. 'That's our location.'

What followed happened so fast that Tayte had trouble taking it all in. His smile dropped instantly as Mavro's door was pulled open with such force he felt the air rush out of the car. As Mavro turned away from him to see who had opened her door a fist thumped hard into the side of her face, knocking her head into Tayte's shoulder. He saw a flash of the assailant's blue denim shirtsleeve as he reached in and grabbed the key from the ignition. Then he saw someone he recognised from the recent prison photograph SAC Reese had shown him. It was Adam Westlake.

Westlake leaned into the car again and this time he wrenched Mavro violently out of her seat, as if she weighed next to nothing. Tayte saw the fear in her eyes and wanted to do something to stop whatever was about to happen, but it was all taking place so fast that he had no time to think.

Westlake pulled a handgun out from the back of his faded grey jeans and pressed the muzzle hard into Mavro's temple. 'Toss your sidearm!' he told her, and a moment later Tayte heard it clatter on to the road at her feet. He felt utterly powerless to do anything but watch, aware that one bad decision right now could get them both killed.

Westlake kicked the door shut. He forced Mavro around the front of the vehicle, holding her firmly by the neck. Given the man's size and obvious strength, Tayte didn't doubt that he could have crushed her windpipe if he chose to. His eyes were locked on Westlake's, and the man was staring right back at him as he came around to Tayte's door. He shoved Mavro away as he reached it, pushing her back towards the cemetery gate.

'Go back inside! Now! Try anything and I'll shoot you both.'

As she went, Westlake pulled Tayte's door open. Now the gun was pointing at him.

'Move over!'

Tayte did as he was told, awkwardly at first, his hands shaking and his heart pounding. He wondered why Westlake was doing this. Was his game almost over? Was this how it ended? As soon as Tayte slid into the driving seat, Westlake got in and tossed him the key. A car approached and Tayte silently prayed that the driver would stop, but either the driver hadn't noticed what was taking place, or just didn't want to get involved.

'Drive!' Westlake ordered, and as Tayte pulled away he risked a glance out of his window, back at the cemetery gate. He caught Mavro's eye. She had her phone out. That was good. She was calling for help.

'Where are we going?' Tayte asked. Out of the corner of his eye he could see the gun Westlake was still pointing at him.

'Just drive. I'll tell you when to turn.'

They quickly came to a crossroads and Tayte began to slow down, awaiting instructions.

'Pick up your speed,' Westlake said, sounding aggravated. 'Keep going straight until I say otherwise.'

Tayte continued to do as he was told, saying nothing until his curiosity to know what Westlake was planning to do got the better of him.

'What are you going to do?' he asked. 'Are you going to kill me? I know you must want to.'

Westlake's top lip curled into a derisive snarl. 'I'd love to put a bullet in your head right now, but that's only going to happen if you push me.' He sat forward and stared at Tayte until the weight of his presence forced Tayte to take his eyes off the road momentarily to look at him. Westlake shook his head. 'You really don't want to do that,' he added, and then he sat back again. 'Do as you're told and I won't hurt you.'

Tayte wasn't sure he believed that. Everything he knew about this man suggested he wanted to hurt him very much, but for now Westlake appeared to be showing restraint for some reason. Tayte wondered why, although he wasn't sure he wanted to know the answer. They continued in silence for several minutes, heading north on 17th Street until they reached a busy intersection with Route 1.

'Turn right onto the highway,' Westlake said. 'Keep to the speed limit.'

'Are we leaving town?'

Westlake didn't answer.

'You know the FBI are going to find me. You can be sure they're already looking for this car.'

Westlake laughed to himself. 'I'm counting on it. Now just shut up and drive.'

They were not on Route 1 for long, which dispelled Tayte's notion that they were leaving DC. They turned off on to Montana Avenue, tracking what appeared to be waste ground on their right, until they followed the road around it on to New York Avenue, which typically was busy with traffic. The area was remarkably run-down given its proximity to the nation's capital. Several buildings in a poor state of repair, some of which were clearly abandoned, lined the street. They came to what had once been a car dealership, and Tayte noticed Westlake's interest.

'Turn off here,' he said. 'Pull onto the forecourt and take the car around back.'

Tayte's palms were sweating as he followed Westlake's instructions. As he came to the back of the low brick building, whose windows were all either smashed or boarded up, he saw that these derelict buildings all backed on to the waste ground he'd previously seen. He thought that if Westlake did want to shoot him, this was a good place to do it.

'Stop here,' Westlake said, and Tayte pulled the car over. He didn't like it that the car, Mavro's car, was no longer visible from the road.

'Shut off the engine and give me the key.'

Tayte hesitated, and the muzzle of the gun Westlake was still holding was suddenly pressing into his temple. 'Do it!'

'Okay, okay.' Tayte took the key out of the ignition. 'Here.'

'Now get out, slowly. I have a surprise for you.'

Chapter Seventeen

Inside the abandoned car dealership, the daylight from the gaps in the boards at the windows did nothing to make the place any more welcoming. Tayte was taken across the debris on the floor of what he imagined had once been a spotless car showroom, still wondering what Westlake had in store for him. A surprise of some sort, and certainly not a pleasant one, given the circumstances. Further in, they passed around the back of what had once been the reception desk, the gun in Westlake's hand trained on Tayte the whole time, and then through a doorway that led into what evidently used to be the service area. There was a stack of old car batteries to his right, and ahead, in the low light, he could see two hydraulic ramps sitting side by side a few metres apart. Any tools left in the place when the business shut down were long gone. There was a single bare light bulb glowing through the window of a small office at the far end of the room. Westlake shoved Tayte towards it.

'Your surprise is in there,' he said, and although Tayte couldn't see his face, he sensed Westlake was smiling.

As they reached the door, Tayte felt Westlake's hand press firmly down on his shoulder. He stopped and turned to face him.

'You can't go in just yet,' Westlake said. 'First I want you to sit in that chair.'

Westlake pointed to a shabby swivel chair by the door. The black fabric was ripped in places, exposing the foam padding, and it had a heavy-looking metal base and castors. Tayte's eyed narrowed as he wondered why Westlake wanted him to sit down.

'I said take a seat!'

Tayte lowered himself into the chair and Westlake stepped closer. There was a small steel filing cabinet beside the chair. Sitting on top of the cabinet was a roll of grey duct tape, which Tayte imagined Westlake must have put there earlier. He picked it up and tossed it into Tayte's lap.

'Now bind your feet and ankles to the base of the chair.'

'Excuse me?'

'You heard what I said. Do it!'

Tayte shook his head. He didn't like where this was heading. 'No, I won't. If you're planning to kill me, I'm not going to make it any easier for you.'

Westlake leaned towards him. 'I already said I wasn't going to kill you unless you push me.' He brought his gun up and pressed it to Tayte's forehead. 'Are you pushing me?'

Tayte stared defiantly back into the man's eyes for a moment, trying to read his intentions, but he couldn't. The only way he was going to find out what Westlake had in store for him was to go along with this.

'Okay, back off.' He bent over his knees and wrapped the duct tape around his ankles and feet, securing them to the chair.

'Good, now strap your left arm to the armrest.'

As Tayte did as he was told, he pondered over this latest puzzle Westlake had set for him and how it had led him to a man who had been electrocuted while working for the Potomac Electric Power Company in 1922. Was Tayte going to be the victim this time? He certainly couldn't shake the idea from his head that he was strapping himself into his own electric chair. It caused him to think back to the Exchange Saloon the day before, when he'd asked himself why Westlake didn't just come after him and be done with it. Now he was telling himself to be careful what he wished for.

As soon as Tayte had finished binding his left arm to the chair, Westlake tucked his gun back into the waistline of his jeans and secured Tayte's right arm to the other armrest. Tayte gave no struggle. It seemed entirely pointless to do so. Westlake then used up the rest of the duct tape, strapping Tayte's thighs to the seat and his chest to the backrest. Once he'd finished Tayte could barely move. He was entirely at Westlake's disposal. Westlake stood back and smiled at his handiwork, then he wheeled Tayte into the office.

As soon as they crossed the threshold, Tayte knew he was not going to be the Genie's next victim. He knew this because he was looking right at the person Westlake had clearly singled out for his next murder. He was a grey-haired man in his late sixties, and most alarming to Tayte was the fact that he recognised him. He'd employed Tayte's services in recent years, and while Tayte couldn't recall his first name with everything that was going on, he knew his surname was Alexander. He was the descendant of John P. Alexander, former employee of the Potomac Electric Power Company. The man was similarly strapped down with duct tape, but not to a chair. He was secured to a large wheeled trolley that was propped up at a forty-five-degree angle against the edge of a table. There was also duct tape across his mouth to keep him quiet.

'Surprise!' Westlake said with a grin. 'You remember George Alexander, don't you? I've made sure he remembers you.'

Tayte drew a deep breath in an ineffective attempt to calm himself as he looked at the unfortunate man before him, knowing there was nothing he could do for him. He was shirtless, and between the lines of duct tape around his body, Tayte could see that there were wires attached to his chest and others connected to his head. Each connection was marked by a pool of dried blood where the wires had been inserted beneath his skin. Tayte could also see a heavy-duty cable running back to the door and out into the workshop area. He recalled the pile of car batteries he'd passed and it was instantly clear that Westlake planned to execute this man by electrocution, killing him in the manner of his ancestor.

'I wanted you to watch him die,' Westlake said, pushing Tayte further into the room. 'I see you're staring at my crude electrodes. Did you know that human skin can offer up to 100,000 ohms of resistance or more? Inside the body, though, it falls to as low as around three hundred ohms, hence the subcutaneous electrodes.'

'Why are you doing this?'

'Come on, Tayte. You know why.'

'His ancestor died in a manhole, nowhere near this place. You're not replicating that death by killing him here. You're cheating your own game.'

'But it's my game, isn't it? I set the rules, and I've decided to throw in a bonus round.'

'So I was never expected to work this one out? I had no chance to save this man?'

'No. The reference I sent you this time was just to get you to that cemetery so I could pick you up and bring you here to watch.'

Not for the first time, Tayte wondered if this really was Westlake's game. He painted a smile on his face in an attempt to put him off his guard, and then playing to his ego, he said, 'I have to commend you on the puzzle you sent me for Tiffany Nelson. That Library of Congress reference really had me stumped at first.'

'But not for long,' Westlake said, sourly.

'No, but even so, I thought it particularly clever of you to hide a clue in the dedication for that book about early settlers of the Midwest.'

'You're not the only smart-ass in town,' Westlake said, offering no contradiction. He pushed Tayte closer to his victim so that Tayte could look into the man's eyes. They were wet with tears and wide with fear, and seeing him like that forced Tayte to focus all his attention on him. Alexander's head seemed to shake, but it was strapped down with so much duct tape that it was hard to be sure.

'I've got over twenty fully charged car batteries hooked up to this guy,' Westlake said. 'I measured their combined output at something close to three hundred volts, but it's not so much the volts that kills you.'

'Don't tell me,' Tayte said with sarcasm. 'It's the current, right?'

Westlake nodded. 'Yeah, it's all about the amps. With DC current, heart fibrillation occurs at between three hundred and five hundred milliamps. Doesn't sound much, does it?'

Tayte didn't answer.

'At five hundred milliamps, with the electricity making the right paths through the body, it can take just a fifth of a second to kill a man, which is why I've plugged my electrodes in so deeply—to literally cut through the skin's resistance. Three hundred volts divided by three hundred ohms of resistance equals a draw of one amp, which I'm sure you've already worked out is twice the lethal amount, just to be sure. Time to death is effectively reduced to one-tenth of a second, so I don't think anyone coming through that door is going to be able to pull these wires out in time to save him, do you?'

'Coming through the door?' Tayte repeated.

Westlake pointed to the top of the door, where Tayte could see a metal box with more wires coming from it.

'It's a simple switch mechanism. It triggers when the door opens, once I've powered everything up, of course, which I'll do on my way out. The switch powers a latching relay, which in turn makes the circuit that fries our mutual friend here.'

'You're a sick man, Westlake. You need help.'

Westlake scoffed. 'Yes, I do, and I'm getting it right now. It's called self-help and it's making me feel a whole lot better already. Is your phone switched on?'

'My phone?'

'Yes, your cell phone. Is it on?'

Tayte nodded.

'Good. I imagine the FBI is close to pinpointing your signal about now. They should be here soon.'

With that Westlake put two strips of duct tape over Tayte's mouth. 'I don't want you calling out and giving the game away.' He went back to the door. 'I'll leave the light on,' he added as he left. 'So you don't miss anything.'

<hr />

As soon as Westlake had gone, Tayte tried to free himself, hoping to exert enough strength to break through the duct tape so that he could reach out and pull those wires from George Alexander's chest and head before it was too late. He figured he only needed to free one of his arms, but they were both strapped down with so much tape that after several minutes of trying and getting nowhere, he realised it just wasn't going to happen. He stopped, panting heavily, and looked at his former client, who was staring right back at him with those fearful eyes. He wanted to tell him that he was so very sorry, and he hoped his own eyes conveyed that as they continued to look at one another. Tayte didn't know how much time he had to save him, but he knew he had to keep trying.

He rested a moment to recover his strength. He looked down at his hands and saw that his wrists were already red raw from the pressure he'd put on them. He didn't care if they were bleeding—a few cuts and bruises were a small price to pay as far as he was concerned. He tried to recall the assignment that had brought George Alexander to call upon his genealogical services, and he remembered that he came from a large family that was going to miss him dearly if Tayte couldn't prevent his murder.

He looked around for something that might offer him a way to do that, but the room was largely empty, apart from a few cupboards and metal shelves. Nothing gave him any inspiration. He had to get out of that chair. Frustration hit him hard and he began to rock from side to side, pulling at the armrests again until his wrists burned. The chair moved a little on its castors, but there was no way to effectively control its direction. He thought to tip the chair over, which he imagined might put enough force on some of the duct tape to at least stretch it, but because of the wheels he couldn't seem to get enough momentum going before the chair began to slide. Tayte stopped again, suddenly disturbed by Westlake's inhumanity, knowing it demonstrated a particular kind of cruelty to have brought him here to watch the murder of yet another victim.

Tayte was breathing hard now from his exertions. It was becoming difficult to get enough oxygen through his nose alone, and Westlake had strapped his chest to the chair in such a way that he was unable to fully expand it. His breathing was accordingly shallow and loud. Over the sound he could hear the hum of the traffic passing by on New York Avenue as the people of DC went about their lives oblivious to what was going on less than a hundred metres from them. Then, as his breathing slowed and the room became quiet again, he heard another sound that chilled him to his core. It was the sound of one or more vehicles approaching. A moment later he heard car doors slam shut and he began to pull at the duct tape again. George Alexander had clearly heard the vehicles, too, because he also began to twist and writhe, but it was to no avail.

Outside the window that looked into the workshop area, Tayte saw the first of the FBI agents enter. He recognised him as Special Agent Jerome Martinez. He was with another agent Tayte hadn't seen before. They were wearing tactical vests and both had their sidearms drawn ahead of them as they came in. Tayte began to shout into his gag, but nothing discernible came out. He was shouting for them to stay back and not enter the room, but all he imagined they saw was a man in peril crying out for help. He began to shake his head vigorously, but it did no good.

'In here!' Martinez called, and as they ran to what they surely believed was Tayte's rescue, all he could do was look back into George Alexander's eyes, and in his mind tell him over and over that he was so very sorry.

Fifteen minutes later, Tayte was sitting in the back of SAC Reese's car with a blanket around his shoulders as more and more FBI and police vehicles arrived at the scene. He was staring vacantly at the headrest in front of him, insensible to the commotion, still shaking from the shock of being forced to witness the grotesque electrocution of George Alexander. Frankie Mavro was sitting beside him to his right, and SAC Reese was sitting half in and half out of the car to his left.

'There's no chance he's still alive?' Tayte asked. He didn't want to believe Alexander was dead, even though he'd seen it happen right in front of his eyes.

Reese shook his head. 'He's gone, Mr Tayte. I'm sorry. We did everything we could.'

'It wasn't your fault, JT,' Mavro said. 'Don't blame yourself.'

The trouble was that Tayte did blame himself, and he would continue to blame himself as long as he lived for everything that was happening to these people. 'I'd like to go and see his family. I want to see the families of all the victims.'

'In time,' Reese said. 'I don't think it's a good idea right now.'

Tayte nodded at the headrest, silently agreeing that he was probably the last person any of the victims' family members wanted to see. He thought most would sooner slap his face than listen to his apologies and words of condolence. He remained silent for several seconds, breathing slowly to help calm himself, thinking back over the conversation he'd had with Adam Westlake inside the building.

He turned to Reese. 'Westlake isn't the Genie.'

'Say that again,' Reese said, frowning.

'This isn't Westlake's game. He's abducting these people, sure, and he's setting up their deaths, but he's not the genealogist behind these puzzles being sent to me. I don't believe Westlake knows a thing about them.'

'Why's that?' Mavro asked.

'I started talking to Westlake about the previous puzzle. I mentioned the book we went to the Library of Congress to take a look at.'

'*Tales of Romance.*'

'Exactly. Only I said it was a book about early settlers of the Midwest. It was just something I thought up at random, but Westlake didn't bat an eyelid. He just assumed it was right because he had no idea. I'm sure he's a clever man, but he's not the genealogist working all this out. The real Genie is someone working behind the scenes, telling Westlake what to do.'

Mavro could clearly see where Tayte was going with this. 'You mean the real Genie is that Frenchman, Michel Levant, don't you?'

Tayte nodded. 'I know it's just a hunch, and I can't prove anything right now, but yes, I believe it's Levant.'

Reese sighed heavily, drawing Tayte's attention. 'We ran all the checks on Levant. We even had Interpol look into him. He's as clean as they come—a law-abiding citizen who just happens to be in DC on business at this time. Do you have any proof to contradict that?'

Tayte didn't need to think about it. He had nothing beyond a bunch of circumstances and his gut feeling about the man. 'No, but he's way too smart to be in any of your files, or Interpol's for that matter.'

'You're a smart man. You're in our files.'

Tayte could feel his shock turning to anger. 'I'm in your files because I don't have any reason not to be,' he snapped. 'Have you thought about that? Maybe Levant's file is just a little too clean.'

Reese stood up and leaned in. 'You'd do well to leave the direct investigation of these murders to us, Mr Tayte. If I were you I'd be far more concerned about saving the lives of your former clients. You need to stay focused. Can you do that? Because you're no good to me otherwise.'

Tayte sighed through his nose. He nodded.

'Good. When you're feeling up to it, Mavro will take you back to the safe house. Stay there until Westlake calls you again. Once we have him, we'll be in a better position to find out who may or may not be behind this.'

Chapter Eighteen

'Reese is dismissing Levant too easily,' Tayte said as he and Mavro headed back to the safe house in the lunchtime traffic. He was cradling his briefcase in his arms, as though overjoyed to see it again, and to know that Westlake hadn't set fire to it or otherwise destroyed it out of sheer spite as he'd left the disused car dealership.

Mavro didn't seem to agree with him. 'Until you've got something stronger than your gut feelings about the man, I don't see what else Reese can do. I think he's right about the need to focus on stopping Westlake.'

'And I totally agree with that,' Tayte said, 'but rather than trying to catch Westlake, which so far we've been hopelessly unable to do, maybe there's another way to stop him.'

'How do you mean?'

'I mean it's about time we stopped playing by the Genie's rules. Westlake knows he's never going to get caught in the act. He sets up his murders so he's long gone by the time his victims actually die. We may be able to get the authorities to the scene early enough to save someone now and then, but I don't think we're going to catch him like this. If we keep playing this sick game his way, it's just going to go on and on.'

'So how do we bend the rules?'

'Simple. We go after the man who's really behind this. Stop the game maker and we stop the game.'

Mavro's shoulders slumped. She heaved a sigh. 'You've really got it in for this Frenchman, haven't you?'

'I'm right about this, Frankie. I know I am. Take a left up ahead onto 6th Street. I want to go to the National Archives Museum. Levant's first event on genetic ancestry begins today.'

Mavro shook her head. 'I think that's a very bad idea. Reese told me to take you back to the safe house and that's exactly what I'm going to do.'

'Okay, take me to the safe house, but I'm going to see Levant. I'll get a taxi.'

Mavro gave another sigh and kept driving. A moment later she said, 'What are you planning to do when you see him?'

'I'm just going to talk to him—ask him a few questions and maybe rattle his cage a little.'

Mavro raised her eyebrows. 'Rattle his cage?'

'Just a little.'

The turn-off Tayte had indicated was coming up fast.

'Come on, Frankie, what harm can it do? I'd sooner have you with me.'

Mavro slapped the steering wheel with both hands. 'Okay, but if something goes wrong and I lose my job over this, everything that's going on here is going to seem like a stroll in the park by comparison.'

'It's just a conversation,' Tayte said as Mavro made the turn on to 6th Street, heading for the National Archives Museum. 'What could possibly go wrong?'

First opened in 1935, and informally referred to as Archives I, the original headquarters of the US National Archives and Records Administration in Washington, DC, was built in the Classical Revival style. It was home to many important records, from the reissued Magna

Carta of 1297 to the formative documents of the United States of America: the Declaration of Independence, the Constitution, and the Bill of Rights. As Tayte and Mavro climbed the stone steps, passing between tall Corinthian columns towards the Exhibits entrance near the corner of 9th Street and Constitution Avenue, Tayte could already feel his blood begin to boil in anticipation of coming face to face with Michel Levant again.

The Exhibits entrance was largely used by visitors with advance reservations, saving the need to queue at the General Public entrance. Mavro showed her badge to the attendant, and once inside the building, they headed across the polished marble floor of the Orientation Plaza towards the David M. Rubenstein Gallery. There were plenty of people around, although the well-lit area never seemed too crowded to Tayte, who had been there more times than he could recall.

'Do you know where you're going?' Mavro asked as they arrived at the gallery entrance before a glowing amber wall panel that read 'Records of Rights'.

Tayte smiled and led Mavro to their right. 'Of course. Levant's event will be in the William G. McGowan Theater. It's on the lower level.'

They passed the myArchives shop on their left, heading for the elevators and stairwells that were located at either end of the building. They took the stairs down, and emerging on the lower level it was immediately apparent to Tayte that the event had either just finished or was breaking for lunch. Throngs of people were coming out from the walkway that led into the theatre. Most were heading away from them, towards the cafe.

'Looks like we just missed his talk,' Mavro said.

'Yeah, that's too bad,' Tayte said, glad that he didn't have to sit and listen to the man for an hour before he could get to speak with him. 'He's drawn quite a crowd.'

They fought their way through the people in the walkway until they came to the theatre, which was steeply tiered with close to three hundred red velour seats arranged in a subtle curve around the stage below. Tayte saw Levant right away. He was standing in front of the stage, wearing a shiny silver-grey suit and tie, surrounded by half a dozen people—no doubt revelling in their compliments.

'Just take it easy,' Mavro warned him, but Tayte was already marching down the steps ahead of her, bent on confronting Levant. All he could think about was the tormented expression on George Alexander's face as he was electrocuted right in front of him, and how powerless he'd been to prevent it. As he reached the bottom of the steps and strode across the red and gold carpet towards the stage, he didn't feel like taking it easy on this man he believed was ultimately responsible for the murders of so many people.

'Levant!'

Every head turned towards Tayte as he called the Frenchman's name. As soon as Levant saw him, Tayte thought he looked uneasy, as if trying too hard to hold on to his thin smile, which began to quiver more and more as Tayte approached.

'*Monsieur* Tayte, what a pleasure to see—'

'Cut the crap, Levant. It's not a pleasure for either of us and you know it.'

Levant's smile was suddenly gone. 'What is it you want? As you can see, I'm very busy.'

'I'll bet you are. Tell me, has Adam Westlake been in touch yet to tell you how the latest murder went, or shall I fill you in?'

'Murder? But what are you suggesting? I've already told you I have no idea who this Adam Westlake is.'

'I'd tell you he was the man the press are calling the Genie, but we both know that's not quite true, don't we?'

Tayte was aware that Mavro had now caught up with him, and that the crowd of people who had previously been standing around Levant had backed away. They weren't leaving though. Mention of murder and the Genie had seen to that.

'Is Westlake paying you to work out these sick genealogical puzzles for him?' Tayte continued. 'Is that it? Or perhaps it's the other way around? Maybe you're paying Westlake to do your dirty work for you just so you can get back at me for what happened in London? Are you on some personal revenge trip to destroy my life?'

'This is preposterous,' Levant said, turning to the people around him. He gave a shake of his head as if to suggest he was being confronted by a madman. Then he offered them a faltering smile and Tayte knew the accusation had shaken him.

He didn't let up. 'I denied the heir hunter his ultimate prize, didn't I? And I've no doubt I lost you a potential fortune in the process. I beat you at your own game and you can't let it go.'

When Levant turned back to Tayte, his brow was set in a deep furrow. He tipped his head back and began to study Tayte, shaking his head as he did so. 'It's a good thing our mutual friend Marcus Brown is no longer alive to see the depths to which you have fallen.'

Tayte didn't like to hear Levant talk about his old friend Marcus Brown. His was another death Tayte held Levant indirectly responsible for, although again, he had no proof. 'Marcus was no friend of yours,' he said. 'I don't care how long you two had worked together in the past. He told me he didn't want to see you that day.'

The Frenchman gave a whimsical laugh as he leaned close to Tayte and, whispering in his ear so that only Tayte could hear him, said, 'Marcus was a very clever man. He should have known when he was in over his head.'

Tayte recoiled at hearing that. He felt his cheeks drain of colour. Had Levant just admitted to being an accessory in his friend's murder? He stared into Levant's eyes, trying to read him. The Frenchman was still smiling. Why was he smiling after saying such a thing?

'You did have him killed,' Tayte said under his breath.

Levant heard him well enough. 'Did I?' he said, his eyes flashing with menace as he spoke.

Tayte gave no conscious thought to what he did next. He grabbed the slight Frenchman by the lapels of his jacket and clenched his fists tightly around the material, squeezing with all his might to quash the anger that had risen inside him before he did the man any harm. Then he lightly shoved him away towards the front of the stage. It was such a light shove that Tayte was shocked to see Levant react as he did. He staggered back, and his legs seemed to slam hard into the low stage wall. He cried out as though in great pain as he tripped and fell up on to the stage. Then he immediately began to clutch at his right leg as if it were broken.

'Security! Somebody call security!'

Tayte went to help Levant up. He hadn't wanted to hurt the man, but Mavro held him back.

'I think you'd better leave him.'

Tayte turned to her. 'This is ridiculous. I hardly touched him.'

Out of the corner of his eye Tayte saw two security guards coming down the steps at the side of the theatre and he figured someone must have called for them as soon as the conversation between him and Levant became heated. Before they could get to him, he turned back to Levant and pointed.

'This isn't over, Levant. I know you're the Genie.'

A moment later, Tayte felt two pairs of strong arms on his and he turned away from the stage. 'All right, I'm going,' he told the security guards. 'There's no need to get heavy.'

He heard Mavro sigh as he was led out of the theatre, and he knew why. She didn't speak to him until they were back in the car, when she turned the key in the ignition, shook her head and said, 'Yeah. What could possibly go wrong?'

The drive back to the safe house was a quiet one. Mavro had said very little, making it clear to Tayte that she was upset with him for turning what was supposed to have been 'just a conversation' with Michel Levant into a full-blown, physical altercation. Tayte had been quiet, too, in part because it took him a long time to calm down afterwards, and because he thought it best to give Mavro some time to calm down, too. She stopped the car a block away from the safe house, as was her habit in case anyone was following them, then Tayte turned to her and broke the silence.

'I'm sorry,' he said. 'I'm not usually like that. I really don't know what came over me.'

'It's called stress.'

'Well, I guess it's getting to me, and Levant just makes it worse. You want to come inside for a coffee?'

Mavro gave a long sigh as she turned to him, as though at last letting go of her anger. 'Sure, why not?' she said, 'Never sleep on an argument, right?'

Tayte smiled. 'It won't happen again. I promise.'

'Be careful not to make promises you can't keep, JT. This isn't over yet.'

They walked the short distance to the safe house in the warm early-afternoon sunshine, taking in the cars that passed and the people around them. No one seemed to care who they were or where they were going.

'He was deliberately goading me,' Tayte said as they went. 'You won't have heard what he said to me just before I shoved him, but do you remember I told you about a good friend of mine called Marcus Brown who was murdered in London last year?'

Mavro nodded. 'Sure I do.'

'Well, Levant told me that Marcus should have known when he was in over his head.'

'If whatever your friend was doing got him killed, he clearly *was* in over his head, don't you think?'

Tayte had to agree that Levant's statement, when taken at face value, was little more than an observation of what was evidently true.

Were it not, then Marcus would still be alive, but he felt there was so much more to it.

'It wasn't just what he said, it was the way he said it. And it was the way he looked at me as he said it—that subtle raise of his eyebrows and the intensity in his stare. Something unsaid passed between us in that moment.'

'Or maybe you read into it what you wanted to read into it because you've convinced yourself that Levant is the Genie.'

There was more logic to that than Tayte cared to admit, but was it true? Was the stress getting to him so much that it was clouding his judgement? He didn't think so. He came back to the idea that Levant had deliberately goaded him, and he wondered why Levant would have done that if he had nothing to hide.

'I barely touched the man,' he said, thinking aloud.

'You're a big fella. Maybe you don't know your own strength.'

'I know it well enough. Levant was play-acting. The shove I gave him was only enough to rock him back on his heels, yet there he was crashing onto the stage and pretending to have hurt his leg. Someone should give the man an Oscar.'

They came to the safe house and Mavro took a last look around before they climbed the steps to the entrance. 'It doesn't really matter whether he exaggerated or not. He's a much older man, and you're twice his size. You were the aggressor. You grabbed him and shoved him, and there were plenty of people close by who witnessed it. You'd better hope he doesn't press charges.'

'I don't care what he does. He got away with things before. I'm not going to let it happen again if I can help it.'

As Tayte opened the door and they went inside, he felt his phone vibrate in his pocket. He stopped and took it out. He had a new text message from an unknown number. When he opened it his breath caught in his chest.

'What is it?' Mavro asked, concern in her voice.

'Oh, Christ no,' Tayte said. 'Not her.' He sat down on the stairs and sank his head into his hands.

'Here, let me see.'

Mavro took Tayte's phone from him and looked at the message he'd been sent. It was an image of a woman Tayte clearly knew. She looked terrified. Beneath the image was the Genie's latest clue.

Tayte looked up again, his face pale and drawn. 'This guy isn't letting up for a minute, is he?'

Having sent his latest text message to Jefferson Tayte, Adam Westlake placed the stolen phone he'd used down on the low stump of a felled tree and crushed it hard several times with the heel of his boot until the phone was barely recognisable. Then he picked up the pieces and scattered them amongst the fallen autumn leaves around him. He stepped out from the cover of trees, towards the railway tracks, and took out another phone from the pocket of his jeans, one he wouldn't have to destroy after he'd used it because the person he was calling had given it to him to facilitate convenient yet untraceable communication between them. There was only one number in the phone's memory. He selected it and made the call.

'It's done,' he said, nodding to himself as the person at the other end spoke. 'That's right. Noon tomorrow, just as you said, but I don't like to change things. I don't like to be rushed, either. Bringing this forward hasn't left much time to prepare.'

Westlake continued to listen as the person at the other end spoke again. Then he turned away from the tracks, back towards the trees in the direction of the car he'd parked nearby. 'Yeah, she's in the trunk,' he said. 'I'm taking her there now.' He listened again, and then he said, 'And this is the last one, right? Then Tayte's mine?'

On hearing the answer, Westlake ended the call, smiling to himself. He'd played the game long enough. He'd made Tayte suffer mentally for what he'd done, and he'd enjoyed watching the genealogist sink lower and lower as he'd murdered so many of his former clients and their family members, at the same time making sure that the people of DC would think twice before employing his services. He'd destroyed his home and most of his possessions along with it, but it still wasn't enough. It wasn't even close to being enough payback for Adam Westlake. As soon as he'd been released from prison he'd wanted to kill Tayte, but as impatient as he was for that day to come, this way really had been far more satisfying. Now the endgame was close at last, and he was all the more eager for it to begin.

Then Tayte will really know what it is to suffer, he thought. *And only then will I kill him.*

Chapter Nineteen

Tayte's hands were shaking as he turned the key in the lock and entered the safe house apartment. Mavro was at his heel, her face lined with concern and curiosity as to why Tayte was so upset about the Genie's latest victim.

'Sit yourself down on the couch before you fall down,' she said as they crossed the living room. 'I'll let Reese know we have another clue while I fix us that coffee, or would you like something stronger?'

Tayte continued to wander across the living room without answering her.

'Hey, JT! Coffee, or something stronger?'

Tayte snapped around, as if he'd only just realised Mavro was there. 'Coffee, strong. Thanks.'

He sat down, and while Mavro was in the kitchen he looked at his phone again, staring at the image of the woman Westlake had just sent him, his mind firmly back in the late 1990s when he'd first met her. Apart from the obvious fear in her eyes and the terrified expression on her face, he didn't think she'd changed all that much since then. Her mid-brown hair was perhaps a little shorter than he remembered, and she was older, of course, but there was no mistaking who she was. Beneath her image were a few words from the man who had abducted her. Tayte read them again, turning them over in his mind.

At noon tomorrow she'll be dead. You have all the clues you need.

'All the clues I need?' he mumbled to himself, screwing his face up as he wondered what this latest cryptic message meant. All Westlake had sent him was the image and the amount of time he had to save her.

Mavro came back with their coffees. 'You really don't look so good,' she said, interrupting Tayte's thoughts. She set their drinks down on the low table between them and sat in the armchair opposite. 'So who is she? I can see she means something to you.'

'She does,' Tayte said, still sitting bolt upright on the edge of his seat, partly lost to his memories. He wondered whether the Genie knew as much. 'At least, she used to mean something to me. Her name's Lauren Emerson. She came to see me one summer, about fifteen years ago, when she was researching her family tree. She'd hit a genealogical brick wall with one family line in particular, around the time of the Civil War, and she wanted my help.'

'And through that you became close?' Mavro asked, sipping her coffee.

Tayte leaned in and collected his mug from the table. He sat back with it and tried to relax. 'Not in any regular sense, but I became very fond of her.'

'And was she fond of you?'

'I think so, but she was the shy type, and I was too afraid she'd say no if I tried to take our friendship any further. I didn't want to lose what we already had.'

'So, you're still good friends, is that it? Is that why you're so cut up?'

Tayte shook his head. 'No, there was this other guy. He was far more confident with relationships than I ever was. To cut a long story short, he swept her away and told me never to see her again. I cared for her very much. I kicked myself for a long time afterwards for not having told her how I felt about her.'

'That's too bad,' Mavro said. 'Can I take another look at the message?'

Tayte handed his phone to her.

'*You have all the clues you need,*' she read out. 'What do you suppose he means by that?'

'I can only imagine that Lauren herself must be the clue. Everything we need in order to find her in time must stem from her.'

'Her assignment file?'

Tayte nodded. 'Perhaps.' He drained his coffee and got up. 'I'll go and see if it's still there.'

In the room where all Tayte's files had been stored, he opened the corresponding cabinet and began to flick through the files, wondering as he did so what further clue Lauren Emerson's file might contain and how he would recognise it at such when he saw it. He was pleased to see the file was there, which gave him hope. He pulled it out and returned to the living room to look at it with Mavro.

'That's a good start,' she said as Tayte sat down. 'I'd half expected it to be missing.'

'I kind of was myself at first, but then I figured this had to be what Westlake meant us to look at when he said we had all the clues we needed.'

He sat forward with the folder and set it down on the table. Emerson's file was thick with records, dating back to the time of the United States' Founding Fathers, and Tayte recalled that because of his affection for her, he'd gone way beyond helping her to break down the brick wall she'd originally come to see him about. He'd broken through it and kept on going, in part trying to impress her, but mostly as a less transparent reason to keep seeing her because he liked her company.

'It could take a while to work out what we're supposed to find in here,' he said, riffling through the records.

'We've got less than twenty-four hours,' Mavro reminded him. She got up, collecting his coffee mug as she rose. 'I'll keep the coffee coming. I'm not sure I'd know what to look for.'

Tayte wasn't sure he did, either. Did Westlake really expect him to go through every record he had on Lauren Emerson's family history?

Without having at least some idea of what he was looking for, surely there was too much data. He had copies of all the records Emerson had researched before she came to him and everything else he'd found with her since. All he needed was a way in to this latest genealogical puzzle and, as before, he figured it would have to be fairly obvious to him once he saw it.

The file index was sitting on top of the records, an overview of the family tree containing all the names and key dates. He smiled to himself when he opened the folded sheet of paper and looked at all those names. In his desire to impress, he'd been so thorough that he hadn't missed a single thing since the early 1800s. He was about to close the sheet of paper again when he saw something that made him sit up. Amidst the sea of names and dates was a lone question mark. Clearly he had missed something, or had hit a brick wall himself.

When Mavro came back into the room and set a fresh mug of coffee down in front him, Tayte scratched at his temple and said, 'I think I might have found it.'

'You have? That was fast.'

Tayte took a sip of coffee and nodded. He offered up the index. 'Whatever we're looking for has to stand out in some way, right?'

'It would have to, or how else would we know?'

'Exactly. Well here, among all this completed data, is just one piece that's missing. It's a date of death for someone called Benjamin Kirkland, which fits with the Genie's game plan. So far all these puzzles have pointed to someone's death record, so that from it we could go on to identify how and where the next victim was going to die.'

Tayte thought back and tried to recall the reason he'd put a question mark against this man's record of death. Clearly he hadn't been able to find one. He hated leaving his research incomplete like that, and he really wouldn't have wanted to leave Lauren Emerson's family tree incomplete if he could help it. He remembered then that it was because of the other man in Lauren's life. Benjamin Kirkland's death record was something he'd intended to go back to, but he never had the opportunity, or rather the desire, after Lauren had told him she could no longer see him.

'So we just have to fill in the blank?' Mavro said, interrupting Tayte's thoughts.

Tayte nodded. It sounded simple, but he doubted it would be because he already knew that this particular family history mystery had stumped him before. He flicked through the records and found a copy of Benjamin Kirkland's marriage to Dorothy Valentine, dated 1907. That was the only vital record he'd been able to find, and he tried to recall why he'd previously been unable to locate any information about his birth or death. He came to another record, a copy of a newspaper report from the *Washington Times* dated Thursday, May 5, 1910. Seeing the headline again brought everything flooding back.

'Of course,' he said. 'Benjamin Kirkland's wife reported him missing. It made the newspapers.' He held the printout up so Mavro could take a closer look. 'He left for work one morning and never came home again.'

'And he was never found? Not even his body?'

Tayte shook his head. 'I searched long and hard for a record of his death. I couldn't find a thing. I also checked the ships' passenger lists for that time, thinking he might simply have run away for whatever reason. There was nothing. If Kirkland died in 1910 and his body was found, he must have died in some way that left him unidentifiable. As things stand, he appears to have just vanished.'

'So how on earth are we supposed to find out where he died?'

'That's a very good question, Tayte said, sitting back with his thoughts. 'Right now, I don't know, but one thing's for sure—Lauren Emerson's life depends on us finding the answer.'

After calling SAC Reese again, this time to update him on their progress, Mavro came into the kitchen and joined Tayte at the table by the window where he'd laid out the key records from Lauren Emerson's family history file. He had his notepad and pencil at the ready, and he'd put on a fresh pot of coffee to help keep them going. It was now after three in the afternoon and he was conscious of the time in case there were any records he needed to see before the record office closed for the day—not that he imagined it would be too difficult to get someone back there under the circumstances.

'You make better coffee than I do,' Mavro said, holding on to her cup as she breathed in the aroma.

'It's the same stuff. I just put extra in. Gives it a little more bite.'

Tayte picked up the copy of the newspaper report and studied it again, focusing on the salient points as he saw them. 'It says in this report that Benjamin Kirkland's wife reported him missing "on Monday last" which was the day after he celebrated his fortieth birthday. It says he left for work wearing his company uniform, as he usually did, and that was the last she saw of him. It also states that she said he worked for the Baltimore and Ohio Railroad as an engineer. They're one of the oldest railroad companies in the country and, if memory serves, they opened a branch in DC sometime in the 1830s. However, to add further to the mystery, the report goes on to say that when the police enquired with the railroad company, they were told there was no record of a Benjamin Kirkland on their payroll.'

'The plot thickens,' Mavro said. 'I can see why you left it there. Does it say whether the police were able to draw any conclusions?'

'No, it seems they left it there, too. At least, I couldn't find any further reports or I'd have them here in my file. Maybe they gave up the search for Kirkland too easily.'

'It doesn't sound like they had anything much to go on. Neither, it seems, do we.'

'That's not quite true,' Tayte said, scribbling into his notepad. 'And we have to remember that the person who set this latest puzzle for us must have found the answers. In that case, so can we. We just have to look in the right places.' He finished writing his notes and looked at Mavro again. 'As I see it, there are two main possibilities. Benjamin Kirkland could have lied to his wife about where he worked. Maybe he'd lost his job and didn't want her to know, so he maintained the illusion that he had a job, when he was really out looking for work.'

'In a B&O Railroad engineer's uniform? I guess he could have obtained one from somewhere.'

'It would certainly compound the lie,' Tayte offered, 'but it seems a little unnecessary to me. He could have made up just about any job and gone out in his Sunday suit.'

'So what's the other possibility?'

'The other possibility, and I believe this is the stronger of the two, is that this man did work for the railroad company, but under another name—his real name. The fact that I couldn't find a record of birth for him fits with this idea, and the lack of a death record corroborates the theory. Whether the police gave up the search too soon or not, back then it's unlikely they would have taken much interest in his vital records, but then, they weren't looking at the case with a genealogical eye.'

'So why did Kirkland lie about who he really was?'

'That's the golden question. If we can answer that and discover his real name, we'll have all the answers we're looking for.'

Mavro laughed to herself. 'You make it sound easy. How do you propose we do that?'

'Let's think about it for a moment,' Tayte said, rubbing his chin. 'The only connections we have to this man are his wife and their children—of whom my client, Lauren Emerson, is a descendant—and the Baltimore and Ohio Railroad. The railroad company would appear to be our best way forward if we're to assume for now that he did work for them, albeit under his real name.'

'So we somehow have to find a match to the real employee, like comparing photos?'

'That kind of thing, yes, only we don't have a photograph of Benjamin Kirkland to compare with, and I doubt there are many photographic records of the railroad company's employees from that time.'

Tayte paused and drew a deep breath, wondering in what other ways they might be able to match Kirkland with another of the railroad engineers. Several quiet seconds passed until his eyes fell on the copy of the newspaper report again.

'Of course!' he said, sitting up with a jolt that startled Mavro. He had a wide smile on his face as he picked up the photocopy and tapped it. 'Kirkland's birthday,' he added. 'Or more specifically, his date of birth.' He read out the date at the top of the newspaper page. '*Thursday, May 5, 1910.* The report stated that Kirkland was reported missing on the Monday of that week, the day after he turned forty.'

'So he was born on Sunday, May 1st, 1870,' Mavro said, taking no time to work it out.

Tayte threw her a smile. 'You're sharp.'

'I'm just glad to be of some use. What can we do with Kirkland's date of birth?'

'Plenty. What are the odds of there being another engineer working out of the DC branch of the B&O Railroad with the same date of birth as our Benjamin Kirkland?'

'Slim to none.'

'Exactly. And there can't have been many employees whose service terminated on the day Kirkland went missing. We can use that information, too. We just need to take a look at the B&O Railroad's employee records.'

'We can do that?'

'Sure we can, to a point. The B&O no longer exists as a company. Their network became a part of CSX Transportation in the 1970s. From then on the company records are private. I've had many assignments over the years that have led to railroad workers in one family branch or another. I know that records for this particular company prior to the Great Baltimore Fire of 1904 were destroyed in the blaze, but that's okay because we're only interested in 1910. The US Railroad Retirement Board records have proven useful in the past, but they hold no records prior to 1937. There is, however, a collection at the Hays T. Watkins Research Library at the B&O Railroad Museum in Baltimore. They have thousands of records from the payroll department, and although they contain very little personal information, I believe that employees' dates of birth are recorded.'

'Are the records online?'

'Unfortunately not. We'd have to go there.'

Mavro glanced at her watch. 'Will they be open? It's almost four and it's about an hour to Baltimore if the roads are clear. At this time of day, we'll likely hit commuter traffic. It could take a couple of hours.'

'I'm pretty sure the museum closes at four,' Tayte said. He began to gather up the records. 'We'd better give them a call, and you'll have to play your government-agency-on-life-or-death-business card to get someone to stay back and help us.'

Chapter Twenty

The Baltimore and Ohio Railroad Museum was located on West Pratt Street, Baltimore, in the city's Southwest neighbourhood. Tayte and Mavro arrived at what was widely regarded as the 'birthplace of American railroading' a little after half past five, having taken the I-95 up through Maryland along with the commuters heading home for the evening. Before they left DC, Mavro had arranged for an archive assistant called Warren Guthrie to stay on and help with their investigation. As they pulled into the otherwise empty public parking area close to the building and got out of the car, they were met enthusiastically by a man in loose-fitting blue jeans, boots, and a white B&O Railroad Museum T-shirt that had a picture of an old Civil War–era steam locomotive on the front. His hair was long and grey, and it was difficult to determine his age, but Tayte thought he was in his mid- to late fifties.

'Welcome, welcome,' the man said as he pumped Mavro's hand, and then Tayte's.

'We're here to see Warren Guthrie,' Mavro said. 'We're with the FBI.'

'That's me. I'm Guthrie. I know who you folks are—been looking out for you.'

'Thanks for agreeing to stay late,' Tayte said. 'We really appreciate it.'

'Happy to help,' Guthrie said, pulling at his wiry handlebar moustache, which was straight out of the Old West. 'Care to follow me?'

Guthrie led them into the main building, part of an annexe that had been built and extended over the years alongside the roundhouse that was now home to several of the museum's historic locomotives and passenger cars. He took them up a flight of stairs to the second floor, then in through a red-framed set of double doors that had the words 'Hays T. Watkins Research Library' on a silver sign above it. Once inside, they were invited to sit down at a table upon which were several microform readers.

'So, you're trying to identify a fella who used to work for the B&O Railroad,' Guthrie said. 'Is that correct?'

Tayte set his briefcase down as he and Mavro sat around one of the readers. 'That's right. We're specifically interested in employee records.'

'Know the fella's name?'

Tayte shook his head. 'That's just the thing. We have a name, but you won't find it in your records. We were hoping to find him via his date of birth, and we also know he was an engineer working out of the DC branch.'

Guthrie twirled his moustache as he gave it some thought. 'A large number of payroll records were transferred to microfilm back in the 1960s, covering the years from 1905 to 1971. They hold the information you're looking for, but they're not complete by any means.'

'This man we're trying to identify,' Mavro said. 'We believe he worked for the B&O Railroad when he disappeared in 1910, so we only need concern ourselves with the first five years of those records.'

'That'll help narrow the search down, that's for sure. The records were stored by their creation date, being the individual's date of employ, give or take. Sit tight there while I go see what I can find.'

'Before you do that,' Tayte said, 'does any of this sound at all familiar to you?'

'How do you mean?'

'I mean, it's possible that someone else has been here recently, looking for the same information—someone with a French accent, perhaps.'

'Canadian?'

'No, not Canadian. I was just wondering whether our research enquiry rings any bells?'

Guthrie sucked his teeth and drew a long breath. 'Nope. I can't say it does. We get plenty of folks drop by, though, and contrary to how it may seem, I'm not always here. Maybe your friend was helped out by someone else.'

My friend, Tayte thought, almost smiling at the grossly incorrect assumption. 'That's probably it,' he said. 'Thanks anyway.'

When Guthrie left them, Tayte turned to Mavro and said, 'That's too bad. I just thought the Genie might have come here looking for answers when he was setting this puzzle. If nothing else, it would at least have told us we're on the right track. Still, I have a good feeling about this.'

'I'm glad to hear it,' Mavro said, 'because right now we don't have much else to go on.'

'It all stacks up too well. The company uniform, the lack of a birth or death certificate in Benjamin Kirkland's name. If that was his real name, I'm sure I'd have found something. This could take a while, though. We need to inspect every payroll record this research library holds over a period of five years.'

Guthrie was gone several minutes. When he returned he produced a roll of 35mm film and held it up. 'If we have a payroll record for the man you're looking for, he'll be on this roll of microfilm. It covers the earlier years, from 1905 onwards. It's a great pity they're not digitised or we could easily have searched for that date of birth you're interested in.'

'That's okay,' Tayte said. 'I knew what to expect.'

Guthrie loaded the film carefully into the reader. 'Know how these things work, or would you rather I manipulated the dials? They can be a mite tricky to get the hang of at first.'

'No, I'll be just fine,' Tayte said, 'but thanks for offering.'

Guthrie nodded and stood back. 'Well, just you holler if there's anything you're unsure of. If you need anything, I'll be in back.'

Tayte and Mavro both smiled at the kindly man as he left them to it. Then Tayte sat forward and began to work the reading machine's controls. Looking at the first record, he saw that these payroll cards contained all kinds of useful information pertaining to the job. They showed the person's name, date of birth, job title, division, department, station, and any changes in the employee's job or salary, including the date of retirement, where applicable, as well as resignations and dismissals. As he scrolled through the records he saw that many also contained salary information, and in some cases the employee's date of death, which he thought could prove very useful.

His eyes quickly grew accustomed to singling out the employee's date of birth, and he kept Kirkland's in mind as he scrolled through the records looking for a match. Mavro scanned the information along with him—two pairs of eyes definitely being better than one in this case—but even so, he had to take it slowly because the handwriting was often faint, and every now and then he would have to stop altogether for a closer inspection, particularly whenever he saw the word 'May' or the year '1870'. An hour quickly passed, at which point Tayte sat back and pinched his eyes.

'You okay?' Mavro asked. 'Wanna take a break?'

'No, I'm good. We don't exactly have time for breaks, do we?'

Another thirty minutes flew by, then both Tayte and Mavro sat up together and pointed at the screen.

'There's a match,' Mavro said, narrowly beating Tayte to it. 'May 1st, 1870.'

Tayte nodded, scanning the rest of the information on the record. His nod quickly turned to a shake of his head. 'Same date of birth, but neither the job title nor station matches.'

'That's too bad. I thought we had him there for a minute.'

'Yeah, me too.'

At that point Guthrie came back into the room. 'Would you folks like me to see if I can rustle up some coffee? The vending area's all locked up now, but I'll see what I can do.'

'That would be wonderful,' Tayte said. 'If it's no bother.'

'No bother at all. I'm about finished back there, and I could use a hot drink myself. Are you getting anywhere with those payroll records?'

'Nothing yet. We're up to 1907, though, so we shouldn't be too much longer.'

'Take all the time you need,' Guthrie said as he made for the door they had previously entered by. 'Police work's important business.'

'And it doesn't get any more important than trying to save someone's life,' Tayte mumbled to himself as he turned back to the microform reader.

He began scrolling through the records again as the payroll dates crept closer and closer to 1910. By now it was clear to him that if Benjamin Kirkland had worked for the B&O Railroad under another name, then he hadn't worked there long before his disappearance. The minutes continued to slip by, and Tayte barely noticed Guthrie come back into the room fifteen minutes later and set a Styrofoam cup of black coffee down at his elbow. Another half an hour passed in silence after that, with Tayte's eyes glued to the blur of records that were passing before him. Then he saw another matching date of birth. It was on a payroll record dated August 1908, and this time both the job description and station tied in with the information they had gleaned from the newspaper report in Tayte's file.

'Got him!' Tayte said, his face cracking into a wide smile. He noticed his cup of coffee then and drained it back. It was cold, but he didn't care. 'There he is,' he added. 'William H. Durant, Engineer. Born May 1st, 1870. That has to be him.'

'Look, there's a date of death,' Mavro said. 'Wouldn't that suggest he died in service?'

'Yes, it would, and look at the date. May 2nd, 1910—the day after his birthday, which was the same day his wife reported him missing.'

It was close to nine and dark outside as Tayte and Mavro crossed the railroad museum car park and got back into the car. Having thanked Guthrie for his time, Tayte was keen to get on the road again and continue the research he hoped would save Lauren Emerson's life.

'At least the traffic should be lighter heading back,' he said as Mavro turned the key in the ignition. 'We should be in DC around ten.'

'Then what?' she asked. 'What's our next move?'

'Well, first we need to prove that William H. Durant is our man. Right now all we have is a probable match, but we need to be absolutely sure. If he is, we need to find out where he died.'

Mavro pulled out on to the main road, heading back to the I-95. 'It's a pity there wasn't more information about his death on that payroll record.'

'That's the thing with genealogy. You rarely find all the information you're looking for in one place, if ever.' Tayte tapped the notebook inside the breast pocket of his jacket. 'I've written down all the information there was on Durant's payroll record. We can use it to confirm that he and Benjamin Kirkland were the same man, and hopefully we can then learn more about him, but to do that we need access to Durant's vital records.'

'We're going to the Department of Health? At this hour?'

Tayte nodded, taking his phone out. 'I don't want to wait until morning unless we have to. I'm going to call Reese. Maybe he can get someone from the Vital Records Division to meet us there.'

Tayte dialled SAC Reese's number. It went straight to voicemail, so he left a message, letting him know what they needed from him and why. 'Fingers crossed he picks it up soon,' he said to Mavro as he ended the call.

They made good progress to the I-95, where Mavro picked up the pace. 'So what do you make of this fella we're looking into? If it's the same man, he was employed by the railroad company as William H. Durant, yet his wife knew him as Benjamin Kirkland. He had to be lying to one of them.'

'I don't think he was lying to the railroad company about who he was. I think it's more likely that he was lying to his wife, which again explains why I couldn't find his birth or death certificate. Just a marriage certificate.'

'You think he was a bigamist?'

'Yes, I do. We know he was with Dorothy Kirkland née Valentine the day he left for work, never to return. If we're right about who Kirkland really was, we also know why he never made it back. He died at work that day, but rather than reporting his death to Dorothy Kirkland, whom the railroad company knew nothing about, they informed his legal wife, Mrs Durant. It fits well enough.'

Mavro agreed. 'Which is why Dorothy Kirkland reported her husband missing, and why the police couldn't make any progress finding him.'

'Exactly. Benjamin Kirkland, who's supposed to have been born on May 1st, 1870, didn't exist. And how do you find someone who doesn't exist? The records could prove it. The 1910 census would tell us who Durant was living with when he died, but we're not interested in proving whether or not the man was a bigamist. When we get to see Durant's vital records, I expect we'll find his birth certificate, his legal marriage certificate to someone other than Dorothy Valentine, and his death certificate, which will hopefully shed more light on how, and perhaps even where, he died. That's what we're interested in.'

'Why don't you try Reese again.'

Tayte made the call, and this time Reese picked up. Tayte put him on speaker so Mavro could hear.

'Mr Tayte, I was about to call you back. I got your message. It's going to take a while, but we're all set. A woman called Pamela Bryant is going to meet you at the Department of Health in about an hour. She's authorised to give you access to anything you need to see. If you get there ahead of her, just wait with security. They're also expecting you.'

'That's great,' Tayte said, recalling that they had met Pamela Bryant on their visit to the Vital Records Division two days ago. 'I'll let you know how it goes.'

With that Tayte ended the call and said to Mavro, 'We can't be more than half an hour away now. Let's grab a bite to eat somewhere nearby while we wait for her.'

They found an all-night diner not far from North Capitol Street where they were heading. It was just after ten as they sat down and ordered. Tayte asked for steak and eggs to go with his coffee, and Mavro opted for salmon cakes. The interior was long and narrow, like a train passenger carriage, with a counter that ran half the length of the diner. To the other side, by the windows, was a line of faded red leather booths, which was where Tayte and Mavro were seated. The place was warm and smoky from the grill area behind the counter. Being busy, it was relatively noisy, although not to the extent that you had to raise your voice to hold a conversation.

'I'm curious,' Mavro said as they waited for their meals to arrive. 'Just how does someone get away with bigamy?'

Tayte turned away from the multi-coloured neon sign he could see over the tops of the parked cars outside the window. 'Actually, it's a lot easier than you'd think, and the further back in time you go, the easier it was to get away with. Back in the early 1900s, of course, they didn't have the electronic communications we take for granted today. There was no Internet or social media, such as Facebook, to catch a person out. Even today, depending on which state you live in, a previously married person isn't always required to prove they're no longer married before they can marry again. That's if they admit to being married in the first place, which is unlikely if they're planning to marry illegally. To commit bigamy, all a person has to do is lie about their marital status and claim they're not already married.'

'So, no one runs a check to see that both parties are legally allowed to marry?'

'No, it's not possible. There's no central US marriage register to check. Bigamists are often only discovered by chance, which, as I've said, is more likely these days than it used to be. If we're right about the man we're looking into, his bigamous marriage has gone undiscovered right up until now.'

Their coffees arrived, and Tayte sat back and turned his head to the window again as a white police cruiser pulled into the parking area. 'Our city's finest on their Twinkie break,' he said with a grin as two bulky police officers climbed out of the vehicle.

Mavro grinned back at him. 'Yeah, all cops eat Twinkie bars on their breaks, and I suppose you think the FBI really does have an X-Files unit.'

Tayte laughed. 'I've never seen the X-Files, so I can't comment.'

'Well, let's see if you're right. If either one of those police officers orders a Twinkie bar, I'll get the check. Otherwise, it's all yours.'

Tayte took the bet. He reached across and shook Mavro's hand on the deal, and then he turned around to get a better view of the two officers as they walked into the diner. One of them, a bald man with a hard face, was looking right back at him. Tayte saw him nudge his partner, who was a shorter, older man with salt-and-pepper hair and a moustache. Then they both looked at Tayte, and Tayte thought their pace quickened as they seemed to recognise him. They didn't go to the counter at all. They made straight for Tayte and Mavro's table.

'Jefferson Tayte?' the shorter, older man said.

'Yes, I'm Tayte. What can I do for you, officer?'

The bald man spoke next, but not to Tayte. Instead, he turned to Mavro. 'Franchesca Mavrothalassitis?'

'What's this about?' Mavro asked, her eyes narrowing as she spoke. 'How do you know who I am?'

'We spotted that silver Jeep Cherokee parked outside. We ran a check on the licence plate and your name came up.'

Mavro asked the obvious next question. 'And just why would you run a check on my vehicle?'

'Because this man sitting opposite you is wanted for questioning in connection with an assault at the National Archives Museum earlier today, and he was seen leaving afterwards in your vehicle. That's how come we knew who you had to be.'

The shorter man spoke again then. 'Mr Tayte, I need you to come with us. If you resist, you'll be placed under arrest and taken into custody. Forcibly if necessary.'

Tayte stood up, but he wasn't ready to leave. 'This is ridiculous! I barely touched the man. He was faking it.'

'Mr Levant is currently walking on crutches, thanks to you,' the bald man said, punctuating his words with a stab of his forefinger. 'He checked out of the hospital with a knee injury and a cut above his left eye, so don't stand there and give us your "I barely touched him" speech. We've heard it too many times before. He's almost seventy years old. You should be ashamed of yourself.'

Mavro stood up. She had her FBI badge out, which she offered up to the two police officers. 'This man is assisting the FBI on federal business. A woman's life is at stake, and—'

The shorter officer cut in. 'Look, lady, we're just doing our job. If you've got a problem with that, you can take it up with the Station Supervisor. No one's above the law. I don't care who he is or what he's doing. I have my job to do, just as you have yours. If you persist in trying to get in the way of mine, I'll take you in, too.'

Tayte was aware that the whole diner had gone quiet around them as conversations fell to whispers. Just about everyone was looking at him. 'How long will this take?'

'That all depends on you,' the shorter officer said. 'Right now you're wasting time standing here talking. The sooner you come with us, the sooner you'll be able to get back to whatever it is you and your FBI friend are in the middle of.'

Tayte reached into his inside jacket pocket, and as he did so both officers stepped back. At the same time, the bald officer reached a hand out towards Tayte. With his other hand he covered the sidearm on his hip, ready to draw it out. 'Don't move!'

'It's just my notebook,' Tayte said, freezing.

'Let me see your hands. Real slow.'

Tayte took his hand out from his jacket again and raised both hands level with his head. The shorter of the two officers stepped closer and patted down Tayte's chest. Then he reached inside Tayte's jacket and took his notebook out.

'See. It's just my notebook.'

The officers relaxed again and Tayte was handed his notebook back. He stepped out of the booth, and as he did so he gave the notebook to Mavro.

'The details on William Durant are in there. Go ahead and meet with Pamela Bryant as planned. Give her all the information we have and ask for copies of Durant's vital records—everything she can find. We'll go over them once all this is straightened out.'

Mavro nodded. 'Try not to say anything to incriminate yourself. I'll call Reese. I'm sure he can help.'

'I hope so,' Tayte said as he was led away. 'Oh, and look after my briefcase, will you?' he called back as he went, passing the waitress carrying his steak and eggs, and wishing they had chosen somewhere else to eat.

Chapter Twenty-One

It was almost eight the following morning by the time Tayte was released from the custody of DC's Metropolitan Police Department. He had been charged under DC law with aggravated assault, to which, under the advice of the lawyer Reese had quickly dispatched to his aid, Tayte had pleaded not guilty. Given that there had been so many people present to witness Tayte laying hands on Michel Levant at the National Archives Museum, however, Tayte had pleaded guilty to the misdemeanour offence of general assault, leaving it down to the prosecution to convince the jury at the DC Superior Court that Tayte had knowingly or purposefully caused injury to Levant. Tayte was grateful to both Reese and the lawyer that their actions saw him released on citation, which meant no bond was imposed. For now, all he'd had to do to become a free man again was to sign a form acknowledging that he was required to appear in court at a later date, when his longer-term freedom would be determined.

Mavro was waiting for Tayte on his release. From her weary appearance as he dragged himself into the car he could see that she hadn't fared much better than he had since they last saw one another, although as she was wearing a black trouser-suit and a cream blouse today, he knew she'd at least had time to go home and get changed. However Mavro appeared, it was quickly apparent that she thought Tayte looked far worse.

'You look like shit,' she said. 'You wanna try and get something to eat again before we go on?'

'How about steak and eggs?' Tayte said, smiling. 'They were unlucky for me last night, but hey, it's a new day.' Mavro's expression remained as unemotional as it had been since Tayte got into the car. 'Okay, blueberry pancakes,' he added. 'A whole pile of 'em, covered in syrup and chocolate sauce.'

'You have anywhere in mind for that?'

Tayte had a few favourites, but right now he didn't care where they went. 'The first place you come to,' he said, and Mavro began to drive.

'Did you bring my briefcase?'

'Back seat,' Mavro said as they filtered out into the morning traffic.

Tayte craned his neck around until he saw it. 'Thanks.'

They continued in silence for several minutes. Tayte couldn't decide whether Mavro was just tired or angry with him. When she eventually spoke, he knew it was the latter.

'You know, you're lucky I'm here to pick you up this morning. Reese went ballistic when I called him last night and told him what had happened. He wanted to see me about it first thing this morning. I've just left him.'

'I was wondering why you're wearing that suit.'

'Well, now you know. He was very quick to point out that by disobeying his instructions to take you straight back to the safe house yesterday, I'd jeopardised the whole operation and put people's lives at risk. I'm lucky I still have a job.'

'I'll talk to him—let him know I gave you no choice.'

Mavro was shaking her head almost as soon as Tayte started speaking. 'No, he's even more pissed at you right now. You'll only make matters worse. Besides, I had a choice, and I chose poorly.'

'I'm sorry.'

'I bet you are. You know what the maximum sentence for aggravated assault is in DC?'

Tayte nodded. 'My lawyer told me. I could get up to ten years and a fine of up to $10,000. It's half that for attempted aggravated assault, although we're hoping for general assault, which carries a maximum sentence of 180 days and $1,000 in fines.'

'I'm glad you were paying attention.'

'It was hard not to under the circumstances. Even 180 days in jail is a frightening prospect.'

Tayte let out a long sigh just thinking about what it could mean for Jean and him, and their wedding plans. He supposed that would now have to be put on hold. That's if Jean had any interest in marrying an ex-con.

'Did you manage to get those copies of William Durant's vital records last night?' he asked, trying to put his impending court hearing aside for now, knowing he had to refocus his remaining energy on saving Lauren Emerson if he could.

'I did,' Mavro said, her voice losing its bitter edge. 'Birth, marriage, and death.' She scoffed. 'That's why I also look like shit this morning. Pamela Bryant took a long time to show and we were there a few hours. I could tell she didn't take too kindly to being called out in the middle of the night.'

'Who would? Main thing is you got the records.'

'Yeah.'

They turned on to 10th Street in the Penn Quarter and parked up close to a short-order diner called Lincoln's Waffle Shop, which was opposite the historic Ford's Theatre, where on April 14, 1865, President Abraham Lincoln was assassinated. The place was busy as they entered, the warm air humming with conversation and the sweet smell of waffles. They found two high stools side by side at a table that was set out like a family breakfast bar.

'It's cosy,' Tayte said as he settled on to his stool, trying not to invade the space of the man eating his breakfast to the other side of him.

Once they had placed their orders, Mavro reached into her suit jacket and handed Tayte his notebook, along with a fold of papers. 'Let's see what you make of these. We'll have to work while we eat. We only have a few hours left to crack this.'

Tayte was all too aware of how much time they had left. He only hoped there was enough, and that his antics with Levant the day before hadn't cost Lauren Emerson her life. He set his notebook down and unfolded the copies of William Durant's vital records. First, he studied his certificate of birth.

'The date of birth tallies with the date on Durant's B&O Railroad payroll record,' he said. 'Also with our calculated date of birth for the man calling himself Benjamin Kirkland. We can't draw much else from it, given that I could find no certificate of birth for Kirkland to compare with.'

He turned to Durant's certificate of marriage. 'This is rather more interesting. Durant married a woman called Elma Brightwater in 1894.' Tayte had brought his briefcase in with him. He pulled it up on to his knees and found the copy of Kirkland's certificate of marriage to Dorothy Valentine. Then he laid them out side by side. 'If these men are one and the same person, he married Dorothy Valentine in 1907, at which time Elma Brightwater had been his legal wife for thirteen years, unless they were no longer married by 1907 for whatever reason.'

He saw something then that cemented his belief that he was right—that Kirkland was really William H. Durant. 'Take a look at that,' he said, and Mavro leaned closer. His index finger was hovering over the heading 'Husband's Birthplace' which showed as Rockford, Illinois. He moved his finger across to the other record, which showed exactly the same.

'So, it has to be the same man,' Mavro said. 'Born on the same day, in the same city, winding up in DC working for the B&O Railroad, and dying on the same day he was reported missing.'

'There's no doubt in my mind at all,' Tayte said, moving on to Durant's certificate of death. 'This confirms that he worked as a railroad engineer and that he did, indeed, die on May 2nd, when Benjamin Kirkland was reported missing, just as it said on his payroll record.' He scanned down to the cause of death and read it out. '*Injuries received by accidental explosion of boiler whilst at work.*'

'His train blew up? Does it say where?'

Tayte shook his head. 'No, there's no place of death shown. I expect the explosion would have made the news, though.'

Their food arrived just as Tayte was dipping into his briefcase again, this time for his laptop. As it booted up he cut into the pile of blueberry pancakes that had been set before him, suddenly oblivious to everyone else in the diner. It was just him and the pancakes, and he ate his way through half of them before coming up for air.

'You really are hungry,' Mavro said, herself having taken only two small mouthfuls of her omelette. 'Didn't they feed you last night?'

'It was paltry, and that's being generous.'

'Well, you'd better finish up your meal before you start typing, or you'll get syrup all over your laptop.'

Tayte just nodded and continued to devour his pancakes as if he were in a race to finish them before his laptop was ready. When it was, he ate the last few mouthfuls and washed it all down with his coffee. Then he brought up Chronicling America, the Library of Congress newspaper archive website he'd used to good effect before, and selected publications for the District of Columbia, 1910. He decided to keep the search simple. He just entered his subject's name, William Durant. He thought that would be enough as it wasn't a particularly common name. Several results came back, but he was quickly drawn to the first. It was from the *Washington Herald*, dated May 3, 1910—the day after Durant died.

'Here it is,' he said, turning the screen around so Mavro could see it better.

She read out the heading. '*Engineer Durant of Baltimore & Ohio Railroad killed and his fireman injured.*'

Tayte continued to read out the rest, just as it appeared in the newspaper. '*The forward locomotive of a B&O Railroad double-header northbound coal train exploded yesterday morning south of the Takoma Park B&O rail station, instantly killing engineer William H. Durant of Woodridge, painfully injuring fireman J. S. Pendleton, also of Woodridge, and scalding, perhaps fatally, Henry Lewis, a negro section hand. Fireman Pendleton was on the forward end of the engine and was hurled a distance of fifty yards. His escape from being killed is considered remarkable. The explosion is believed to have been caused by water in the boiler running low. The locomotive was reduced to scrap iron. Engineer Durant leaves his wife, Elma, and their three children.*'

'It's amazing what you can find,' Mavro said.

'It sure is. And here's solid proof that Durant was a bigamist. He married Dorothy Valentine in 1907, yet this newspaper article confirms he was still married to his first wife, Elma Brightwater, when he died in 1910.' Tayte tapped the screen. 'This is what we're looking for, though, the location of the explosion.'

'*South of the Takoma Park B&O rail station.*' Mavro read out again. 'Shame it doesn't say how far south.'

Tayte agreed. 'There was clearly a B&O rail station at Takoma Park, Maryland, in 1910, although I don't think it's there now. There's a Metrorail station this side of the boundary in Takoma, so I guess we're looking for somewhere south of that.'

'Could be a lot of track to cover,' Mavro said, checking her watch. 'It's after nine. We have less than three hours left.' She took out her phone. 'I'll call Reese and let him know.'

'Tell him we'll meet him at Takoma Metro. He's going to need all the help he can get.'

Chapter Twenty-Two

It was close to ten by the time SAC Reese had mobilised a team of FBI agents and police officers to meet at the Metrorail station at Takoma, which was on the edge of DC's Northwest quadrant. There were just two hours to the deadline Westlake had set, when, according to the rules of his deadly game, Lauren Emerson would be blown into oblivion. They had to find her in time. The overground rail line had been suspended, and Reese and his team were standing at the southern edge of the platform, preparing to walk the track. Beyond agreeing to Tayte being there with Mavro—on the basis that it was better to have him around and not need him, than to need him and not have him there—Reese had so far said little else to him. For now, there were more important matters to deal with than giving him a hard time over Michel Levant.

'Remember,' Reese called to the team. 'We don't know exactly what we're looking for or where this is likely to happen, so stay sharp, eyes peeled. I want inspections of all trackside buildings, and anywhere else Lauren Emerson could be concealed. And be careful. We know how the Genie plans to kill Lauren Emerson and I don't want any mistakes. If you suspect you may have found her, call it in. Leave the rest to the bomb techs. We have two hours, so let's move fast and be thorough.'

It was a warm, bright morning with a clear sky and a light breeze as they set off along the track, no one saying much. Dogs trained in explosives detection were up front with their handlers. Reese and several other agents in shirtsleeves and blue FBI tactical vests were close behind them, and Tayte and Mavro were at the rear. They were accompanied by a handful of police officers and track maintenance engineers in white hard hats and orange high-visibility jackets, who had been called upon for their local knowledge and expertise should the need arise. They had already advised Reese of two potential locations for the killing: a track maintenance shed about half a kilometre down the line, and a disused signal box that was scheduled for demolition.

Tayte removed his jacket and slung it over his arm as they walked, revealing the bullet-proof vest he'd been made to wear, taking in the surroundings left and right as his loafers crunched over the coarse gravel beside the track. He wondered what Adam Westlake had planned, and it occurred to him that as the Genie couldn't know exactly where in 1910 the B&O Railroad locomotive had exploded, he could have chosen just about anywhere close to the track. He doubted Lauren would be out in the open, though. A small building, such as those pointed out to them by the track maintenance engineers, or a room within a larger building seemed more likely, although he knew nothing could be ruled out where Westlake was concerned. After all, the man had already hanged one of his victims from Chain Bridge in broad daylight.

As much as he tried not to, Tayte began to picture Lauren Emerson tied up somewhere with explosives strapped to her, perhaps watching a digital clock readout slowly counting down to the end of her life. He wished the search party would move faster, but Reese was right. They had to be thorough or risk missing some vital clue as to where she was. High concrete walls lined the track for a while, yielding little but wild trackside shrubbery. Everything had to be closely inspected, which ate into the precious time they had left, slowing them down. After the concrete walls, the sidings were lined with wire fencing, topped with barbed wire, through which Tayte could see the rear of factories and businesses to one side, and residential housing to the other. There was nowhere to hide anyone here, so they pressed on.

The first half-hour passed quickly, and then a call went out from the front. It was Special Agent Martinez, and Tayte couldn't help but notice Mavro's eyes light up at hearing his voice.

'He's found something,' she said to Tayte, at the same time quickening her step to see what it was.

Being taller and at a better angle relative to the curve of the track, Tayte could already see what it was. 'It's the track maintenance shed the engineers told us about.'

Everyone came to a standstill as the dog handlers and bomb techs went on ahead to inspect the building. Tayte checked his watch and noted that they still had almost an hour and a half to the deadline, and he silently prayed that they were about to find Lauren. If she was there, he figured there was plenty of time left to disable any explosives Westlake had set up and get her to safety. Tayte and Mavro crept forward to get a better view, and the tension became palpable as Tayte looked on with the rest of the team while the shed was inspected externally. Then one of the track maintenance engineers was called forward with the keys to the building and the first of the bomb techs entered the brick and corrugated steel structure. Tayte had been watching the dogs with interest. He'd noted no change in their behaviour, so when the bomb techs came out again a few minutes later, he wasn't surprised to see one of them shaking his head. Lauren Emerson wasn't there.

Everyone relaxed again and they moved on, passing more wire fencing and trackside foliage. The repetitive landscape seemed to stretch on and on as they progressed down the line, offering few suitable places to conceal someone. They crossed above an underpass that was busy with late morning traffic, then the buildings that had previously run close to the curve of the tracks became more distant, yielding to a wider expanse of land beyond the wire fence, where there were trees to one side and open ground to the other.

One of the track maintenance engineers sidled up to Tayte. He was a portly man with an Irish-American accent. 'I'll bet you fifty bucks he's got her tied up in the old signal box a little further down. That's where I'd take her. It's no more than a shell. Doesn't even have a door.'

'I hope you're right,' Tayte said. 'Is it much farther?'

'Ten or fifteen minutes, maybe. We should see it soon. The track straightens out after the community gardens on the right there, just past the trees you can see up ahead.'

Tayte followed the line of the man's arm towards the trees, and through the wire fence before them he could see the section of land he'd referred to, which was largely in a tilled state ready for winter crop planting or had been freshly sown. There were some wooden sheds close to the wire fence and he saw that a few agents were on their way over to inspect the area, presumably to see whether the fence had been breached. He noticed then that he'd fallen behind Mavro and most of the police officers while he'd been talking to the engineer, so he quickened his pace to catch up.

Then something stopped him altogether.

An explosion no more than fifty feet away almost shook him to the ground. It ripped through the wire fence as if it were made of nothing more than paper chains. Everyone instinctively ducked as debris from the explosion came at them and black smoke began to plume skywards from the garden sheds that had now been reduced to matchsticks. Tayte's eyes immediately sought Mavro out, just in time to see what appeared to be a large piece of timber flying straight at her.

'Mavro! Look out!'

He was too late. It all happened so fast. He saw the timber slam hard into her. The next moment she was down.

'Frankie!'

Tayte's pulse began to kick harder as he rushed to her, but he was narrowly beaten by Special Agent Martinez who was quickly at her side.

'Are you okay?' Tayte heard Martinez ask her.

'I think so,' Mavro said, patting herself down.

'You had me worried there. I saw that beam hit you and all I could think was that I might never have the chance to ask you out.'

'You want to ask me out?'

Martinez smiled as he grabbed Mavro's hands and helped her to her feet. 'I thought you knew. I just didn't think you were interested.'

'Are you kidding?'

Reese's voice suddenly cut through the air. 'Agent Martinez! Get over here!'

Martinez let go of Mavro's hand. 'We'll talk later.'

As he left, Tayte stepped closer. 'Are you sure you're okay?'

Mavro nodded. 'I just had the wind knocked out of me, that's all.'

Tayte held up his watch. 'It's barely eleven. We had a whole hour left according to the deadline Westlake gave me.'

'Maybe something went wrong,' Mavro offered. 'Either that or he never meant to give us until midday. Maybe he saw us coming and panicked. He could still be here.'

They both looked around, but Tayte was distracted by the debris and the general aftermath of the explosion. He could see that those agents closest to the blast hadn't fared so well. One was sitting up clutching his arm. Two were still down and neither was moving. He began to run towards them to offer any assistance he could, but as he drew closer, he stopped cold. The immediate area around the site of the explosion was covered with blood. It was on just about every piece of debris he could see. When he saw a low-heeled woman's shoe in the midst of it all he fell to his knees and wept, knowing he had to be looking at what remained of Lauren Emerson.

Chapter Twenty-Three

Two hours later, Tayte was with Reese at the FBI Field Office on 4th Street, sitting opposite him at his desk. He'd been called in so that Reese could update him on what had been found at the scene of the Genie's latest murder, and because Reese had some news for him, sensitive enough that he wanted to talk to Tayte about it in person. Knowing how close Tayte had once been to Lauren Emerson, Tayte thought he knew what Reese was going to say.

'You're going to confirm Lauren's dead, aren't you? I think I already knew as much.'

Reese looked hot and very bothered as he finished rolling up his shirtsleeves. He sat forward on his elbows and sighed to himself, as if contemplating how best to handle what he was about to tell Tayte. 'I'll spare you the details, but yes, we've had positive confirmation that Emerson is dead.' He paused, avoiding eye contact with Tayte until the silence began to make Tayte feel uneasy. 'But that's only a small part of why I wanted to see you.'

'A small part?' Tayte said, surprised, wondering how anything could be worse than the death of the woman they had been trying so hard to save.

Reese nodded. 'Along with what remained of Lauren Emerson, another body was found at the scene.'

Tayte screwed up his face. 'A second victim?'

'No, it wasn't another victim. It was Adam Westlake. We found a cell phone on him, but it was too badly damaged in the explosion to get anything out of it. It was probably stolen, just like all the others he's been using to contact you.'

The news knocked Tayte back into his chair. 'Westlake's dead? How could that be?'

'We have a few theories. The most likely is that Westlake got careless with his explosives, or maybe the timer was faulty. The explosion occurred almost an hour before it was supposed to, by which time Westlake should have been long gone. He wasn't as close to the blast as Emerson obviously was, so perhaps he was leaving as we arrived, but he was close enough for the blast to kill him. It's not how anyone wanted this to end, but it's a mercy it finally has.'

Tayte was confused. 'Are you sure?'

'There's no question that the body we found was that of Adam Peyton Westlake III.'

Tayte shook his head. 'I mean, are you sure it's over? Westlake has always been so meticulous—so careful.'

'They all make mistakes sooner or later,' Reese offered. 'Westlake's luck just ran out.'

Tayte couldn't quite believe it, any more than he was ready to believe that the Genie's reign of terror had at last come to an end. The reason he didn't believe it was because he still didn't think Westlake was the real Genie. Tayte chewed at his lower lip before saying what he really thought. He didn't want to bring Michel Levant up again so soon after the incident at the National Archives Museum, but he couldn't stop himself. Some things had to be said.

'What about Michel Levant? What if I'm right and he *is* the real Genie?'

Tayte thought back to his time in London the year before, and he thought this was just Levant's style. He used people, and when they were of no further use to him, they wound up dead, but never in any way that could be connected with him. It still sickened Tayte to think that the last time it happened, Levant had come out of it looking like a hero.

The expression on Reese's face was less than encouraging. 'Mr Tayte, I didn't want to say this after everything you've been through today, but your obsession with this man, Levant, has to stop right now. Don't you see that Lauren Emerson might still be alive if you hadn't gone after him at the National Archives Museum like you did? If you hadn't given the man cause to bring charges against you—serious charges, I might add—we may well have had enough time to save her.'

Tayte did see. It had been eating away at him since he saw Lauren's shoe lying amongst the debris following the explosion that had so violently killed her. He would take back that visit to the National Archives Museum if he could, but nothing could change his instinct about Levant.

'Look, Mr Tayte,' Reese continued. 'Right now, you have more important things to concern yourself with. As I said, I have some news for you.'

'You mean that wasn't it, either? There's more?'

'I'm afraid there is,' Reese said with such gravity that it made Tayte sit up again.

'Westlake is dead,' Reese continued, 'but that's the only good news to come out of this. I'm afraid the rest of what I have to tell you is right up there with your worst nightmares.'

Reese opened his desk drawer and produced a transparent evidence envelope, inside which Tayte could see a sheet of paper.

'This was found in Westlake's pocket. It was inside an envelope with your name on it. Presumably he meant to leave it someplace for us to find. Maybe that's what he was about to do when the explosives went off.'

Reese placed the evidence envelope on the desk and slid it across to Tayte. It was a typed list of all the victims' names, with the most recent at the top, going back to the first victim to be discovered. The surnames came first and the first letter of each name was in bold. At the top of the list was a question mark.

?

EMERSON, **L**AUREN
ALEXANDER, **G**EORGE
NELSON, **T**IFFANY
SHAW, **S**AMUEL
UTTRIDGE, **K**ELLY
MASTERSON, **B**OBBY
MASTERSON, **L**EE
EDWARDS, **R**ANDALL
ROGERS, **A**NNABEL

As Tayte read down the line of bold lettering, his breathing became rapid and shallow. It was suddenly clear to him why the Genie had chosen these people from the great many members of his former clients' families. They had been selected for no other reason than because their names fitted with the killer's ultimate objective: Jean Summer. The Genie's sick game had been pointing to her all along.

Tayte's mouth was suddenly so parched he had trouble swallowing. He coughed before he read out the message at the bottom of the note. *'The last round of the game is simple. Guess the missing letter. It's a pity she doesn't have a sister, or perhaps you could have married her instead.'*

A cold sweat broke across Tayte's forehead as he pulled out his phone to call Jean's number. When his call went straight to voicemail he thought he was going to be sick. Why hadn't anyone spotted this pattern emerging? Why hadn't he? The simple answer was that he'd never for a moment considered Jean to be a target. These were all local murders in DC. Jean was so far away, and up until now every single one of the victims had been a former client or one of their close relatives.

He understood now that this hadn't been about any of them, or about Jean. It was about him. It had always been about him. The Genie clearly wanted to destroy Tayte's life and everything in it, including the woman he loved.

He tried Jean's number again, recalling that she'd said she was travelling home from her seminar in Scotland today, and that she was going to stay with her parents over the weekend before returning to London. Once more, his call went straight to voicemail and he feared the worst. Knowing that the Genie had intended for his note to be found at the scene of Lauren Emerson's murder could only mean that he'd arranged Jean's abduction beforehand. Tayte quickly found her parents' number in his phone's address book and dialled it, breathing hard as he waited for someone to answer because he knew in his heart that it was already too late.

PART TWO

PART TWO

Chapter Twenty-Four

South Coast of England. Three months later.

Just a few more steps and all this would end.

Above the hurried wind all Tayte could hear was the ceaseless sound of the waves crashing over the chalk scree more than five hundred feet below him. It was a cold, miserable January, made colder by the creeping damp of the British winter and the howling onshore wind that came at him in gusts, as if trying to push him back to safety, but Tayte was having none of it. He took another good slug of Jack Daniel's from the bottle he'd taken up to Beachy Head with him, and then he took another small step towards the cliff edge, knowing he would soon be at peace. And how he yearned for it.

It was late afternoon and already close to dark. The grey, featureless sky had brought the day to a premature end, but ahead of him, out over the brooding, turbulent sea, he could still make out the horizon. All he had to do was focus on that and keep walking. He tried to take another step, but either out of fear or some primal instinct to survive, he was suddenly unable to lift his loafers from the sodden grass that blanketed the clifftop. To steady his resolve, he took another slug from his now half-empty bottle, wondering if anyone would miss him. He shook his head. Misery was his only companion now, and how he'd grown tired of its tormenting voice constantly telling him his fiancée's death was all his fault.

Jean . . .

Another tear fell on to Tayte's cheek as he thought about her again, and for the umpteenth time he wondered what had happened to her. How could he go on without knowing? The pain was too much to bear. He thought back over the past three months, as he had done many times since leaving DC in search of answers—in search of Jean. Following the death of Adam Westlake, it hadn't taken the FBI long to close the case. As far as SAC Reese was concerned, the Genie was dead. The killings had stopped and that was an end to it. He'd smoked his damn cigar. Tayte hadn't much cared for Reese's appraisal of the situation with Jean at the time, even if it had most likely proved to be an accurate one.

'I know this isn't what you want to hear,' Reese had told him a few days after Westlake's death, 'but realistically, whoever this man hired to abduct your fiancée probably cut and ran as soon as he heard what had happened. It's not a good sign that she still hasn't turned up. Whatever's happened to Jean Summer is a matter for the British police.'

Frankie Mavro had been far more sympathetic. 'Anything you need, just let me know,' she'd said, squeezing Tayte's hand as he'd waited to board his plane for England. As kind as it was of her to offer her help, Tayte couldn't see what she could do, so he'd kissed her on the cheek and bidden her farewell, glad to know that she now had someone special in her life, even if he was on the cusp of losing the one special person in his.

Tayte was still unable to shake the idea that Michel Levant was the real Genie behind it all, which had given him some small hope at first because if he was right about Levant, it stood to reason that the Frenchman had to know where Jean was. Two other things about Levant had served to compound his theory. The first was that Levant had dropped the assault charges against him—and it occurred to Tayte that he'd only brought the charges in the first place to obstruct Tayte's attempt to save Lauren Emerson. The second was that Levant had apparently left DC immediately after dropping the charges. Having checked Levant's further seminar dates at the National Archives Museum, bent on confronting him again despite what had happened on the previous occasion, he'd been told that all of Levant's future talks had been cancelled. It was clear to Tayte that someone had been working with Westlake. Why not Levant? He was, after all, a man who had every reason to go after Tayte looking for retribution.

Tayte's legs began to feel leaden as he braced himself against the wind, but he managed to take another tiny step closer to the edge of the cliff, willing this purgatory to end. Until he took his final step he knew it would not. He thought back to when he'd gone to see Jean's parents after he'd returned to England, at their home near St Albans. Jean's son, Elliot, had been there, and while everyone seemed pleased to see him at first, glad of any information he could give to them and to the police, as the days wore on with no positive news, their feelings towards Tayte turned to resentment. After that, his stay with Jean's family had been short-lived. He could still hear Jean's father's parting words, which, true as they were, had added to the burden of guilt that was now drawing him steadily closer and closer to the edge of the cliff.

'If you hadn't come into her life, none of this would have happened!'

Tayte sighed and raised the bottle of Jack Daniel's to his lips again, and this time he held it there until he began to sway. He'd told the British police about his theory regarding Michel Levant, but they had been no more interested in pursuing the Frenchman than had the FBI. Tayte pictured the detective in charge of the missing persons case, DI Rutherford. He was a short, clean-shaven man with appropriately tidy hair for a policeman and a face that seemed to Tayte to be set in a perennial frown. Tayte had quickly become a thorn in his side during the first month of the investigation.

During that time, thanks to CCTV footage, he'd learned that Jean was last seen at a motorway service station along the M1, not far from the St Albans turnoff, and that therefore she must have been abducted somewhere between there and her parents' home. The hire car she'd been driving took longer to find, since it had been abandoned and burned out in a field near Dartford in Kent, delaying identification. Because of the connection with the killings in DC, it had been a high-profile case, with television and newspaper coverage for several weeks, but as the weeks wore into months with no further progress, Tayte's hopes of ever seeing Jean again began to fade. He'd been told that most people reported missing were found within the first forty-eight hours, and he got the underlying message. Statistically, after three months the odds of Jean turning up alive, if at all, were unlikely.

Tayte wiped another tear from his cheek as he stepped to within three feet of the cliff edge. He could see the white chalk face to his left and right now, like a ghostly shadow in the near darkness that spread beneath him to the sea. He tried to peer over the edge, but he couldn't see the bottom, which he was thankful for. He could only hear it as the waves continued to make their thunder below.

He'd been walking up to Beachy Head this past week while staying with Marcus Brown's widow, Emmy, who had moved out of London to live with her sister, Joyce, in Eastbourne after Marcus's death. He'd poured his heart out to both of them, telling them everything that had happened since he and Jean had visited Germany the previous summer looking into his own family history, and how Jean had proposed to him before they left. How he wished he could wind the clock back to that happiest of days.

Tayte pictured Jean's smile as she'd asked him to marry her, and as he took another small step closer to the edge, he imagined she was there and that he was going to her. He raised his bottle of Jack Daniel's to her memory and took another sip. Then, as he raised his right leg to take another step—his last step—he heard a faint voice calling to him on the wind.

Jean, he thought. *I'm coming, Jean. Wait for me.*

He completed the step, and was now so close to the edge that he could feel the wind rushing up at him. Then he heard the voice again, louder this time.

Jean? No, it can't be. Jean never calls me Jefferson.

The voice came for a third time. 'Jefferson!'

Tayte was sure now that it was a man's voice, coming, not from in front of him, but from behind. He slowly turned around, staggering a little as he did so, as much from all the Jack Daniel's he'd consumed as from the battering wind. When he saw who was standing there, not ten feet away, his brow set into a confused furrow. He recognised the man's features immediately: his blond hair, piercing blue eyes, and that narrow strip of beard that ran down the centre of his chin.

It was his brother, Rudi.

Chapter Twenty-Five

'Rudi! What are you doing here?'

Rudi stepped closer, his usually coiffed hair now dancing wildly in the wind. 'I could ask you the same thing,' he said with a British public-school accent that belied his German upbringing. He reached out his hand and his long grey overcoat began to flap as a gust of wind caught it. 'Come away from the edge.'

Tayte swayed in the breeze, but his feet remained firmly planted. 'I mean, what are you doing here in England? How did you know where to find me?'

'You left my contact details with a woman called Emmy Brown yesterday. Apparently you told her I was your next of kin. She called and said you'd been coming up here all week and that she was worried about you. I've been calling you. Why didn't you answer?'

'What's the point?'

Rudi frowned. 'I booked a last-minute flight and came as soon as I could. Good thing I did.'

'It's too late,' Tayte said, slurring his words. 'Did Emmy tell you about Jean?'

'Yes, but how can you be so sure she's dead?'

Tayte waved his bottle of Jack Daniel's at Rudi as if dismissing any other possibility. The sudden action almost unbalanced him.

'I just know,' he said with an air of despondency. 'It's been three months.'

Rudi took another step towards Tayte, and Tayte was reminded of just how athletic his brother was. They were both tall, though Rudi was marginally taller. His thighs were as big as Tayte's, but where Tayte's were soft, Rudi's were thick and muscular—strong like tree trunks. As for being fraternal twins, Tayte thought Rudi had got the better deal when the genes were being handed out, although Tayte couldn't deny that Rudi had undoubtedly looked after himself better over the years.

'So you're just giving up?' Rudi said. 'Is that it? Do you always give up so easily?'

Ordinarily Tayte had never been one to give up on anything. If something was wrong or out of place, he had to put it right, or at least try to, whatever the risk. He'd spent his entire adult life trying to find out who he was, trying to identify his bloodline, and he hadn't given up on that. But his parents were dead. His only true friend, Marcus Brown, was dead. Now Jean.

He took another gulp of Jack Daniel's. 'I have no one left to live for.'

'Really? Now you're hurting my feelings.'

Tayte's shoulders slumped. He hadn't meant it like that. Of course there was Rudi, but he'd only recently made his acquaintance. Nevertheless, Rudi was his brother, and it was a timely reminder to Tayte that he did have someone left to live for, however little they knew one another at this fragile juncture in their lives.

'Look,' Rudi said, holding out his hand again, clearly hoping Tayte would take it and come away from the edge. 'Even if you're right. Even if Jean is dead. Don't you want to know what happened? Don't you want that closure?'

Tayte shook his head as another tear came to his eye. 'It won't change anything.'

'Or it just might. Now come with me and let's find out together.'

Rudi stepped forward again until they were both dangerously close to the edge of the cliff. His hand was still outstretched and it was now well within Tayte's grasp.

'No!' Tayte said. 'Stay back! This is for the best.'

'The best for whom? Has it occurred to you that this is precisely what someone wants you to do? You've been driven to this.'

'Yes, and I give in. I can't play this game any more.'

'That's just the bottle talking. Give it to me.'

Tayte held out the bottle of Jack Daniel's. Then he began to turn away to face the sea and the peace he longed for. As he did so, instead of taking the bottle, Rudi grabbed Tayte's wrist, and with all his considerable strength pulled him back from the edge, sending them both tumbling until they came to rest several feet away.

'You're squashing me,' Rudi said, sounding short of breath.

'Let me go and I'll get up.'

'If I let you go, do you promise to stay away from that edge? I know Emmy would like to see you again. I took a taxi as far as the road would allow. Do you have a car nearby?'

'No. I walked up from Eastbourne. It's not far. I've been walking a lot lately.'

'Well, a little more air won't hurt us. What do you say we take a stroll back to Eastbourne and get ourselves a hot drink? Then in the morning, when your head's clear, we'll figure out what we're going to do, one step at a time.'

Tayte swallowed hard. He gave a sigh. 'And what if I don't like what we find? Do you promise not to try and stop me again?'

'I'm your brother, Jefferson. You know that's a promise I can't make.'

'Okay, then will you at least stop calling me Jefferson? Only Marcus called me Jefferson.'

'What's wrong with Jefferson? I think it suits you, and who knows? Maybe someday we'll be good friends, too, as well as long-lost brothers.

Then we'll look back and see how fitting it was for me to go on calling you Jefferson, just as your good friend Marcus did.'

Tayte sighed again. He still felt so very low, but somehow this interruption had, for now, taken the edge off his desire to kill himself. He gave a nod. 'Okay, just let go of me. I'll roll off you and you can get up first.'

Tayte felt Rudi's arms go limp and he rolled to one side, his back to the grass now as he looked up into the blackening sky, wondering how on earth they were even going to begin their quest to discover what had become of Jean.

'Come on,' Rudi said, offering his hand again.

This time Tayte took it, and with relative ease Rudi pulled him to his feet.

Tayte still had the bottle of Jack Daniel's clenched tightly in his other hand. There was a good measure left in the bottom. Rudi gestured to it and Tayte handed it over. Then as they began to head back down, to calm his own nerves, Rudi drained what was left and hurled the empty bottle out over the cliff, sending it spinning into the sea below.

Parked in a lay-by off Beachy Head Road, Michel Levant was toying with the large gold ring he always wore on his left index finger: his Sun King ring. It was the size of a full sovereign with black enamel detail, and in the centre was engraved the likeness of King Louis XIV of France, surrounded by a flaming sun. It was no ordinary ring. As lethal as a bite from the most venomous of snakes, it held a deadly secret that had served him well in the past, having saved his life on more than one occasion, which was why he never took it off. Amongst the kind of people Levant so often found himself keeping company with, he never knew when such a beautiful yet deadly trinket might come in handy. He pursed his lips, admiring himself in the rear-view mirror as he continued to wait. He was bored out of his mind, but the wait was worth it.

Levant often hired people to follow and watch others for him, but he'd wanted to be here in person this time and, despite his boredom, being so close to Jefferson Tayte at what was surely his untimely end was worth any hardship. He'd watched Tayte head up to Beachy Head several times that week—Beachy Head, where around twenty people commit suicide every year. To have driven Tayte to such hopeless desperation was the ultimate prize the game he'd been orchestrating had to offer, and to Michel Levant, nothing denoted more power than the ability to rob a man of his will to live.

He thought back to the start of the game, which he considered to have begun in London after he'd effectively had Marcus Brown killed for the contents of his briefcase. When Marcus's American friend had sought to make sense of his death, he had denied Levant so much.

'Deny me! Michel Levant!' he said under his breath.

He couldn't believe the nerve of the American, but now it was his turn—now he had denied Tayte. He had denied him everything he held dear, his home, his work, and his bride-to-be.

'Or not to be,' he said, smiling to himself. 'That is very much the question.'

He sat up from the slump his ageing yet outwardly youthful frame had slipped into and peered out of the windows to see if anyone was around. It was fully dark now, and with the darkness in such places came solitude. A few other cars periodically passed on the road that led down to Eastbourne, but this was a scenic route and there was little now to see. There was still no sign of Jefferson Tayte, which he took to be a victory.

He considered the excellent part Adam Westlake had played in the game, and how he really couldn't have achieved this fine ending without him. Levant had spent months going through the US newspaper archives looking for mention of Jefferson Tayte, trying to identify anyone he felt had an axe to grind with the genealogist. He'd found a few possible candidates, but none so perfect as Adam Westlake. Westlake had been so hungry for Tayte's blood when Levant first went to see the man that it had been difficult at first to talk him around to his way of thinking—to playing his game. As the game progressed, however, he knew Westlake had enjoyed making Tayte suffer, just as he would have enjoyed the large payment he'd offered him on completion of the game, had he lived long enough to claim it.

Levant's eyes were back on the rear-view mirror. 'Ah, such a pity,' he told his reflection. 'I could have used a man like that again.' He genuinely hoped Westlake hadn't suffered too much when the time came to terminate his employment, rigging the explosives timer he'd supplied Westlake with to detonate an hour early, catching him at a time when he knew he would still be close to the centre of the blast.

He looked away from the mirror, but as he did so, movement drew his attention back to it. He sank lower in his seat again, and moments later he heard voices, growing louder. One of them was American, he was sure of it.

'*Merde!*' he cursed.

Very slowly he peered over the edge of the door, and through the glass he saw a familiar tan suit. His first thought was to question why anyone would go up to a place like Beachy Head in January without a coat. Then as it sank in that this was indeed Jefferson Tayte, walking and talking and still very much alive, his blood began to boil. If he'd had a gun in the glovebox he knew he would have leaped out of the car right there and then and used it, but to Michel Levant, guns were a loathsome vulgarity.

He took a series of deep breaths to calm himself. *Who is that with him?* he wondered, knowing it was highly unlikely that Tayte had just bumped into someone on Beachy Head in the dark by chance. *Someone knew Tayte was there. But who?*

Levant had no idea who this man with Tayte was, but he planned to find out. He watched the other man put his arm around Tayte's shoulders momentarily as they passed, pulling him towards him as if to embrace him. The gesture told Levant they were close, and that excited him. If there was now someone else whom Tayte cared for, someone else he could use to prolong Tayte's suffering before his end, then this man's appearance served only to make the game more interesting.

Chapter Twenty-Six

If Tayte was ever asked to pick a colour for January, based on his latest visit to England, he'd have to choose grey. It was already mid-morning the following day when he surfaced from his bedcovers, and in his stars-and-stripes boxer shorts opened his curtains to a rain-streaked window and yet another suffocating sky bereft of contrast or delineation. It was as if one enormous cloud had fallen over Eastbourne, bringing with it the kind of damp chill that he imagined would remain in his bones until spring.

He trudged to the small washbasin in the corner of the spare room he'd been staying in at Emmy's sister's house, part of a small development of mock-Tudor homes on the southwest outskirts of town, and splashed cold water in his eyes to wash the sleep from them. It had been another fitful night, made worse on this occasion by the bottle of Jack Daniel's he'd all but finished the day before. He'd been troubled by nightmares, the kind no one should have to endure, about Jean and the terrible things his subconscious mind continually conjured for him. He tried to block them out, as he did every morning, but this time, the harder he tried, the more his head ached with the dull, continuous throb that had greeted him upon waking.

Peering at himself in the small mirror above the washbasin, he shook his head at his reflection and knew he had to get his act together. His face was unshaven to the point where the dark stubble could almost pass as a beard, and his hair looked as if it hadn't seen a comb in weeks. He felt as rough as he looked. His eyes were red and he was cold, almost to the point of shivering, despite having just left the warmth of his bed. He'd given himself a chill, plain and simple, but he brushed it off as he ran a comb slowly through his hair and began to dress, thinking only that if he'd known he would be coming back down from Beachy Head the night before, he would have dressed more appropriately.

Tayte could smell fried bacon as soon as he opened his bedroom door and stepped out on to the landing. As he headed down the stairs, he hoped he hadn't missed breakfast because, while he felt there were many things wrong with him that morning, there was absolutely nothing wrong with his appetite. He found Rudi in the living room, looking quite the lumberjack in fitted chinos and a blue checked shirt with the sleeves rolled up. He was on his knees tending the log burner. He supposed Emmy and her sister were in the kitchen.

'Good morning,' Tayte said, feeling more than a little embarrassed at his behaviour and the reason Rudi was there. 'Look, I'm really sorry,' he added, meaning to go on, but Rudi stopped him.

'There's no need to apologise,' he said as he stood up. 'You've been through a lot. I understand.'

'But I've dragged you all the way over here, and—'

Rudi stopped him again. 'I came because I wanted to. If you have an apology to make it's for not telling me sooner. Perhaps I could have helped.'

'Perhaps,' Tayte said, nodding thoughtfully. 'At least accept my thanks. In the cold light of a new day I almost missed, I'm glad you came.' He undid the button on his suit jacket and sat in one of the armchairs by the fire, crossing his arms as he did so for extra warmth. His head continued to thump. 'So, who's looking after the gallery while you're away?'

Rudi sat in the armchair opposite him. 'No one.'

'You closed your art gallery to come here? Weren't there any auctions scheduled?'

'I expect so, but it's no longer my concern. I sold it a month ago. Everything.'

Tayte fully understood why Rudi wanted no further part in the business. Tayte's visit to Munich the year before had heralded a difficult time for his brother, but he hadn't expected to hear that Rudi had sold everything.

'I gave half the proceeds to various charities,' Rudi added. 'The other half I haven't decided on yet.'

'I know you worked hard for that business, however it was founded,' Tayte said. 'You shouldn't leave yourself short.'

Rudi smiled. 'Half is still more than enough. For now, I'm happy to follow my interest in mountaineering, which is something I've had very little time for of late. And who knows? Maybe I'll find myself a wife, settle down and raise a family.'

The door opened then and both men stood up as Emmy came in carrying two colourfully patterned plates, which matched well with the room's bright and cheery decor. Now in her late sixties, she was a short, full-figured woman with ash-blonde hair styled in a bouffant to give her extra height, and a round face that to Tayte always seemed close to a smile.

'I thought you'd need a bacon butty, seeing the state you were in last night,' she said. 'It was all Marcus ever wanted the morning after he'd had too much wine.' She gave them each a plate of sandwiches, adding, 'You had me so worried, JT. If my knees were better, instead of calling your brother I'd have gone up there after you myself.'

'I'm really very sorry,' Tayte offered. 'Did I apologise last night?'

'No, you had a quick cup of tea and Rudi put you straight to bed.'

'Tea! I must have been in a bad way.'

'Tea is what you needed. It's no use drinking coffee before bed. Especially as much as you drink. All that caffeine.'

'I thought tea contained more caffeine than coffee.'

'Not as a drink. Mind you, I doubt much would have kept you awake, the state you were in. How are you feeling? You look terrible.'

'I feel about as well as I deserve to,' Tayte said, and then he bit into one of the sandwich triangles and knew exactly why this was all Marcus ever wanted whenever he'd had too much to drink. 'This is good,' he added as soon as he came up for air. 'Thank you, Emmy. You're too kind.'

Emmy gave him a warm smile. Then she leaned in and kissed his forehead. 'Someone's got to look after you, haven't they?'

'Where's Joyce?' Tayte asked. 'I need to apologise to her, too.'

'You'll have to wait until this afternoon for that. She's gone to her Women's Institute meeting.'

Tayte gave a nod, his mouth full again.

Emmy continued to smile as she watched them both eat. 'Look at the pair of you,' she said. 'You're like chalk and cheese. Who would have guessed you were twins?'

'I couldn't believe it myself when Jefferson first told me,' Rudi said. 'But he has the DNA test report to prove it.'

'How Marcus would have loved to see that,' Emmy said. 'It would have made him so happy.'

'It sure would,' Tayte agreed, smiling back at her.

'And to have met you, Rudi. Marcus had been helping JT to look for his family for such a long time.'

'I'm only sorry I never had the chance know him,' Rudi said. 'But I'm very glad to know you. Marcus was a very fortunate man.'

Emmy laughed to herself. 'You'll have me blushing if you keep that up. Now, I must get on. I've got the kitchen to clear up and I promised Joyce I'd go and buy some more winter pansies to fill in some of the gaps in the garden this morning.'

'Please leave the kitchen to us,' Tayte said.

'It's no bother. Can I get you something hot to drink before I go out?'

'We can manage, Emmy. Please. You've done enough.'

'Okay. Well, I'll see you both later.'

With that Emmy left them to finish their sandwiches by the fire. Once they had, Rudi said, 'Now then. Let's get down to business. Tell me everything that's happened.'

While they cleared up in the kitchen, Tayte began to fill Rudi in on the events that had called him back to Washington, DC, in October the previous year, leaving nothing out. During their conversation he began to feel considerably better, which he put down to the warm environment and Emmy's bacon sandwiches. With some degree of hesitation, Tayte also told Rudi about Michel Levant, and for a change it was good to have someone listen to his theory about the man he believed was the real Genie without dismissing the idea out of hand. Tayte made an instant coffee for himself and a mug of tea for Rudi, and as they sat by the log burner in the sitting room with their drinks, Tayte finished the story of how he came to be standing so close to the edge of the cliff at Beachy Head the night before.

'So it's all a game to whoever's behind this?' Rudi said. 'He kills someone and leaves a note, giving you a clue as to who will be next, and how and where this person is going to die if you can't save them in time.'

'Exactly that,' Tayte said. 'Only the last note, the note that was found on Adam Westlake when he was killed, only told me who the next victim was going to be. Jean.'

'But that's out of keeping with the rest of the game, wouldn't you say?'

'Yes, but the game was pointing to Jean all along. The clues were there, building murder by murder, only I was too blind to see it. There would have been time to save her if the pattern had been spotted sooner, but when Lauren Emerson was killed, and Westlake with her, time ran out.'

'Are you absolutely sure?'

'How do you mean?'

'I mean, as all the other notes and text messages carried clues that allowed you to try to save each of the victims, perhaps there was something on this last note that gave you the chance to save Jean. Did the note say anything else?'

'Just a personal jibe, letting me know I wasn't going to marry Jean after all.'

'Perhaps there's more to it. Do you have a copy? Can I see it?'

Tayte felt a cold sweat wash over him. What if Rudi was right? What if there was more to the note and he'd missed something vital, and along with it his chance to save Jean? The thought did nothing for Tayte's already delicate state of mind. If he had missed something, he knew he would blame himself entirely for Jean's death.

He stood up. 'I'll go up and get it. It's in my briefcase.'

When Tayte returned he handed his photocopy of the note to Rudi. Having read it to himself again on his way back, he could draw nothing more from it. The last part was just a throwaway quip to twist the knife after letting him know Jean was going to die next.

Rudi read the note aloud, slowly, as though making sure to take every word in. '*The last round of the game is simple. Guess the missing letter. It's a pity she doesn't have a sister, or perhaps you could have married her instead.*'

'You see,' Tayte said. 'There's just that jibe at the end.'

Rudi was silent for several seconds. Then he asked, 'Does Jean have a sister?'

'No. At least none either Jean or her parents have ever mentioned. If Jean had a sister I'm sure she would have told me. We made a guest list for our wedding. There wasn't any sister on it. The note even says it's a pity she *doesn't* have a sister.'

'She doesn't have a sister,' Rudi repeated, thoughtfully. A moment later, he added, 'Not now, perhaps, but did she ever have one? Maybe a sister who died?'

The potentially devastating connotations of that simple question struck Tayte dumb. He couldn't answer. He didn't know, but he realised it was a possibility and that worried him deeply. If Jean did once have a sister who had died, then in keeping with the rest of the Genie's game, he knew that would potentially give him a past family member whose manner and location of death was to be replicated with Jean. It would be a recent past family member, but it would still fit the pattern.

Tayte felt numb as he reached into his suit jacket pocket, suddenly in a hurry to find out. 'I'll call Jean's parents and ask them,' he said, looking up their number in his phone's address book.

His call was answered so promptly that he wondered whether Jean's parents were still waiting beside their phone, as they often had while he was staying with them, in case the police called with news of their daughter. If that were true, Tayte was sorry to disappoint them.

It was Jean's mother who answered. Her tone was unsurprisingly melancholy.

'Hello, Linda Summer.'

'Hi, Linda, it's Jefferson Tayte.'

'Oh,' she said, coldly. 'What do you want?'

Tayte paused before telling her, fully aware that in her current fragile state, the last thing she needed was to be reminded of the other daughter she'd lost, if there had been another, but he had to ask. 'I need to know if Jean was your only daughter, or whether perhaps she has, or once had, a sister.'

The line went silent for several seconds. Tayte's eyes were locked on Rudi's as he waited to hear the answer. Then he heard a sigh, followed by a single word that shook him to his core.

'Yes.'

Tayte swallowed hard as he gave Rudi a nod, letting him know he was right—that the last part of the note was indeed a clue that might have led him to Jean in time to save her. But he had failed to see it.

'Yes, she *has*, or yes she *had*?' Tayte asked. 'Can you tell me about her?'

'We never talk about her. It's too painful, even now, and I certainly don't want to talk about her with you.'

'But it's very important that—'

'Haven't you done enough damage to this family?' Linda said. Then she ended the call.

Tayte lowered his phone and stared at it, thinking that he'd done far more damage than Linda Summer knew. She had just confirmed that he'd had a chance to save Jean, and he'd blown it. How could he live with himself knowing that?

Rudi sat forward. 'That didn't seem to go too well.'

'No, it didn't,' Tayte said, putting his phone away. 'All I managed to get from the conversation was that Jean either has or had a sister they never talk about. I suppose that's why she never told me about her.'

'Perhaps she would have, given time.'

'Yes, perhaps. Linda said it was too painful to talk about Jean's sister, even now, so it seems likely that she died and that whatever happened to her happened a while ago.'

'Can we find out about her some other way?'

Tayte thought about the newspaper archives, although as he hadn't managed to get the name of Jean's sister from her mother, he knew they didn't have enough to go on yet. Jean's family history records could tell him more, but it would take time, and not being a family member or having been employed by the family, and without the backing of the authorities, as had been the case when he was trying to stop Adam Westlake, he knew there would be obstacles in his way.

He shook his head. 'What good does any of this do? It's been three months. Jean's dead. Finding out how she died isn't going to bring her back.'

Rudi stood up. 'You've got to stop this. You don't know what you don't know, and until you do you have to keep an open mind.' He still had the copy of Westlake's note in his hand. He tapped it, drawing

Tayte's attention back to it. 'Something else stands out about this note that's worth mentioning.'

'Go on,' Tayte said. 'Tell me what else I missed?'

Rudi gave him a sympathetic smile. 'Look, don't be so hard on yourself, Jefferson. In your position, I would likely have written off this comment about Jean's sister just as you did. You were too close to see it. Sometimes it takes an outsider.'

Tayte drew a deep breath. 'Being hard on myself is how I deal with things. Just let me get on with it. Tell me what else stands out.'

'Well, from what you've told me about the killings in America, the clues to help you save the victims came with deadlines, didn't they?'

Tayte nodded. 'That's right. All the clues sent directly to me, that is—the phone calls and text messages.'

'Exactly,' Rudi said. He held out the note again. 'But this clue comes with no such deadline.'

Tayte could see where Rudi was going with this. 'You mean because there's no deadline, there could still be time to save Jean?'

'Why not? If no deadline has been set, logically, as per the rules of the game, there must still be time. If we're to go on, you at least have to believe that. And you must have hope, whatever we may ultimately find.'

Tayte desperately wanted to believe there was still time to save Jean, but the last three months had made it difficult for him to trust in hope. Now that they had a way into the game again, through Jean's sister, he decided to trust in his own ability to find out what had happened to Jean instead. He was about to suggest they start digging in the archives to see what they could turn up when his phone rang.

He checked the display. 'It's Jean's mother,' he said to Rudi. 'Maybe she wants to talk after all.' He answered the call. 'Hi, Linda, I'm glad you called back, I—'

'It's Keith,' the voice said. 'Linda just told me you'd called. She said you were asking about our Cathy, and I'd like to know why you thought it was important.'

'Keith, hi. I'm sorry if I upset Linda, but I think there could be a connection with Jean's disappearance.'

There was a brief pause. Then Jean's father spoke again. 'You'd better come and see us right away,' he said. 'It's best if I show you what we have.'

Chapter Twenty-Seven

It was mid-afternoon by the time Tayte and Rudi arrived at Jean's parents' home, in a car they had hastily hired for the week. The house was a modest semi-detached property not far from London on the northern edge of the rural village of Sandridge, near St Albans. It backed on to more of the same open farmland they had passed on their way there. They were greeted on the doorstep somewhat coolly by Jean's parents, Keith and Linda Summer, who were both in their sixties. Tayte thought their faces looked older and considerably more drawn than when he'd last seen them. Having introduced Rudi, they were led through an uncomfortably warm living room to the dining room at the back of the house.

Keith took his blazer off and hung it over the back of a chair. 'Have a seat,' he said, and everyone sat around the table.

'How have you both been?' Tayte asked, meaning well, but seeing it for the dumb question it was as soon as he'd asked it. Linda, who had been a petite woman when Tayte first met her, now seemed so thin and frail. 'And Jean's son . . . How's he holding up?'

'Not good,' Keith said, fiddling awkwardly with his glasses. 'Elliot's back with his father now.'

No drinks were offered, and it quickly became clear to Tayte that Jean's parents wanted to get this over with as soon as possible. So he began by showing them his copy of Westlake's note again, explaining why they now believed Jean's disappearance was connected with her sister, Cathy.

'If there is a connection,' Tayte continued, 'then learning more about Cathy could help us find Jean, or at least find out what happened to her.'

There was a tatty old shoebox in the middle of the table. Keith pulled it towards him and opened it. He took out a photograph and set it down on the table before sliding it across to Tayte and Rudi. The photograph was of a young girl in a light-blue dress with a navy cardigan over the top. She had mid-brown hair, tied back in a ponytail, and a dimpled smile that reminded Tayte of Jean. There was an emblem of some kind embroidered into the cardigan, which led Tayte to believe that he was looking at an old school photograph.

'Cathy was Jean's older sister,' Keith said. 'This picture of her was taken over thirty years ago, just before she went missing.'

'Missing?' Tayte repeated, glancing at Rudi.

'She was only eight years old,' Linda said, wrapping her long grey cardigan tighter around her. 'She was out playing with her friends in the street one day after school, as she often did. One of her friends lived further down the road, no more than a hundred yards away. When the police asked her about Cathy, she told them Cathy had gone in for her tea. She always came in around the same time. I never had to shout for her or go out and fetch her.'

'But she didn't come in for her tea that day,' Keith said, gravely. 'It's believed she was snatched right outside our front door, or close by.'

'I'm so sorry to hear this,' Tayte said.

'Yes, well, you can understand why no one in the family likes to talk about it.'

'Was she found?' Rudi asked.

At hearing the question, both of Jean's parents seemed to sigh at the same time. Linda sank her head and began to shake it from side to side as Keith said, 'No, not to this day. That's what goes on hurting inside us. It's not knowing where our baby is, only that she's dead. Now it's happening all over again.'

At that point, Linda burst into tears. She stood up, and without saying a word she almost ran from the room.

'I'll make no apology for my wife,' Keith said as soon as the door closed behind her. 'I'm surprised she could even sit down at the table and talk about Cathy in the first place.'

'I understand,' Tayte said, and now with Jean gone, he truly did.

'Of course you do. I'm sure this has been very hard for you, too. I'm only sorry we couldn't bring ourselves to be more supportive.'

Tayte wanted to say he understood that, as well, and that he'd been blaming himself so much for everything that had happened that he didn't want to be around himself any more, either. But he didn't want to talk about his recent visits to Beachy Head. He wanted to stay focused. 'You said you knew Cathy was dead. I know it's been a long time, but how can you be certain if she was never found?'

'I'm certain because I heard it from the horse's mouth, so to speak. I know who killed her. His name's Donald Blackhurst, and he admitted to it soon after the police caught him. That was early the following year. My Cathy wasn't his first victim. Neither was she his last.'

'Another serial killer?' Tayte said.

Keith nodded, frowning. 'The very worst kind. All his victims were young girls about the same age as Cathy. They were just children.' He reached into the shoebox again, and this time he pulled out several newspaper cuttings. 'I collected these at the time. Don't ask me why. I suppose it helped to make me feel more connected, as though I was doing something useful, although Linda didn't like it. She thought my interest in the other victims was too morbid, and maybe she was right, but I've kept this shoebox all these years. As painful as it is, I never want to forget.' He paused, indicating the cuttings. 'There are four other victims mentioned in there, all since my Cathy was taken, of course. I had no reason to collect anything before then. The police told me Cathy was his third known victim, making seven in total, although after the trial Blackhurst admitted to more.'

Tayte began to look over the newspaper cuttings, noting that the report for Cathy's abduction was dated April 1982. He passed each of the cuttings to Rudi as he worked his way through them, and he quickly learned that the missing girls had been abducted over a two-year period from villages and towns in rural areas around London, from Hertfordshire, where Cathy was taken, Essex, Kent and Surrey. The cuttings all focused on the families of the missing girls, offering no clue as to what might have happened to them or why, other than to suggest a probable connection with the man the press had dubbed the 'Ring Road Killer' because he was thought to have used the North and South Circular ring roads that ran through the Outer London suburbs to both select his target areas and to make good his escape.

'When you told me this man's name,' Tayte asked, 'you spoke in the present tense. Is Donald Blackhurst still alive?'

'As far as I know, more's the pity. He was sentenced to life imprisonment with a recommendation that he should never be released. Last I heard he was in Broadmoor.'

Tayte wasn't familiar with the name. 'Broadmoor?'

'Yes, it's a high-security psychiatric hospital in Berkshire, not far from London. It's home to several of Blackhurst's ilk.'

Tayte took his notepad out and wrote down the name of the place. He also wrote down a name he'd read several times in the newspaper cuttings. 'I kept seeing mention of a police detective, DCI Philip Wendholt. I take it he was running the investigation?'

'That's right. I met him a few times. He was very kind and supportive, as everyone was. He was hell-bent on catching the Ring Road Killer from the outset, and it's a blessing he did, before too many other girls were taken. Heaven knows the first was already one too many.'

'Do you know if Wendholt is still alive?'

'I really couldn't say. He was close to forty then, so if he is, he'd be retired now. He was based in London. The Metropolitan Police might be able to help if you think it would be good to talk to him.'

'I'm sure it would,' Tayte said, noticing the nod Rudi gave him, affirming that he also thought the former detective chief inspector could prove to be a good source of information.

Keith waved a hand over the table. 'You can keep all this,' he said. 'I don't know if it's of any use to you, but it's high time I let it go.' He reached across the table and placed a firm hand on the back of Tayte's. 'Find out what happened to Jean,' he added. 'From what she's told me about you, I know you're not one to give up the search once you've got your teeth stuck into things. And I know it's a lot to hope for, but maybe along the way you'll also find out what became of Cathy. It would ease our hearts to know.'

Tayte gave Keith a firm nod. 'I'll never stop,' he said, and he meant it. 'You have my word.'

He gathered the items from the table and put them into his briefcase. He stood up to go, and perhaps it was because his brother was with him and that he was no longer alone in this that he felt suddenly re-energised and strong enough to go on again. His sense of determination to know what had happened to Jean, for his sake and for the sake of her family, could not have been stronger.

Tayte shook Keith's hand. 'Goodbye, and thank you. I know how difficult talking about Cathy must have been, and please say goodbye to Linda for me. I'll be in touch.'

With that, Tayte and Rudi headed back to the car. As they went, Tayte thought over what Keith had said about also finding out what had happened to Cathy. *Along the way*, he'd said, but Tayte knew it was imperative they find out what had become of Cathy first if they were to have any chance of discovering what had happened to Jean. According to the rules of the Genie's game, knowing the location and manner of Cathy's death was vital, yet hearing that Cathy's body had never been found had come as a major blow. It appeared that the only person who knew where she had died was the man who had killed her—Donald Blackhurst, a criminally insane murderer who had kept the location of Cathy's remains to himself all these years. As Tayte climbed into the driving seat of the car, however, he had to remind himself again that to play this out, the Genie must have discovered where Cathy had died, and if the Genie had found out, there had to be a way.

Chapter Twenty-Eight

Tayte and Rudi spent a quiet evening at a hotel in St Albans, getting to know one another better, talking about nonsense much of the time, which Tayte thought was mostly just Rudi's way of distracting him from the painful thoughts that would creep into his mind whenever he had nothing else to occupy it. He already had Rudi pegged as a pragmatic man, whose strength transcended his obvious physical attributes, and he thought that was just the kind of friend he needed right now. He felt glad to know him at last, and to have his companionship through this most difficult of times.

Having tried in vain to obtain any contact information from the Metropolitan Police for former Detective Chief Inspector Philip Wendholt, which he thought was entirely understandable, Tayte had called DI Rutherford, the detective working on Jean's disappearance. He'd told Rutherford about the possible connection with the abduction of Jean's sister and how imperative he believed it was that they speak with Wendholt about the case he'd been in charge of over thirty years ago. By early evening Rutherford had called back with positive news. Wendholt had agreed to see them to discuss the Ring Road Killer, Donald Blackhurst, the following day. Tayte had sensed that Rutherford wasn't entirely happy to hear that he and his brother had taken it upon themselves to investigate Jean's disappearance, but knowing that Tayte had previously helped the FBI, and that there was some correlation between the two investigations, he'd simply advised Tayte to be careful, and to let him know straight away if any new evidence concerning Jean's disappearance came to light.

The meeting had been arranged for midday at a village pub in Surrey called the Queen's Head, and it was close to twelve when Rudi drove into the car park. It was another chilly day, the ground damp and the sky that same shade of dove grey Tayte had become accustomed to. It wasn't actually raining, but he figured it would be by the time the meeting was over.

The interior of the pub was darker than Tayte had expected, in part due to the overcast sky, but also because of the low ceiling, the small windows and the black oak beams that traced a web-like pattern across the walls and ceiling. It was unusual to see candles glowing in their glass dishes on the tables at midday, but the effect served to brighten the otherwise dull atmosphere. It was relatively quiet, but it was early yet, Tayte thought as they moved further in, looking for the man they had gone there to meet. There was an open fireplace at one end and they migrated towards it. A man was sitting at one of the tables with a pint of ale in one hand and a newspaper in the other. He appeared to be around seventy years old, which was about the right age for Wendholt, so they approached, drawing his eye as they stepped closer.

'Mr Wendholt?' Tayte asked, smiling.

The man rested his paper and his pint, which he'd almost finished. 'Mr Tayte?' he replied, and Tayte nodded.

'This is my brother Rudi,' Tayte said, shaking Wendholt's hand.

'Can I get you another beer?' Rudi asked.

'That's very kind of you. I'll have a pint of Speckled Hen. Thanks.'

Rudi looked over at Tayte. 'You want to try one, Jefferson?'

Tayte hadn't had anything alcoholic to drink since that bottle of Jack Daniel's up on Beachy Head, but he'd acquired something of a taste for British cask-conditioned ales of late and he hadn't tried this one.

'Sure, why not?' he said, pulling out a chair to sit down.

Philip Wendholt was a stocky man with dense salt-and-pepper hair, and a thick grey goatee. He wore glasses, perhaps just for reading, and he had a kind, almost jolly face that immediately put Tayte at ease. His dark-green Barbour-style coat was hanging over the back of his chair, and there was a pipe and tobacco pouch on the table in front of him, which Tayte thought he must have recently prepared, perhaps for his walk home again once the meeting was over.

'Thank you for agreeing to see us,' Tayte began. 'We'd like to talk to you about Donald Blackhurst. Among others, he abducted and murdered a young girl called Cathy Summer in 1982, and I believe there's a connection with the recent disappearance of her sister, my fiancée, Jean Summer.'

'I know precisely who Donald Blackhurst is, Mr Tayte, and why you're here,' Wendholt said. 'DI Rutherford gave me the details. You've been working with the FBI in America on an investigation into a serial killer that's led to the disappearance of your fiancée. Now you're of the opinion that Blackhurst is the key to finding her.'

'That's it in a nutshell,' Tayte said. 'We'd be glad to hear anything you can tell us about him.'

Wendholt finished what was left of his pint. 'And what exactly are you hoping to achieve from this line of investigation?'

'I want to know where Blackhurst killed Jean's sister—where her remains are.'

'And how do you propose to discover that? Blackhurst certainly won't tell you. Believe me, we tried for years. He didn't seem to care so much about the others, but he'll never give up Cathy Summer.'

'You mean he's told you the locations of some of the other victims?'

'Over the years he's revealed every one of them, except Cathy's.'

Rudi returned to the table with three pint glasses clutched in his large hands. He set them down on the table, lowering himself into one of the spare Windsor chairs as he did so. 'Did I miss much?'

'Cathy is the only one of Blackhurst's victims he won't talk about,' Tayte said. 'The only one whose location he won't give up.'

'Really. Why's that?'

'I was about to ask the same thing,' Tayte said, turning back to Wendholt.

Wendholt raised his glass to them before taking a sip. He set it down thoughtfully, and said, 'To better explain, I should begin by giving you some background on Blackhurst, and what drove him to abduct those girls in the first place. He had a younger sister called Stephanie. She was eight years old when she died. At the time, her death was recorded as an accident—death by misadventure. She'd been out playing in some nearby woods with Donald, who said she'd fallen from a tree they'd been climbing. The coroner's report showed that she died from massive haemorrhaging due to the fall, and the injuries sustained to her skull were in keeping with Donald's account of what had happened. It wasn't until much later, after Blackhurst had been caught, that he admitted to his sister's murder along with the rest. He said she hadn't fallen from the tree at all. He said she looked so pretty he wanted her to stay as she was forever. Apparently she told him she was going to grow up to be just like her mother because that's what she'd heard other people say, so he took a rock to her head to make sure she wouldn't.'

Tayte shook his head. 'The crazy bastard.'

Wendholt nodded. 'Oh, he's crazy all right. There's no doubt whatsoever about that.'

'So the girls he abducted,' Rudi said. 'They reminded him of his sister Stephanie?'

'Yes, apparently he saw his sister in all of them, so he snatched them off the street, as if to make things right again as he saw it. There was his sister, just as she was, not having grown a day older.'

'So why did he kill them?' Tayte asked. 'If he thought he was putting things right, that is.'

'The illusion didn't last,' Wendholt said. 'Eventually he'd snap back to reality and realise the girl wasn't his sister after all, so he'd kill her. He liked using rocks and other heavy objects. Most if not all of the remains we managed to locate showed extensive trauma to the skull. I imagine Cathy Summer shared a similar fate. As to why he won't give her up, it's because he said she was special to him. If I could show you a photo of Cathy

Summer and Stephanie Blackhurst side by side, you'd be hard pushed to tell them apart. But again, sooner or later, the illusion had to end. It's just that with Cathy, because she and Stephanie were so alike, he chose to keep her to himself. It's not believed there was any sexual motivation. It was simply that he wanted to be with his sister again. Whatever was going on in that deeply troubled mind of his, and still is, for all I know, it was as if it gave him some inner peace, until the illusion ended, of course.'

'I see,' Tayte said, wondering where this left his line of investigation. Under the circumstances, it seemed that Blackhurst wasn't about to tell them what he'd done with Cathy after he killed her. But if he was right about this, surely he must have told someone. He must have told the Genie. He then wondered whether it was at all possible that he could go and see Donald Blackhurst. 'Jean's parents told me Blackhurst was being treated at Broadmoor Hospital,' he said. 'Would it be possible to arrange a visit so I can talk with him?'

Wendholt smiled to himself. 'You're not easily deterred, are you? You'd have made a good detective.'

'Leave no stone unturned and all that,' Tayte said. 'We may learn nothing from the visit, but I don't want to miss anything just because I didn't try. I'm realistic enough about this to know he's not going to tell me where he killed Cathy, or what he did with her body afterwards, but I'd like to ask him just the same, so I know it's covered. I believe he's told someone recently. I don't know why he would do that, but I feel I need to go and see the man if it's at all possible.'

'It's definitely possible,' Wendholt said. 'It'll take time to arrange— five days' notice is the usual minimum requirement for Broadmoor— but if you'd like, I'll see if I can use my once formidable influence in the Met to pull a few strings.'

'That would be great,' Tayte said, reaching into his pocket for a business card, which he handed to Wendholt with a smile, hoping the visit wouldn't take too long to set up.

Chapter Twenty-Nine

Two days later, Tayte and Rudi arrived at Broadmoor Hospital, one of three high-security mental health hospitals in England, accommodating over 240 male patients, including several high-profile serial killers. Known as the Broadmoor Criminal Lunatic Asylum when the first patient was admitted in 1863, the sprawling complex had been expanded and modernised over the years, although it still retained much of its Victorian architecture, including the iconic arched entrance now referred to as Gate 60, with its central clock set between two three-storey-high towers.

During their wait, Tayte and Rudi had returned to Joyce's house in Eastbourne, where Rudi spent many hours walking on the South Downs, and Tayte learned more about Donald Blackhurst from the online newspaper archives, which included an interesting profile that spoke of a violent family background. His parents were Terry and Maureen Blackhurst. Tayte read that the young Donald Blackhurst had often witnessed his father beating his mother, sometimes savagely, until their relationship finally ended in divorce. That was soon after the death of Donald's sister, when he'd been placed into foster care, subsequently undergoing psychiatric treatment for a personality disorder. Tayte thought the signs were all there, but as informative as his research had been, it had given him no further insight as to where Cathy had been murdered. It had, however, served to help keep his mind focused until the expected call from Philip Wendholt came through, confirming their visit to Broadmoor Hospital at eleven o'clock the following day.

Tayte and Rudi were taken to the Visits Centre, a large high-ceilinged room, painted white with blue squares fixed here and there to the walls, pale-beech woodwork and blue desks. There were fifteen desks in total, each accommodating up to four people, including the patient. Sitting opposite a man capable of doing the things Donald Blackhurst had done, Tayte was all the more glad to have his brother beside him. Blackhurst was a small, rather ordinary-looking man, but just the same, Tayte was also glad that the two highly trained members of staff who had brought them to the Visits Centre were standing close by, watching over them.

Now in his early sixties, Blackhurst had a balding pate with short brownish hair at the back and sides. He had small, wide-set eyes and shiny skin that was red like a rash around his mouth and nose. He wore a pale-blue shirt, which Tayte imagined had been issued to him by the hospital, since he'd been told that Blackhurst never received visits from family members, only from the police and from journalists looking for a story. It had piqued Tayte's interest to learn that a journalist named Joshua Evans from a local newspaper called the *Bracknell Times* had visited Blackhurst in recent months, not least because he had also been told that visitors of any kind were extremely rare when it came to Donald Blackhurst.

'My name's Jefferson Tayte, and this is my brother Rudi,' Tayte said. The man opposite him just stared back, his face still as a mannequin.

'We'd like to talk to you about Cathy,' Rudi said. 'Cathy Summer?'

Blackhurst's eyes drifted across to Rudi. 'You want to know where my sister is, don't you?'

Blackhurst had a calm, slow voice, and at first Tayte couldn't decide whether it was naturally slow like that, or whether it was because of the medication he was on. His eyelids were certainly droopy, as though he constantly had to fight to keep them open.

'Can you tell us where she is?' Tayte asked, thinking it was as well to get the big question out of the way.

Blackhurst's eyes drifted back to Tayte again with all the speed of an old tortoise who seemed indifferent to the world beyond his shell. 'Have you tried calling for her?'

'Excuse me?' Tayte said, smiling awkwardly.

'My sister, Stephanie. She's always hiding under her bed. I'd look there if I were you.'

Tayte glanced at Rudi with raised eyebrows, unsure whether Blackhurst was just putting on a show for them, or whether he really did believe his sister was still alive, still the young girl he had known when they were growing up together. Before Tayte could think what to say next, Blackhurst spoke again.

'I was excited when they told me I was having a visitor,' he said, his eyes still fixed on Tayte. 'You have a funny accent. Are you a cowboy? Like in the movies?'

Tayte had to stop himself from laughing at the suggestion that every man who spoke with an American accent had to be a cowboy. 'No, I research people's families—their family histories.'

'And what are you?' Blackhurst asked, turning surprisingly sharply now to Rudi, seeming to show no interest in Tayte's profession, which came as no surprise to him, given what he'd read about this man's own family.

'I used to be an art dealer,' Rudi said. 'I—'

'My sister likes drawing pictures,' Blackhurst cut in. 'Maybe she's in the playroom with her crayons.' To Tayte he added, 'Have you tried looking there?'

Tayte gave a gentle sigh. They had been with Blackhurst less than five minutes, but he could already see that they weren't going to get anything sensible out of him about Cathy Summer. He wasn't ready to stop trying just yet, though.

'Cathy Summer,' he said, trying to refocus the bizarre conversation. 'You remember her, don't you?'

'Summer . . .' Blackhurst repeated, drawing the word out. 'No, I don't think so. We had a frost the other morning. I saw it from my window.' He shook his head. 'It can't be summer.'

Rudi caught Tayte's attention. He was shaking his head as if to say they might as well get out of there.

'You had another visitor recently, didn't you?' Tayte said, still not quite ready to throw in the towel, now that he was sitting face to face with the man he knew had the answer he was looking for. 'He was a newspaper reporter,' he added. 'What did you talk about?'

Blackhurst's eyes were still on Tayte. He didn't answer straight away, and before he did a wry smile creased his lips. 'Do you like puppets?'

Tayte scrunched his brow.

'We do, my sister and I,' Blackhurst said. 'We love puppets.'

Rudi stood up then. 'Come on, Jefferson. Let's go.'

Tayte sighed again as he followed Rudi's lead and stood up. The interview was over. Tayte turned his back to Blackhurst and headed for the door, and as he went he heard faint laughter begin to rise behind him.

'We're all his puppets,' Blackhurst said, laughing more fully as they left.

Driving back to Eastbourne with Tayte in the passenger seat, Rudi asked, 'What do you suppose Blackhurst meant when he said we were all his puppets? It was an odd remark.'

'Yes, it was,' Tayte said, still thinking about the journalist who had gone to see Blackhurst recently. 'But then just about everything the man said was odd.'

'That's true. He's in the right place, that's for sure. So where do we go from here? How are we going to find out what he did with Jean's sister?'

'That remains a very good question,' Tayte said, and it was one to which he had no immediate answer. 'I'd like to talk to the reporter who went to see Blackhurst. Maybe he managed to get more sense out of him than we did.'

As Rudi turned the car on to the M3 and they picked up speed, Tayte took out his notepad, into which he'd previously written the journalist's details. His briefcase was between his feet. He reached into it and pulled out his laptop, partly out of habit, but mostly because he preferred its larger screen over his smartphone. He wanted a contact number for the newspaper he'd been told the journalist worked for: the *Bracknell Times*. He was pleased to see that his laptop had a good charge and that his phone, through which he could access the Internet, had a 3G data connection. He soon found the number he needed to call.

'I'm going to see if I can reach that journalist,' he said. 'Maybe he'll agree to see us.'

His call only rang twice before it was picked up. He found himself speaking to a young woman in the editorial department who introduced herself as Amber. Her tone was clipped and somewhat unnatural-sounding, Tayte thought, as if she were putting on what she considered to be a posh phone voice.

'Hi, my name's Jefferson Tayte,' Tayte said. 'I'd like to speak with a reporter who works for your newspaper if that's at all possible. His name's Joshua Evans.'

'Joshua Evans?' Amber repeated.

'That's right. I believe he was working on a story about one of the patients at Broadmoor Hospital a few months back.'

The line was silent for a few seconds. Then Amber said, 'Are you're sure he works for the *Bracknell Times*?'

'That's what I was told.'

Silence again. Then, 'I'm sorry, but I can't find any employees called Evans in the system.'

Tayte sighed. 'Perhaps he left the newspaper recently. Can you check?'

'One moment please.'

The line was silent again, this time for close to a minute. When Amber came back she was apologetic again. 'No one by that name has worked for the *Bracknell Times* in the last twelve months,' she said. 'I'm afraid you must have been misinformed. Perhaps he's freelance or maybe he works for another newspaper.'

Tayte's eyes narrowed thoughtfully. He knew he couldn't have misheard the name of the newspaper, or the man's name. He could still vividly recall the member of staff at Broadmoor Hospital telling him. 'Maybe that's it,' he said, going along with the suggestion, but thinking that whoever had gone to see Donald Blackhurst must have lied about his identity. 'Thanks for your time,' he added, then he ended the call.

Turning to Rudi, he said, 'The newspaper has no record of a Joshua Evans working for them. Not now, or within the last year.'

'That's odd. Maybe the hospital made a mistake.'

'It's possible, but I'd imagine such a high-security establishment would be very thorough when it comes to recording visitor information.'

'So, if Joshua Evans didn't work for the *Bracknell Times*, who was he?'

'That's another very good question,' Tayte said, considering that the man who had gone to see Donald Blackhurst in recent months might not have been a journalist at all. Maybe he was the real Genie, the mastermind behind everything that had happened, having gone there to hatch the rest of his deadly game.

Chapter Thirty

It was mid-afternoon and raining heavily by the time Tayte and Rudi were back in Eastbourne. They were sitting opposite one another at a table by a window in the back room of Joyce's house, both looking out through a layer of condensation over a small garden. It was colourful for the time of year, trying in vain to bring cheer to an otherwise gloomy month. It had turned colder over the last few days, and now the rain drove icy sleet against the window. Tayte watched it slide down the glass, lost to his thoughts as he wondered what to do next.

'What do you usually do when you're stumped?' Rudi asked, breaking the silence that had settled over them since Joyce had brought them both a hot drink some time ago.

Tayte drew a deep, contemplative breath. 'I grind it out,' he said. 'Sometimes for days, even weeks, on end. I go digging in the archives. I go back and talk to my client's family members in the hope that I'll see or hear something new that might open another line of investigation.'

'Well, since that newspaper reporter turned out to be bogus, we've run out of people to talk to,' Rudi said. 'What about these archives? Can they help?'

'Maybe, but we have to know what we're looking for.'

'We're looking to find out what Blackhurst did with Jean's sister, because the Genie plans to replicate her death.'

Tayte gave a sombre nod, thinking about Jean again and whether or not Cathy Summer's death had already been replicated. He still couldn't shake the idea that three months was too long for there to be any hope of finding Jean alive. 'That's the big question,' he said, 'but as Blackhurst isn't going to answer it for us, we need to look for some stepping stones.'

'Stepping stones?' Rudi said, raising his brow.

Tayte nodded again, more enthusiastically this time. 'We need to take smaller steps toward our goal. Answer some other, smaller questions in the hope that they'll lead us to the bigger answer we're ultimately looking for.'

He stared at the sleet on the window again as his thoughts turned back to their conversation with the retired detective who had worked on the Blackhurst case. He recalled that Wendholt had told them Cathy Summer was the only victim Blackhurst hadn't given up. He reconsidered the reasons Wendholt had given.

'All we have to go on for now is what we've heard so far,' he said. 'And most of what we've learned about Blackhurst has come from Jean's father, my research, and Philip Wendholt. He told us that of all Blackhurst's victims, Cathy Summer looked the most like his sister. That's the reason why Blackhurst has never given her up.'

'Cathy was special to him,' Rudi said.

'That's right—special. So we could be looking for somewhere that was special to Blackhurst and his sister before he killed her. Wendholt suggested that Blackhurst took these girls because in his mind he felt he was bringing his sister back, undoing the terrible thing he'd done. For a time, he felt as if he were with his sister again, so maybe he took them to places he and his sister used to go.'

'It's logical,' Rudi said. 'Although, I should think the police would have checked all the places Blackhurst frequented.'

'I'm sure they would have, but they could only have checked the places they knew about. This goes back to when Blackhurst and his sister were children, years before he abducted his first victim. What if there was someplace extra special to them both back then, a happy place and time where Blackhurst might take the one child who looked so much like his sister that, according to Wendholt, you'd be hard pushed to tell them apart?' Tayte paused and smiled at Rudi. Then he reached down into his briefcase and pulled out his laptop. 'I think that little stepping stone just gave us our new line of investigation.'

It was barely after four in the afternoon, but beyond the window it was already growing dark thanks to the short winter daylight hours and the heavy clouds that continued to drench the already sodden land with yet more rain. Tayte stared at his laptop in contemplation of how best to go about finding such a special place in Donald Blackhurst's childhood; a place, perhaps, where fond family memories had once been made with his sister. The birth, marriage and death indexes were his usual starting point, but this search was somewhat different from his usual routine, and apart from knowing the names of Blackhurst's immediate family, his parents and his sister, he had little else to go on. Building an accurate family tree for Blackhurst would take time, and on this occasion Tayte didn't feel that it was the right way to proceed, given that he didn't exactly know what he was looking for.

He looked up over his laptop screen at Rudi. 'I think a general search for the Blackhurst family name is going to be the best place to start,' he said. 'Maybe I can find a connection to someone or somewhere that way.'

'Is there anything I can do?'

'Not really, unless you brought your laptop with you.'

Rudi shook his head. 'All I have is my phone.'

'It's probably a little small for this kind of work,' Tayte said. 'It's too bad Emmy and her sister aren't hooked up to the online community, or maybe you could have borrowed one of their laptops.' He slid his mug across the table and gave Rudi a coy smile. 'I could use another coffee.'

Rudi stood up. 'So my status has been reduced to tea boy, is that it?' he said in good humour as he collected their mugs.

Tayte winked at him. 'Just think of the greater good, Rudi. Keep that coffee coming.'

As Rudi left him to it, Tayte turned back to his laptop, thinking that he'd quickly Google 'Blackhurst' in case any pertinent connections to Donald Blackhurst came back, but by the time Rudi returned with their drinks, he knew he was wasting his time. Rudi pulled a chair up alongside him and sat back with his drink.

'That doesn't sound very promising,' he said in response to the long sigh Tayte gave as he too sat back in his chair and sipped his drink.

'Too much data,' he said. 'I need to narrow it down. Maybe there's something in the newspaper archives I started looking at while we were waiting to see Blackhurst.'

He brought up the British Newspaper Archive website, where he'd previously read about Blackhurst's family background. The fast-growing archive boasted access to over sixteen million pages covering two hundred years of history. Because of the serial killer's notoriety, the search still returned too much data as far as Tayte was concerned. He'd read some of the articles already, which helped, and he'd glanced over others to some degree, but there were so many more that were new to him.

Time to grind it out, he thought as he selected one of the articles and began to read, hoping that sooner or later something would stand out. An hour quickly passed, and he soon wished he had a bag of Hershey's left to munch on. Rudi had fallen asleep in his chair, no doubt from boredom and the hypnotic patter of rain at the now black window.

Most of the articles Tayte read were understandably about Donald Blackhurst's crimes and his family background. The case was so widely reported in the press during Blackhurst's reign of terror that Tayte soon found himself going over familiar information in one newspaper and then another until his eyes began to tire. He was about to go and make himself another mug of coffee, not wanting to disturb Rudi, when he saw something that made him sit up.

'Touchdown!' he said, loud enough to wake Rudi from his slumber.

'What is it?' Rudi said, suddenly at Tayte's elbow.

'A pretty obvious connection if you ask me. It's just the kind of thing I've come to expect from all the previous puzzles I've had to solve.'

'What have you found?'

Tayte tapped a single word buried within the article he'd been reading.

Rudi leaned closer. '*Puppets,*' he said, raising his eyebrows as he made the connection.

Tayte nodded. 'This particular article is about an interview Blackhurst gave soon after he was sent to Broadmoor. It reads much like parts of our conversation with Blackhurst earlier, in that he tells the reporter, again in answer to an unrelated question, that he and his sister liked puppets.'

'So, maybe he's been leaving clues as to what he did with Cathy Summer all along, only no one picked up on it.'

'It's possible. It might still be nothing, but my instincts tell me it's worth exploring.'

'*We're all his puppets,*' Rudi said. 'That's what he told us as we were leaving. All whose puppets?'

'If I had to hazard a guess, I'd say Blackhurst was referring to the man who had gone to see him, and if that was the Genie, as I now suspect it was, then Blackhurst could see him as the man who was pulling all the strings in this sick game he's playing. Maybe he told Blackhurst all about it in exchange for information about Cathy Summer and it excited him enough to talk. Or maybe the Genie was fed the same line about liking puppets and he went ahead and worked the rest out for himself, as we're now doing.'

'Either way,' Rudi said, 'it seems that Blackhurst's visitor was persuasive enough to have him pass on that message as we left. Assuming for now that's what it was.'

Tayte agreed. 'I think this could be the connection to Blackhurst I was supposed to find, but what to do with it?'

'A puppet show?' Rudi offered. 'We're looking for somewhere that was special to Blackhurst and his sister. Maybe they used to visit somewhere as children.'

'Or someone,' Tayte said, thinking that every puppet show had its puppet master.

Rudi nodded. 'So, I suppose the next step is to look into puppet shows?'

'That's right. Follow the clues and see where they lead, and this particular clue takes us to the entertainment industry. There are some key publications we can look at. Back home we have *Variety* magazine, but here in the UK we need to look at *The Stage*. It's been going since the late 1800s, and fortunately, they have a comprehensive online archive.'

Tayte brought up another browser screen and was soon looking at the website for *The Stage* archive. He clicked the search button, selected to view all clippings and entered the keyword they were interested in: *puppet*. The search returned results dating from 1950 to 2005. All were advertisements of some kind, many of which were from puppet theatres looking for puppeteers to drive hand puppets and marionettes. There was one for an international puppet festival in 1963, and another for Puppeteers' Day in 1983. Tayte's eyes scanned through every one of them, but he was unable to make a connection.

'Isn't there anything further back?' Rudi asked. 'There's a big gap between 1880, when it says the archive begins, and 1950.'

'I think it's because I've only searched for *puppet*. I'll try another term—*marionette*.'

He clicked the back button and entered the new keyword to search for. This time the results dated further back, and once again there were several advertisements, this time more for marionette shows than for puppeteers. As he scanned through them he read about the Marionette Follies from 1946, and the DaSilva Marionettes from 1964. Tayte read through each one, growing more and more disheartened as he came closer to the bottom of the results page. Then he found something that set his pulse racing.

'Look at this,' he said, enthusiastically tapping the screen as his skin began to tingle. He was looking at an advertisement for a marionette theatre, dated 1937. At the bottom of the advertisement was the proprietor's name.

'*Vincent Blackhurst*,' Rudi said, reading the name aloud. His face was suddenly beaming. 'That's it!'

Tayte was now smiling along with him. '1937 is long before Donald Blackhurst and his sister were born, of course, but maybe the theatre was still there when they were growing up. It would appear to have been owned, or at least run, by one of Donald Blackhurst's ancestors—his grandfather or a great-uncle, perhaps.'

'There's an address in Broadstairs,' Rudi said. 'I've heard of it. It's a seaside town in Kent that I read about during my English literature studies.'

'Broadstairs,' Tayte repeated. 'A puppet show at the seaside.' He was still smiling. 'Now that must have seemed like a very special place to visit as a child.'

'Yes, but I shouldn't think the theatre's still there. The building perhaps, but puppet theatres have long been out of fashion.'

'I think we need to go there first thing in the morning and take a look,' Tayte said. 'But before we do, I want to learn some more about Vincent Blackhurst, particularly whether he still has family living in the area. I'd like to prove his relationship to Donald, just to be sure. If Vincent is part of the same Blackhurst family, maybe one of his relatives will recall the young Donald Blackhurst. We may even be able to find out whether he used to visit Broadstairs with his sister.'

Chapter Thirty-One

Hindered by the morning rush-hour and the lack of a fast motorway, it took Tayte and Rudi around two and a half hours to drive the eighty-mile journey from Eastbourne to Broadstairs the following morning, having passed through umpteen towns and villages, often on painfully slow single-lane carriageways. The heavy rain of the previous evening had thankfully stopped, but the overcast sky remained to set another dreary outlook for the day. It was after ten o'clock as Tayte pulled into a kerbside parking space on Western Esplanade, as close as he could get to the walkway that led down from the cliffs to the harbour. His hopes of arriving any earlier had been dashed by both the traffic and the hearty breakfast Emmy and her sister had insisted he and Rudi ate before they left.

A chill breeze greeted them off the green-grey sea as they got out of the car, causing Tayte to pull his jacket collar up. He didn't like wearing a coat because he often felt too warm with one on, whatever the weather, and he never knew what to do with a coat when he wasn't wearing it. It was just something else to carry or remember not to leave behind whenever he went out, although today, Rudi's lime-green waterproof mountain-jacket seemed like a good idea.

'Don't you want your lovely warm scarf?' Rudi called to him from the other side of the car, grinning as he held it up.

Emmy had loaned it to Tayte that morning, and he hadn't wanted to offend her by refusing to take it. It was baby pink with little white sailboats embroidered on it. He hadn't planned to wear it, but now he was here in that bitter winter wind, he was glad to have it, whatever the colour. He raised his hand and Rudi tossed it over the car roof for him to catch. As they set off down the walkway in search of the address they were looking for, he wrapped it twice around his neck and tucked the ends snugly into his jacket, not caring what he looked like, or that he now smelled of English Rose perfume.

Tayte had his briefcase with him. Rudi had a map of the town that he'd bought at a petrol station just outside Broadstairs when they stopped for fuel. On it he'd marked the approximate location of Vincent Blackhurst's marionette theatre, and he was studying the route as they made their way alongside the metal railings that fringed the edge of the cliff, overlooking Louisa Bay.

'It should be just along here,' Rudi said. 'Before we come to Victoria Gardens.'

Tayte could see the gardens up ahead. Before them, to his left, the view seemed far from promising. He was looking at a series of balconied apartments that overlooked the sea, four storeys high. It was clear from their modern design that the existing properties had been recently redeveloped.

Rudi stopped walking. 'It should be right about here,' he said, looking up at the apartments.

'There hasn't been a puppet theatre here in a while,' Tayte said, sounding disappointed if not surprised that such real estate had since been turned into profitable sea-view apartments.

'Where does that leave us?'

Tayte was wondering the same thing. 'If Donald Blackhurst brought Cathy Summer here after he abducted her in 1982, and if this is where he concealed her body after he killed her, I should think there's every chance her remains would have been found when the site was redeveloped. As that doesn't appear to have happened, I'd say this is probably not the right place. If it was, it would also be nigh on impossible to know exactly where the puppet theatre was amidst all these apartments. We couldn't specifically know where the Genie had taken Jean. It's all too vague. It doesn't feel right to me.'

'I agree. So now we go to plan B?'

Tayte gave a nod. 'We go and talk to the family. That's if Vincent Blackhurst's family will agree to see us.'

Before Tayte had turned in for the night, he'd carried out several searches on Vincent Blackhurst, and he'd found his obituary in the newspaper archives. From that he'd learned that Vincent left behind a wife called Elizabeth, and a married daughter whose name was Georgina Budd. The obituary had given Georgina's age as twenty-nine when her father died in 1973, making her seventy-three years old today. Armed with this information, Tayte had then used an online directory service to obtain a telephone number for Georgina, along with her address, which, according to Rudi's map, was on the other side of the harbour on Dickens Road.

Tayte headed back to the car. 'You drive,' he said. 'I'll call ahead and see if I can set something up.'

'Drive? It's not far. What's wrong with your legs?'

'Nothing, I just thought it would be quicker if we took the car.'

'Nonsense, the sea air is good for you, and so is the exercise. Come on, you'll have plenty of time to make that call and I'm sure you could use a cup of coffee on the way.'

It was a little after eleven by the time Tayte and Rudi turned off Eastern Esplanade on to Dickens Road, having kept the sea to their right all the way, first along West Cliff Promenade and down to the harbour at Viking Bay, where they had coffee, and then along East Cliff Promenade before heading up again to the road. Tayte was still a little out of breath as they came to the house they were looking for, although he tried to hide it, sensing that Rudi was hungry for the exercise and would have liked to step it out more than they had. Tayte's telephone call to Georgina Budd had been well received and, intrigued by his and Rudi's interest in her late father, she had agreed to see them as soon as they could get there.

The three-storey house looked as if it had been there since before the war, although that wasn't true of all the houses they passed on their way there. It had a terraced porch, painted white, with a balcony above it, and mock-Tudor beams on the upper front gable. Tayte opened the gate and they stepped up to the door. He knocked, and as they waited for Georgina to answer, Rudi pointed an index finger at Tayte.

'The scarf,' he said, grinning. 'I wouldn't want her to get the wrong idea about us.'

Tayte had barely managed to snatch it off and stuff it into his brief-case before the door opened, and they were greeted by a golden-haired woman of medium height and build, dressed from head to toe in navy-blue casual wear. She was smiling so enthusiastically that Tayte instantly felt as if he were visiting with a dear friend whom he hadn't seen in a long while.

'Mr Tayte?' she said, straightening her glasses.

Tayte returned her smile. He shot out his hand. 'Thanks so much for agreeing to see us, Mrs Budd. I can't begin to tell you how much I appreciate it. This is my brother, Rudi Langner.'

Rudi stepped closer. 'It's a pleasure to meet you, Mrs Budd.'

Georgina shook his hand and invited them both in. 'Please, call me Georgina,' she said as they went inside. 'Would you like some tea?'

They were led into the living room, which faced the street through a wide bay window, the view through which was blocked by a thick net curtain. The decor was busy with floral-print wallpaper and furnish-ings, and more antiques and ornaments than Tayte could count. It was a homely room, filled with more than one lifetime of character. They were invited to sit on the sofa and Georgina then left them, returning several minutes later with their drinks, having found an old jar of instant coffee for Tayte.

'You say you're brothers,' Georgina said as she sat in one of the armchairs opposite them and sipped her tea. 'You're not both from America, though, are you? And you have different surnames.'

'It's a long story,' Tayte said, 'but to cut it short, we were adopted as babies into different families. We only found one another recently.'

'It was you who found me, Jefferson,' Rudi said. 'I can take no credit for it.'

'How lovely,' Georgina said, and Tayte agreed, recalling that night up on Beachy Head, and shuddering to think what might have happened if his brother hadn't been there for him.

'Your phone call left me intrigued, I must say,' Georgina said, bringing Tayte's focus back into the room. 'How did you come to know about my father and his marionettes?'

Tayte didn't want to talk about Jean unless he had to, or that they were there because of a possible connection to a place Donald Blackhurst might have brought her sister before he killed her. Neither was he sure of what Georgina knew about Donald Blackhurst, so he thought it best to establish that before getting to the crux of their visit. He also wanted to confirm the relationship between Donald and Georgina's father.

'We came across Vincent Blackhurst while we were looking into someone called Donald Blackhurst,' he said. 'Do you know whether you have a relative called Donald?'

The smile that had never been far from Georgina's lips since their arrival suddenly left her. 'Assuming you're referring to the infamous Donald Blackhurst, yes, he's my cousin.'

'And I guess you know what he did?'

Georgina frowned more fully, as if recalling the events of the early 1980s. 'I heard all about it, yes. The whole country soon knew what

Donald Blackhurst had done, but it's not something one wants to be associated with, is it?'

'No,' both Tayte and Rudi agreed.

'I never knew him, and I don't actually recall ever meeting him,' Georgina continued. 'I do know that Uncle Terry, Donald's father, used to bring his family to Broadstairs in the early 1960s. The marionette theatre had closed by then and my father was reduced to giving Punch and Judy shows on the beach.'

'Your father must have been great fun to grow up around,' Tayte said.

'Yes, he was, although I moved away from the area soon after the theatre closed. I would have been in my late teens in the early sixties when Uncle Terry and his family used to visit. I married young and my husband's work took us to Bristol for a time, which is why I never knew them. I moved back here with my husband, may he rest in peace, soon after my father died and I inherited the house. I suppose it's a mercy my father never came to know what a monster Donald turned into.'

Rudi sat forward, his eyes narrowing into a quizzical expression. 'If you never knew Donald, or hadn't even met him, how is it that you know the family used to visit Broadstairs? I suppose your father told you about them?'

'More than that,' Georgina said. 'Amongst the many things my father left in this house when he died was a box full of old photographs. I came across them one day while sorting through everything.'

Now Tayte sat forward, eager to see them. 'Do you still have those old photos?'

'Yes, I have them,' Georgina said. She waved a hand across the room. 'As you can see, I'm a bit of a hoarder.'

Tayte liked hoarders. The things people kept in their families, their heirlooms, were often invaluable to his research. He was about to ask if it would be possible to see them, when Georgina stood up.

'I'll go and fetch them,' she said. 'It's true that a picture can paint a thousand words, don't you think?'

Tayte did, and more besides. He knew that photographs could tell you things that people couldn't. Once Georgina had left the room, he turned to Rudi and said, 'So we know for sure that Donald was Vincent Blackhurst's nephew, and that the family used to visit here in the sixties. That's a good start.'

'Yes, but with her father's puppet theatre gone, I still don't see where that leaves us.'

'I'll ask about the theatre when Georgina comes back. Maybe she can tell us some more about it.'

Georgina wasn't gone long. When she came back into the room this time, she had a large mahogany box cradled in her arms. Rudi, who was closest, shot to his feet and helped her with it, setting it down on the coffee table between them.

'I'll swear that old box is getting heavier every year,' Georgina said, smiling. She sat down and opened the hinged lid. She began to rummage inside. 'I keep meaning to sort these out,' she added. 'There are several pictures in here somewhere of my Uncle Terry's family.'

'Please, take your time,' Tayte said. 'We're in no hurry.'

Georgina continued to browse through the photographs, discarding the majority of them on to a pile to her left, every now and then smiling to herself as she placed one to the right. By the time the box was empty, one half of the coffee table was scattered with unrelated photographs, while the other contained a small, neat pile of perhaps six or seven black-and-white images. Georgina handed them to Tayte and began to put the rest of the photographs away again.

'That's everything I have of Uncle Terry's family,' she said. 'I think they only visited for a few years. When my father died the family connection was broken, I suppose, as so often happens.'

Tayte thought the reason the visits had stopped had to be related to the violent break-up of Donald's family and the death of his sister, Stephanie. He looked at the first of the photographs before handing it to Rudi. It had a date on the back: 1962. He quickly calculated that Donald would have been six years old when the photograph was taken. His younger sister was four. The picture showed the family on the beach, all smiles and happiness, and having just walked past the harbour, Tayte recognised the distinct line of two-storey beach huts that were set below the cliff at Viking Bay.

The second photograph Tayte came to was in a similar setting, but this time it was a close-up of two small children sitting on the sand, eating ice cream and getting most of it on their faces. It was dated 1961, a year before the previous picture, and inscribed with the names Donald and Stephanie. When Tayte looked at Stephanie, whose ice cream seemed almost as big as she was, he couldn't help but feel sad for the innocence he knew was all too soon to be lost.

The third photograph was very different. It was not taken at the beach, but inside what Tayte at first took to be the marionette theatre that had brought him and Rudi to Broadstairs. Then he remembered that Georgina had said the theatre was no longer there by the time Donald and his family came to visit. Wherever it was, there were several puppets visible in the background: Snow White and the Seven Dwarfs, one of which was perched on Donald's shoulder as his sister sat beside him, laughing. According to what was written on the back of the image, this picture was also taken in 1962, and it led Tayte to his next line of enquiry.

'Where was this taken? Did your father open another puppet theatre?' he asked, quickly going through the rest of the photographs and noting that they were all happy pictures of the two children in the same location, surrounded by puppets. 'Apart from his Punch and Judy show, I mean.'

Georgina finished putting the last of the other photographs away and closed the lid. She squared her glasses on her nose as she took the photograph back from Tayte to take a closer look. 'No, this picture was taken at my father's shop.'

'His shop?' Tayte said, glancing at Rudi, suddenly excited by the prospect of there being another location associated with Vincent

Blackhurst's marionettes—another place where happy childhood memories had perhaps been formed in the young Donald Blackhurst's mind.

'Yes, my father ran a shop where he sold puppets and carried out repairs. He was quite well known for it. Puppeteers and other theatre companies used to visit him all the time.'

'What happened to your father's shop after he died?' Rudi asked, beating Tayte to the same question.

'My son ran it for several years. He tried to keep the puppet theme going for a while, although it was more of a novelty shop, mostly selling jokes and magic tricks—hand buzzers and squirting neckties, that sort of thing. I kept all the original marionettes, though.'

'Is the shop still in the family?' Tayte asked.

'No, it was sold a long time ago, complete with all the stock. It wasn't making much money and my son eventually lost interest in it. I don't think the new buyer was too impressed with his profit margin, either, because it had closed down by the following summer.'

Tayte was growing more anxious by the second to go and see the place. 'Is the building still there?'

Georgina nodded. 'As far as I know, although it was boarded up the last time I saw it. I wouldn't be surprised if it's been sold on again by now. It's just off Harbour Street.'

Rudi produced his map from his jacket pocket. 'Could you please circle it for us?'

'Of course. It's not far. It shouldn't take long to get there.'

'Thank you, Georgina,' Tayte said, hurriedly getting to his feet, impatient to find out what was there. 'You've been very helpful.'

Chapter Thirty-Two

The building Georgina Budd had directed Tayte and Rudi to was along a narrow cul-de-sac off Harbour Street, not far from the beach. Although close to the harbour, Tayte could see why things hadn't worked out too well for those owners who had tried to run the place as a novelty shop for the summer tourist trade. There was no through road and no other shops evident along the quiet little street; it would have been all too easy for people to pass it by without ever knowing it was there. He imagined there had once been a sign on the main road, but clearly it had not been enough.

The building was painted white with royal-blue window frames. The lower windows had been boarded up, as Georgina had said, both to the front of the building and along the short alleyway Tayte could see to the right-hand side. To brighten things up, the boards had been painted with colourful seaside murals, although the general paintwork on the bricks and window frames was faded and flaking, and the upper sash windows were so dirty it was doubtful anyone could see out of them. The general impression Tayte got as he stood alongside Rudi, briefcase in hand as he took everything in, was that it looked as if no one had been there in years.

'I have a good feeling about this,' Tayte said, stepping closer.

'Me, too,' Rudi said. 'So perhaps we should be careful.'

'Do you think we should call the police?'

Rudi shook his head. 'And tell them what? I think we first need to satisfy ourselves that this is the right place.'

Rudi stepped up to the door, which was painted the same shade of blue as the window frames. It had a brass anchor in the centre for a door knocker and he knocked twice. While they waited Tayte looked back along the street. There was no one around, but then it was January and the weather was far from encouraging—it still looked as if it could rain hard at any minute. He turned back to the door. There was no sound from within, and given the state the building was in, he didn't expect anyone to answer. Rudi tried to push open the letterbox, but it appeared to have been sealed shut.

'No one's home,' Rudi said, stepping back.

They moved around to the side of the building. The alley was no more than a tight cobbled track that had once served as access to the walled rear gardens of the buildings facing Harbour Street further down. It was evident that there had once been gates in the walls, but the openings had since been bricked up, giving the alleyway no purpose other than to provide an unhindered space for weeds to grow. It was accordingly even quieter here, and Tayte and Rudi realised they were all but hidden from view. Rudi went up to one of the painted window-boards and began tapping at one of the lower corners.

'What are you doing?' Tayte asked him, speaking in a loud whisper.

'I want to see inside. I think this board's loose.'

Tayte looked around again to make sure no one could see them, and then he joined Rudi at the window, just as Rudi gave the board a tug and it fell away. He felt as if he were up to no good, but he had little choice other than to help Rudi catch it, and together they lowered it to the ground. Behind the board was a tangle of cobwebs and scurrying spiders.

'I'm really not sure we should be doing this,' Tayte said, still whispering.

'Can you think of a better way to find out if this is the right place? If we call the police it could take ages—perhaps too long. Are you prepared to risk that?'

Where Jean was concerned, Tayte wasn't. The only thing keeping him going right now was the hope that she might still be alive. If she was, then as far as he was concerned every second counted. He leaned in and began to brush away the cobwebs, which clung to his fingers as countless spiders of various sizes began to fall to his feet. Rudi helped to clear the cobwebs away and they rubbed at the dirty glass to get a better look inside.

'It's too dark,' Tayte said, cupping his hands over the glass. 'I can't make anything out.'

'Look,' Rudi said, pointing to a gap along the bottom edge of the window. 'It's not closed properly.'

'Or maybe someone left it open for us,' Tayte offered, thinking that if this was the right place—the place where Cathy Summer had been murdered and her body hidden all these years—the Genie would have to be sure they could get inside in order to find Jean.

Tayte took a deep breath as he and Rudi slid their fingers into the gap and began to lift the old sash window open. He reminded himself that over three months had now passed since Jean was abducted, and the thought conjured vivid and terrifying pictures inside his head. Was he about to find her body, decomposed and covered in flies? As the window continued to rise, he tried to block the image from his mind, hoping with all his heart that Rudi had been right when he'd pointed out that the clue hidden in the Genie's last note had given no time limit to finding her, meaning there was a faint hope that she was still alive.

With the window now fully open, they were able to see inside a little better, although on such a dull day, it was still difficult to make out any detail beyond the first few feet. Tayte poked his head inside and was thankful that he couldn't hear the sound of buzzing flies, or smell the sickly putrid stench that would have drawn them to this place had there been a dead body decomposing nearby. Instead, the air had a dry, musty odour to it that made him cough.

'Dust,' he said. 'Everything's covered in dust.'

'Here, give me your foot,' Rudi said. 'I'll help you up.'

Tayte's brow knotted. 'Help me up?'

'We have to go inside. In for a penny, and all that.'

Tayte knew his brother was right. They had come this far and they still hadn't seen enough to know whether this was the right place or somewhere else they could dismiss. He sighed, suddenly wishing he was elsewhere, yet knowing he had to go in.

Rudi squatted down and cupped his hands. 'Come on, before someone sees us.'

Tayte shook his head as he put his briefcase down. He put his hands on to the window frame, ready to pull himself up, then he put his left foot into Rudi's hands. Before he knew it he'd swung his other leg up and was sitting awkwardly half in and half out of the window.

'You're coming in after me, right?'

Rudi shook his head. 'We can't leave the window like this. I'm going to put the board back and keep watch.'

'That's just great,' Tayte said under his breath. Then he swung his left leg inside and lowered himself down on the other side.

Rudi already had the board in his hands. 'You can use the torch on your phone to see by,' he said as he began to lift the board up. 'Knock when you're ready to come out again.'

Tayte took a deep breath, nodding. 'Look after my briefcase,' he said, and then he was in darkness.

Standing inside Vincent Blackhurst's former marionette shop, Tayte could already feel goose bumps on the backs of his arms. He wasted no time getting his phone out to switch on the torch, which cast a wide silvery beam over the room and its contents. The dust he'd seen from the window was everywhere, giving the place an eerie glow, muting all the colours. He shone the light down at his feet to see where he was going, and he was immediately puzzled. Unlike the rest of the room, the wooden floor was relatively clean. It told him someone else had recently been here, and he supposed that whoever it was must have wiped the floor before leaving to hide his tracks.

'The Genie,' he said under his breath.

Tayte moved further in. There was a large round table in the centre of the room, on which he saw an assortment of some of the larger novelty items that had once been for sale. Around the table were rotating racks containing some of the smaller products. To his left, towards the front of the old shop where the main boarded-up display windows were, he saw a fully dressed window, just as he imagined it must have looked decades ago.

He went closer and took in the faded, dusty outline of a magician's top hat, complete with a white rabbit poking out from the top. Around it were packs of playing cards and several ready-made magic tricks. To the other side of the window display he saw some of the novelty and joke items, such as a set of wind-up gnashing teeth, transparent red and blue water pistols, and a number of face masks. Taking pride of place in the centre of the window was a handful of once colourful puppets, suspended by their strings in various poses. Everything Tayte saw suggested to him that very little, if anything, had been touched since the shop last closed its doors to the public.

Turning back into the room, he began to wonder why. Surely whoever had bought the shop from Georgina Budd after her son lost interest in it wouldn't have just abandoned it when it failed to turn a profit? He supposed the new owner could have died, but what of their relatives? Why hadn't it been sold on to someone who wanted to make better use of it? A thought occurred to him then that made perfect sense.

What if the new owner was none other than Donald Blackhurst?

There were ways to buy property without putting your own name on the deeds. Georgina had said that the property was no longer in the family, but perhaps she hadn't known it was her cousin, Donald, who was behind the purchase. How better to preserve a place that held such special childhood memories than to buy it yourself? It would have been easy for Blackhurst to bring that one special person here: Cathy Summer. It would also explain the state of the place today, because Donald Blackhurst had been incarcerated for the past thirty years, with no chance to visit.

Tayte went over to the shop entrance, where he fully expected to see a pile of old mail, but there was nothing. He recalled then that he'd been unable to open the letterbox from the outside, which explained it. He wondered how a building could go unoccupied for so long without questions being asked, but he supposed the basic services had been cut off a long time ago, keeping bills to a minimum, and that any local council taxes due were being paid via direct debit ad infinitum, or by someone else. Perhaps Donald Blackhurst wasn't so completely alone in the world, after all. If this was his property, he considered that perhaps someone was helping him to keep it going. That's if it was owned by Donald Blackhurst at all, Tayte reminded himself. It was all mere speculation that just happened to fit.

Moving to the back of the shop, where he saw an old-style till behind a small shop counter, Tayte began to wonder what he hoped to find. If Cathy Summer's remains were here, he was sure it would take more than a quick scan of the place to make such a discovery. He was rapidly concluding, however, that one thing was certain—Jean wasn't here. At least, not in this room. The place was already beginning to give him the creeps, so it was with some reluctance that he was about to go through the doorway at the back of the shop, to see what lay beyond, when a sound startled him, setting his nerves further on edge. He spun around, a flush of adrenaline surging through him. He could hear laughter, muted as if coming from another room—only it wasn't coming from another room: it was in that room with him. It sounded jolly, yet maniacal, repeating over and over like a laughing-policeman toy whose pull-string voice box had broken.

Cautiously, Tayte retraced his steps, listening intently as he went, in an attempt to locate the source of the sound. Part way towards the display window he stopped, sure that it was coming from the table in the centre of the room. He shone his light over it. There were more puppets hanging from the ceiling over the middle of the table, and there were several boxes, colourfully painted beneath their layers of dust. He bent down and leaned his ear to them, convinced the laughter was coming from one of them. He opened one. It was empty. Then he opened another and caught his breath as a jack-in-the-box puppet shot up at him, almost hitting him in the face. His heart rate shot up with it as the laughter became instantly louder. It was a telephone ringtone. Fixed to the puppet with elastic bands was a mobile phone, its display glowing brightly. On the display he saw an alert that told him there was an incoming video message.

Tayte was breathing rapidly. He closed his mouth and swallowed drily as he reached for the phone, uncertain of what further surprises lay in store for him. He freed the phone from the jack-in-the-box puppet and accepted the incoming message. A video began to play. The time-stamp told him it had been recorded several weeks ago. It began with a close-up of a grotesque mask—a woman in a white lace bonnet with exaggerated features painted with garishly bright make-up to match her red nose and cheeks. The image began to zoom out. It revealed a spotted light-blue dress and a white apron. The character was Judy, from a Punch and Judy show. She was tied to a chair in a small, dimly lit room, and in her lap was a board on which was written 'BXCB 378569'.

Jean?

There was no way Tayte could be sure it was her, but as this was clearly another clue from the Genie, surely it had to be. The timestamp worried him, though. The video had been recorded soon after he'd returned to England to look for her. It was almost three months old. But what did that mean? Obviously the video had to be pre-recorded; the Genie could have no way of knowing when he would turn up, but if he was too late—if Jean was dead—why bother to send it now? He drew a deep breath, and at the same time he felt suddenly light-headed to think she really could still be alive after all this time, especially if this message meant that he now had a chance to save her.

The video was still playing, and now Tayte gasped as someone else came into view. The similarly grotesque figure was dressed as Punch. First the mask came in close to the camera, and then as the figure backed away he saw the unmistakable red jester's motley and tasselled sugarloaf hat. The figure stood to attention beside Judy for a few seconds, one hand on the chair, the other behind his back. Then in a flourish Punch produced a long, broad-bladed knife and held it to Judy's throat.

Tayte felt his palms become clammy as he watched Punch move around behind Judy, rocking the blade from side to side, causing it to catch the light from the video camera. Judy was shaking her head now. She began to struggle, but it did her no good. With his free hand, Punch reached down towards Judy's lap and flicked away the message board. There was another message behind it.

'*You have twelve hours,*' Tayte said under his breath as he read it. After which time, as was evidently clear from the video, whoever was sitting there in that Judy costume would die.

The video ended abruptly, and Tayte felt both elated and relieved to know that Jean was probably still alive, yet he was terrifyingly afraid that he wouldn't be able to save her.

Twelve hours . . .

He checked the time. It was approaching midday, which meant he had until just before midnight. There was no time to waste, now that the countdown had begun. He wondered then what had triggered it. The Genie had to know he was there in order to send the video message at just the right time, telling him that the Genie had to be watching.

He shone his light around the room again, now looking higher up towards the ceiling, and there in the corner by the display window was a small video camera, far too modern to have been installed when the shop was in use.

Tayte dashed back to the window he'd entered by and knocked on the board, eager now to leave. He had to get started on this latest deadly puzzle the Genie had set for him as now it seemed that Jean's life was once again at stake.

———

Sitting in a pair of paisley silk pyjamas in the penthouse suite of a luxury hotel two hundred miles away, Michel Levant closed his laptop and let out a long, satisfied sigh. The IP camera he'd had one of his more unscrupulous associates install at Vincent Blackhurst's former marionette shop, with its discreet night vision, had worked perfectly, alerting him to Tayte's presence, signalling the recommencement of the game. He only wished the camera had sound so that he could have heard Tayte's surprise when the jack-in-the-box had popped open.

Levant was over the disappointment he'd felt that night at Beachy Head, where he'd been watching Tayte personally, waiting in his car in the hope that this time Tayte would not come back down from the cliffs—that this time he would read about the American's tragic suicide over a cup of herbal tea with his morning newspaper. He was also over the displeasure of knowing that he hadn't quite managed to drive Tayte to self-destruction through the cleverly constructed and executed series of genealogical puzzles he'd devised, causing the piece-by-piece ruination of Tayte's life through the destruction of everything he held dear. The game was back on, and Levant was confident that the grand finale he now had in mind would be an even more satisfying end to Jefferson Tayte's life.

He threw his head back into the settee's soft cushions and stared up at the chandelier as he thought back over the few months since Tayte had come to England in search of the woman he loved. How pathetic he thought Tayte's attempts had been, when for so long he had missed the clue he had placed right under his nose. But Michel Levant was a patient man. Had he not been so patient—had he tried to hurry Tayte along with some other clue—he would have missed the pleasure of watching him suffer day by day from the loss of his bride-to-be.

He thought about the man he'd seen walking down from Beachy Head with Tayte that night, and it did upset him that, for all his contacts, he still had no idea who he was. Not that it really mattered. If this man had helped Tayte get back into the game, then good for him. He was someone to be thanked, otherwise the game's grand finale might never be realised, and now that it was so close he felt child-like in his eagerness to see it play out.

Levant smiled to himself. How he had waited to settle the score between them. Tayte had upset his plans when they first met in London over a year ago. The American had lost him a small fortune, and had almost got him caught in the process—and if Levant had been caught he would have been imprisoned, which was something he could never face. To strip away the finery of life, particularly the life he had become accustomed to, was to take the life itself as far as Levant was concerned. When he'd first met Tayte, the American had little more than his reputation to lose. Now he really had something special, or rather someone special in his life, whom he would soon die for.

Levant's smile broadened. He couldn't wait to test the power of love, but first there were more preparations to be made—the final preparations. He stood up to get dressed, thinking that Tayte would not want to waste a second trying to solve the last clue in time, and he truly hoped he did. He was the Genie after all, the game master, and he wanted his game to be played out to the end.

Chapter Thirty-Three

The inevitable rain had begun to pour by the time Tayte and Rudi were clear of the old marionette shop. Having followed a sign for the town centre, they found shelter in a welcoming cafe that smelled of sugared doughnuts, although Tayte didn't imagine they were selling many today. It was lunchtime, and the place was all but empty, thanks to the inclement weather and the time of year.

'Are you going to tell me now?' Rudi asked impatiently as they sat down at a table somewhere in the middle of the cafe, away from the entrance and the draught. 'What's got you so excited? What did you find?'

'I found it was the right place,' Tayte said. 'We need to let the police know that Cathy Summer's remains could be concealed there.'

'How do you know it's the right place?'

Tayte produced the mobile phone he was meant to discover and navigated to the video message. He handed it to Rudi. 'It was inside a jack-in-the-box. Watch the video. It has to be Jean in that costume. It was recorded a while ago, but I think she could still be alive.'

'I told you to never give up hope, didn't I?'

'Yes, and I'm glad you did.'

'Are you going to tell the police about this message, too?' Rudi asked. 'That you think it's Jean?'

Tayte shook his head. 'Not yet. The police can't solve this. The FBI couldn't, either. They brought me in because they needed an expert in the field of genealogy. I'm best placed to work this out, and apart from Jean and her family, I've got the most to lose if I fail. Calling the police in now would slow things down for sure. We only have twelve hours. By the time I'd explained everything it could be too late for Jean.'

Rudi nodded in agreement. As he began to watch the video message, Tayte took his laptop out from his briefcase and connected to the cafe's free Wi-Fi, ready to get started on the Genie's latest clue.

Rudi paused the playback and looked up at Tayte. 'Do you know what BXCB 378569 means?'

'Yes, I do. That's the easy part. It's a birth registration number.'

'And what are you supposed to do with it?'

'That, I imagine, is going to be the hard part. The Genie would know that someone in my profession would recognise the reference. It's what it points to that's important.'

'Don't you mean *who* it points to?'

'Perhaps. I need to see a copy of the birth certificate this number references, but unless the Genie has left a trail of breadcrumbs for me to follow online, that's not going to be easy. I'll probably have to contact the General Register Office to find out.'

'You can't just run an Internet search?'

Tayte shook his head. 'The searchable archives and indexes are mostly name driven because that's what people know—the names of their relatives. For England and Wales, you use names and dates to identify GRO index reference numbers in order to obtain the various birth, marriage, and death certificates for the individual you're interested in. It's usually only once you have a copy of the certificate that you know what the birth, marriage, or death registration number is.'

'I see,' Rudi said. 'And what then?'

'Then the challenge really begins. As with all the previous clues, the game's all about discovering the place and cause of death of someone in the victim's ancestry. This time the victim is Jean, but which ancestor's death is the Genie planning to replicate? That's what this birth registration number should ultimately lead us to.'

'If we can work it out.'

'Yes, and in less than twelve hours,' Tayte reminded himself.

A waitress came over to their table and they ordered hot drinks: a coffee for Tayte and a pot of tea for Rudi.

Rudi tapped the menu. 'Are you ordering food?'

Tayte shook his head. 'Maybe later. I don't have much of an appetite.'

Smiling at the waitress, Rudi said, 'Just the drinks for now, thank you.'

As Rudi bowed his head and continued to watch the video message, Tayte turned back to his laptop. He thought he'd try a general search for the birth registration number first, just in case there was a reference to it online, as was sometimes the case when other genealogists and family history enthusiasts made their own research public. No matching results were returned and he figured the Genie had probably set this opening clue up as a time-waster, knowing Tayte would have to call the GRO for more information, and that it would be a challenge in itself to get to see the birth certificate the registration number related to in time.

Tayte was just reaching for his phone to call them when he noticed that Rudi was still watching the video message. He thought he must have played it back several times over by now. He seemed to be scrutinising something he'd seen.

'What is it?' Tayte asked.

Rudi began to shake his head. 'I'm not sure. It could be nothing. How do you feel about playing this game by a different set of rules?'

Tayte had had those thoughts already, back in DC. It had led him to a confrontation with Michel Levant and nothing good had come of it. 'How do you mean?'

'I mean there could be another way to reach the conclusion we're looking for, other than working out this clue.'

In light of the challenges the birth registration number presented, Tayte was all ears. 'Go on. What have you got?'

'Well, you just said that from this clue you ultimately had to find a location—somewhere one of Jean's ancestors died.'

'That's right. It's always come down to that.'

Rudi turned the phone around to face Tayte. He'd paused the playback at the point where the Punch character was holding the knife to Judy's throat, having moved around behind her, tilting the blade so it caught the reflection of the video camera light. Tayte leaned across the table to get a better look.

Rudi pointed to the blade. 'There appears to be something written here,' he said, 'But it's too small to make out, and it's almost washed out by the glare. The background is also telling. It looks industrial, don't you think? There's a lot of ironwork.'

'The video wasn't shot in someone's basement, that's for sure,' Tayte said, beginning to see where Rudi was going with this. 'You think if we can work out what those words say, we might be able to identify where Jean is and cut a few corners?'

'Exactly that,' Rudi said. 'You told me you had a friend who works for the FBI.'

'Frankie Mavro,' Tayte said, nodding.

'Well, perhaps she could have the image enhanced enough to see what these words say.'

Tayte reached for his phone to make an international call to Washington, DC, and he was thankful that, with the five-hour time difference, his nation's capital was just getting ready to start the day.

⌣

An hour passed slowly. Outside the cafe, the rain continued to beat relentlessly at the windows, keeping Tayte and Rudi glued to their seats while they waited for Frankie Mavro to call back. It had been a simple matter to forward the video message to her, and she had been keen to help, but despite all the technology Mavro had access to, Tayte wasn't pinning all his hopes on her coming back to him with a positive result.

They ate lunch while they waited, and during that time, Rudi called DI Rutherford, the detective in charge of Jean's missing persons case, suggesting they make a thorough search of Vincent Blackhurst's former marionette shop for the remains of young Cathy Summer. Tayte contacted the General Register Office, still trying to solve the Genie's latest clue the hard way, in case the words Rudi had seen on the video came to nothing.

Tayte's call to the GRO had been a frustrating one, yielding little to no chance of seeing the information on the corresponding birth certificate in time, so he'd continued to work away at the clue on his laptop, having reminded himself that the Genie had to know it could be solved within the twelve-hour timeframe he'd set, or his game would be impossible to play. If only Tayte could work out how he'd done it. With no online information about the birth registration number the Genie had given him, the GRO seemed the only option.

He was just considering whether to go against their decision to keep the police out of the loop for now and call DI Rutherford again to ask for his help with the GRO, when his phone began to ring and vibrate on the table in front of him. The screen told him it was Mavro, and he almost dropped it in his haste to answer her call.

'Frankie, please tell me it's good news,' he said. 'I'm pulling my hair out over this.'

'It could be,' Mavro said, sounding upbeat. 'The Computer Analysis Response Team I fired the video off to managed to enhance the image enough to see what those words were, but I'm not sure how useful it's going to be to you.'

'What does it say?'

'It's a warning sign. It reads: *Danger. Lift shaft.*'

'Lift shaft?' Tayte repeated, more for Rudi's benefit. 'So the video was shot someplace near an elevator?'

'A dangerous elevator at that. Looking at all the old exposed steel-work in the background, I think you can rule out hotels and high rises. I think you're looking for something industrial, a kind of mine, perhaps?'

'A mine,' Tayte mused, looking across the table at Rudi as he spoke. He could certainly imagine the video having been shot in such a place. From what he could see of the steel framework in the background, he thought it could very well be part of an open lift cage. But what kind of mine, and where was it located? He knew Mavro wasn't going to be able to tell him that.

'Thanks, Frankie,' he said. 'I really appreciate it.'

'I just hope you find her. If there's anything else I can do, you let me know, okay?'

'Sure,' Tayte said, adding hopefully, 'Hey, maybe I'll bring her over for pasta someday.'

'You do that. Anytime.'

Tayte nodded to himself, fighting his emotions, wanting with all his heart to make that happen. 'Okay then,' he said. Then he ended the call.

To Rudi, he said, 'It looks like Jean could have a mining ancestor or two.'

'How do we find that out?'

Tayte closed his laptop and stood up. 'We go back to basics and follow the first rule of genealogy. We go and talk to the family.'

Chapter Thirty-Four

Tayte and Rudi arrived back at Jean's parent's home near St Albans feeling positive about their visit, despite the fact that they were now almost four hours into their twelve-hour deadline with no concrete progress to show for it. Rudi had driven the hundred or so miles through heavy rain that seemed to cover the entire southeast of England, and along the way Tayte had called ahead and spoken with Jean's father, Keith, about the possibility of there having been a mining ancestor in the family. His answer was the reason Tayte felt so optimistic as he and Rudi were invited to sit down in the living room.

'I'm sorry Linda isn't here,' Keith said. 'She has a doctor's appointment this afternoon. We think it's anxiety. She's having trouble sleeping, among other things.'

Given the circumstances, Tayte fully understood. He knew firsthand what it was like to be incapable of sleep. Over the past few months there had been times when he'd gone for days on end with no more than a couple of hours sleep here and there, his body finally shutting down from sheer exhaustion until the next nightmare woke him again. 'I'm sorry to have missed her.'

'Yes, well perhaps it's for the best that she's not here at the moment. I take it from your call you've found something? Are you any closer to finding Jean?'

Tayte didn't want to raise anyone's hopes too high just yet, any more than he wanted to lose any of the precious time left to them through explaining everything that had happened since their last visit. Hopefully there would be time for that later.

'I believe she's alive,' he said, 'but time is critical, so please excuse me if I don't go into any details right now.'

'I understand,' Keith said, nodding attentively. 'I've dug out some more photographs for you to see.'

'Of the mining ancestors you spoke about on the phone?'

'That's right. There aren't many, I'm afraid, but I thought you'd like to see them.'

It hadn't escaped Tayte's notice that Keith already had them in his hand. He passed them across the table. There were only three, all in faded black and white, with curled edges. The first showed two men with shiny blackened faces, wearing safety helmets and dark overalls, their white smiles gleaming. It had obviously been taken at a colliery somewhere.

'Who are they?' Tayte asked, handing the image to Rudi.

'The man on the left is my paternal grandfather. That's his brother, my great-uncle, beside him. My family's from the West Midlands, the Black Country, although I've never lived there myself. My father was the first to move away from the area, looking for alternative work when the coal mining industry began to collapse.'

'Do you know the name of the mine where your grandfather worked?'

'I'm afraid not. I'm sure I'd know it if I heard it, but I've been trying to recall the name since you rang. I may have only heard my father mention it once or twice. I do know that my grandfather died in a pit disaster back in the 1940s. A tragic accident. Many lives lost. Sadly, such incidents were all too common.'

Tayte and Rudi both looked at one another, understanding that if they were on the right track they had just heard something of the manner of death the Genie intended to replicate for Jean if they were too late.

'The other photos you have there are of the same two men,' Keith said. 'As you can see, they were also taken while they were at work.'

Tayte looked at them, but they offered no further clue as to where in the West Midlands the colliery was. It didn't matter. He now knew the area and decade in which Jean's great-grandfather had died, and such a tragic mining accident was sure to have been widely reported and documented. He reached down into his briefcase and took out his laptop.

'You said this part of West Midlands is called the Black Country?' he said to Keith as he fired up his laptop.

'That's right. It was appropriately named, too. There were hundreds of small coal pits in the area at one time.'

Hundreds, Tayte thought, knowing that wasn't going to help when it came to identifying the one they were interested in. He brought up Google and searched for mining disasters in the Black Country. The number of results was overwhelming.

'Do you know when in the 1940s your grandfather died?' he asked, knowing he had to be more specific.

Keith paused to think about it. Then he shook his head. 'Sorry,' he said. 'I have a copy of my father's death certificate, but nothing for my grandfather. I'm not being of much use, am I?'

'You're doing just great,' Tayte said. He brought up another browser screen. 'Perhaps with a little more information I can find the year your grandfather died via the birth, marriage, and death indexes.'

Rudi, who had been listening quietly up until now, sat forward then and indicated Tayte's laptop. 'There are only ten years in a decade, Jefferson. Why don't you just search for each year specifically. There may have been many colliery accidents in the Black Country in the 1940s, but I doubt you'll find many that could be described as disasters during any given year.'

'That's a good point,' Tayte said, once again glad to have his brother with him, not least because he seemed to see things with such a logical, common-sense eye. It was a refreshing alternative to his own tried and tested way of thinking.

He ran the search again starting with 1940. There were still many results, and while he expected any wholly relevant match to be on the first results page, he wanted to be thorough, so he kept looking in the hope that one of the colliery names would jog Keith's memory, or at least match with the kind of disaster they were looking for. Most were of no interest, and the more pages of results they looked at, the less relevant they seemed to be. Tayte moved on to the next year, and the next, scanning the information in the links that came back. He became interested enough to open a few of the links he saw, but nothing seemed to fit. Time passed, and it wasn't until he came to 1947 that things took a positive turn.

Keith sat up with a jolt. 'There,' he said, pointing to the screen. 'Westborough Colliery disaster, 1947. That's where my grandfather worked. I told you I'd remember the name if I heard it.'

Tayte followed the link, which was to a blog detailing the events of the tragedy. 'Thirty-eight miners lost their lives,' he said, and the hairs on the back of his neck began to tingle when he read that the accident was due to a lift-shaft collapse, which had effectively entombed the ill-fated miners below.

'This has to be the place then,' he said, turning to Rudi. 'The type of accident also fits perfectly with the words Mavro managed to get enhanced for us. "Danger. Lift shaft." The Genie plans to entomb Jean in this mine, just as her great-grandfather was entombed there in 1947.'

'Please no!' Keith said as the shock of what Tayte had just said hit him.

Tayte put his hands up. 'I'm so sorry. I forgot where I was for a moment. We still have several hours. We can prevent this, I'm sure we can.'

He quickly read on and discovered that the Westborough Colliery had closed in 1959, and that only a few pithead buildings and the engine house now remained, protected by Grade II listed building status so that the site's past would be remembered.

'To the Black Country then?' Rudi said.

Tayte gave him a nod, thinking he could find out where the site of the former Westborough Colliery was along the way.

'It'll be dark soon,' Keith said, standing up. 'I'll fetch a couple of torches. I'd like very much to come with you, but I need to be here for Linda when she gets home.'

'I understand,' Tayte said. 'And perhaps it's for the best. If we're right about this, it could be dangerous.'

'Well, do be careful,' Keith said. 'If you call the police I'm sure they can meet you there.'

Chapter Thirty-Five

Westborough Colliery was located between Walsall and Wolverhampton, close to a now-disused railway line that had previously conveyed the pit's coal production to service the area's once booming industry. It had taken two hours to drive there, and Tayte was glad to have left the rain behind as he and Rudi approached along an empty road that was no more than an unlit, potholed track. It was just after six in the evening as they climbed out of the car to better take the place in. As it had been dark now for almost an hour and a half, however, with no moon or stars visible in the blackness above them, they were unable to see much more than a silhouette of the engine house and the sheave wheel that sat directly above the lift-shaft head frame. It was eerily quiet.

'Are you sure you don't want to call the police?' Rudi asked in a whisper, continuing a discussion they had begun in the car on the way there.

'No, I'm not sure at all,' Tayte said, questioning the rationale that had seemed logical enough to him in the relative safety of the car. 'But it's like I said. This isn't going to stop unless we stop it. The Genie has made it very clear that he wants me to suffer, and he doesn't care who he uses to achieve that. If this doesn't end tonight, one way or another, it'll never go away. I'll be looking over my shoulder the rest of my life, worrying myself sick about everyone I ever care about. The way I see it, this is my best chance—maybe my only chance—to make it all go away.'

Tayte checked the beam on the torch Keith had lent him. 'I don't know if the Genie's still here,' he added, 'but if the police show up with their lights flashing and their sirens wailing, it's sure to scare him away if he is, and there's no telling what might happen to Jean if he thinks the game's up. We have almost six hours left before the deadline. That has to give us some kind of advantage.'

'Okay then, we'll play it by ear,' Rudi said, checking his own torch. 'Let's go and see what's there.'

The surrounding area was lightly wooded, screening the former colliery from the rest of the world. Shining their torches into the darkness Tayte saw that they were in a clearing that was covered with tall grey weeds long since gone to seed. They set off slowly towards the sheave wheel that loomed above the tree line, a relic of the area's industrial past, crunching gravel beneath their feet as they followed the rusting iron railway tracks for a time. Then they headed across the clearing and the brittle weeds that snapped and crackled at their every step. If the Genie was there, despite their slow and steady approach, Tayte thought he would hear them coming a mile away.

As they approached the head frame, Tayte shone his torch over the small red-brick building that surrounded it. 'The lift shaft's in there,' he whispered.

'And look,' Rudi said. 'There's a gate.'

They went closer to inspect it. The gate was offset to the right of the building's centre. It was painted black with large padlocks at the top and bottom, securing thick steel bars to the frame. The whole thing looked heavy duty, having been added to the structure after the pit had closed to seal off access. Beyond the gate was an arched brickwork opening that led to the shaft, through which the miners would enter and the coal would be brought out. There was no light from within. Tayte could hear no sound. He shone his torch through the arch and saw a glimpse of the iron support girders and more exposed brickwork.

His attention was drawn to Rudi then as he began to shake the gate. 'What are you doing?'

'If this is the right place, there has to be a way in,' Rudi said, and as soon as he'd finished speaking, the gate nudged open.

They stared at one another with their mouths agape. Closer scrutiny of the locks, which remained intact, revealed that the bars they were securing to the frame had been cut clean through.

'Cordless angle grinder,' Rudi said. 'Noisy, but what would that matter out here?'

Tayte pushed the gate and it opened further, emitting a loud grating sound from the rusty hinges. He quickly stopped it from opening any further and heard roosting birds flapping in the nearby trees. He looked back at Rudi and winced.

'Sorry. I should have expected that.'

They both looked around, shining their torches across the clearing towards the car. It seemed they were still alone.

'Open it quickly,' Rudi said. 'That's usually best.'

Tayte stood in the gap and in one swift movement he forced the gate wider. The hinges squealed briefly, and then all was silent again apart from the sound of his own heavy breathing.

'Do you want to go first or second?' he asked Rudi, shining his torchlight through the archway.

'You're nearest,' Rudi said, his lips creasing into a smile. 'After you.'

Tayte swallowed the lump that had risen in his throat as he stepped inside. He flicked his torch beam ahead of him, illuminating an ironwork cage in the middle of the room that was partially surrounded by sheet-steel walls. The framework extended up through the top of the structure, above which was the sheave wheel they had seen from outside. He moved closer, to what he imagined was the front of the cage because he could see steel tracks laid into the ground to facilitate the mine carts. The tracks, which once ran from the lift-shaft entrance out of the building, now ran to a brick wall where the opening had been permanently sealed.

The cage became more open as Tayte drew closer to the front, and there he saw several lift-shaft warning signs and was reminded of the video message. He was aware of Rudi beside him then as he turned to face the cage entrance, lifting his torch as he did so, unsure whether he was about to meet with a life-size Judy doll or nothing at all. What he saw caused his hands to shake and his breath to catch in his chest.

It was Jean.

'Jean!'

Tayte dropped his torch and ran to her. Rudi was right there beside him. Jean didn't stir and Tayte silently prayed she was alive. Her head was tilted forward, there was a gag around her mouth, and her arms and legs were bound to the chair she was sitting on at the back of the cage. The Judy costume and hideous mask were gone in favour of the blue jeans and ankle boots he was used to seeing her wear, and she had on a thick, shabby winter coat that Tayte didn't think belonged to her. He imagined the Genie must have put it on her to ward off the cold, knowing she would be sitting there for some time.

'Jean!' Tayte called again. He was close to tears—tears of joy at seeing her again. He gently lifted her head and her eyes slowly opened. He smiled and her eyes closed again. 'Jean, it's me. It's JT. Everything's going to be okay.'

'She must have been drugged,' Rudi said. 'Let's untie her. We'll carry her out.'

Tayte removed Jean's gag while Rudi began to untie her left arm. Then, as Tayte went to untie her right arm, he froze. 'Wait! What's that she's holding? It looks like a baton of some kind.'

They looked more closely. There was a polished metal bar protruding from the chair's right arm. Jean's hand was wrapped around it, secured to it with duct tape so she couldn't let go.

'There's a wire running from it,' Rudi said.

Tayte knelt down to get a better look. Beneath Jean's hand he could see a black cord coming from the end of the metal bar. It ran up inside the coat she was wearing. His breath quickened as he carefully undid the buttons, fearing the worst, imagining that Jean had been strapped with explosives that would go off the second they tried to move her. He carefully undid the last of the buttons and held his breath. Then he slowly lifted the coat open. Beneath it, hanging by a chain around Jean's neck, was a timer, its glowing green digits counting down the seconds to the deadline he'd been given. It showed they had five hours, forty-two minutes and seven seconds left. Tayte quickly checked Jean over, but he could find nothing other than the timer, the wire, and the steel bar it was connected to.

'I think we're in luck,' he said. 'There's plenty of time to get Jean out of here before this thing reaches zero and sets off whatever the Genie had planned for her.'

Rudi wasn't so sure. 'Why is her hand taped around that bar?'

Tayte shrugged. 'I don't know. It's not like she could go anywhere. The chair's bolted to the floor and to the back of the cage, and Jean's tied to the chair.'

'I don't like it,' Rudi said. 'There must be a reason. Why is the bar Jean's holding connected to the timer?'

Jean mumbled something then, but she was still half asleep. It was difficult to make out what she said.

'Ti . . . er.'

'What was that?' Tayte asked. 'Jean?'

She didn't answer.

'Who did this to you, Jean? It was Levant, wasn't it?'

Still no response.

Tayte patted her cheeks, but she was out cold again. 'Come on,' he said to Rudi. 'Let's finish untying her.'

They untied the ropes. The only thing keeping Jean in the chair now was the duct tape securing her hand around the bar at the end of the chair's right arm.

'What now?' Rudi asked.

Tayte shook his head, trying to imagine what was going to happen when the timer finished its countdown. 'The timer must be rigged to set something off wirelessly.' He studied it again, following the wire out from the hem of the coat to the polished metal bar Jean was holding. 'Unless the timer causes something to happen to the bar, something that could kill Jean.'

'I suppose it's possible. A lethal injection perhaps?'

Tayte shook his head. 'That doesn't fit with the cause of death the Genie plans to replicate here. Jean's mining ancestor died in a shaft collapse, but I don't see any explosives.'

'Then I'm at a loss.'

So was Tayte, but right now all he wanted to do was to get Jean out of there, away from that timer and the metal bar her hand was taped to. 'We have to undo the tape,' he said. 'I don't see that we have any choice. If we don't, Jean will still be here when that timer runs out.'

He began to undo the duct tape and his touch stirred Jean again. She began to rock her head from side to side. 'Ti . . . er,' she said again, still shaking her head.

'What is it, Jean? What are you trying to say?'

'Tri . . . er,' she said, and this time her eyes opened. 'Trigger,' she added, more coherently this time.

'It's a trigger?'

Jean nodded. She was coming around.

'Will something bad happen if you let go of the bar?' Rudi asked.

Jean nodded again, more emphatically this time.

Tayte sighed. 'That's just great,' he said to Rudi. 'So how do we get her out of here if she can't let go of the trigger?'

Half an hour slipped by, during which neither Tayte nor Rudi had managed to come up with a satisfactory solution to the question of how to get Jean out of the lift cage without triggering the timer, and whatever else the Genie had planned.

'One of us could take her place,' Rudi said, breaking a particularly long period of silence.

The thought had already crossed Tayte's mind, and he'd already decided that if anyone was going to do that it would be him, but it was a far from satisfactory option. 'It doesn't eliminate the problem.'

'Okay, so maybe you or I could leap clear of the cage just in time. Let go of the trigger and jump.'

'The Genie would have thought about that. Whatever's going to happen is likely to happen in a split second. The chair is at the back of the cage, and the cage is too deep. I strongly doubt I'd make it out in time.'

'Maybe I could.'

Tayte shook his head. 'And maybe you couldn't. This is all on me, and as I see it, the last thing we need to do is to make a rash decision. We still have plenty of time to think about this.'

'I'm going outside,' Rudi said, sounding frustrated.

Alone with Jean, Tayte held her free hand and kissed her forehead. 'I'm going to get you out of this if it's the last thing I ever do,' he told her, smiling as best he could to reassure her that everything was going to be okay.

Jean's eyes opened slowly. 'JT,' she said, and now she managed to smile back at him, although he thought it a sad smile.

Rudi was only gone five minutes. When he came back to the cage he didn't enter right away. Instead he remained just outside. Through the gaps in the ironwork, Tayte could see him closely inspecting the frame.

'What is it?' he asked. 'Did you find something?'

Rudi stepped into the cage. 'Yes I did, and it's not good. There's an old ladder rail attached to the building around the back. I used it to climb up on top of the head frame. This lift cage is supported by a steel cable that runs over the wheel above us and down to a winch inside the engine house next to this room. I saw a lot of explosives. There are charges attached to the cable above us in several places. It's an old cable. I shouldn't think it would take much force to break it.'

'Can you remove the explosives, or at least disable them?'

Rudi shook his head. 'There are wires all over the place and it's bound to be tamper-proof. I wouldn't know where to start.'

Tayte slapped the side of the cage, venting frustration. 'Surely the lift shaft was made secure when they closed this place down.'

'That's what I was just checking. You're right. It was. Steel plates were welded between the cage and the frame to prevent it from dropping.'

'Don't tell me. The Genie cut through the plates with a cordless angle grinder, same way he got through that gate outside.'

'I'm afraid so.'

Tayte shook his head. 'So we're in a lift cage that's going to drop hundreds of feet down into the mine when that timer hits zero, or as soon as Jean lets go of that trigger.'

They both drew a long, deep breath and held on to it.

'Perhaps now is the time to call for help?' Rudi said a moment later. 'The police?'

'I don't see why not. I'm sorry, Jefferson, but the Genie isn't here. The main thing now is to get Jean to safety. As I see it, we need to remove this chair and carry the whole thing out with her still sitting on it. We don't have the tools to do it ourselves.'

Tayte knew Rudi was right. He glanced at the timer. It now showed they had just over five hours left, which was plenty of time to get the help they needed. He took his phone out, turning to Jean as her eyes fluttered open again.

'I'm calling for help,' he told her, and he was about to do so when Jean began to shake her head again.

He paused and looked at her quizzically. 'No?' he said. 'You don't want me to call for help?'

Jean shook her head again. 'Watching,' she said, still slurring her words a little, yet becoming more and more alert by the minute. She raised her free arm, pointing to somewhere higher up behind them.

Tayte turned around to see what she was pointing to as Rudi flooded the area with torchlight. There was a small CCTV camera fixed high up in the corner of the cage, just like the one Tayte had seen at the marionette shop in Broadstairs.

'The Genie's watching us,' Tayte said.

Suddenly his attention was drawn back to the timer around Jean's neck as it beeped and the countdown speeded up. It was now counting down so fast that hours were being wiped out in seconds.

'Christ!' Rudi said. 'We have to get her out of here!'

Tayte didn't think about it. He didn't have time to. He began to undo the duct tape. 'Hold her hand around the bar so she can't let go,' he called to Rudi.

Jean protested. The drugs she'd been given were wearing off fast now. 'No! We'll die.'

'No, we won't,' Tayte assured her. 'I'm going to take your place.'

Jean shook her head. 'Then you'll die!' She was almost shouting, borderline hysterical at the idea.

'It's the only way to get you out of here.'

Tayte finished undoing the duct tape. Then another beep drew his attention back to the timer. With less than twenty minutes remaining, it began to slow down, settling back into its regular pace with just fifteen minutes to spare. Everyone seemed to let go of the breath they were holding.

'He's given us more time,' Tayte said, 'but he's made damn sure any help we call on will get here too late to be of any use.'

Rudi agreed. 'And it didn't matter how quickly we solved this puzzle. The Genie's controlling the timer remotely. He could trigger the charges to go off at any moment.'

Tayte shuddered to think what might have happened if they had brought the police along with them. He imagined the charges would have been triggered while they were trying to free the chair, sending everyone in the lift cage plummeting to their deaths.

'The Genie is still in control of the game,' Tayte said under his breath as the timer reached fourteen minutes.

Rudi, whose hand was still holding Jean's to the bar so she couldn't let go, was on his knees taking a closer look at it, as if to see how the trigger worked. He carefully lifted Jean's fingers, one at a time, to better see the bar beneath them. 'There are several rubber O-rings going around the bar at intervals. It appears to be some sort of touch sensitive switch, relying on conductivity from the skin. Jean's hand is completing the circuit.' He looked up at Tayte. 'Are you sure you want to do this?'

'Honestly, I would have liked a better outcome,' Tayte said, managing a slight smile, despite the almost certain probability that once he sat in that chair in Jean's place, he was going to die. 'This is what the Genie wants. It's what he's wanted since the beginning and from where I'm standing, I don't see that I have any choice.'

Tayte heard a sob then. It was Jean, now clearly fully aware of what was going on.

'I can't let you do it,' she said. 'Get as far away from here as you can, both of you. I was told the whole area was rigged to blow up, not just the lift cable.'

'Did you see who's doing this?' Tayte asked.

'No, a hood was put over my face whenever anyone came to see me.'

'You must have heard his voice, though. Did he have a French accent?'

'His voice was distorted. I could barely make out what he was saying.'

Hearing that only compounded Tayte's belief that Levant was the Genie. Why else would he have felt the need to disguise his voice? It had to be someone Jean would otherwise have recognised.

'Just go, JT!' Jean said with urgency. 'I don't want you to die.'

Tayte shook his head and smiled at her. 'It's okay,' he said calmly, placing his hand over hers. 'You have family to go home to. Your son needs you more than you know.' Slowly, he began to work his fingers on to the bar until his hand was also completing the circuit. 'Were you well treated?' he asked, both to satisfy his burning desire to know, and at the same time to take Jean's mind off what he was doing.

'Yes, given the circumstances I was treated very well. I was kept in a nice room with an en-suite bathroom, and I was well fed. I've no idea where I was. I don't think I've been here long. I remember having lunch, then being told I had to be moved because you were coming to save me.'

As she spoke, Tayte gently but forcibly removed Jean's hand from the bar, feeling from her resistance to let go that it was against her will to let him die in her place. Jean was sobbing as she stood up. She hugged Tayte hard and continued to cry into his chest. Tayte didn't want to let her go, but he knew he had to. Time was running out. He stepped back, holding her away from him as Rudi removed the timer from around her neck. Then Rudi placed it around Tayte's, and Tayte sat in the chair in Jean's place.

***

'*Très bien!*'

Michel Levant was positively glued to his laptop screen, watching his grand finale unfold with great pleasure via the CCTV camera he'd set up in the lift cage. Other than the glow from the screen, he was in total darkness, sitting in his car close by, from where he had a direct line of sight to the old colliery buildings. He hadn't been foolish enough to wait there for Tayte to arrive, not knowing who he might bring with him. Initially, he'd been watching discreetly from the main road, knowing Tayte had to turn off on to the track that led to the former coal mine. If the police had been in tow, Levant would have monitored the proceedings from a safer distance, but then he wouldn't have been able to use the powerful night-vision binoculars that were hanging from his neck, through which he'd watched Tayte and his friend arrive.

He toyed excitedly with his Sun King ring, turning it round and round on his finger. Beside his laptop on the passenger seat was another device, a palm-sized black plastic box with a short aerial protruding from the top. The glowing green digits on the remote trigger's display told Levant that the game would be over in eleven minutes and thirty-one seconds. He could hardly wait.

'Not much time left for Jefferson Tayte now,' he told himself.

Looking at his laptop again, he could almost make out the beads of sweat on Tayte's brow as he sat motionless in the chair. He was the only person in the lift cage who wasn't in some way animated by the proceedings, and Levant was pleased to see that the injection he'd given Jean Summer had now all but worn off. He wouldn't have wanted her to miss Tayte's touching farewell gesture. Equally touching was that Jean was clinging to Tayte's arm, unable to leave him to his fate. He could imagine the tears in her eyes, and once again he wished the camera had sound so that he could hear the drama as it played out.

He watched the man who had gone there with Tayte go to Jean and gently encourage her away. He watched Jean bow her head, cupping her face in her hands as she sobbed. Words were exchanged at extraordinary length, Levant thought, given that time was fast running out. Ordinarily, lengthy goodbyes bored Levant to death, but not this time. This was one goodbye he would savour for the rest of his days. He saw the man and Jean turn away then, and suddenly the camera could no longer see them. They had left the lift cage—left Jefferson Tayte to die because he, Michel Levant, had given them no other option.

He put the remote timer in his pocket and closed his laptop, plunging the car's interior into total darkness. Then he opened his window, raised his binoculars to his eyes, and watched the gate. He sank lower in his seat as he saw the man bring Jean outside. Even now it was clear that she desperately wanted to return, perhaps to die with her love.

Had Levant been a sentimental man, he thought the scene might have brought a tear to his eye. As it was, he just smiled to himself as he continued to watch them head for the car. When he saw it turn around and head back towards the main road, if Levant had been standing he would have given a little jump of joy.

This was all going so delightfully well.

Levant watched until he could no longer see or hear the car. Then he took out the remote trigger to watch the countdown. It now showed that Tayte had just three minutes and twenty seconds of precious life left. He opened his laptop again and saw that Tayte was staring right into the camera. There was a look of resolved defiance on his face that did him credit, but it was of no consequence now. In three minutes the game would be over, and the game master would have won.

Chapter Thirty-Six

Three minutes . . .

A bead of sweat ran off Tayte's brow and he let out a long sigh. It was so quiet in the cage, and he savoured these last moments of silence, knowing it would all change when the timer reached zero, detonating the explosives above him. He might have felt alone in his last moments were it not for the CCTV camera above him. He still had his torch, which he shone up at it, wondering whether the Genie was still watching.

Of course he is.

Tayte was in no doubt that the true Genie and Michel Levant were the same person, and he knew the Frenchman would not want to miss his moment of triumph.

But what did any of that matter now?

This was the cruellest end to the game Tayte could imagine, carefully planned so that it would always come down to him having to give his life to save the woman he loved, or watch her die. Either way, it was a game he was destined never to win. When Tayte had thought Jean was dead, he hadn't wanted to go on living himself. Now that he'd found her again, he did not want to die. He supposed that at least his death would not be in vain. He had been going to end his life anyway that night at Beachy Head. At least now he'd managed to do some good with it before he went. He'd saved Jean.

Two minutes . . .

As the seconds continued to count down, his mind began to drift through the happy, yet all too brief time he and Jean had spent together. He hoped she would not shed too many tears for him, but he knew she would. They had become very close since their visit to Germany the year before, and he wished with all his heart that he could spare her the emotional pain. The only way he could do that was to stay alive, but the odds were turning more and more against him with every passing second.

Tayte drew a deep breath and stared up at the camera again. He thought back to the day these terrible events began—to the day he was called back to Washington, DC, to assist the FBI. He pictured the faces of Adam Westlake's victims, his former clients and their close family members who had been murdered simply to make him suffer. He glanced down at the timer to see one minute, eleven seconds remaining. It briefly entered his head that maybe it was possible to leap clear in time, just as the timer expired, as Rudi had suggested, but he doubted he'd make it. When the timer reached zero, the lift cage would begin its immediate and rapid descent, and he shuddered to think what would happen to him if he made it halfway out. He'd be cut in two. He stared down at the timer again and braced himself, wondering if he would feel any pain when the lift cage reached the bottom of the shaft. He imagined that if he did, it would be fleeting.

One minute . . .

Tayte closed his eyes, counting down the remaining seconds in his head. Then as his own countdown reached zero, he clenched every muscle in his body and shouted, 'I love you, Jean!'

But nothing happened.

He opened his eyes and looked down at the timer again. It showed that there was still one minute remaining. The timer had stopped. When he looked up he saw why. Standing ten feet in front of him, just outside the cage, appearing pale and ghostly in the glow of the torch-light, stood the Frenchman, Michel Levant.

———⌣———

At seeing Levant standing before him, Tayte instinctively leaped out of the chair. With his free hand he tried to grab him, but despite his long reach he might as well have been chained to the back of the lift cage for all the good it did. Without letting go of the steel bar—the trigger—he was unable to make it even halfway.

'Levant!' he said, shining his torch more fully at the man, seeing his thin smile and wanting all the more to go out there and knock it clean off his face.

Levant had on a long grey overcoat that seemed to drown him. His hands were thrust deep into his pockets, but now he took them out and shone his own torch back at Tayte. 'I couldn't resist saying goodbye in person, *Monsieur* Tayte. I hope you don't mind.'

'Why don't you come in here and we'll talk about it.'

The idea seemed to amuse Levant. He laughed to himself and gave a sly grin as he stepped closer, until he was at the very edge of the lift cage. 'That was a very touching scene I just witnessed through the camera lens as your friends were saying goodbye. By the way, who is this new acquaintance I keep seeing you with?'

'He's none of your business,' Tayte said, thinking it best not to let on that Rudi was his brother—someone else he cared about.

'It's such a pity they had to leave you,' Levant said, 'but I suppose Jean must have told you all about my explosives and the extent of the damage they will cause. I'm afraid I lied to her so you would send her far away from here. My explosives are only set to break the steel cable holding this cage in place, little more than that.'

'Just so we could be alone together,' Tayte said. 'I figured you couldn't resist letting me know it was you.'

Levant pursed his lips. 'At least now you won't have to die alone, as you have lived so much of your life.' He raised his other hand then, revealing the remote trigger he'd used to pause the countdown. 'And I suppose you could say that your life is now in my hands.'

'Does that make you feel powerful?'

'Oh, yes. Very much so. I simply press this little button and you have sixty seconds to live.'

Tayte shook his head. 'Why are you doing this?'

Levant scoffed. He threw his hands in the air. '*Mon Dieu!* Where do I start? It began in London, of course, when our mutual friend, Marcus Brown, was murdered.'

'He was no friend of yours.'

'Perhaps not when I had him killed, but once upon a time.'

Tayte clenched his fists. He'd always thought Levant was behind Marcus's death, but to hear the Frenchman confirm it so coldly made his blood boil. 'All you wanted was the contents of his briefcase. You could have just taken it. Why have him killed for it?'

Levant drew a sharp breath through his teeth. 'When you send a killer on an errand, you have to expect that someone will die. I'm sorry it had to be Marcus, if you can believe that.'

'No, I can't. I don't believe you have a sorry bone in your body.'

'Well, it's of little consequence now, isn't it? Marcus is dead and very soon you'll be joining him. Did you really think you could cross me as you did, deny me the prize I had worked so long and so hard to attain, and then go on with your pathetic little life as though nothing had happened? The audacity! My reputation could not allow it.'

'So why not just kill me and have done with it? Why have Westlake go after my clients first? This had nothing to do with them.'

'You still fail to see it, don't you?' Levant said, smiling that thin smile to himself again. 'I loathe you. I wanted to destroy your life piece by piece for what you had done! And I must confess that once started, the game became something of an addiction to me. I enjoyed pitting your genealogical mind against mine, setting my little puzzles for you to solve, if you were able to.'

'You're as much a psychopath as Westlake was, if not worse,' Tayte said, thinking that Levant was certainly the more calculating.

'Ah, poor Adam Westlake. He was just another pawn in the game, of course. He was an easy man to manipulate because of his blind hatred for you and our common desire to see you suffer. He would have killed you as soon as he was released from prison had I not gone to him first and offered him a more satisfying solution to his problem.'

'Don't expect any thanks from me,' Tayte said. 'And what about Donald Blackhurst? How did you manipulate him? I knew it had to be you posing as that journalist who went to see him.'

Levant nodded. 'I was heavily disguised, of course, so I couldn't be recognised by the security cameras. Once I'd explained to Donald why I was there he became very excited, and he laughed and cried with joy by the time I left. It was easy to draw him into the game. All I had to do was play to his madness. I showed him a photograph of Jean Summer and I told him it was his sister, Stephanie. He thought Jean bore such a striking resemblance to the woman he imagined his sister had grown up to become that he readily believed it was her, just as he'd previously believed that Jean's sister was Stephanie. He became so excited when I told him I could take Stephanie to their special place one more time, if only he would tell me where it was. Manipulating people is easy. You simply have to understand their needs.'

'What are your needs, Levant?' Tayte asked, both out of curiosity and the desire to keep him from pressing that button.

'Very complex, *Monsieur* Tayte. Far too complex for the little time we have together. I've no doubt your fiancée, or that new friend of yours, has already called the police, but I'm afraid they will arrive too late. Now I must bid you *au revoir*.'

With that, Levant held up the remote trigger to recommence the countdown, but suddenly, just as he was about to press the button, Rudi appeared behind him.

———

Rudi had not left in the car with Jean. He'd climbed into the passenger seat, but he'd slipped out again unseen, losing himself in the darkness amidst the cover of the tall grey weeds just before Jean drove off. It had been a gamble for both Tayte and Rudi, and Tayte had doubted several times over the plan they had quickly hatched with Jean before she left him as he sat waiting in that chair, willing Levant to show. As Rudi reared up behind Levant, Tayte revelled in the shock that registered on the Frenchman's pointy little face.

'As I said, Levant, I figured you couldn't resist letting me know you were behind all this. It was something I literally bet my life on, but I knew your ego wouldn't allow you to walk away without stopping by for a farewell gloat.'

Rudi grabbed Levant's arm, but the small Frenchman was spritely for his age. Before Rudi could snatch the remote from his hand, Levant had dropped his torch and pressed the button. The timer on Tayte's chest continued its countdown.

'Fifty-nine seconds!' Tayte called to Rudi.

'He's slippery as an eel,' Rudi called back.

By the light of his torch, Tayte could only sit and watch the action unfold in front of him, his life now firmly in the balance again. He saw Rudi's strong arms restrain Levant. Then just as Rudi reached for the remote again, certain to get to it first this time, Levant dropped it.

'I don't mean to pressure you, Rudi, but this thing says I've only got fifty seconds left!'

Rudi let go of Levant and dropped to his knees, grabbing for the remote, just as Levant kicked it away from him. Tayte watched it slide across the dusty floor towards him, and he hoped it would slide far enough for him to be able to reach it. He stood up, ready to grab it if it did, but when it reached the gap between the lift cage and the frame, it caught on the edge of the cage, which was slightly raised. Then Tayte could only close his eyes and sigh to himself as first the slim body of the remote trigger, and then the aerial, dropped from sight. It had slid through the gap, and for all Tayte knew was now on its way to the bottom of the lift shaft, where he would also be heading in exactly forty-six seconds.

All eyes had been following the remote, and now everyone froze. Tayte saw Levant and Rudi staring at one another as if wondering what to do next. Rudi had two options as far as Tayte saw it. He could grab Levant and detain him until the police arrived, but in doing so he would seal Tayte's fate. Or he could go for the remote in the hope that somehow he could retrieve it. Levant only had one choice open to him and he quickly took it. He turned and ran.

Rudi snatched up the torch Levant had dropped. He leaped to the gap where the remote trigger had last been seen. The timer on Tayte's chest was now down to thirty seconds.

'Can you see it?' Tayte asked, holding his breath as he waited for the answer.

Rudi shone the torchlight down into the gap. 'I can! There's a narrow ledge. The tip of the aerial is resting against the cage. It seems to be the only thing that's keeping it from falling into the shaft.'

Breathlessly, Tayte asked the all-important question. 'Can you get it?'

Rudi was already trying. 'It's tight. I can only fit my little fingers through the gap.'

Tayte didn't think it would help Rudi's nerves to know that the timer now showed that he only had twenty seconds left, so he gritted his teeth and kept that information to himself.

'I have to be very careful,' Rudi said. 'If I knock the aerial the remote could tip over. If it does that it's going to drop.'

A few more seconds passed and Tayte could feel beads of sweat forming on his brow again. He tried to breathe slowly to calm himself, his eyes now glued to the timer as the seconds ticked away.

Fifteen . . . Fourteen . . .

'It's hard to see what I'm doing,' Rudi said. 'I need both hands free and the torch is too big to hold in my mouth.'

Eleven . . . Ten . . .

When the timer entered single digits, Tayte couldn't keep quiet. 'If you're going to get it at all, it has to be now!'

'Almost!'

Tayte closed his eyes and drew a deep breath.

Seven . . . Six . . .

'Five seconds!' he called.

'Got it!' Rudi answered, sitting up with a smile on his face.

Tayte watched him lift the remote back into view by the tip of its aerial, clasped between his two little fingers. As Rudi pressed the button, the timer on Tayte's chest froze again with just two seconds to spare. Then every muscle in his body seemed to sigh with relief as he sank down into the chair.

'Is it safe to let go of this bar now?'

Rudi raised a cautioning hand. 'Wait! Not yet.' He studied the device with his torch. 'It's still active. I have to disable it first. If I can just get this panel open, I'm sure there has to be a switch.'

Tayte watched him take a coin from his pocket, which he used to pop the panel open.

'Here it is,' Rudi said, flicking the override switch inside. 'You can let go now.'

Tayte did so very slowly. When nothing happened, much as he would have liked to go over and hug his brother, he stood and ran out after Levant, hoping there was still time to catch him. He knew Levant had the means to make himself disappear if he didn't, and then he'd be back to looking over his shoulder again. He had to end this. He reached the gate and paused as he heard a car rev into life somewhere nearby. He ran out, following the sound. A moment later he saw the car's headlights, and with all the strength he could muster, he ran through the crackling grey weed stems on an intercepting course, his eyes on those headlights the whole time. He noticed that the car wasn't able to move very fast for now, and he knew Levant had to come back to the track he and Rudi had arrived by.

Tayte quickly reached it, just as the car slid out on to the gravel, its tyres losing traction as the engine revved harder. Tayte was so incensed by all the terrible things Levant was responsible for that he gave no regard to what he did next. He leaped at the car as it screamed towards him and landed flat on the bonnet with a thud, blocking Levant's view. The car immediately began to swerve on the loose gravel, but Tayte managed to hold on as the steering became wilder. A second later the car veered off the track, cutting down through the dead vegetation.

It didn't get far.

One of the wheels must have hit something hard. There was an almighty crunch and the car came to a sudden, jarring halt that sent Tayte flying. He rolled into the brittle weeds for several feet, and when he sat up again and looked back at the car, he realised the engine had stopped running. He stood up. One of the headlights was out, broken in the crash. He blocked the light with his hand, and through the windscreen he saw that Levant was trying to start the engine again. It turned over several times, but it wouldn't start.

Tayte clenched his hands into fists and strode up to the car. He saw Levant fumbling with his seat belt. Then just as he opened the door and began to climb out, Tayte ran at it. He kicked it into him, pinning him between the door and the body of the vehicle. He saw Rudi approaching from the rear of the car, but seeing that Tayte had the situation under control, he held back. In the distance, Tayte heard the wail of police sirens.

'It's over, Levant!' he yelled. 'You hear that sound? It means you're going away for a very long time, and I hope they never let you out for all you've done.'

Levant groaned, the weight of the door and Tayte's determination to keep him there causing him to grimace, but he still managed to smile weakly through the pain he clearly felt, despite the fact that the tide had now turned so forcefully against him. 'So, you win after all, *Monsieur* Tayte. You must allow me to congratulate you.' Levant offered his right hand for Tayte to shake, drawing Tayte's attention to it, misdirecting him as he quickly raised his left hand and swiped it at Tayte's face.

Tayte saw it coming. He grabbed Levant's wrist just in time, preventing contact. He thought the blow would have been weak at best and he wondered why Levant had bothered to try something so futile, but then he looked more closely. He twisted Levant's hand around until it was facing palm up. Levant immediately began to groan again, and it was then that Tayte saw the ring Levant was wearing on his left index finger. Protruding from the band he saw a small needle, and he could only imagine what might have happened had Levant managed to prick him with it.

'Poison?'

Levant pursed his lips awkwardly. It was a mannerism Tayte noticed the Frenchman displayed whenever he became overly flustered or perturbed. 'Succinylcholine chloride,' Levant said. 'It's a synthetic form of curare.'

Tayte had heard of curare. He'd read that the natives of South America used the naturally occurring poison to tip their deadly darts and arrows. He kept a firm hold of Levant's wrist.

'The dose would have been strong enough to paralyse you in seconds,' Levant added. 'Your lungs would cease to function and you would quickly suffocate.'

Rudi had come to Tayte's side. 'We should shut him in the car until the police arrive.'

Tayte nodded. He released the pressure on the door, and still holding Levant by the wrist, as if holding a deadly snake by the neck so it couldn't lash out and bite him, he pulled Levant aside so that Rudi could retrieve the car key. Once he had, Tayte shoved Levant into the car and kicked the door shut behind him. There was a clunk as Rudi pressed the button to lock all the doors for good measure, and just in case Levant tried to open them again from the inside, they stood one to either side of the car, leaning against them.

'I've been wanting to ask you,' Tayte said to Rudi across the car's roof. 'What kept you back there?'

'How do you mean?'

'I mean when Levant turned up and paused the timer, you can't have been far behind him. Why did you leave me sweating for so long?'

'You kept asking questions,' Rudi said. 'I thought you'd like to hear the answers, that's all. I'll admit I was also curious enough to want to hear them myself.'

Tayte laughed through his nose, knowing he'd have been just the same. He saw the flash of police lights approaching along the track and he bent down to look in on Levant for one last time, just to see his disappointment. What he saw made the smile drop from his face in an instant. He swallowed hard, unable to do anything more than stare into the car in disbelief. He wrenched open the door and reached in to check the Frenchman's pulse. His face was noticeably pale and his hands were tellingly clasped together in his lap. Rather than spend the rest of his natural life in prison, he'd intentionally pricked himself with his own lethal ring.

Michel Levant was dead.

Chapter Thirty-Seven

Six weeks later

Jefferson Tayte and Jean Summer were married on a fine Tuesday morning in early March. They left the St Albans registry office full of smiles to a barrage of confetti and cheers from the intimate gathering that had been invited to witness their union. On the bride's side were Jean's parents and her son, Elliot, and on the groom's side there was Rudi, Emmy Brown and her sister, Joyce. Tayte had offered to hire a dark suit for the occasion, but Jean wouldn't hear of it, and being Jean she had gone out the following day and bought herself a tan trouser suit to match Tayte's, saying that she thought it the perfect attire for someone whose initials would also soon be JT. The degree of light-hearted amusement it afforded them had been just the tonic they needed after their recent ordeals, although Tayte was having a hard time trying to forget.

During the month that had passed since Michel Levant took his own life, ending the Frenchman's nefarious activities for good, DI Rutherford had called Jean's family to confirm that Cathy Summer's remains had been found at the former marionette shop in Broadstairs. It had come as no surprise to Tayte to learn that Donald Blackhurst was the true owner, having bought it from his cousin, Georgina Budd, via a limited company so as to keep his identity from her. Because of this, the authorities had not connected the property to Blackhurst after his arrest. Nothing could bring Cathy Summer back, of course, but Jean and her family were now able to lay Cathy to rest at last, and Tayte hoped it would help Jean's mother in particular to finally know what had become of her daughter.

The wedding photographs were taken in the gardens to the rear of the registry office, the former Victorian gatehouse providing a pleasing architectural backdrop to the setting, with its arched mullioned windows and patterned red and black brickwork. Jean was on Tayte's left, and Rudi, his best man, was on his right. As they waited in between photographs, Rudi leaned closer to Tayte.

'I have a wedding present in mind for you, Jefferson. How would you like to do something really useful with the money I have left over from the sale of my gallery?'

Tayte gave his brother a wary smile. 'What did you have in mind?'

'Well, you're a genealogist. How about starting a school of family history, for young people perhaps? It could be good for you.'

Tayte thought it would certainly afford him a welcome change of pace. He could name it after his late friend, Marcus Brown. He thought it would be less hazardous, too, and he'd had enough adventures for the time being. All he wanted to do now was to be close to Jean.

'I almost forgot!' Rudi said, breaking formation just as the photographer was about to start shooting again. He ran off to the side of the gathering, and a moment later he returned with something that brought a smile to everyone's face. It was Tayte's briefcase. Rudi thrust it between the bride and groom. On the front he'd written 'JUST MARRIED' in bold white lettering.

As the photographer began shooting again, more confetti was thrown into the air, and in that moment Jefferson Tayte felt as if he were the happiest man alive. He turned to Jean and kissed her softly on the lips. Then, as if his heart were not full enough, she leaned close to his ear, and through her smile she whispered, 'I'm pregnant.'

Tayte's heart could have burst with joy right there and then. His breath caught in his chest. He could have laughed and cried at the same time were it not for Rudi, who in his other ear said, 'Give my wedding present idea some thought, Jefferson. Family is so important. Don't you think?'

Tayte smiled knowingly. 'I do,' he said for the second time that day, gazing back into Jean's wide eyes as the camera shutter continued to click. They were about to start their own family history together, and that was one adventure Tayte welcomed, knowing it would surpass all others.

Acknowledgments

My continued thanks go to Katie Green for her editorial advice and guidance in helping to tell this story, to my copy editor Julia Bruce, to Emilie Marneur, Jane Snelgrove, and all of the team at Amazon Publishing for the many things that have gone into producing this book, to all the proofreaders who strive to make sure this work is as error free as possible, and I would also like to thank my friend, Kath Middleton and, as always, my wife, Karen, for the invaluable input that goes into creating every Jefferson Tayte story. I would also very much like to thank you for reading this book. I hope you enjoyed it.

About the Author

Credit: *Karen Robinson*

Steve Robinson drew upon his own family history for inspiration when he imagined the life and quest of his genealogist hero, Jefferson Tayte. The talented London-based crime writer, who was first published at age sixteen, always wondered about his own maternal grandfather. "He was an American GI billeted in England during the Second World War," Robinson says. "A few years after the war ended he went back to America, leaving a young family behind, and, to my knowledge, no further contact was made. I traced him to Los Angeles through his 1943 enlistment record and discovered that he was born in Arkansas . . ."

Robinson cites crime-writing and genealogy amongst his hobbies – a passion that is readily apparent in his work. He can be contacted via his website, www.steve-robinson.me, his blog at www.ancestryauthor.blogspot.com, and on Facebook at www.facebook.com/SteveRobinsonAuthor.